The Lure

Stillwaters Runs Deep Book Two

By Frank Talaber

Photo By SueB Photography

Digital ISBNs
EPUB: 978-1-77362-372-6
Kindle: 978-1-77362-373-3
WEB: 978-1-77362-374-0

Print ISBN: 978-1-77362-375-7
Amazon Print ISBN: 978-1-77362-376-4

Dedication

To my mom, Judy, whose unconditional love and off-the-wall being and humour guided my life and inspired me to be a writer.

To Jacquie, whose editing skills and strong 'I ain't taking this crap as writing' moulded me into a better and tougher writer and who introduced me to Jenny, my wife.

To Rory, my son, and the driving force to make me a better and very proud father.

To Ashley, my daughter in heart and soul, whose youthful outlook guided my trying to keep in touch with a changing world.

But most of all to my wife, Jenny. Who's knowledge of police procedures not only aided and abated me in writing this book and made it not only possible, but somewhat accurate. She's the rock in my life, my lover, my laughter, and the one who puts up with all (okay most) of my quirkiness, and with me. She took the brave chance to come out to Canada to be with me and knew, like I did, the first time we met, it was meant to be.

Acknowledgements

To E. Pauline Johnson (Tekahionwake), if it wasn't for her recording Chief Joe Capilano's [also known as Joe Mathias or Sa7plek (Sahp-luk)] oral history of the Vancouver and Stanley Park area in Legends of Vancouver, this book would not be possible. It was her poem (As Red Men Die) I've used near the end of this book. A pioneer that went beyond the boundaries of race and gender. She allowed nothing to hold her back. I wish that to everyone who reads this book

Praise For The Lure

Damn Frank – this writing is as tactile as a 1955 T-Bird. Very nice descriptions, good dialogue, a thinking man's book but one that can be read entirely for pleasure. Good work.

Michael Arkin/Judicial Indiscretion

Paranormal fantasy, mystery thriller rolled into one. The Lure is a well-crafted story that builds suspense through flowing narrative, life-like characters, and believable dialogue. If you're a fan of any of the above mentioned genres, or if you're just looking for a page turner to get lost in, The Lure will not disappoint.

Cris Pasqueralle/Destiny Revealed

A gritty book flavored with primitive urges and mysticism. As I followed Carol's foray into the realm of shamanism, I realized that it took a special touch to pull off a complicated plot the way you did. Your prose was concise, powerfully descriptive, the dialogue lively, and your photographic mastery of the fixtures and streets in Vancouver's hub, in clear evidence.

Kenneth Edward Lim/The North Korean

Carol, the head detective, has to solve several murder cases: with many twists and turns. There's Shamans, Animal Spirits, and "The Lure" thrown in for good measure. No wonder, Carol wanted to resign! Yes, this novel is a roller-coaster ride, with the author cleverly hinting along the way, ending with a roller coaster ride! Read this book. It is different. It's as if Elmore Leonard has risen as a shaman, to guide others to write about Indian lore.

Nancy Bridgeman

Prologue

Carol's hand quivers closing around the cold metal of her revolver as she stares at the middle-aged man sitting at the bar. Sunlight filtering in from behind, casts his face in shadow and highlights the cigarette smoke curling around his head as he ignores the incessant nattering of the old native lady sitting beside him. He pulls another reluctant drag. His hand shakes, red flares from the end of the tobacco, and regret oozes forth in cloying streams of grey haze. Carol flicks off the safety and rises to erase months of searching.

In the background a hard-rock song rages.

Its guitars crying ... ...like Harleys in heat, drenched in the blood of betrayed bikers.

Memories of a cold October night spring to life, like bats born in hell returning to roost, playing themselves over in her head once again.

Table of contents

Chapter One

Carol looked out over the seawall from the knoll in front of The Teahouse near Stanley Park's Third Beach scratching her head. "Not a bloody clue to who killed Vancouver's Mayor." The restaurant behind her dark and cold, the parking lot empty this time of night. The ground beneath her boots squelched; a typically damp Vancouver fall night.

Somewhere in English Bay a tugboat sounded its horn, seagulls squawked in response. Mist rose in clammy waves threatening to engulf the city and the park, reminiscent of scenes from *The Fog*. So far the only disturbance was a family of raccoons foraging, stopping their prowling to stare at her like a thief caught in the headlights. Through the trees the occasional duck and Canada goose honked from Lost Lagoon, as if laughing at her cold plight. Vancouver sounds she'd grown to know, having patrolled the park in a cruiser many times before recently graduating to the rank of detective.

She sipped from her to-go designer coffee cup and sucked back another drag on her cigarette, hoping the wildlife wouldn't report the recently outlawed activity. "Pretty soon I'll have to go out of the city limits just to have a drag." Exhaling, she realized a good slow smoke was something a non-smoker could never understand. The languorous effects of the sheer senses-numbing inhalation of nicotine was comparable to the heady effects of wine's more lubricous and seductive aspects during moments of intimacy or pleasure. Sometimes a cigarette was better than sex, she thought, even when you can get it with a decent partner. Which wasn't often; being a cop and single didn't exactly add up to a full date calendar. Only the cigarette didn't help this time.

Nearly three a.m. Twenty-some hellish hours since the body of the City's mayor, Cole Bridge, was found near the memorial to Pauline Johnson in a sheltered glade next to The Teahouse Restaurant. Yellow police tape cordoned off the area behind her where he'd been found brutally butchered, by what forensics knew was a hunting type knife. So far no leads—no clues.

His daughter and wife were now known to be missing, but whether they were victims, hostages, or possible perpetrators was still an unknown. The city sat waiting for grim answers as Carol thought the worst and shivered, from the damp but also from her fears sinking in. The more time that elapsed, the greater likelihood the news wouldn't be good.

Still, it was at least peaceful here. The swish of cedar and pine aromas filling the air with an earthy sensuality and saltwater spume gurgling against shore rocks belied the fact that they were actually in the middle of a bustling city. Somewhere out there, on the misty waters, ocean tankers sat like squat walruses dreaming of engorging on salmon runs. Whoever preserved Stanley Park, probably some stuffy old English lord, was a genius. It had become a focal point of beauty, enticing many tourists, and was a major contributor to making Vancouver one of the most beautiful cities in the world. But in this case, the woods definitely had its darker, secluding aspects of malevolence.

Her first big case and, while being a detective had its fun moments, she'd already learned that most of her time was to be spent on obs, shivering in the dark. Waiting. It took boring to a whole new level. With the cleanup crew not scheduled until the morning, she'd volunteered to join the graveyard shift police over the thoroughly investigated crime scene in order think over what happened here. Last thing they needed was the dead mayor's blood pool on the front pages of the tabloids. The two on duty uniformed cops had gone off to grab coffees.

Carol yawned and butted out her smoke. Sipping her cooling coffee she tugged the belt of her overcoat tighter, wishing she'd put on another layer. A glance at her watch told her she had another couple of hours here. Lost in the frantic pace of forensics and media, a clue existed, always did—

only she hadn't found it yet. There had to be something they'd overlooked, something she'd missed.

Grabbing her flashlight she started toward the Memorial again when a voice cracked the air.

"But one can't keep a watched pot from boiling over forever." An elderly voice shattered the stillness.

Carol jumped at the stark gruffness from the direction of the darkened trail that broke her dulcet meanderings of being at peace. Her right hand instinctively set down the coffee and reached for her gun. *Most of the people around the park at this time of night were usually crackheads. Trouble of some sort, anyway.*

An elderly native man shuffled forward into the dim glow cast into the fog by a nearby lamppost. Leaning heavily on an ornate Orca-headed cane, twin braids of white fire streamed down his back from under an old, outdated Expos baseball cap heavily studded with various pins. A blue-jean jacket and pants that needed washing weeks ago if not pitching in a dumpster, together with a western-style, checkered shirt, completed the ensemble.

"Most interesting death." He hummed and hawed walking around the area, careful not to tread beyond the official yellow tape. Noting that the statement didn't elicit a response from the detective, other than a disapproving glare, the native man added, "Nice night, if it don't rain." His breath rose in white mists, dispersing into the chill of the night, and still eliciting no overly enthusiastic response. "You're not very chatty. Sea Otter got your tongue or are you bound by those inane legal contracts that says you can't comment to the public?"

What would an elderly native fellow be doing out at this time of night and how'd he sneak up on me? "Look, buddy, this is a crime scene. Detective C. Ainsworth."

She flashed her badge. "No offence, but you need to beat it."

"I know, on both parts," he grunted, "and none taken. Caught you on the TV." He turned his gaze back to the night sky. "But I guess rain only matters if you're not aquatic or amphibious."

He changes subjects in mid-sentence; probably a little mad, touched in the...

"Touch the stars, you can, on nights like this." He waved his cane over his head, even though there wasn't a single star to be seen in the overcast sky. "Charlie Stillwaters, native ska-ga or, as you white folk affectionately call us, shaman. A term originally meant for Mongolian Healers, but I think, as you can see, I'm not Mongolian, nor even remotely Chinese. Although I do fancy a good egg foo yung. Can't beat the Chinese for food. You ever wonder what they eat for takeout over there? Shall we go for some Canadian tonight? Ohhh, I'd murder for some back bacon and pancakes smothered in maple syrup." A disgusted frown crossed his face as he stuck out his tongue in a feigned display of throwing up.

"Look old man." She rose, not in the mood for banter to distract her from deliberations, realizing he was either whacked out on alcohol-laced mouth wash, Ecstasy, or just plain whacked. "I don't mean to be rude, but I'm here on police business and would prefer to be alone. It's been a rough day and tomorrow doesn't look much brighter. So like I said politely earlier, you need to leave this area."

"Hmmm. No clues then," he said, turning to stare back at the old trees along the trail, apparently losing interest in Carol. "It's been written 'We cannot choose what we are—yet what are we, but the sum of our choices?'"

Carol experienced a mental double-take. The eloquent voice didn't match the image before her of some grubby old hobo. He talked in the slow, clipped native tones, but it was becoming obvious to her that more intelligence resided under that ball cap than the originally estimated two pinches of blue smirf shit.

Catching her interest she decided to engage him in conversation. Besides, the park bench and pine trees of the local environment weren't exactly much company. Even the raccoons had left her. "Yes, I think I've heard that quote. Aristotle or Shakespeare?"

"No, Rob Grant, co-writer of the *Red Dwarf* series. Brilliant stuff, English TV, smart comedy too, 'specially compared to American comedy. The Brits play more on words and make you think, highbrow stuff. However I suppose I should let you go. Busy day and all."

He was flaky, but no dummy. "Yeah, you're right. Tough day and still no answers." His words rattled through her head; without her realizing, she'd spilled some of the case out. "Hang on, what made you think of using that quote?" She'd hated philosophy in college, preferring the more direct hands-on courses, like the sciences.

"Simple. Someone in your situation can't be greater than the choices you made to arrive at the sum of your parts to get to this point in your life. In other words, you can't look outside the box if you're not conscious enough to know you're stuck in one. Of course, that doesn't explain the whole synchronicity thing. Great album. By the Police, oddly enough. Good night, Detective." He started back down the dark trail, leaning on his cane, as the mist began to swallow him into its shifting curtains.

What a load of crap. Okay, reserve judgment on the soundly intelligent part, there were some brains there, but the man sounded borderline psycho. More pressing matters. Where to start tomorrow? We haven't any clues and there isn't anyone left to check out, at least not until we find the wife and daughter. No one at all. God!

And she feared the worst, sensing the wife and child were also here, as their house revealed no-one and the family SUV had been discovered in the parking lot near the memorial.

"Only it's whom or, more precisely, what," Charlie called out from the shadows edging the light cast by the lampposts. "We have a native saying that when you're chasing squirrels there's more than one tree to climb and more than one squirrel to chase. Some just hide in better places, or in their case, trees."

"Then you got any bright ideas, non-shaman shaman man?" Carol shielded her eyes from the glare of the bulb, squinting into the dark, trying to pick out the old man.

Weary of his baiting and bantering, suddenly the company of only trees and park benches seemed appealing and sedate.

"No, Detective Blinders, but if you know where to look, I'm sure you'll probably find your killer of these folks. Sorry for wasting your time." Carol just caught his image highlighted under the bright moon ghosting through the mists and scattering clouds. Carol blinked, swearing as his figure wavered, thinning, blending into the mists as if it wasn't really there.

"Crap!" She rubbed her eyes. "Either too much coffee or not enough sleep. What a nut job. A few poles missing in his teepee..." Retrieving her cup Carol gagged on the now-cold coffee. His words echoed back at her. He'd said folks? She clicked on her flashlight and marched down the trail. "Hang on, old man."

* * *

Two vans accelerating wildly shatter the serenity cast by the Harley's beefy growl cruising along the open highway. Its skull-capped rider glances in the mirrors hung on the long-handled chrome bars. Windows darkened with tint; they pull alongside him, one slightly ahead, forcing him closer to the metal guardrail on his left. The roar of a third van gunning its engine behind him sends a lurch into his guts. His Sunday cruise has gone terrifyingly wrong.

The lead van accelerates, moves over, and blocks his escape to the front. Another glance in his mirror reveals the one behind is closing the gap fast. He hits the brake, attempting to dodge behind the van on his right before this avenue is blocked too, but the last van is too quick; it swerves into his lane. Four barrels open in a hungry, air gulping roar.

"Oh shit."

Reminiscent of starved hyenas chasing down an injured gazelle, the van's throaty carbs cackling in glee as they close the space between him and freedom on all three sides.

Ben tries to hug the guardrail at a hundred clicks an hour. Sparks ignite in a myriad of colours as he contacts the rail, trying to buy even an inch of freedom. Only that inch doesn't exist in this lifetime as brakes fry on steel and the very air shoots skyward as day vanishes in a haze of GMC obscuring chassis.

Metal groans under protest, pain screams its voracious voice, legs crumple backward, bones popping like guitar strings and the raw stench of fuel from rupturing tanks fills his lungs, along with blood and betrayal. Glass shards splatter like neon fireworks and cold asphalt caresses his body with its sandpaper claws, tearing away life and consciousness.

* * *

Ben lurched awake. "Why? Why can't I get this dream out of my head?" He gulped down water and stared into the shadows cast by the dim nightlight. "Two nights in a row. It's so bloody real."

Wiping his forehead, Ben realized he'd awoken at the same point last night.

Crushed up against the guardrail, body being grated into hamburger. "Why a bike?" He preferred a more luxurious ride, like his BMW, and had never ridden a bike. Hated them, actually.

Only two hours to get some decent sleep before his workweek began. Ben yawned and turned off the light, preferring darkness to the wavering shadows. Some psychobabble believers would, he knew, insist this nightmare represented some horrendous past event. Only whose? Because it sure as hell wasn't his.

* * *

Across town a woman cries as she packs a few belongings, preparing to leave the house, her home, for the last time. Swollen lips throb; she's had enough from a man who says he loves her but doesn't know how to show her. Instead he allows his anger to get in the way of explaining his emotions, and reverts to his fists and brute force to exert his will. She wipes away the tears, wincing at the shooting pain from her darkened eye.

She stares at the last letter he'd written to her, explaining how he loved "his Dear Yolanda" and would do anything to earn the money to make her happy. It took her years, but she realized he was a dreamer and always would be. Maybe that's why he carried that inane hunting knife in his belt. He never went hunting. She feared that knife. The letter was two days ago. She sobbed, it was so hard giving up. Replacing her sunglasses she zips shut the final case and marches down the stairs to the waiting taxi.

"Where to?" The cab driver pretends he doesn't notice her battered features leaking into his rear-view mirror. He's learned not to get into things he's seen too many times before.

Tears stream down her face. Outside, the day is pleasant. Children play in sprinklers, lawnmowers hum, and the tang of fresh-cut grass hovers over the edge of quiet suburbia while inside her own world hell drags its razored talons through her heart yet again.

Yolanda stares into the street, unable to answer.

* * *

Lightning's jagged voice shrieks through nerves. Thunder bellows retribution's rage like Harleys shifting gears into the night. Strings yanked taut holding him begin to snap. In the darkness hyenas cackle in gleeful mirth. Tendons of reality tear away like cobras striking.

Larry spun away, experiencing the sickening sensation of falling through unending darkness. He's flung around like tissue paper in a gale, as the final umbilical cord tethering him to purgatory's demons recoiled away.

Tumbling.

Too late, oh so too late, for in hell's all-consuming hunger even angels die.

Betrayal's stench burned vengeance in his mind like tattoos etched in acid.

A crying woman holding her crushed cat, its one eye dangling.

Fires erupting within, licking at his soul and all he once held dear.

Naked blood of innocents; his own families, spilled.

Memories that stopped him from leaving and dragged him back here. The need to exact his revenge on the despicable man who performed the deeds holding him in this time and place. Not to mention the code. The Devil's Spawn bikers always stuck together, even in retribution.

He refused to go, someone had to pay.

A final staccato echo of gunfire.

He gasped for air, like a drowning man. Heart thumping in response.

Guts heaved heavenward. Raw whisky's reek burned down his throat.

Reborn.

He could taste again. Through the pounding in his head, Larry fought to focus. Opening his eyes to neon light as urine's vileness caught in his nostrils and the porcelain-white toilet stared back. He threw up again.

Time's mistress played harsh games with revenge, and to time's abeyance of his soul. He dry-heaved what little was left of bile and alcohol, wiped his mouth and staggered to the sink. His head throbbed in migrainic pulsing. An unrecognizable reflection glared back from the pockmarked mirrors. Swaying on his feet, he gripped the counter top, trying to gain his bearings as the world spun around and hell slowly vanished into the thrum of pounding background music. A cold splash of water on his face, a couple of deep breaths, before trying a few nervous steps. The pounding in his brain subsiding, Larry headed for the exit.

He was back.

Chapter Two

S weat beaded his forehead as Ben Carlton lurched up, switched on his nightlight, and gulped from the glass of water on his nightstand. He squinted, rubbing his eyes, trying to adjust to the light. Glancing at his clock again he noticed it was nearly time to get up for work and he felt like he hadn't slept a wink all night.

The same bizarre dream, like earlier.

It always started the same, cruising down a highway, at peace with the hearty throb of a Harley-Davidson in full throttle. The rhythmic rumble of the world's biggest vibrator, a biker once told him. No wonder girls loved riding on back; better than riding a horse bareback, a female biker also had told him. Being a reporter meant dealing with, and interviewing, some odd people; good ones, lowlifes—the whole spectrum of humanity. He'd learned some weird facts, but he hadn't dealt with anything or anyone related to bikes lately. Other than the bikers he'd seen at the pub on his date with Brandi on Saturday night. So where did this dream come from?

He'd nicknamed Harley riders GGG's, geriatric granddads at the gynecologist, as most of the riders seem to be guys in mid-life crisis mode searching for some long lost potion of testosterone-fueled youth and the position of the rider's legs on the foot-pegs bought to mind a woman spread before her doctor for an exam.

So what had prompted this dream? The only thing out of his normal routine had been the date with Brandi. Other than the fact he'd had too much to drink, he didn't think the date had gone all that badly. Although, thinking about it, he had wound up passed out in his car, alone. With no memory of how he got there, nor, actually, any idea how Brandi had got home. He hadn't heard from her, though.

Maybe it hadn't gone that well after all. He thought hard, trying to remember what went on that evening and drew a blank—odd.

Crawling out of bed he slowly put on his sweats. He still had time for a quick jog through Stanley Park, which he did most mornings. If that didn't clear his mind, maybe a couple of espressos would.

* * *

Carol crawled from her unmarked cruiser in the early light. She'd barely slumped into her bed in her downtown Vancouver condo when the call came. Even her second Starbuck's Venti couldn't keep her from yawning.

"Are we keeping you awake?" Police Chief Commissioner Dan McKinney bellowed as she sauntered up to the gathered officers. He had a few nicknames, some profoundly derogatory as he wasn't muchly liked by anyone that worked with him on the police force. One of his nicknames though, Double Patty, came courtesy of the rumour, although rarely said to his face, that he'd solved one of his biggest cases sitting on stakeout at Micky Dee's, home of the double arches, enjoying one too many of their finest. Although he was a big man, around six-two, and someone she wouldn't dream of being able to wrestle to the ground, over the years on the force Dan managed to put on weight in one area, his gut. His gut protruded like he was six months pregnant.

Carol searched for a cigarette. "No sir, sorry. It's been a long night and I barely…"

"Can the shit. I know you just got off shift. Tough break. Welcome to the detective ranks. Little sleep and even less sanity. Besides, you probably slept half the night on that cold bench on stakeout."

"I never sle…"

He waved her objections aside. Double Patty, or as some less brave on the force mentioned, Big Mac, was a very hard-nosed but fair chief. He had the respect of most under him, having risen honestly from the ranks of beat officer over fewer years than most. Carol preferred to call him simply Big Dan, out of respect.

Carol said nothing. Further apologies, she knew, made her look weak in the world of men and of the police force.

"Body's over here."

They marched up the earthen trail into the park's gloomy centre. Dodging squirrel shit and slimy slug piles of snotty goo she struggled to keep up to the marching commissioner, all the while trying to balance the coffee and keep it from spilling. "Shit! Hot!" she gasped at one point as she failed miserably and scalding coffee washed onto her hand.

"Try Timmy's next time, they don't heat the buggering bejeezus out of the stuff," he growled. Near a running creek that released the waters of Lost Lagoon to flow under a concrete footpath bridge, they settled in amongst several constables milling about in a small clearing surrounded by half-a-dozen or so age-old cedars. "Body's over here." Big Dan motioned for Carol to follow him.

Stepping back across the narrow path, Mac led Carol behind the root-ball of one of many toppled giants, spread out like twelve foot fans, the work of the windstorm of 2006. Several CSI types, who, contrary to the popular TV series, didn't walk around in designer outfits, quietly took pictures and samples in their white coveralls.

Carol nearly gagged as she caught sight of a severely mutilated and partly naked woman's body lying under the trunk of the fallen cedar. So many crime scenes, but still the sight of human remains sent revulsion screaming up her throat. One of the main reasons she became an officer was to right such heinous wrongs. A strong need drove her to be like her father, always trying to make the world a better and safer place.

Other than the long, coiffed blonde hair one couldn't much make out the fact the body was female. Her head had been stove in, crushed beyond recognition. Carol gritted her teeth, if this was Cole's wife, she'd taken a severe beaten. All she knew was that Cole's wife was a blonde, and a real looker, as one reporter once described her.

"A jogger found her this morning, his dog ran off the trail and he followed. Judging by the faint drag marks in the soil and the traces of dirt on her shoes and legs she was dragged to this position." Carol had already noted a faint outline of track marks in the soft, mossy soil.

"Blunt force trauma, probably a rock judging by what appear to be fragments of granite imbedded in her skull," one of the white coveralls muttered as if reading her thoughts. "We're having that analyzed, but no rock around here seems to fit the bill, especially one with brain matter and blood stains on it."

Carol tried to hide her revulsion as they picked through the remains of the poor woman's head. "Hit her several times, way more times than necessary to kill her. Usually signifies a crime of passion," he continued into a microphone.

"Crap," the gruff commander muttered. "No matter how many stiffs I see it still unsettles the guts." As tough as he appeared Big Dan was very similar to her in that respect. She said nothing, clenching her guts, trying to stay analytical.

"Yeah, interesting." One of the CSI members, wearing the nametag Jenkins, lifted his hands as if pretending to ram a rock down into her head. He walked back over to the glade and pointed down. "Depressions here and here suggest they squatted over the body." Imitating the killer, and careful not to touch the ground, his knees seemed to naturally set virtually the same distance apart as the two indentations in the mossy earth. "Mostly likely male, similar to me in size. Looks like he incapacitated her elsewhere, dragged her into this glade, and finished her off here, judging by the brain and blood cast-off we've found." Jenkins pointed to an area several feet away. "The sheer ferocity of the blows suggests the attacker was acting out of anger or revenge rather than self-defence or a need for drug money."

"Possibly a lover? Maybe he offed her, and then killed the husband? We need to look at all the angles. Definitely dealing with pent-up emotions here," the Chief spat, disgust curling his lips. "The only thing I've got pent up right now is puke and hunger pangs. I'm off to grab some chow and coffee at the nearest Mac station. Ainsworth, you're in charge until I get back, while these analytical types scour the area for clues. DNA evidence has been sent off, that needs a day or two, her fingerprints will be quicker. If she's in any of the databases we'll find her." He wrinkled his nose at one of the forensics people picking through her bashed brains.

"Too bloody clinical for my liking."

He stormed off before Carol could even give a curt "yes, sir" response. But she knew what he meant. Some of the officers in the CSI squad seemed to relish putting together the pieces of crime scenes. Performing the actions over and over, like an actor learning what goes through the mind of the character they have to portray.

"Male perp?" she pondered, already ruling out the possibility that Cole Bridge did this, as his body was too hacked up to have been self-inflicted.

"I'd say. Whatever rock they used was heavy and packed quite a wallop. Most women wouldn't be able to lift it." Jenkins held his hands apart trying to judge the size of boulder needed to cause the damage to the dead woman's head.

"Mrs. Bridge?"

"No identification on her body, except this great hunk of rock." One pointed to her ring finger.

"Well, that rules out mugging," Carol muttered, glancing at the glittering ring she thought appeared to be well over a carat in size.

"Whoever married her had big bucks to buy her bling that size and I don't need DNA to prove this is his wife." Another of the white-garbed group sauntered up.

"I've a twenty that says it's her," Jenkins retorted.

"Hey, you're on," the one leaning over her body responded.

"And the daughter?" She sipped at her coffee. It took a special breed of person to be able to dig through human remains and keep down their dinner from the night before. She wasn't one of those, and found it even more morbid when they did things casually like betting on results. Her stomach turning, Carol spun away before she contaminated the crime scene with last night's meal or this morning's coffee. She dug in her pockets finding a light and her pack of smokes.

"No sign yet, but I'll double the wager on the fact she's here also," one said smartly.

"You're on again."

As she took a long disgusted drag from her cigarette the incessant click of a camera shattered the tableau. "What the... I said don't let anyone near this site yet." Carol spun around. "Especially..."

A lean, fit-looking man threw his one hand up waving his press card. "Ben Carlton. Just happened to be out jogging along Cathedral Trail behind us this fine morning. Gotta love these cell phones with built-in cameras."

"...the press." Carol appraised Ben quickly, already seeing herself being raked over the coals by Big Dan. The jogging outfit and sweat streaming down his face confirmed his story. She caught sight of the jut of dimpled chin and that flash of darkness in his brown eyes she so liked in men. The dark, smoldering look that could take you to the edge and beyond whenever he wanted. Many in the TV and newspaper business with that savvy, handsome look were definitely gay, so she didn't hold out much hope in having the right equipment to grab his fancy. She snatched his press card and matched the sweating face to the smile in the photograph. "Jenkins, verify this man is who he says he is." She handed the card to another detective who ran it through a scanner.

Unperturbed, he smiled and stuck his hand out, obviously used to police harassment or questioning. "You know, I'm familiar with most of Vancouver's finest. Can't say I've met you."

"Detective Carol Ainsworth, newly appointed. Now I'm going to ask you nicely to put the cell phone away or I'll have you arrested and the phone confiscated," she said, feeling the warmth in his hand and noticing how one lip curled up when he smiled, giving him that childish grin she found most attractive. His eyes had that penetrating quality that could cut away and reach deep inside; strip her to the bone. A shiver ranged down her back at the thought of him undressing her. *Way too many lonely nights recently.*

He switched off the cell and stuck it in his pocket. "Only because you're gorgeous and you asked nicely."

The remark stunned her. Maybe not gay then. She hadn't showered in two days, didn't have time for makeup, barely dragged a comb through her hair, and used espresso coffee to gargle. She ached; her entire body felt like the Canadian army used it for a boot scraper. A blush crossed her face. Definitely way too many lonely nights.

"He's legit." Jenkins handed the card back to her, eyeing the reporter as she handed it back to Ben.

"Although, you gotta wonder how'd she end up here and her husband over by Third Beach. The two locations don't jive. You'd think someone would see the mayor, of all people, staggering along with his throat cut," Ben pondered, casting his eyes around.

"Good point," Carol acknowledged, taken a bit aback. She hadn't thought that far ahead. The cigarette and coffee for breakfast hadn't awoken her cognizant skills yet. Although they were usually pretty alert, maybe they'd been put off guard by Mr. Handsome.

"Oh well, might as well continue my morning run then, if you don't mind." He raised his arms over his head, stretching back and forth.

"Hang on. What paper are you with? In case I've some further questions I need to ask. Like what are you really doing out here at this time of day?"

"I go jogging early in the morning, usually through the centre of the park, couple times a week. Get the blood pumping, good for story ideas. Relaxes the mind and it's the *Province*." He zipped up his sweater and pumped his muscular, long legs twice before proceeding back in the direction he most likely came from.

"Oh, and I meant it, the 'gorgeous' thing."

He smiled at her. Carol caught the glint in his eye, the hint of promise on his lips, the subtle widening of his pupils. He liked what he saw and so did she. She smiled back as he bounded down the trail, disappearing into the darkness of the woods.

Before she could continue the wild fantasy unfolding in her mind, Big Dan McKinney came striding back up, taking his usual two of her steps in one of his. "What the hell was that, Ainsworth?"

"Jogger. Happened to also be a reporter, Ben Carlton. Says he was out on his usual morning run and stumbled on the crime scene by fluke. Got where he works if there's any further questioning needed," she blurted, being jolted from her thoughts of what she'd do to Ben if she had him in cuffs.

"Great! I'll bet we'll be splattered over the front pages before we can spit. I just heard from the labs, thought I'd tell you first. The fingerprints match Mrs. Cole."

"All right." One of the forensics in the background blurted out. "Looks like you're buying breakfast, sucker."

"We're gonna verify with DNA too, obviously. I've put a priority on the test. Any sign of the daughter? Cindy, isn't it? Hope not, but more than likely now," Big Dan asked Carol, shooting a mildly disgusted look at the CSI.

"Not yet. But she's also here, I can just feel it." As soon as the words left her mouth, Carol knew it was the wrong thing to say, especially to someone like him.

"Yeah, that's some fucking woo-woo thing you've got there. Stick to the facts and leave conjuring to the magicians. The rest of the press will be here in droves, you need to get ready for whatever comes your way. Detective …" He paused for a moment as if at least contemplating an apology; then continued, "the media relations officer will answer all questions. You'll be in the background. But if you get cornered and asked anything follow their lead. Just remain calm, look confident, and stick to the facts. Let the public know beyond question; we *will* get who did this."

He span around and pounded his way back toward his cruiser, his big size twelve or thirteen black police-issue leathers tearing up the trail.

"Can be a real prick sometimes," a fellow officer spat out.

"Maybe," Carol replied. Concerned but emotionless, he was like one of those over-protective 'dads from the fifties. Mental hugs from a distance and support with stilted phrases, like "well done". "But at least pricks can be useful. Sometimes."

All within earshot laughed. Carol stood there a moment surveying the scene, allowing a little of the fright regarding her first live TV interview to fade. Dan didn't trust just anyone to lead any of his investigations and even less to talk to the press about it. He either trusted her or was testing her. Or both.

Carol took a deep breath and reached for another smoke. If she kept this up she'd need to get another pack before the reporters arrived, or keel over with lung cancer. Crap. She looked a right sight too.

Leaning against one of the steady old cedars, she calmed herself and pondered what to say to the reporters and cameras.

Idly, she glanced around at the trail, the one Ben had jogged away on, and the position of the body. Inside, her guts were telling her to get some food and put some makeup on. She had a travel kit in her car, mainly for stakeouts, when she needed some freshening up. She should probably go back there quickly before anyone showed.

But there was more here. Something that didn't fit. More than the two crime scenes. At least one more; this was a secondary, she knew they were widening the search area right now.

But one thing was right, the fact her native visitor from last night knew Mrs. Cole's body was here, and she knew the daughter's was as well. She pondered how he'd just disappeared into the forest's mists. It didn't help that the memorial had been erected at the convergence of several trail heads, but the man had vanished like he wasn't there. She hadn't told Dan, or anyone, about him. Probably chuck her back to street beat if she did. The shaman more than likely knew the daughter was here somewhere, in probably the same condition as Mrs. Cole. Only who would believe her? Did she even truly believe herself?

Big Dan had left her in charge, and if her guts were telling her the third body was here; then it probably was.

"Jenkins, I want the park sealed off and searched. The daughter must be here as well." They had at most a day to find the girl before media-induced paranoia set in.

And if they found the last body, then the question remained; was the native involved? He was undoubtedly whacko, or had he actually seen this happen? Or worse?

* * *

Larry puked once as he stared into the white of the toilet bowl. He slowly stood up, his head throbbing, stomach reeling, like being stuck in a sauna with the mother of all hangovers while someone cranked the music full blast. He steadied himself, letting his guts settle down. The headache would subside after a while, it was just so intense, like most other physical sensations that were beyond him. In the background the repeated thump of techno music jolted through the walls of the building. He hated techno, didn't care for most music, actually.

He stared at the face he didn't recognize and moved his head, arms, and feet, getting used to the feel of this man's body and slowly walked out to the bar area. As he stood at the bar requesting a bottle of whisky to take home, a dark-haired woman approached him. He blinked as she smiled at him.

Larry took one glance into her eyes and knew who was inside her. "Freaky, scary bitch." He grimaced. The one from the trail in Stanley Park. Larry inadvertently shivered. He didn't like her any more than he liked Ryley. Which was less than a pinch of coon shit.

"Don't I know you from somewhere?"

"Beat it. I ain't your type."

"True." She leaned in to give him a light kiss on the cheek. Her tongue flicked out for the briefest of moments across his earlobe. "You were rather delicious at the time. Thanks anyways for releasing me."

He'd had enough of her. "Yeah, whatever." He was more used to women doing what they were told. Domination may be okay for some guys; not him.

She smiled and turned her attention to the older man standing beside her, the faint indent of a ring on his finger. "Care to buy me a drink, good-looking?"

Larry shivered again as he paid for the liquor and walked out, memories of that fateful night flooding in.

* * *

Carol fumed as she sat in her cruiser and headed home. Another full day spent trudging through Stanley Park in the cold and wet. They'd found no daughter, although an officer did find an IPod they sent out for prints. Could be Cindy's. Dan hadn't been happy about her calling the area search, although he did say he'd probably have done the same. "You're in charge. I'm letting you call the shots on this one. Just remember you've me to answer to. Screw up and I'll have you pulling beat detail on Hastings." Definitely the considerate, fatherly type.

She couldn't stand being put under the thumb of a man, especially one as rude and dominant as Big Dan. Some of the men spat out the word dyke when she rejected their advances. Carol laughed in their faces; she much preferred sausage over fish sauce any day. But it wasn't easy being tough, always on the edge of wanting to let out your emotions and not being able to in a very male-dominant work force like the police department. She'd learned that lesson a long time ago.

No body. Was the shaman real? Or was he some sort of hallucination brought on by lack of sleep, mild hypothermia from the night on a cold bench, and too much caffeine? If she hadn't conjured him up he had been right about the wife, and the girl was out there too, she was sure of it. If he was real, she had to find him. Carol yawned, shivering, as the car's heater kicked in. She needed to buy some warmer thermal undergarments, the detective ranks weren't a walk in the park this time of year. She laughed. "Oh yes, they are! I've just spent two days walking everywhere in that damn park. Could probably identify every single tree trunk and stump in a police lineup by now. Time for some sleep and a decent meal." She was muttering to herself again, a habit from living alone so long, but it helped organize her thoughts, reason things out.

As her car pulled out of Stanley Park, she glanced over at O'Shanahan's Bar and Night Club. Caught on the edge between suburbia and nature. "Funny location." She'd never been to the sports bar, more blue-collar crowd than executive. It was rumoured that a lot of biker types did though, including the local ~~Spawn~~' leader, Ryley McLaren.

One side of the bar dark with the stillness of nature and the other full of city lights bouncing off it. "Never been in there, heard they do a great business on Saturday nights and have a thumping light show and DJ." She smiled sadly and caught her tired reflection in the rear-view mirror. "Not this weekend for sure. Maybe another." Sadness hid in her eyes, crying out with "when, when are you going to allow yourself to relax and have some fun." She signaled and joined the stream of flowing cars, lost in the haze of smog and daydreams. Over the radio a song's lyrics spoke of not getting old, just older. She didn't like being either, especially alone.

Chapter Three

"Hold the Front Page"! An age-old cliché, but one Ben was happy to yell at his editor when he burst into his office at the *Province* earlier today. Sometimes even the most mundane pastime, like jogging, could have unexpected rewards and it was his paper, his byline on the exclusive, that had scooped all the others. He'd have to thank Carol for not putting a gag hold on him, nor confiscating his cell phone although he was pretty sure she'd be after his balls when she realized her error. Pity to get *so* on the wrong side of her, as he'd have liked to ask her out. There was something about a woman in charge that excited him. He was musing his day's good fortune as he put the finishing touches to a follow-up article.

"Abandon me at the bar? Never even call to apologize? You, Ben Carlton, are a complete asshole." Ben jumped as Brandi stormed into his office and stood there fuming. He'd forgotten about their date. This wasn't going to be pleasant.

Ben closed his eyes as she tore a strip off him, uttering expletives he'd never dreamed of, let alone heard from a supposed lady. Then again, he did break his motto, "Never date a colleague and never date skinny women," one that now he wished he'd stuck to. He liked curves and softness, probably should have been born in the fifties and sixties when attractive women looked like Marilyn or Raquel and not paper thin as the likes of Keira Knightley. When was a woman supposed to sport a six pack? And when you take a woman out to dinner isn't she supposed to have more than cola and cigarettes?

"Look, I'm sorry. I must have had too much to drink and passed out or something. I can honestly say I don't know what happened." He struggled again to remember, like he'd done nearly every night since last weekend's date. Other than the haunting dreams of crashing on a highway, smeared into a guardrail, nothing.

Just hazy recollections. He'd not seen Brandi since, and after the scathing message she left on his answering machine and office email, had managed to duck her on a few occasions until now. She'd obviously worked herself into a lather and wasn't about to let it fizzle out.

"Don't know what happened? I'll tell you what happened. You 'go to the washroom' and never come back. I looked all over for you in the bar and even went out to the parking lot. Your BMW was gone. You, you bastard, drove off. Probably ducked out the washroom window, or picked up some ho. If you weren't interested after all you shoulda just let me know. Not just bugger off. I've never been so humiliated in all my life. You sure seemed pretty excited when we were pressed together dancing, and so was I, I woulda jumped your bones if you took me home. Hope she had VD and crabs to boot. Men! Can't figure 'em out." Brandi seethed like a volcano about to explode, arms crossed, looking not at all attractive. Ben couldn't say he actually disagreed with her. It was a rotten thing to do to anyone and now wasn't the time to try some sort of trumped-up lie to back up his story. She'd probably slam his computer into his head. Besides, he had another story deadline to make.

"Look, I apologize. I can honestly say I don't know what happened. I must have blanked out or something, or maybe someone spiked my drink with a drug. Don't know. I don't remember leaving the bar, getting in my car, or anything. I didn't leave with anyone else and was itching to get you home myself." That part he at least could recall. He must have driven off somehow. His deadline loomed ever closer. "Again, I'm sorry."

"You can apologize until Armani is sold at the local Sally Ann's but this woman will never ever, ever go out with you again. Next time you get horny and want to take a girl out for a good time, save yourself the grief and stay in with the Palm Sisters. In fact you can beat off for the rest of your life for all I care. You, Ben, aren't worth my time." She stormed out and slammed his office door so hard the glass rattled. Other people looked up from their cubicles. Ben smiled apologetically as he rose and checked his door, to make sure it was still attached. At least other than a fight, no one heard what went on. Was he losing it? What did happen the other night? He tried again to remember. It was embarrassing, actually; the last memory he had was staggering into the washroom. The date played itself out in his head.

All he really wanted, after all, was a night out, a few drinks, some dancing and, if he got lucky, well that was the bonus. Being single and a reporter was great, except for the lonely nights and cold, empty bed. Everyone from the office told him don't go out with Ms. Pins 'n' Splinters, the young stick-creature from his work. Stick to real women, his buddies told him. They all told him she was a bit crazy. Maybe being strung out on Perrier and green salads did that to people. Although, he knew she was interested in him and crazy sounded like a lot better idea than reruns of *Sex And The City* or renting porn movies for another night.

Brandi had suggested O'Shanahan's. He knew it had a rep for being a biker's bar in its earlier days and now more a hard-edged rock/sports bar for blue-collar types. A place on the edge of safety and danger. He wanted to be out there, living life wild and crazy for once, instead of writing about it.

He didn't care where they went to drink, he only hoped by the look in Brandi's eyes and the promise on her lips where they would end up.

"Weird things happen there," Brandi had said. Ben laughed at her, knowing she frequented the place. Never laugh at the devil dressed in drag, he once was told, or he'll come back and reserve tanning rights on your hide for the rest of your life.

Then again, maybe she said that to interest him and get him to go out with her, and it worked. Weird places and events spurred him on, that was the whole reason for his existence as a reporter. The possible-story bug that haunted him all his life. The need to know and the "what if." His all-time favourite TV series ever since he was a kid was the cheesy *Kolchak, Night Stalker* reruns. The more bizarre and weird the story, the greater his interest.

Experiencing the edge of life, as a reporter Ben smelled it as soon as he walked in. "Story" sunk into every brick and dark, curved-oak banister in the place. The bar had atmosphere—ancient atmosphere—lacking in most bars and pubs on this continent. He recognized it from his travels in England, from their real, old pubs and inns; some dating back further than the twelfth century, older than that even. Laughter, cavorting, and socializing oozed from the timbers, ingrained into the very wood from over the centuries, where ghosts still sauntered up to the bar, mixing with the clientele. Why hadn't he visited this place before?

But his mind was more focused on her body that night as they pounded back several rounds of drinks, both nervous over this, their first date and his first in a long while. Ben didn't date at the drop of a hat, unlike most guys. But the mood had struck and why not? What harm could a night of fun do?

He remembered her asking for shooters. Girls always like the sweet stuff, never mind that it made for wicked hangovers, and should you throw up, disgusting vileness in the great white telephone.

"Let's have a couple of Screaming Orgasms and Sex On The Beach before we leave." Brandi sidled up beside him. "Then you can take me to my place, we can throw down my beach towels, a hot lamp and pretend we're at the seaside and work on the orgasms. Screaming or not." Her hand ran suggestively down the inside of Ben's leg. One of the guys at work told him she was a screamer and liked to thrash around a lot when she made out. He'd already pictured it in his mind. One of his previous girlfriends was very vocal and he couldn't say he didn't enjoy it just a little.

Ben remembered dancing together, his hands fondling her rear. If she had panties on, they were sheer G-strings. Her lips on his neck, an ache between his legs, and her hands caressing that throb. Yup, she was wonderfully uninhibited and crazy. Probably more than he was comfortable with, almost feeling like a virgin led to a vampire banquet.

"Take me home now. I want you," she said through the pulse of his hardness and the thump of the music.

"Wait here, I'll be right back. Need to use the can and call a cab. I've had too much to drink, won't drive home in this state." He sweated. Ben left Brandi propped against the railing lining the dance floor. He vaguely remembered staggering into the john.

And…

And…

A nightmare repeating itself like a broken tape flapping on a projector, him sitting helpless before a blank screen.

Them dancing, him entering the john. Then nothing.

Blank. Complete blank.

Except the dream of someone dying on the highway. Someone not him. Repeating over and over, while the broken tape of his memory flapped away, unable to view a scene from his life that seemingly had been edited or deleted. Or rendered nonexistent.

Maybe he had one drink too many, or worse, perhaps someone spiked his drink? Nothing added up, especially when the next morning found him passed out in his car, on a street in an area of town off Hastings, a street in Vancouver he never frequented, especially that time of night.

No Brandi, just a pounding headache and an empty whisky bottle on the seat.

He hated whisky and he knew he'd never drive if he had too much to drink. Which also meant that he couldn't have had his drink spiked, because he'd never be able to drive, unless she had done something to him. Or maybe she was only a tease, setting him up. Brandi seemed genuinely wanting. No sense, nothing made any sense.

But why? It seemed rather far-fetched Brandi would drug him, although seeing her seething outrage a few minutes ago he wouldn't put it past her now. She seemed genuinely pissed off and hurt that he abandoned her. She was your typical self-absorbed young adult, like one of the bachelorettes on TV he liked to watch. More interested in making sure all of her nails were done right instead of wondering what the possible ramifications of involvement in Iraq will be.

The in-between still remained a blur, like he'd shut down and another Ben Carlton took over. Too many questions and no answers. Some people blank out when drinking, others switched personalities, became belligerent. Was it the whisky? Maybe it knocked him out. Allergic reaction? But that wasn't the case here, was it? This was different. He'd never done anything like this before. Maybe there was something wrong with him; a visit to the doctor might be in order. It was probably too late to verify if someone had spiked his drink or…?

He laughed, going from sublime to ridiculous. Only one logical explanation left, one that made absolutely no sense; *it was like someone else had taken over my body*. Like many people say when they've had one drink too many.

* * *

Virtually crawling from bed to shower, Carol ached. That deep, weary ache of doing far too much in too little time on too little sleep.

Invigorating, tepid-to-cool water worked its magic, nudging exhausted nerve endings, massaging Carol back to full consciousness. She scrubbed her face and let the water cascade over her dirty-blonde hair. She'd the luxury of sleeping undisturbed for six hours, the most in the last four days. But still no clue to the identity of the possibly male suspects, no daughter, and only some wavy apparition of a native elder, who may or not exist, to go on.

Which is the only thing that made any sense. How someone with a limp could have disappeared so fast, leaving no trace of his existence except in her head. Only hallucinations didn't give you their names or talk about British TV series.

"So I investigate the mirage, then," she muttered, shutting off the shower and gently squeezing the excess water from her shoulder-length hair. The force didn't really lend itself to having one's hair extremely long and Carol wished she could grow it halfway down her back. It made for feeling more female, more woman, which in this job, surrounded by mostly macho males, wasn't always easy. Besides, long hair was something for criminals to grab onto if you ever got into a fight.

She'd already searched all known databases and there was no record of a Charlie Stillwaters anywhere, no birth or marriage record or even a police file. "Ska-ga. He called himself a ska-ga." She'd never heard that term before. It was the one scrap of a clue she had to go with. Carol emphasized the harsh, more guttural notes, being used to how most natives naturally talked in her dealings with them as an officer in the rougher areas of Vancouver, where street sweepers swept more needles than leaves. One ability she had honed to a fine art, in her years in the force, was the ability to recall conversations virtually word for word.

"Off to the BC Museum of Anthropology at the University then." If they knew which native language *ska-ga* was from then perhaps she'd at least narrow him down to a certain tribal grouping of perhaps a few villages. If he existed, he'd most likely been born near here or somewhere along the coast.

She checked her messages, none, for a change. Big Dan had given her a breather after the press conference and failed park search, he knew she needed it. "Some rest will help. A tired mind leaves you not thinking straight and you'll know better how to proceed after sleeping on it."

He was right. Pretty cagey for a miserable bastard. After all, that was probably why he was commissioner. She dressed quickly and scribbled on a little face paint, feeling more human and more feminine for the sleep and the makeup. "Grab a hot Venti and off to the museum I go." If he existed she'd find him.

* * *

Voices; whispering incantations just beyond the realm of hearing. Trouble. Charlie closed his eyes. "Damn. Right when I was about to catch the ballgame too."

Spirit voices calling usually meant trouble. Charlie set the VCR to record. "It's not easy being a shaman when you can pick up ethereal distress calls. I really should get an answering service. Wonder if any recently departed ghosts are looking for work, like Anna Nicole Smith. Nay, don't make enough dough for the likes of her. John Candy, now he'd do a wonderful job with that laugh of his."

He clicked off the TV and left the back room of his cabin, the only room that had electricity, and entered the small living room. His fireplace oozed a warm glow as wood crackled away in a slow dance of flames. Smoke penetrated most areas of the cabin giving it an air of natural, earthy incense, aromas reminiscent of campfires full of the sharp tang of pine and aromatic cedar. He slumped into his favourite chair and relaxed, letting his mind clear.

The tugs he'd been feeling all afternoon, building like a barometer to an escalating thunderstorm, settled all around him, urging the shaman to a place that needed him. "Couldn't wait 'til after the game though, could ya."

He released his aura from his physical shell, so easy for him with all the years of practice. Doing what some refused to believe even existed and others deemed impossible. The shaman allowed his astral self to be whisked along the tendrils of ethereal currents, like nervous excited kids discovering some obscure hidden treasure. They tugged and prodded the elderly native's aura along.

Seconds later and hundreds of kilometres away, Charlie appeared before a trail. Several tall and ancient cedars that once stood crowded around in a near semicircle had now been toppled over. Charlie knew the place all too well, had been there in the past. The Cathedral Trail in Stanley Park.

Memories licked at his senses of another time, another seductive woman's arms. Not to mention her breas…

"Snap out of it," he muttered. Whatever happened here recently was not good.

The remaining standing trees rustled in agitation. Charlie looked down and spotted the bare piece of earth where once resided the object these gentle spirits had been elected to watch. A white rock set with blotches of black crust like acid was absent. He projected his aura around the glade. No rock and worse, all spectral traces of her were gone.

The witch, The Lure of Stanley Park, had escaped.

"She's done a walkabout, right out from under the branches of those who were supposed to be guarding her. How is this possible?" Charlie's essence shivered, remembering his first dealings with the evil, flirtatious witch. "This isn't good."

She had been trapped by nature and now due to the fierce windstorms on the West Coast it appeared that nature might have released her. The trees swayed in agitation. They had no answer either, which was why they'd called him. They didn't do memories, at least not of the human cognizant kind, and perceived time by a whole different set of values. Brief time to them meant seasons and individual ring growths. There were other ways of searching, but not in spirit form; he'd have to make a trip to Vancouver to investigate further. "Oh, I hate being in the big city. So rush, rush. Hard on the soul it is."

The shaman surveyed the area and caught sight of crushed vegetation. Foulness and death sang its vile cadence down his chakras. Charlie drew himself back to his body in the cabin just outside of Skidegate. "I sense there is much more travesty committed in that clearing than her mere escape. But how could she? She was transformed into the rock. Even if someone picked up the rock and took it away, how could she escape? She is spirit-tied to the guardians of the grove," he grumbled, knowing the ball game would have to wait now. The elder pulled himself upright, waited a second before rising, and grabbed his cane. "Oh, what to wear for a long trip? I hate packing."

He grabbed his ball cap from the floor where it had fallen. "Found ya! Best tell Brook before I go, could be awhile. Someone will have to water my plants."

He stared out at the portal tree in the backyard. Not sure if he was ready for this, or if his old bones could handle it. "Not good. Not good at all."

* * *

Larry stood at the edge of the dark trail just outside the edge of O'Shanahan's parking lot, waiting in the bushes for Ryley to leave. The three Harleys indicated that as usual he had his two bodyguards, Stumpy and Greasy, with him. They were heading for their bikes. He'd already checked the man's pockets of the body he was in and found only apartment keys. His ID confirmed he lived only a couple of blocks away.

Stumpy and Greasy. He knew the two thugs well. Ruthless, efficient, and brutal. Willing to do Ryley's dirty work at the snap of a finger. Much like he did— once. Another pulse thumped in his head. Larry closed his eyes as a mini-migraine faded slowly away. Residue from descending tonight, he thought, although not usually this late after assuming someone's body. He also knew, in the body of this guy that he took to be a middle-aged accountant, he stood no chance of getting close to Ryley. There had to be another way, but other than follow them back to the clubhouse, he didn't know what to do. Not to mention there was still the matter of the other two. Time was running out tonight. By daylight either this body would start sobering up or pass out in exhaustion. He was tireless; the physical dimensions of a different human's body he'd discovered were not the same, there were limits to what he could and couldn't do.

"Degob, it goin' widout sayein, ye doin' wan guard at a tyme." A voice, hauntingly familiar, whispered from behind him as he had virtually the same thought.

"What the…?"

Larry glanced around in the dark. There was no one behind him, or on the walkway.

"Follow me trail of fairy sparkles. Begorra, if ye cain hear me, ye cain see t'em." A small, barely indistinguishable figure flitted from tree to tree.

"Fairy what?" A faint line of lights shimmered, dancing in the darkness. The voice—it reminded him of someone from long ago.

The three choppers in the parking lot started up, their baritone growls unhindered by mufflers, shattering the sounds of the bar, music still thumping away between the staccato snaps of the beefy bikes as they accelerated, fading into the background.

Larry took another long swig of whisky and began stumbling after the fluttering lights. Might as well check out this bizarre change of events, he had no chance of cornering Ryley tonight. He'd put it down to another night of reconnaissance. Looking, prodding for the weakness in his armour, trying to get closer to Ryley. When he was in the club, he noticed Ryley seemed rather occupied with keeping an eye on his cell phone, checking it often and at one point received a call he kept guarded from the others. There was a way to get closer to Ryley— through Greasy. He cringed, not certain if he could take over the body he needed to. But he'd do anything, and had so far, in order to bring Ryley's world crashing down around him. He had to get his hands on that cell phone.

He wandered along a small earthen footpath following the beacon of lights bouncing along like gay little pixies in front of him. He'd encountered some odd things while being held in the vortex, but nothing like this. Intrigued, he followed the tiny dancing figures. Like Irish fairies. He recalled pictures of these from his childhood, now long proven to be fakes. The Cottingley photographs, taken by some English woman in the twenties. What was her name?

Only these imps cavorted gaily like they'd imbibed too much pixie dust or magic mushrooms. Enchanting! There wasn't much these days that made him smile. His grandmother was Irish and she'd tell him folk stories, of them and of the Leprechauns.

"Wy there laddie, Seamus O'Leary I be called."

It wasn't possible! A red-suited figure with white, frilled cuffs and black breeches materialized. Curly hair, stuffed askew, barely contained under a green top hat topped off the man. A scruffy beard nearly hid a pipe, which hung precariously as he talked, jiggling before him like a three-year-old having to go to the washroom. A two-and-a-half-foot leprechaun; the character from his childhood books and his grandmother's tales stood before him.

Larry stood on the edge of a small glade. A circle of lights gleamed all around the perimeter, flittering under the brush like glow flies in mating dances. Darkness cast itself in the glade under the gaze of the surrounding cedar trees.

"Come! And don't be believin' al dis foolish fairy tales. I found it, after aul dis time." He giggled, genuinely excited with what he'd discovered. Dancing around a white rock, golden light bounced all around the rock.

"Found what?"

"The goold at the end of the ranebow." He giggled.

Larry stepped forward, both feet entering the darkness of the glade. "That's impossible."

"Wy there laddie, it's not only possible, but rale, all these 'ears and 'ears of looking, and I've found it and buried it under dis white rock." He smirked. "Help mesilf lift it. Begorra, me old bones aren't what tey wance were. Me brogues need mending and even me Charlie horses need splints to get me old bones a moving." He crippled over grabbing at his back, leaning over his buckling cane, pretending to be feeble.

Larry chuckled, and without thinking, bent over and touched the old rock etched with moss, lichens, and black spots like acid burns. The well-meaning leprechaun had the same amicable way of cavorting along he used to giggle to as a child. Memories of his old grandmother pretending to be Seamus bouncing around made him smile. He couldn't remember the last time he'd laughed, it had been too long.

A surge of light erupted from the cool, porous surface of the stone. Cold, like the granite he touched, surged inside. The green sprite lifted his cane and an evil smile crossed his face as he jabbed the cane in Larry's face. "Got ya, you of al should know there is no goold at the end of the ranebow."

Larry blinked, his eyes stinging from the cane's butt end smashed into his face. He tried to pull his hand away from the stone, but couldn't. His hand remained glued as the green character slowly vanished in a haze of mist and the lithesome figure of a native woman dressed in veils of silky gossamer erupted from the earth.

She stepped forward shedding all her shimmering wisps of clothing.

The Lolita of his early teenage years. His grandmother told him about her as well. Cunning, sensual, and…

"Deadly." She snickered at Larry, who, as hard as he tried, couldn't pull his hand away from the rock's surface. "I haven't much time, already they awaken." She stretched and lunged forward flowing into the body Larry occupied. He shuddered as the coldness flooded in.

He felt himself thrust aside as the woman flooded into the man's body. She was strong; very strong. This was all a trap. He staggered back, his hand suddenly free. Convulsions ran through the body they occupied. The man buckled to his knees as all the sparkling fairies and dancing lights quickly swirled toward him and sucked themselves into the host body. His heart slammed in his chest at the strain. Was this too much for the man? Stress-induced endorphins tore across his body, his heart convulsed.

The glade itself returned to the dark forest, smelling of dank earth, moss, and cedar as Larry commanded the body to stand up; he had to return to the club. "No," he yelled. "This can't be happening, this body is mine."

"What, another resides in here as well? How is this possible?" The witch glanced around, staring at the cedars swaying in the darkness. "I don't have time for this. Leave the glade immediately." She commanded the body to move against Larry's wishes.

"Explains why I could sense this one's soul was missing and it was so easy to possess." She sneered, as the body staggered drunkenly along like some long limbed alien bug creature strung out on fermented fruit. Larry fought to control the man's body, battling for possession and control of its limbs. Intense pressure pounded at Larry, the man was experiencing agony; what if he keeled over with a heart attack on them both?

"He's mine. Somehow you read my mind and lured me in here with some of my own childhood fantasies."

"Yes, silly man. So full of revenge that you'd ignore reason and caution, so easy to read your thoughts, and that is why I was so able to possess this body. Only I didn't realize your thoughts were not those of the real owner. The native tribes around here called me The Lure. You may call me your mistress." She laughed a little too hard for Larry's liking. How long had she been trapped in that glade?

"Crazy bitch, that's what I'd call you. Get out of here." Larry heaved all of his mental might at her, thrusting a wall of energy. The host staggered, twisting back toward the glade. Blood began to ooze from his ears and nose. Whatever had trapped her in the first place, Larry knew, was the one thing she was afraid of and the one thing that could get rid of her.

"No." A third voice sounded in the air. The host was awakening, undoubtedly due to the tremendous strain the two other entities were exerting on his body.

"Quick, I must be quick. I cannot fight both them and you." She grabbed Larry's essence by the throat. Her long nails dug in, pain lanced through him. *How is this possible?* Somehow blood spurted from the man's neck. "If you ever want to return again to exact your revenge, do what I say now!"

Larry fought, but he couldn't escape her grasp. He was far stronger than her, physically, but not in this mental state of being. Heart palpitations raced through the body, how hard on him would it be if he tried returning to the void above the bar from this distance? What he'd give to have his real body back now, all six feet, two hundred and fifty pounds of it. He wasn't adverse to backhanding a woman; on the other hand he wasn't sure he'd even classify her as female, which made her more than fair game.

"Now, show me how you got in this man's body, and quick."

"Never."

A long hush fell in the forest behind them. The Lure's intense fear ran through the host. A scurry, the sound of millions of hungry rats churning the forest floor, began to flood down the trail. A virtual river of rampaging rodents swept toward them. Larry froze. This was the one fear he carried from his childhood; he hated rats. His parents lived in a very poor neighborhood of Vancouver along the wharves, just off Hastings Street. More than one night he awoke to the scurry of rats in his room and occasionally one trying to bite him. Perhaps that was what made him tough and mean as he grew up.

"They will gnaw on your soul forever. I know, they did mine," she uttered in a deep breath.

He gulped. She knew his deepest fears. Yes, she did, she could read his mind. She'd brought Seamus to life from his childhood memories; that stab of pain earlier in the night. "No, I won't. This is another trick."

"I don't have time for this." The sounds vanished instantly. Larry had been right; she could read his thoughts; that was how she seduced him with the mad little Leprechaun.

Through the corner of their vision he shared her sight as she caught six ominous shadows approaching.

Larry caught her thoughts for a moment, as she let her guard down. Her captors were coming. The reason she couldn't escape in all these centuries.

"It's only because you're in here, distracting this being, that I can enter. Here I thought he was soulless, easy pickings. Now, show me how you got in here. Or die and never reach the goal you are willing to go through the hell of remaining on this plane of existence to achieve."

Larry screamed in agony, just as if her nails dug into his physical skull.

She was right. More than fighting her off, he wanted to get his revenge on Ryley. He'd endured too much agony to remain here. The cost on his soul was tremendous, he needed to concede and hope to get out of here somewhat intact. Besides, the original body's owner was starting to awaken under the strain and they could both be tossed out.

The shattered bodies of his wife and kids flashed to mind, Home burned to the ground. Cat held in his hands, one eye dangling. Perhaps it was her playing with his head again. Pulling up his deepest hurts. What did he care if she was released? He knew why he was here, who he needed to get even with and that was all that mattered. "I got here through a rift over the dance floor in the tavern called O'Shanahan's," Larry capitulated and gave the answer she demanded of him.

"How is this possible? A dance floor, ancient spiral, witches circle. Show me and hurry. Otherwise you'll spend eternity as my plaything, and I get bored very easily." Her free hand swept down Larry's body and grabbed him between the legs, squeezing hard.

Agonizing pain swept through him. How could she do this? She was only a spirit. He gave up; in this form she was stronger than him. There was only one thing he wanted to do above anything else. "Okay."

A tongue licked at his ear as her hand relaxed her grip on his scrotum and slowly caressed him. As hard as he tried to deny it he could feel his arousal. "I knew you'd see some resemblance of reason."

"Crazy bitch." The host spun around and began marching toward the thumping noises of the bar. Cold, clammy sweat beaded his forehead, his breathing ragged. The internal struggle was taking its toll. Larry could sense she was partly occupied with keeping the man unconscious.

Behind him the six dark shadows churned, unable to penetrate the wall of light cast by the parking-lot lights. The definitions between natural and manmade world were sharp. Electric and neon light pierced the veils of night's darkness. "Interesting," she muttered, "they don't like the modern world." Larry caught her thoughts.

* * *

Too late, unwilling to enter man's world they hovered at the edge of darkness, unsure what to do next, until they retreated to the glade. They had no means of dealing with the unnatural world. Only those who sent The Lure into entrapment possibly could. They were old, maybe powerless in this time like the guardians, unseen except in long-ago times. The guardians didn't even know if they still existed. But there was one other who'd visited in the past. He'd dealt with her before, they'd contact him first.

* * *

In the pounding of music, strobe lights flickering, no one really noticed the disoriented man staggering in. Eyes bulging, sweat streaming down his face, he stumbled into the middle of the dance floor, lost in the sea of bodies.

The Lure stared up into the dark maw of churning smoke and haze. "A portal. Clever man! Now I understand." She smiled and turned toward Larry. "What's the expression they use here? Why yes, I will indeed come to your place tonight for a good time." Her body started to shimmer as she pulled herself out of the host they occupied. He blinked, returning to consciousness.

"My head." The host grasped his face, doubling over.

"You will come with me. This will ensure there's no trickery on your part."

A tug and, as hard as he tried to resist, Larry was pulled free of the host as well.

"Forget resisting. Let's just say it has been far too long since I've had a male. And what's to say a girl can't reward a man for saving her life," she cooed.

As they pulled clear the host fell with a heavy thud onto the vibrating dance floor. Tongue protruding from his mouth. Lips blued. He lay still. Some patrons screamed, others continued trying to dance, oblivious to what was happening, lost in their own drug or alcohol-induced worlds.

Bouncers rushed forward.

"But?"

"I said I'd let you live. Not him. No loose lips, no evidence. Isn't that the way of the members you hail from?"

Larry knew the laws of the Devil's Spawn only too well.

One burly bouncer checked his tongue and felt for a pulse before yelling into his earpiece. "He's dead. Get the ambulance, possible coke OD."

She smiled, pulling her helpless captive into the swirling darkness over the dance floor.

A hot, wet tongue licked at Larry's ear.

"Playtime darling."

Chapter Four

"John Denton, curator of the UBC Museum of Anthropology. How may I help you?" He stuck out his hand.

"Carol Ainsworth, I called you from the VPD office earlier." Her policeman's mind immediately registered the clammy handshake. Obviously a law-abiding citizen. He had that nervous demeanor, like he was about to be busted for an overdue parking ticket. She got that emotion frequently from honest citizens. In her experience it was usually only the innocents who were in awe of the police. Criminals, obviously, were not overly concerned. They had their own different nervous dispositions; they didn't care if they were breaking the law.

"Don't worry, I'm not about to bust you or any of your staff, although the janitor over there looks pretty shifty. I think I've seen his face on our wanted posters." She smiled, trying humour to break some of the ice. Carol found the warm fuzzy approach drew better response from people than the stern "scare the crap out of them" like Big Dan often used.

John laughed nervously. "You're only joking, I hope. We screen all of our staff very tightly." He ran his finger inside his highly starched collar, obviously still a little on edge despite Carol's good-cop routine. Her first instinct was "good guy" but you never knew. He could still turn out to be spending museum expense money on hookers. Even bit-part players had to prove themselves to her cynicism.

"Just kidding, police humour. I'm trying to track someone down. A possible suspect. Can't name names but claims he's a ska-ga. Does that mean anything to you?"

His thin face lost some of its pallor. You couldn't say the colour returned, as she rather doubted it ever did. A holiday in his eyes probably meant cramming two weeks into scouring the shelves of Oxford Library instead of lying on the beaches of Hawaii in a suntan-lotion-slathered, alcohol-induced stupor. That was her fantasy.

"First, all our vast museum resources are at your disposal, I'm only glad to be helping one of our detectives on the hunt for felons. Has this anything to do with the big case regarding the death of our mayor and his wife?"

"His wife? How'd you hear about that? Haven't officially released details yet."

An image came to mind; a warm feeling south of her navel. The reporter.

"Hold on. Let me guess; the *Province*."

He nodded. "Splashed all over the morning edition."

Damn. Ben worked fast. "As you can understand, I'm not allowed to divulge any information. Now, let me ask you again. A ska-ga. Does that mean anything to you?" She spoke more harshly than she meant to, irritated now. But not with this poor man, only with her own judgement. Mustn't take it out on someone who could help.

As they walked down the slope, leaving reception behind, Carol admired the ancient totems, recognizing the likeness of Thunderbird, whose massive wings were said to beat out booming thunder. Spilling out into the grand open area, many more poles and native memorabilia were positioned, magnificently lit by the sun beating through the massive, thirty-foot windows. One of the twenty-some foot poles had a jutting beak nearly as long as the totem was tall. Carol admired the workmanship, swirling colours, and ovoid, staring eyes. She'd forgotten just how imposing and awe-inspiring the statues were, having visited the museum on many school expeditions. Representing deities and gods, they were meant to frighten or intimidate enemy tribes, and they did. The scale of the carvings was immense. Through a vast expanse of glass a replica beach set, complete with native longhouses nestling in a white sea of crushed abalone shell, was visible. Carol remembered one school visit in particular, bent at the waist searching the clover for a four-leafed variety. The curator's voice bought her back to the present.

"Yes, the term ska-ga is very familiar to me. It was used by the same people that built these incredible totems from Ninstints." He indicated to his right. "Means shaman, although it's rarely used these days."

"Ninstints? He's a Haida? But that's up in the Charlottes. What would he be doing here?" That threw a curve into things. She'd assumed he was from one of the local tribes, Squamish, or possibly Coast Salish.

"Correct. It's possible he most likely lives somewhere in this area. Walk this way." Squashing the immediate reaction to imitate his gait, she swallowed a smirk and followed him to the right into another gallery. The circular room was overwhelmed by an eight-foot raven perched on top of a clamshell that appeared to be attempting to spill out its cargo of humans.

The raven's eyes seemed to follow her as they walked past. She caught sight of one of the humans perched with his family jewels dangling out of the shell. "Well, they make sure everything is anatomically correct."

"Some of the Haida have quite the sense of humour. That statue was carved by Bill Reid. It represents Raven, their creator god, opening a clam-shell on Rosespit beach releasing the first Haida to the world," he stated, rocking back and forth with his hands behind his back, reminding her of an old English bobby's questioning stance. He was obviously very proud to have the magnificent statue in his collection; curators always thought of the museum's exhibits as their own.

"Humour, you say. Sounds like our man is definitely Haida. Now what exactly do ska-gas do? Are they like witch doctors? That sort of thing?"

"In some respects. Let me show you this mortuary box we originally found near Ninstints. This might explain better." He led her past the display, but still, all the while, Carol held the freaky feeling Raven was studying her out of the corner of his overly large eyes. They entered a part of the museum not normally accessible by the public. Several people were crammed into one corner while someone blabbered on about BC this and AD that. School; a classroom of some sort. She'd disliked school, especially history and socials, preferring Phys ed and mathematics. "Sorry, the session is in, I can't disturb them. But I can show you the shaman's totem we've put up in the main gallery. It will definitely explain better some of what Haida shamans could once do."

He strode over to a totem standing in the corner of the main gallery, all by itself, as if isolated on purpose. "This is a ska-ga totem."

Carol observed the grimacing human holding a wooden three-by-two-foot box above his head. John pointed out the smaller sideways human figure wrapped around the larger's belly. "Probably meant to show he had been eaten for daring to violate the bones of the sacred and holy," John explained. On the tall figure's head were five carved, once-white, horn-like bones pointing upward and piercing the box. As she peered closer, Carol could make out that each bone had another grimacing face carved on it. "A final warning, to those foolish enough to touch the box or what was within." John finished.

Very faint symbols were painted on the sides, similar to the other boxes she'd seen out in the museum. "This totem is one of the few we've found containing the actual bones of a Haida ska-ga. They were always erected on the edge of town, sometimes overlooking it, as if observing the townspeople from wherever they'd passed on to. Death to a shaman simply meant another stage of life's journey. Even in passing, a ska-ga's magic was very powerful. It was believed his or her spirit, even in death, would look after his people."

Carol's eyes opened at the last bit, she didn't realize the women could be shamans as well. "Magic? They some kind of medicine men, then?"

"More like wise holy men. They were very powerful people. To disturb the bones of a ska-ga meant madness and possible death. They controlled spirit beings and, similar to the Aboriginals' dreamtime, often dwelled in altered states. The ska-ga went on spirit quests to overpower and control spirit beings. Some would guard their bones after dying. They could extract diseases and bad spirits from the sick and infirm and advise the chief on the outcome of important situations."

"So you're saying it's possible he could enter some kind of altered state and engage in spirit travel? Like a transcendental state? An out-of-body experience thing and travel around as some sort of ghost being?" This was leading somewhere she didn't really want to think about. He looked so real that night, but could he have been some sort of transcended being? Able to travel around at will? In any case Carol shuddered; she hated ghosts.

"If you mean could they leave their bodies and astral travel, yes. Common among the shamans of many tribes. There are numerous stories, some verified, of such journeys. I can think of a couple. Would you like to hear them?" he asked, tapping his fingers over his chin.

"If you have time. Sure, why not, might help wrap my head around this character." As preposterous as it sounded, was it possible that he was there that night in some sort of astral state? A ghost that communicated with her? Carol shivered. She hadn't any dealings within the esoteric community, except in the movies, and believed in keeping it that way. Besides, how would you arrest a spirit? Let alone put it in a cell.

"I've reports of shamans sending their bodies into journeys and reporting back their results. The most verifiable one was back in 1764 after Canada passed from French to British hands. Sir William Johnson, the chief British Indian Agent at the time, wrote in his journals that he sent messengers to invite the Chief of the Ojibwas to sit down and enter into Peace Treaty negotiations at Fort Niagara. The chief was unsure of the British intentions, so he had his shaman send his spirit over to check if the British were honest or a setting a trap. He reported back saying that indeed there were very few soldiers there and many gifts assembled for them. I've other stories of shamans finding lost people, and one recently from Fort Churchill involving a supply ship. Long overdue, possibly lost, the community leaders were worried that with winter fast approaching they would face starvation. They asked an elderly shaman, Shonkelli, for help, who sent his spirit to investigate. He reported the ship was fine, but had to rescue the crew of another floundering ship from an ice floe. The next day the vessel appeared and the supply ship's captain reported the exact same story, including the name of the rescued ship. All documented and reported cases." He stared up at the shaman's mortuary box, "And yes, in case you were wondering, that box is only a replica; no bones."

"Not to mention that you'd probably not want some angry ska-ga dude haunting away your visitors."

He smiled. "Possibly, although back in the fifties when they brought this to the museum they were a lot less reverent regarding native religious beliefs. The original, bones and all, probably for the sake of keeping everything complete, was installed out here. And don't forget, like I said, not all shamans were male. This one was female. The Haida were a matriarchal race, not like our society."

"Interesting." She pondered whether or not to tell him. If she did she'd have to mention the location and the fact it involved the biggest news story to happen in many years. "Okay, I'm not a believer yet, Mr. Denton, but what if I said I may have possibly had such an experience recently. This is totally off the record so I'm trusting you not to repeat it to anyone." John nodded in agreement and Carol explained what happened the other night at the death scene.

"Fascinating. You're here then, because you believe an ancient shaman visited you. Don't get me wrong, I agreed to secrecy, but I am the curator and a scientist first and foremost. Many of us, after years of study, have begun to believe that there are many sides to life on this planet. Not all of it explainable or even remotely believable. So, while I tend to take the orthodox approach, I've come to realize there is an awful lot the natives understand about this earth and beyond that we haven't even scratched the surface of. Back in the forties and fifties, we scientific lot would probably have laughed in your face, but today it's a different story." He stopped and peered around making sure no one was listening. "I'll share this if you also swear to secrecy." Carol nodded.

"Originally, like I said, the bones were out here in the original box. We had many instances, usually at night, of disturbing happenings that began after we retrieved this shaman's totem from Ninstints in the fifties. Guards were freaked out by the moving of heavy objects and chanting. They'd say they heard the faint murmurs of a woman in the main gallery. After quite a few incidences, and very high staff turnover, we removed the bones and recently, under Haida accompaniment, they were shipped back to Haida Gwaii. The museum made a replica of the box to put on display. "

"And since then, you've had peace and quiet?"

"Oh, yes."

"Interesting." She could tell he was being more than honest with her. "Only this ska-ga wasn't ancient. He spouted a quote from the *Red Dwarf* TV series, which I've never seen but looked up online and found out it was on BBC TV from 1988 to 99."

"Now that is interesting. I've not heard of any modern day shamans, Haida or otherwise. I'd have thought they all were laid to rest long ago in their own little boxes." He pondered for a moment tapping his finger to his lips. "Although, come to mention it, that's triggered something. Wait here, I've got to check our files. I do recall reports…" He wandered off, more thinking out loud and muttering to himself than talking to Carol.

Under the ever-observant eyes of the watchmen assembled in the gallery, Carol wandered around viewing the totems and other statues. Sunlight beaming in the huge expanse of window lit the entire area. She especially liked the carving of the spirit bear catching a salmon in its mouth. Peering at the small plaque she noticed it was also by Bill Reid, a prominent Haida carver and craftsman. A sharp cry from outside caught her attention.

"Look, honey! I believe that's a bald eagle." She heard someone in the gallery, obviously a tourist, exclaim while pointing into the sky in front of the museum. The other person beside them nodded. Carol just caught the sight of wings spread out on wind currents before they circled away. She looked over and caught the carved face of a wooden eagle glaring down at her. Its haughty eyes were captured magnificently in the cedar, a look of permanent disdain on its face. John came walking back up to her. From his enthusiastic gait she knew he'd found what he searched for. Carol pointed to the pole before her. "Is that Eagle on top?"

"Yes, very observant. You can tell it's Eagle because his beak is crooked and the eyes slitted. The Haida lineage and tribes were ruled by either eagles or ravens, so there was some animosity between the two, and even wars. Now, if you'll follow me I'll show you the new gallery and the display we're putting together. It depicts the creation of the Gwaii Haanas National Park in 1993 and the modern day involvement of the Haida to stand up for and protect what they believe in."

He stood before a section of wall, behind them the ancient gods cast from old-growth timbers sat with wide eyes watching her, like Eagle did. This place gave her the creeps. It seemed they were studying her as much as she them, that they were just as curious. Perhaps deciding if she was as bad as the rest of the whites who virtually annihilated their race. The only one she felt any sympathy for, or familiarity to, was the great eagle. It was like her; always observant, missing very little in its harsh penetrating gaze that cut the truth from lies, a trait which served her very well as a law officer.

Her mind raced. What if it were like those movies where museum artifacts come to life at night? She knew one thing, you couldn't pay her enough to work here as security guard. Carol shivered. No chance, not with these morphic beings carved from wood staring out, their shapes moving across the walls under shifting moonlight. Especially when the female ska-ga spirit had wandered these halls at night, who knew what else might be? Besides, she was so used to being the one doing the watching, and hated that jumpy feeling being watched always gave her.

A map of Haida Gwaii hung from a wall screen. Several pictures adorned the concrete surface of the museum walls, some of the open devastation of gutted hillsides bleeding ruddy soil. Massive scarred stumps and branches, like severed human limbs, littered the ground. Others depicted the natural beauty she assumed was in the park. Trees bigger than houses, people gathered in protest blocking idling logging trucks, loggers angry their jobs and livelihood were on the line. All of them waiting to cut down forests, hundreds, if not thousands, of years old, and most of all, police arresting proud native elders. Heads held high under tall, handmade cedar hats, adorned in red and black, button-ornamented cloaks, Raven and Eagle crests emblazoned on the back. Hands pounding on drums; chanting. Pride on their faces, determined to save their dwindling world, knowing that a stand must be taken someplace. Here, in this, the homeland they were given to protect for future generations, was where they were going to do it. Some of this was evident in the photos, the rest written in little cards adjoining them. "From the reports I've read I do recall one such person. Claimed he was a card-carrying member of the local shamans, local member number three or some such silly thing. No one took him seriously of course. Probably thought he was mad."

John scanned the pictures, but before he could indicate the one he was searching for Carol caught the button-festooned Expos ball-cap-wearing individual in the background of one picture in which police were rounding up several elders. A wry smile on his face, as if he knew a joke on those there that everyone else had missed.

They both pointed to the man leaning on his cane at the same time. "That's him!"

"Oh my." John beamed. "I believe I may have found your man."

Chapter Five

The old canoe sailed effortlessly into English Bay and rounded the corner of Siwish Rock. Four men, garbed in headdresses of cedar boughs and ferns, their bodies adorned in painted colours and further attire of grasses and ferns, stared up at the span of Lion's Gate Bridge which towered over them as they glided under towards Coal Harbour. A low fogbank had crept into the inlet virtually hiding them as they entered the inner waters of the port. Cars zipped by overhead in a relentless stream. "The world has changed since our last visit."

"Indeed, a lot," the other three nodded. They sailed farther and caught the sails adorning Canada Place. "What a large canoe."

"So massive."

"Such change."

"So little time." Another gawked as they spoke in harmony, one after another in singsong repetition as if the four minds were really one. "I think not made of wood." He added from the head of the canoe, frowning. "Unnatural."

"Agreed." The others nodded in unison.

"Let us return to our objective."

"Yes, return. To those who called."

"Trouble brews."

"Not good, not good."

The one sitting in the prow of the canoe set his paddle into the waters of English Bay and stroked. "It's been a long time."

"Too long."

"Yes, a long time," the others replied, mouths gawking at the trappings of a modern city of lights blinking from a thousand buildings. Like four kids entering Disneyland for the first time.

They turned the canoe as easily as otters twist through the kelp plants that once thrived in the waters and headed for Stanley Park. Once ashore they quietly headed toward the cedars of Cathedral Trail, the mist edged their passage so others were oblivious to their presence.

A car honked at a jogger, earphones blaring away, as they crossed the road running through Stanley Park.

"So much change." One began and the others all chimed in.

"Much has also gone." Another added. "Many things, not of earth, unnatural."

"I sense little life within this forest. None of those of the old ways dwell here.

The villages of our followers are gone, covered over."

He leaned over and touched the earth. "Much destruction and death." A tear bled from his eye for the ones buried in the memory of the soil.

"Much strangeness, mountains erected by transformers as powerful as ours." They all nodded staring at the skyscrapers edging the south of Stanley Park.

"We have been away such…"

"A long time." The others added in.

"Caution. It is best to blend in."

"Observe first."

"Wise judgment," they added to each other.

* * *

"I think you have our mysterious ska-ga." Carol stared at the image, the entire conversation with Charlie rattling through her head, like he was standing next to her. She peered closer. "The picture is poor, dark, but that's definitely him. Can I have a copy of this sent to my office? Now, how do I find out who he is?"

"Surely. Let me jot down this file number and we'll search our records for what was noted about the people on this photo. We do a very meticulous job in recording everything that enters the museum," he said with evident pride, obviously feeling very cocky about himself as he started to wander off. Carol smirked. Probably has a small grow-op in his basement like half of Vancouver.

"Mind if I wander about while you do that?" She yelled to his retreating back.

"Go ahead. It might take me several minutes to get the information needed."

Carol quickly jotted down details in the pictures while she waited, noting that Charlie was only in the one photo. She walked back down into the sunlit area of the main gallery and stared again at the shaman's totem, sitting by the large, full-sized statue of a Sea Wolf, a salmon in its mouth. Not a bear, as she surmised earlier, according to the plaque in front of it. The carving by Bill Reid was amazingly like those of the ancient carvers of the Haida ancestors he'd studied under. Maybe their reborn spirits guided his hands. Getting bored, she decided to walk back towards Raven and the clamshell; it was the direction John had disappeared off to. She sat on the dais and stared blankly at Raven perched on top of his clamshell. He reminded her of the other three usually adorning most Haida poles. They were the watchmen, she knew. All of them seemed to watch her as John came walking out from the student area flipping through a huge bound book.

"Charlie Stillwaters of Skidegate."

She hadn't mentioned his name to John, now it didn't matter. "How was it that there was no mention of his arrest? I searched police records," she wondered out loud to John.

John spent several more moments, finger spearing across notes left to right. "Ah here we are, Mr. Stillwaters. Claims he was just passing by, upset that the road to his favourite nudist beach had been blocked. Thought this would be a great place to open up a HaidaBucks coffee house, or at least a big-name, American fast-food joint. The police didn't arrest the man, thinking he was obviously mentally challenged or deranged, but took his statement down."

Which a proper police officer would do. The more notes and records the better, especially in large cases like this where it's possible that future court proceedings might be involved. "Well, that would be Charlie, sounds loony enough. It doesn't explain what he was doing there. I thought he was mental at first, too. But that man is smarter than he lets on. If he wasn't arrested that explains why I've no record of him on file. I searched Government birth records and social insurance numbers and he's not registered anywhere."

John walked over to a copy machine and punched several numbers in. "Not unusual, many natives are born at home, not in hospitals, even today. Hence, no records, unless they choose to be registered. He was probably there advising a local chief, either invoking success or adding his powers of observation to the behind-the-scenes actions, which is what the shaman did in the old days. Here's your digital copy of the photo, Detective. I'd guess if he just lived off the land like a real shaman, he'd not need to work, other than fishing, perhaps. Now if you don't mind, I do have other pressing matters of the museum to attend to. So unless I can help in any other way?" He handed her the picture, his face beaming, obviously proud he could be of assistance.

"No, you've done more than enough but I'll keep your card should anything else come up. Don't think Crime Watchers has a reward out on him yet, but if they do I'll let you know. Thank you."

"Just doing my mere civic duty to keep this a law abiding town. Don't forget to make a donation to our museum charity on the way out. Takes a lot to keep this place going." He shook her hand.

65

"Will do. Thanks again." Carol put twenty dollars in the coffers as she exited. A little on the cheap side, considering what she'd discovered from him and his archives, but she didn't make much as a detective. "Barely able to keep myself in coffee and smokes," she muttered as she left, asking the front desk for a receipt, intending to claim it as an investigation expense. She glanced at her watch. "Now what, a trip to Skidegate?"

* * *

Brook looked up as Charlie nudged the front door open with his cane and wandered into the office of the *Northern Islander Report* in the summer village of Tlell. "Well, I see you've spruced up the place since you and my niece Chelen bought the only newspaper in Haida Gwaii. Seen any mischievous, big black birds grubbing for food recently?" Brook had met Chelen and Charlie when he was investigating a story involving the cutting down of The Golden Spruce last year. He'd needed Charlie's shamanic powers to help defeat the Haida's creator God, Raven.

Brook looked up from the computer he was working on. Bundles of old newspapers, books, and magazines littered the whole one side of the reception area. Two chairs, a plain coffee table, area rug, and coffee machine, all very tidy and clean, sat on the other side of the room. Brook eyed Charlie as he stared around the coffee-machine area. "Don't even joke about Raven. How's it going, Charlie?"

Brook glanced at his empty coffee cup, pushed his slightly disheveled hair back from over his eyes, and put on his glasses as he stood up. "Care for a coffee?"

"Thought you'd never ask. I decided to stop by before getting on the ferry for the mainland. Goodness, for one who never believed in the mystical stuff you've sure changed your tune."

Brook poured them each a cup. "Well, fighting six-foot Ravens will alter one's perception of life in the big cosmic scheme of things. Business trip? Or chasing some old flame!"

"Funny you should mention old flame, in a way you could say that. I'm off to Vancouver, some trouble I need to investigate involving some crazy woman locked away in a rock. Probably wants to jump these old bones in the worst way."

Brook laughed. "That's good. You really should consider finding someone to share your life. It must get lonely up in that old cabin sometimes. You know, a warm body to keep you cozy under the covers." He knew Charlie had been heartbroken since his childhood sweetheart, Lucy, had died. He'd not, to Brook's knowledge, ever been with another woman since.

The elder smiled back, grimacing at his coffee cup. "Man, this stuff packs a wallop, made it this morning or yesterday? I'm not lonely, and if I was, I could always take afternoon naps with my spirit animals. Although the bear snores, wolf lets off the occasional howl and the buchwuss, well, he drools."

Brook shook his head and chugged a swig back. "Yeah it is harsh isn't it? Yesterday's or Monday's I think. Usually tastes okay if I reheat it."

"Yeah, so does tar the third time around."

"I'll brew up a new pot. Speaking of unchanged, don't you ever change your outfit?" He nodded at Charlie's jean jacket and checkered shirt. "You remind me of the story about Einstein when a reporter went to his house for an interview and found out he had seven identical outfits of shirts and pants in his closet."

"Does Superman change his cape?" Charlie stood as Brook sauntered off to the back room with pot in hand. "I'd pour that straight into your half-clogged toilet bowl instead. That stuff would be better than drain cleaner."

"Hah! You really should have called first, we could have done lunch. I was just about to head out and meet Chelen over by the Pesuta Shipwreck trail." Brook poured away the thick, black coffee, its overdone acidic smell filling his nose. "Yeah, I must remember to put on a new pot of this stuff every day. Nasty. Oh sorry, I forgot you don't believe in having a telephone."

"Who needs a telephone when they're connected to the natural flow of the earth? It tells me everything I need to know, like this trouble brewing over in Stanley Park. When you listen to the right frequencies it's like a homegrown version of those tweeter things, constant chatter. Can you keep an eye on my place, water the plants, and make sure the old VCR catches this week's ball game?"

Brook knew Charlie had electricity only in the very back room of his cabin and that was only to watch his beloved baseball. Although it wasn't the same since his adored Montreal Expos had abandoned him for Washington D.C. to become the Nationals. "Sure, no problem. And it's Twitter. We're settling in just fine. The waiting area was Chelen's doing," he explained as he poured new water in the top of the coffee machine and reached for the bag of ground beans.

"Although, she's been acting weird lately. Bit grumpy in the morning."

"Pregnant." Charlie said, while Brook leaned over the coffee pot, adding the new scoop of beans over the old ones. "And you really shouldn't reuse the beans like that, leaves a bitter taste, not good for you neither. Filters don't cost more than a sixteenth of a cent each."

Brook spilled the scoop of coffee all down the side of the pot. "What?"

"Beans get as bitter as the coffee if you re-use…"

"No, the other bit."

Charlie gave him that apologetic look. "Well, I guess that wrecks the surprise. Sorry, it's hard to fool a shaman, you know."

"Yeah, got it. In touch with the universe and everything." Brook took a deep breath. "Next thing you're going to tell me we've got twins or something."

"No, just one, a ..."

"Stop! I want some sort of surprise. If you're telling me the truth." His eyes grew large as he thought for a moment. "You know you could make a mint with skills like that."

"Yeah, and I wouldn't have to pee on a stick to do it, either." Charlie helped

Brook clean up his mess. "Sorry, didn't mean to spoil the fun. She's about two days in. And you know I can't sell my abilities, only use them for ..."

"Good and the betterment of fighting evil, blah, blah, blah." Brook shook his head and spilled another spoon of coffee all over the table as the realization really began to sink in. "I'm going to be a father." He breathed deeply, hand shaking and took off his glasses.

"And I'm never going to get a cup of coffee am I? You better sit down and let me do this." Charlie set his cane aside as the shell-shocked Brook fell into one of the chairs.

"A kid? A dad?"

"Yup. I'd bring some cigars back from Vancouver only I don't smoke."

"No, that's my job." Brook's face went a little paler as Charlie chucked the paper filter out and refilled the coffee machine.

"Oh, yeah. I'll add an extra scoop, think you could use it." "I could use a straight double rye about now."

* * *

Carol landed at the Sandspit airport. It was one of two airports on the Charlottes and while on Moresby Island, the lower of the two main islands and necessitating a ferry ride, it was much closer to Skidegate than the airport at Massatt at the top of the Charlottes.

She'd sent Dan an email letting him know she was going on a lead, but didn't say where. No point in him thinking she was barking, or even just barking up the wrong tree. If he bawled her out for leaving no details then so be it. Carol trusted her gut instincts and they were telling her Charlie either knew more than he was letting on, or was involved in the murders somehow. Besides, there had only been a narrow window to book the police plane for the flight, and Big Dan was always banging on about time being of the essence. It was also the only real lead on the biggest case in the city. Even with the discovery of the second body whose prints matched Mrs. Coles, all they had for the daughter's whereabouts was an IPod. Carol was certain they'd eventually find Cindy, but it wouldn't be good. With no ransom note or contact of any kind, it was doubtful the girl was alive after all this time. Even if she had been kidnapped, both the parents were dead. Kidnappers would probably have got scared and offed the poor kid. Most likely dumped her in the waters of Coal Harbour, or nearby Lost Lagoon. When she'd left they'd already begun dragging the lake after failing to find any real sign of the kid.

Making for the car-rental office Carol fought the queasiness in her stomach from being bounced around in the updrafts as they tried to land the twin-engine Cessna. She hated flying in little planes. Felt about as sound as the balsa-wood gliders she used to buy from the toy store for a few cents when she was young. They broke apart after only a couple of landings and she always feared the Cessna would do the same. Once cocooned from the winds in the hired vehicle, Carol made for the ferry, MV Kwuna, which would take her across the Skidegate Straight to Graham Island and Skidegate itself. Charlie lived on the outskirts of the small town, near the new museum. Carol didn't have a hope of trying to pronounce the name, but the English translation was Sea Lion Town. She actually found it incredibly easy to find him, once she thought to simply look in the telephone directory.

Waiting on the ferry, she stared at the sleepy-looking houses dotting the coastline of the narrow straight. Islands sprinkled the waters, laden with cedar and spruce, the trees spilling into the bay. So enchanting; she'd have to come back for a holiday. Actually, it was something she'd always wanted to do. Although with a husband, minus the two-point-five kids, was more the hope. She sighed, work, work, work; there always seemed to be work. Little time for dating, even less for herself.

The wait gave time for remembrances of growing up in Vancouver to surface; visiting the Sunshine Coast, enjoying time on Sechelt beach with her family.

Memories flooded in of visiting little fishing villages, and whale watching.

She made a mental note to phone her dad, Paul, for one of their chats. A retired Canadian Army General, he'd served in several of Canada's peace-keeping ventures and was very proud of the fact his daughter was in the police force. Although she knew he'd always wanted to see her in the army. But if she joined anything it would have been the Navy, which would have mortified him. The pictures at the museum stirred memories of old photos she'd seen of her dad's.

He'd been based for a brief spell up at Masset, at a place they called the elephant cage. It was a giant round of antennas designed to pick up long-distance communications, waiting for the Russian attack that never came. The place looked like a holding pen for some incredible creatures the size of elephants or dinosaurs. He told her how beautiful it was then, being virtually on the edge of the world. Amazingly, with all the logging, it still was. When you live in paradise, why do you cut it down? Maybe that's why the Haida took a stand with the Gwaii Haanas Park. In essence she always thought about visiting just to see what her dad meant. *Never thought it would actually happen.*

Her mom passed away five years ago. Cancer had riddled her body.

Carol phoned her dad often, knowing he was very lonely without his right hand, as he called her mom, Catherine. She never really got close to her mom. Catherine was English, with some Celtic and Welsh in her family as well. Carol always thought that side of her ancestors was a little too odd. Catherine would bind one strand of hair in a braid. Reminded Carol of the hippy folk she caught pictures of in the sixties. Still her mom was nothing but kind and loving. A gentle soul, her dad would always say.

She actually wished Dad would find himself another mate, if not for anything else but the company. Yet out of some sort of self-imposed veneration for the woman he spent his lifetime adoring, she knew he wouldn't. In some respects Carol admired him for that and wished she'd find such a man. They didn't make them like that anymore; this generation was different. Values were different and ideals of the fifties were long put to bed. Funny, she wanted that ideal, "women knew their place then, at home, dressed up, cooking the meals for man and family," yet here she was loving this typically male job, on the edge of danger and excitement. Double standards.

She missed her mom, but if one of them had to go first it she was glad it wasn't her father, as horrible as that thought was. He was her rock as she grew up. Still, she couldn't understand how any woman could stand to be parted from her husband for months on end while he was away on overseas duty. She wondered if her mom had actually truly loved her dad. Carol certainly did, they went everywhere together when he was in town. He'd send her all kinds of letters and postcards from wherever he was stationed on active peace-keeping duty.

The whistle of the ferry as it approached Skidegate made her jump. Unfortunately this wasn't a pleasure trip, but she promised herself she would return, perhaps with a hubby in tow and, she cringed, kids. She loved children, but the idea of actually having one terrified her. She'd seen the *Alien* movie series way too many times to trust what was in wouldn't come bursting out.

Minutes later she drove up to an unassuming little cabin in the middle of the woods at the end of a dirt road. There wasn't a neighbor in kilometres, which in some respects didn't seem like a bad thing. As she got out and walked by an old red Ford pickup she felt the warmth radiating from the hood and the creak of metal cooling down told her someone had very recently driven the truck. So Charlie must have been home, although that would mean he had a driver's licence. She'd checked that avenue too and knew he didn't. But he was in the phone book.

She knocked on the door noting there wasn't a doorbell nor anything that looked like an entrance light over the creaky doorstep to the ramshackle cabin. She knocked twice and quickly stepped back as heavy footsteps thudded inside, just in case anyone decided to swing the door open quickly. A police-trained instinct, like never parking your cruiser directly parallel behind someone you've pulled over, and instead, leaving a half vehicle width over, so that anyone approaching would not be able to hit you as you stood talking to the offending person. The heavy tread of footsteps told her the person answering the door was most likely male, but she didn't expect the yuppie-type, blond-haired, be-spectacled gentleman who stared out, grimacing into the sudden glare. A near replica of Daniel Jackson from the *Stargate* TV series, one of her favourite shows before it was cancelled. Her practiced look of "gotcha, didn't figure I'd ever find ya," vanished before it could plaster itself on her face. He was definitely not her man.

"Hi, Detective Carol Ainsworth VPD, looking for a Charlie Stillwaters." She flashed her badge, as he looked rather perplexed. "Or have I got the wrong address?"

"No, this is his place. Bizarre. He's out right now. Is he in trouble?" the startled man queried.

"No, I just want to ask him a few questions." She purposely hadn't called ahead, hoping to either catch him off guard or prevent him from doing a runner. Maybe even impress him with her ability to track him down and wipe some of that amused smile off his face.

"Funny you should just arrive here when he just headed off for Vancouver. Something about an old flame, hot date, and rocks or something like that. I wasn't paying much attention at the time."

"Was he driving?" She thought, how oddly funny, he'd be halfway there by now and she was here.

"No, hitchhiking actually. Charlie doesn't have a licence, he drives, just no licence. Like a lot of people out here."

Why did that not surprise her? "Do you happen to know where in Vancouver he's going?"

"Ah, no. One thing you should know about Charlie. If he wants you to find him you will and if he doesn't, well, good luck. He's not your average run-of-the-mill native. He's a…"

"Ska-ga." They both blurted at the same time and laughed. It broke the ice. Carol could tell by his eyes the man was being very honest and didn't have much, if anything, to hide.

"Right, then you've met him already. Brook Grant, by the way." He extended his hand for Carol to shake.

She responded and returned his greeting. "I have met him briefly and let's just call this research. I need to ask him some questions regarding Shamanistic practices and powers. Thought he could give me some answers. Might help with a case I'm on."

"Well, he doesn't normally say much, but wind him up and off he goes. Bent sense of humour though." Brook smiled and opened the door farther.

"Yeah, I got that all right and he seems to love baseball."

"Not so much since the Expos abandoned him, Mainly Blue Jays these days, but yeah, still watches. Come on in, the door's never locked. In fact there's no locks on the doors at all. You can come and visit anytime, not that you probably would. Don't know if he even has any coffee around here."

"Really?" She glanced at the shrubs surrounding the doors.

"We don't need them out here and besides, he has his own unique security system."

"Plants?" She remarked, "As in the *Attack of the Killer Tomatoes*?"

"Yes, sort of. That's spiny devil's club. It's for keeping out evil spirits. I asked the same thing the first time I visited."

"Let me guess, one prick and you'll be flat on your back for hours in a state of total paralysis." She couldn't help herself, even though she had been trained over and over not to put personal comments into a situation when interviewing as it often slanted a person's statements. "He's serious about this stuff?" She picked at the plant wondering if it would lash out at her like some plant space creature from *Day of the Triffids* or *Little Shop of Horrors*.

"Very. You don't know Charlie very well, then. But do be careful, one sting from that plant and you'll die a screaming, horrible death." Brook tried to keep a straight face, then laughed. "Just kidding. Yeah, it works for him."

"No, obviously not." Carol smiled as she entered the cabin. Brook seemed harmless enough. The smell of wood smoke and cedar hung in the air. Reminding her of log cabins she'd been in the past, and old holiday resorts. It was dim and she immediately looked around for the light switch.

"Don't bother, no electricity, except in the room in the back. He likes to watch the news and his baseball. Uses a lot of candles and coal-oil lamps. Give your eyes a minute to adjust."

"He lives here alone? In the dark? No heat or lights?"

"For the most part, yes. He's a few relatives around besides Chelen, his niece, my wife. He believes electricity breaks up the natural flow of energy in the earth." Brook walked around. "He does things like cut firewood only from trees already dead on the ground and thanks the provider for it. He does watch other TV shows sometimes. Besides the ball games he seems to like a lot of educational and documentary programs. He often comments about shows and says things like 'that David Suzuki, he's got it all wrong.' Or 'they've finally got that theory correct, it only took them ten thousand years and computers to catch up to the Indians.'"

"But he has a phone, I found him in the local directory." She was puzzled as she looked around.

"No, you found him listed in the phone book. He just likes to see his name in print. He doesn't actually own a phone. Number's bogus."

"Very odd fellow." Perhaps he was more than just a little nuts, she pondered.

"I used to think so too. But Charlie, well he's just different. Looks at life from a slant quite uniquely his, the kook part hides his depth and pain."

"A front for something." She'd learned more from Brook in the last few minutes than a month's worth of investigation would dig up.

"Yup. He's really the most amazing man I've ever met. A little crazy, I'll give you that, but I think being a modern day shaman, maybe you've just got to be. I've gone on journeys with him and let's say he's... how do I say? Much more than he lets on and much more than most of us even begin to appreciate. I think the only reason he took up this business of hocus-pocus was to try to reconnect with Lucy, the love of his life. Hoping to bring her back to him somehow. And I don't think he'll ever give up trying."

"Who's this Lucy?" She reminded herself she was here looking for Charlie, but any information into his background and/or character was very welcome. Was Charlie another one, like her dad? Brook seemed a fountain of info, obviously a little in awe of this fellow. She wanted to know why, when she thought he was most likely just some strung-out native.

"She died when Charlie was young. Late teens I think. As far as I know he's never been with another woman since."

"Teenage sweethearts." Carol walked around. It looked like just what it was; a rustic backwoods cabin. The smell of smoke hung in the air, along with dampness. The walls were merely logs; the wooden floor creaked as she walked. Gas lanterns hung here and there.

"A part of him died inside when she died. They were more like soul-mates actually, and that term I wouldn't have believed until I met Chelen and fell head over moccasins in a heartbeat. But you can see it in Charlie's eyes when he talks about Lucy. That faraway look and I don't mean woo-woo stuff here."

"You're also very observant. What field of work are you in?" Old animal furs hung on the walls and the smell of wood smoke tugged at her constantly.

"I own the only paper on the islands, but I used to do investigative reporting with the *Toronto Star* and the *New York Times*. You should stop by and grab a copy. Our office is just up the road in Tlell. Not sure how long you're staying but don't let the locals allow you to drink the water at St. Mary's spring."

"What?"

"The legend has it that if you do, you'll end up returning to stay. I came out here to do an article. Met Chelen, drank the water, and set up shop."

"Thanks for the tip. I'm not big on water, prefer a good strong coffee or espresso." She smiled. The timbers in the walls were old and sparse, moss or mud wedged in the cracks between the logs. He definitely wasn't rich and judging by the amount of dust on everything, not one to spend time cleaning house often.

He laughed. "Try HaidaBucks, pretty good stuff."

"Yeah, already heard of it, was heading there next. If I give you my address and contact info, would you please ask Charlie to contact me if he should do some sort of hoodoo act and mysteriously appear?" She pulled a card from her pocket.

"Thanks, but he won't need it. If he wants to find you he will. He has his own guidance system."

"GPS?" She walked toward a back-room wall, now that her eyes had adjusted to the darkness.

"No, the earth. He claims he can travel within the earth and uses it as his homing signal."

"Oh! Really?" That was new. She bet even Whacko Jacko couldn't pull that one off. Carol surveyed the masks adorning the log cabin's back wall, along with old pictures of totems that once used to decorate some of the local villages. Memories. He lived in a state of the past, she surmised. "Mind if I look around? Interesting masks." He had not only native masks, but Japanese theatre masks, some Hawaiian and Maori as well, and others obviously of some sort of African origin.

"Go ahead. You're probably as fascinated as I was my first time here. Just don't touch anything. You don't want to know what he uses for an alarm system."

"Let me guess, giant black widow spiders high on peyote or mad beavers that smack you to death with their tails."

He laughed. "Good imagination. Close, probably worse."

Carol gazed at the old prints of empty villages. Totems with ovoid eyes and grimacing teeth glared back. Haunting images of bygone times and another age reeked from the photos. That and other unexplainable things in the pictures. She stared harder in the dim light. Blurred, ghostly images. Carol moved aside and looked back; they seemed to watch her. Dispossessed spirits drew her in as if their essence was still there, held in abeyance on silver-oxide prints. What would make a man live like this?

Perhaps he really was nuts. Probable schizo. She made a mental note; Google aspects of shamanism and schizophrenia. Several of the totems had the three Watchmen crowning them, along with several other creatures. Some were meant to awe, others to terrify, she wasn't sure which. "I'm sure the winters up here must be cold. How does he keep warm?"

Brook shivered. "Very rainy and the winds are fierce. As far as I know that fireplace is all he's got, apart from long underwear and several blankets.

No space heater or miracle-fiber, Teflon-coated shorts."

"So when did he visit Vancouver before?" Carol asked. She liked Brook's sense of humour; in some respects it reminded her of Ben. A reporter's literary humour, she gathered.

"What do you mean? He just left yesterday. As far as I know he's been in Haida Gwaii all winter." Brook look puzzled.

"Yesterday? I saw him a few days ago in Vancouver, on the night of the fifteenth to be precise." *Or so I thought.* "Are you sure?"

"Yes. He stopped by to say he was leaving and to let me know my wife was pregnant."

"Pregnant? Is he a practicing doctor of some sort also?" She never thought to look into the doctors' database to track him down.

"No, just a shaman. The rest you figure out. I'm tired of trying to understand how he knows impossible things."

Carol scratched her head and glanced at Brook, dumbstruck, not sure what he was getting at.

"I mean he just does stuff like that all the time. He dwells in dimensions, realities we barely realize are out there. He told me Chelen was pregnant only two days in, the fancy pee sticks at the stores we tried this morning are still saying she's not. We'll try again tomorrow and my money says he's right."

"You can't possibly outguess science." She knew Brook believed the old man, he really did. Carol remembered John Denton's conversation regarding the shaman's powers. Could he have visited her in some out-of-body state? And why?

"To be honest, I'd give my life to Charlie. If he says she's pregnant, then there's no doubt in my mind he's correct." Brook looked upset that she'd doubt him.

"Where's the room with the electricity?" She thought she'd change the subject. Brook looked agitated, she wasn't sure why. He pointed over his shoulder.

Carol walked past Brook into the back room. An old eighteen-inch Sony sat in one corner and under it a VCR that looked even older. She followed the cord attached to the front of the VCR to a remote. "Wired remote, late-seventies vintage."

A single lamp on a night stand jiggled as she walked up to it and went to sit in his cloth-padded ottoman. A heavy animal skin was draped over the chair and a folded blanket beside it. Just behind it she spied an electric heater. "Cheater. So much for roughing it."

She sat in Charlie's chair as Brook walked into the room, trying to get a feel for what he saw from this chair, maybe get a feel for the man himself.

"Yeah, that's weird." Brook muttered as Carol felt the air around her virtually still. Calming her, pulling her away. Displacing her. She looked at the view through the window into the backyard full of trees. One in particular caught her eye.

"I only sat in that chair once. He says he bought this cabin for that particular view."

"Of trees? He must be a real nature lover, then."

"Mainly of that tree with the double trunk, he calls it a portal tree. Very rare and sacred."

Carol got up, sauntered over to the window, and glanced out before leaving the room. "Charming. You really believe he can do crazy, weird things?" She glanced back at the space heater. Well, he had Brook buffaloed.

"I've seen it, experienced it. Nearly drove me mad with some of the shit he's done. I mean." Brook grabbed Carol's arm and stared deep into her eyes. "Look. You train yourself to be a cop. To track clues, hunt down criminals, analyze crime scenes, know when someone is lying to you, and study criminal patterns, etcetera. So you already know I'm telling the truth. He brought Chelen back from a place where she should have been dead, under the ocean." Brook started to break a sweat. "I can never thank him enough for that."

Carol nodded at him. He was either telling the truth, was a damn good liar, or was a little crazy himself. Although she didn't really feel threatened, she was ready to grab his hand and forcibly remove it. Even though in body mass he was larger, she could drop him in three seconds flat, and would if needs be. As if reading her thoughts, Brook let go.

"Sorry about that. Look, he does the same with spirit beings. They have life and existence to him. That's what he has spent his life practicing, walking in worlds we only glimpse in dreams."

"A practicing shaman? Rare these days. Do you think he's capable of heinous actions?"

"No. He's a very lonely man, but as honest, kind, and as just as anyone you'll ever meet. And more perceptive than Houdini. Don't bet against him. I'd trust him more than my wife. Nuts, yes, he showed me things that still give me nightmares and he lives there every day amongst them. I figured that would twist your mind just a little. I couldn't do it without cracking."

"Look, I have to go." Carol moved away from Brook. He wasn't lying; there was genuine fear in his eyes. "You've my card if he should show up or if something comes up." She'd seen enough to know Charlie wasn't one to mess around with, nor be trusted. All joking aside, there was one part of him that made her cringe and question whether she should turn out her lights at night.

"And here's mine."

Carol took Brook's card and walked out the door. For a moment she was a little disturbed by his adamant behaviour, but he was okay, just freaked. She knew one thing for sure. The man was definitely telling the truth. She'd loved to find out what Brook experienced but time was of the essence and it wouldn't help the investigation, only perhaps make Brook come unglued. What would Big Dan say if she had to detain or arrest the man, or worse, get arrested herself for some incident in the middle of nowhere?

"Thanks." She strolled out to her rental. *Okay, other than let him come to you, how do you track down a shaman?*

* * *

Located just a few kilometres outside Prince Rupert the same day, a driver pulled over by the tree of Lost Soles. He smiled at the sight of the old man bent over his cane. Perfect, he thought, he could use some roughing up and that cane could fetch a few bucks.

"Need a ride, do ya?" The young, burly male in tattered T-shirt asked as he slowed down, staring at the tree. "Quite a sight isn't it. Crazy people have been dumping their shoes here for the last twenty years."

Charlie limped toward the truck. He stared at the tree littered with well over a hundred pairs and odd single shoes; even skis, pants, sandals, and a hubcap had made their way to nearly thirty feet up the tree.

"Yeah, interesting," he said. One couldn't be too choosy being a hitch-hiker these days, Charlie thought. All those news stories about senseless murders, muggings, and gang violence were getting to people and it was getting much harder to get a ride. He'd been standing out on the pavement for nearly two hours after getting a short ride from the ferry.

"Sad state of affairs, people don't even want to pick up a helpless old man." As he crawled into the truck Charlie felt the vibes from the late twenties male weren't good. It had nothing to do with the death's head carved into the dash, the dozen or so coffee cups abandoned on the dashboard, or the beer bottles he'd left scattered on the floor amid empty cigarette containers. Charlie couldn't help but wonder what the guy's house looked like.

"Do you get the double entendre?" he said, smiling as he settled into his seat, unsure if he should buckle himself in. Instead, he rubbed his medicine pouch and muttered a few words in Haida to it. Wisps of smoke curled out into the cab.

The fellow growled back, "Yeah, play on words, intellectual mind crap, isn't it."

"Not really. Do you ever think about who once wore those shoes?"

"Don't really care. I know whose feet are in these shitkickers." Charlie picked up the veiled threat.

"Don't you worry, old man? About getting rides from strangers and having someone mug you and beat you up?" Charlie caught the sly smile the much-younger man gave him from under his cowboy hat.

"No, I don't worry. I've got my guardians." He hated doing it, but knew there were times being a ska-ga definitely came in handy. He opened the flap on his bag. A very fine mist rose, quickly swirling into the back of the crew cab.

The man was reaching for the length of broken baseball bat Charlie knew he kept by his seat. He hesitated for a moment as the word sank in. "Guardians? What kind of guardians would an old man have?"

"This old man is a shaman, actually, and we usually have totem animals we carry with us all the time. I've gone on quests and established control over certain creatures. Once done, they protect us and do our bidding."

"What a load of shit!" He smirked.

"Don't believe me? Before you touch that bat look in your rear-view mirror."

"How'd you know I was going for my ba…" He inadvertently looked up as the pungent aromas of canine sweat and bear musk washed over him and caught the images staring back in the mirror. The great black Wolf and spirit Grizzly glared back at him, teeth glinting menacingly. Wolf growled. He turned and caught the sight of the empty rear seat of his quad-cab truck, nearly swerving into the ditch. Charlie lurched in his seat and grabbed the steering wheel, steadying the vehicle.

The rank aromas of unwashed animal filtered through the air. "Christ, what was that?"

"My spirit guides, who come to my aid when I'm threatened. Kinda the opposite of vampires, they can sometimes be seen in reflected light. But usually only to those who mean to harm me."

"Ah! Look, old man, no harm intended, I'm just giving you a ride." The man looked up again, colour draining from his face. The deep eyes of the dark wolf bored into him. The white grizzly merely shook its muzzle, drool splattered the back seat. Obviously not happy being cooped up.

"Although it's not them that usually give me trouble, it's the one on the roof. I've just acquired him and he takes a lot of effort to control. Not sure if he's as docile as the others. So I'd keep your hands on the steering wheel, my friend."

"Roof?" The nervous man swerved the vehicle slightly as he tried peering over the edge of the windshield.

"He hates being enclosed, not to mention they have this very pungent musky odour, I think they use that to attract each other. If that's the case, then you can smell a rutting bigfoot twenty miles away. Phew!" Charlie pinched his nose in disgust. "Kinda smells like rancid skunk and it doesn't help they have this thing, like cats, about taking baths and being wet. Usually, though, he's pretty docile most of time."

The truck's thin metal roof buckled as something huge shifted above them. The man turned twenty-pound-paper white and tried not to swerve again as the realization hit that there was a good possibility he could be ate.

"Most people don't know that Buchwuss, or Bigfoot, as you might call it, likes the wind in its face. Like a typical dog, really. Blow in its face and it'll nearly bite your head off. Stick it in a vehicle and it sticks its head out the window." Charlie smiled.

"I've a...what on my roof?" He glanced in his side view mirror working the electric controls to bring the view from alongside to the top of his vehicle.

A large, hairy hand, nearly as big as his size-eleven feet, grasped the edge of the door. A hand that could crush him in a second. Charlie saw his eyes widening in panic as he caught the reflection of a hairy, apelike face in his side mirror. He was prepared to grab the steering wheel again if needed.

"Mother of God! Ah, look man, I don't know what the hell is going on here. But maybe you want to get out. Honest, man, I ain't going to hurt you. Get it?"

Charlie talked on, ignoring the panicked man. "Yeah, they can be a little intimidating at times. Get bored rather easily, too. But since you did offer me this ride out of the goodness of your heart and all, I should be kind enough not to turn down the offer and offend you. I think I'll stay until we get to Prince George." He slumped low in the seat and pulled his ball cap low over his eyes, a slight smile of his own on his face. He hated flaunting his powers, but he'd never be able to fend off the man if he swung his bat at him like he was going to. "If you don't mind I'm rather tired and think I'll grab a little shut-eye. My guardians rarely need sleep. Well, except the bear. After a good load of spirit-salmon stew he's out for days at a time."

"No offence intended, old man. Be my guest," the man stuttered, grinding his teeth, beads of nervous sweat dripping into his T-shirt, white-knuckled hands gripping and re-gripping the steering wheel.

"And it's Charlie. Don't worry, you'll be okay as long as you keep both hands on the steering wheel and hold her at a steady speed."

The driver glanced at the sawn-off bat and the back of the cab shifted under the weight of the massive grizzly. "Hey! That's just for checking tire pressures on the truck." The wolf quietly stared at him again in his mirror. "What if I have to signal or stop for another leak or something?" He squirmed. Charlie caught the fear in his thoughts of being mauled, especially by something as large as Bigfoot.

"Well, now that would be quite a problem, I suspect. Reckon you should see how big a bladder you've got. Oh, and the griz, he also hates the smell of tobacco, gets him really grumpy. You'd probably not like to see him grumpy. I did once, he demolished the inside of a thirty-foot Winnebago, gutted it completely. Never did find most of the body parts. You know they can eat a lot in one feeding."

"Why'd he go berserk?"

"Like I said, tobacco pisses him off."

"Thanks for letting me know. Although I could really use a smoke right about now." Sweat continued to roll down the man's face.

Charlie was hoping he wouldn't wet himself; he never cared for the stench of urine. "Yeah, no doubt. But I wouldn't chance it myself. Look, I'll only be taking a power nap. Light sleeper and all, good night. And if they give you any grief, yell loudly, before you get blood all over the place." The shaman smiled, he thought he might as well rub it in real thick. He wiggled himself into a more comfortable sleeping position and pulled the ball cap even lower over his eyes. He'd already deduced the driver had probably assaulted more than one hitchhiker. While as a shaman he'd sworn to help others, he knew he couldn't correct everything in this world, but he'd make sure this fellow never wanted to try this stunt again.

* * *

"Yeah, sure." Jimmy wondered what kind of a kook he'd picked up as fetid breath washed over him. This was the last hitchhiker he'd ever pick up, let alone beat on. "Can never tell what kind of nut cases were loose in this world," he muttered to himself, licking his lips as nicotine's harsh cravings jangled at his nerves and the rank musky smell of animal kept his sweating hands glued in a death grip to the steering wheel.

"That's for sure," Charlie muttered under his breath. "You never can tell if you might meet someone slung from lower on the nut tree than yourself."

Chapter Six

CLarry staggered out into the parking lot of O'Shanahan's, shaking off the vile memories of that night gone wrong and the hideous things The Lure made him do. Maybe some men were partial to it but he was definitely more of the standard macho male. Subservience to the every whim of a woman was not to his liking. He cringed whenever he saw pictures of men on their knees being whipped or forced into pleasuring them. Damn, he didn't need to be forced but he did need to be the dominate one. Sure, they were all created equal and had the same rights. He was okay with all that, but in the marriage, what the man said, went. And unless he wanted her to, he got on top. Others might have called him a redneck, but he always assumed a man was a man and a woman was meant to be a woman.

It took, surprisingly, very little concentration to run the unconscious bodies, which was good, otherwise tasks like driving a car would be murder. He'd purchased another bottle of whisky, just for insurance, as the longer he kept the person impaired the better. He felt in his, or rather his new rides, pocket for keys. Tangents of memories would slip through on occasion, but usually the owners were out for the count.

"Damn, no remote. Have to do this the hard way." he growled with a voice he didn't recognize. Too high-pitched. It was sometimes eerie hearing your words in someone else's voice. "Ford, I think." He slowly approached every Ford in the closest row, trying the keys in the door.

"Hey, what the fuck do you think you're doing, pal?" swore a big brute of a man as he approached the older Mustang Larry was trying his keys on. Dressed in ball cap, blue jeans, and T-shirt, his Saturday best no doubt, the man lumbered toward him. Judging by the fact he was leaving alone, he was also unable to get lucky.

"Aw, sorry. Wrong car. Too much to drink," he slurred, staggering down the row, laughing, "don't remember where I parked." Not normally one to back away from a fight, Larry decided it was the best option this time. In this slip of a male, he'd lose. In his own body he'd tell the guy to piss off and make mincemeat out of him.

"You really should call a cab, loser." The man laughed as Larry staggered away. The throaty roar of an engine and rubber squealing in protest let Larry know he'd left. He had more luck with the second car, a newer-looking Taurus. He chugged a long pull from the bottle, allowing the rawness to tear down his throat and felt in the man's pockets again. "Damn, no cigarettes. Doesn't smoke. Could sure use one though." He put the idling car in gear and headed for the convenience store around the corner. It was funny that even though the body's real owner didn't smoke, the mental addiction of nicotine in his head and nerves still remained. "I guess some things do reach beyond the grave."

An hour later, Larry parked in front of the clubhouse. The crazy woman had a good point. Ryley had taken out his whole family, raped his wife before killing her and torching his house. All while he was recovering in the hospital after being sideswiped on the highway. Three months later he left in a wheelchair, body crushed, no family, and no life, only to be shot dead as he sat in front of the burned remains of his house. With his dying eyes he remembered the van's plate. The same one Ryley used to run him over on the highway. His hands gripped the steering wheel tighter. They'd come back to finish the job, and now, so had he. The Spawn stick together; attack one and you attack them all. The code they all swore allegiance to.

He watched Greasy and Stumpy leave the nightclub. He knew they'd only followed orders, but still, they did what they did, and they were once friends. He'd hung out with them, had them over many times for drinks and poker. How could they have done this?

Supposed friends. Treacherous bastards.

That made the hurt even worse. He knew only one man was ultimately

89

responsible. He took another long swig of whisky and knew who'd pay.

Another couple of hours until the sun came up and he had to leave. The sunlight did something, he didn't know what, didn't care; only knew the pain of remaining inside another's body was too intense after that. A weight in the man's coat tugged at Larry and he pulled out the wallet and looked inside. Two kids, boy and girl, smiling sweetly and innocently. He pulled it free and on back was scrawled, "We Love You, Dad." Tears tumbled down his face. So like his own, Cassandra and David, only eight and seven. Both taken away by Ryley. That hurt worse than the betrayal. He'd never hurt or abused a youngster in all the years of being Ryley's main enforcer. He'd seen what jail did to kid beaters; and it wasn't nice. The favour had to be returned. For the kids more than anything, he'd settle up.

Larry grit the man's teeth as one of the bikes started up. He could tell by the Harley's growl it was Stumpy's. He'd inherited his nickname from falling off his bike many years ago and losing part of his right foot, causing him to walk with a pronounced limp. Brothers-in-arms they once called themselves\. He couldn't remember how many adventures, good or bad, they'd been on together. Still, they'd carried out Ryley's betrayal and he had to end this. His family came first, always did. Greasy went back into the nightclub. Good, now he could tail Stumpy alone.

Larry slumped down in the seat and waited about twenty seconds before following. He knew where Stumpy lived, Hastings Street, and knew which stretch of road would be deserted this time of night.

Sure enough, as they got off Hastings and onto Heatley he was right behind.

Larry watched him glance in his side view mirror, perhaps beginning to suspect he'd been tailed. Before the burly biker had a chance to think about it Larry floored the gas and whipped around the biker like he was about to pass. Stumpy glared at him. "Now the shoe is on the other foot, you back-stabbing bastard." Larry smiled as realization crossed his former compatriot's face for a moment. Larry swerved and slammed into the big bike, forcing him off the road into the path of an oncoming dumpster.

Stumpy tried to swerve out of the way, but the bulky Harley wasn't one for maneuvering. The bike skidded, slid sideways, and slammed hard into the dumpster; Stumpy's body flopped like a rag doll. Metal shattered against metal, the rider's leg trapped beneath.

Larry screeched to a halt and got out. He looked up and down the street; there was no one at this time of night. "That was for Sally, Stumpy, or should I say Tom Braden," he spat as he walked up. Although the bike still lay atop Stumpy's leg, Larry noticed that his foot pointed in the wrong direction, bent beyond where it was meant to go. "You ain't running away from this one."

"Who the fuck are you? How do you know my real name? Only gang members know..." Blood gurgled in his throat, maybe internal injuries, too. Larry thought he didn't have long. "Do I know you?"

"Take a wild, fucking guess at who I am." Larry dug down and relaxed the host's vocal chords, allowing as much as possible of his own deeper voice to come through.

"How? It's not possible." Truth cried from his eyes as Death's scythe swung down. Despite the broken leg and five hundred-odd pounds of Harley squashing him, Stumpy tried to crawl away, denial running his reasoning like a race car into a brick wall.

Larry stuck his face closer and lowered the tone of the host's voice to match his own natural voice. "Look closely, 'cause you ain't going to heaven to sit at the right hand of the big guy and St. Peter."

"Larry? Not possible. You're dead. I made sure of it."

"Actually, yes, you backstabbing piece of shit. Only dead don't mean gone, loose ends, you know? Now, you're going to hell, the first of many. I'll get you all. Unlike you, this Spawn honours his code."

"How?" He coughed one last time. The wheeze of death's grip, Larry knew, was on him.

"How? I'll tell you in purgatory. Where the dead will spend eternity peeling your foreskin off to use as the devil's handkerchief forever, you prick."

He grabbed the biker's head and gave a quick, efficient twist. A harsh crack rang out. Stumpy quivered twice and lay still. He waited until the biker's eyes glossed over and his head fell backward. The only one he wanted to really suffer was Ryley. A jolt from the body told him he needed to be quick. Convulsions ran through the host. Even while unconscious the sight of death stirred some strong reaction from the straight-laced, probably law-biding man he'd used tonight.

"Gotta get back to the club." He guzzled half the bottle when he got back to the car, hoping it would settle the battle inside. He waited a moment, watching the man's hands blur as the alcohol kicked in. Larry flung the empty bottle away, allowing it to shatter against the wall, getting rid of evidence, and then cleaned up best he could with a box of baby wipes he'd bought earlier. He threw it in the empty bag that had contained the bottle and tossed it all in a dumpster a couple of blocks down. He needed to use the host bodies to get back at Ryley, but he didn't want any more innocents destroyed by the scum, so the less evidence the better. There was only one man that would suffer. A lot.

If his luck held he'd make it back before this one came to. The alcohol was working, but the host was putting up a strong fight.

Only two more to go.

* * *

Sparks erupting in a crescendo of fireworks; black rubber protesting its ability to stop; tarmac vanishing into the GMC van; breath crushed from his body and the raw stench of erupting fuel. Then flames. The hot lick of flames.

Ben lurched awake. Another sweat-filled night.

He grabbed his pen and pad and began scribbling frantically before it all faded away. Only this time it wasn't as strong as last time, almost like an infection slowly washing out of him. It would soon be gone and he, Ben, would forget. He knew something terrible had happened to someone and now he knew it wasn't him. So why? Why him?

Details. Look for details. The vision of a licence plate glared but the digits were obscured by smoke and exhaust fumes. Ben kept writing until there was nothing left, folded up his pad, and dropped his head back down. He would concentrate and try again. At least this time he'd noticed the van had BC plates but now he had to get the letters and numbers.

As he drifted back down into sleep the intense feeling of betrayal stayed with him. Someone had died horribly and he needed to find out before it left him.

* * *

As she started up the SUV a bird cried out piercing the silence. In her rear-view mirror an image shifted, quickly, like a vision between blinks. Again a sharp cry; the flutter of dark wings. A raven. Or something larger?

Carol glanced around; something was watching her she could feel it. If she didn't know any better, she'd have guessed Charlie was here. Eerie. This was beginning to get way too bizarre and freaky. "You hang around long enough in a graveyard and sooner or later you begin to see ghosts." Big Dan once told her. It was time to go before she got totally freaked.

"So what exactly do shamans do?" She turned around in the driveway, half expecting a semi-naked shaman to come bouncing out of the woods, chanting incantations and waving some voodoo doll at her. His hair full of grass, grubs, and twigs, like the natives in some of the pictures on his wall. "Time for a strong espresso and some literary research."

She'd heard about the clash a coffee shop called HaidaBucks had with Starbucks years ago and headed to the café. "Let's see if theirs is as good as the real McCoy."

She glanced at her watch as she strolled into the café. Still had over four hours to catch the next ferry back to the airport. "Is there a good bookstore around that would have books on native beliefs, particularly shamanism?" she asked the native girl serving her. Most of the Haida natives didn't seem to have the same features as other ethnic tribes; they seemed to more closely resemble Hawaiians, Samoans, and that lot. A few might match them pound for pound on the rugby field, too. Like the burly New Zealand All Blacks she'd seen doing the Haka on the sports channel one day. Funny, except for one letter or two the word was the nearly the same. She'd gone to New Zealand, Australia, and Hawaii with her parents one year. Some of the totems and their grimacing faces, they could be cousins.

Just then her cell phone rang. The pilot from the Sandspit airport. "I'll be right back." Carol said to the lady at the counter as she was preparing her coffee.

"What, you've got an emergency? Okay I'll book a commercial flight." The police department needed the plane and had commandeered it. She'd have to book the next available flight back to Vancouver. Carol called the airport. "Well, that's synchronicity, I'm trapped here until the early hours of the morning," she muttered as she booked the only flight out. Man, this wasn't going to make Big Dan any happier.

"There's a couple bookstores over in Charlotte City," the girl informed Carol gruffly as she walked back in. Obviously not willing to be overly friendly with someone not from the island. Of course, she didn't trust whites or strangers and would probably trust her even less if she knew she was a cop.

"Hey, this shit beats Starbucks." She smiled. "And I don't need a second mortgage for refills either." She hoped to set the waiter at ease by lowering herself to a basic level. A little humour might loosen the girl up.

"Don't worry about it. Refills are on the house."

"Got any T-shirts left that might fit my skinny white ass?"

The girl laughed, "Just native medium, which is probably Three-XL for you white eyes," she retorted. "You probably need Three-XS." They both laughed and exchanged names.

"Raseen Eaglefeathers. I could pronounce my Haida name but you'd not understand it anyway. Think it means big girl high on caffeine."

Carol laughed, she'd definitely broken the icy front. "The only good bookstore on the islands is just out of town in Charlotte City. Murdocks. He's got lots of old books on native studies. But if you really want to understand the Haida, go up to Rosespit."

"Rosespit. I've heard of the place. Something about Raven and opening clamshells, releasing the Haida. Where is that?" She lied on purpose, trying to strike some semblance of conversation and interest now she'd broken the ice.

The image of Raven hovering over the first Haida scurrying out from their imprisonment ghosted through her mind. She could still see him watching her. Staring through his eyes; like the watchmen perched on the top of the poles. Carol blinked. It was like he was still watching her with a hypnotic gaze. A creepy eerie feeling swept over her, like at Charlie's cabin.

"The very top. A piece goes out for miles at low tide. You can find crystals and agates, the beach is littered with them. Magical, it is, where the Haida began. Or so legends say." The girl's dull eyes sparkled, coming alive.

"Is that the source of the sculpture at the UBC Museum? The one Bill Reid did?" She was hooked and wanted to experience more of that twinkle in Raseen's eyes, the wonder lust she felt inside. If time presented itself, she'd go to Rosespit.

"Yes, I believe it was. He's Haida, buried at Tanu with his mother. She was born there."

"Do you know how to get up there?" Carol didn't know why but she knew she had to go. This was as close, perhaps, to a shamanic experience as she would ever have. She wanted to experience what Raven did, what Charlie felt.

Magic. It was non-existent in her own life. And more than that, in order to track down a shaman, you need to feel what a shaman feels, do what he does and think, act like one. Something she learned from many of the great crime books she'd studied. Many of the greatest detectives in the field said the same thing. "Get in their heads and know what they're thinking in order to know intuitively what their next move is." She had to go there now.

"Well, as it works out, I've several hours to spare anyways, due to the change of plans." Carol said.

"Follow the highway to Massett and take the Tow Hill exit. Follow that to its end at Hiellen campground. There the road goes onto the beach and you four-by-four it, girlfriend, all the way to the end." Raseen told her.

"Off to Murdocks, then I'll buzz up to Rosespit maybe. Thanks for the info and oversized T-shirt. I'll probably drown in it but if I ever have a boy-friend over we can have a snuggle party inside it, together."

Raseen laughed. "Have fun, girlfriend, and pick a few crystals for me."

* * *

There were two policemen on duty around the area where the mayor's wife's body had been found. The area itself was still roped off and Ben was only allowed to walk around the perimeter. He smiled at the officers and continued slowly walking down the trail. Carol, unfortunately, wasn't there and the tent setup had been cleared of the white-garbed CSI types. It was useless talking to the two officers; they were just grunts and knew nothing.

Ben was really hoping Carol would be around, he'd been going to ask her out for a coffee or something. He walked around the site to the back of the trail area where the old cedars stood like guardians. Out of the corner of his eye he spotted four shadows moving. "What the...?"

"He sees us. Unusual."

"A familiar."

"See who?" Ben muttered, wondering what four old creepy guys would be doing here at the death scene, hiding in the shadows.

"He has been in contact with one who has seen her."

"Residual energy."

Four aged, bizarre-looking men parted the shadows, letting the darkness wash off them. Beads and shells hung from one, others had moss and rotting vegetation dangling off them. Roots intertwined in clothing and hair. Earth and dirt shook loose as they moved, smelling of dampness and age.

Ben stopped, blinking in shocked disbelief. "Jesus, you guys. Some bizarre hippy cult? Return to your roots and all that? Or environmentalist, live-off-the-land types?" Yup, he'd seen it all now.

"Too conspicuous."

"Much has changed."

"Need better disguise."

"Blend in with the times." They muttered to each other, finishing each other's sentences. Ben wanted to run but couldn't. One waved at him and he remained rooted to the spot. Compelled to find out what and who these strange men were. Or he assumed they were male, perhaps actors. "Like bloody Men in Black by the way they hung in the shadows."

"We need newer image."

"Match the times."

"Blend in."

"Less conspicuous."

One waved his hand and they transformed themselves into four men dressed in long black overcoats, black fedora hats, black shoes, and black wrap-around sunglasses.

"Hey what the…how'd you do that?"

"Forget us."

"No memory."

"Better this way."

"We will watch him." One waved his hand and they vanished into the background. "Yes, he's got the stink of a familiar," they all replied. "She may find him again."

"Most peculiar." Ben stood on the trail scratching his head. Not sure why he said that or even why he was standing there. He returned to the walkway, leaving Stanley Park. There was something odd about that area where they'd found the mayor's wife's body. Things just didn't jive, didn't feel right. Or maybe it was simply because he hadn't slept well the last few nights. "A good movie, some cheap wine, and a few laughs might be in order," he muttered, since Carol wasn't around to ask out. "Yeah, could relax with *Men in Black* again."

One of his favourites, he thought, wondering what made him think of that movie. He'd watched it a dozen times, helped him focus on the fact that everything wasn't what or how it seemed to be on the surface. "Imagine! Bizarre aliens living here amongst us. Wonder if that would be possible."

* * *

Carol drove over to Charlotte City and found the little bookstore tucked in just out on the edge of town. Murdock's opened up inside and she found herself mesmerized by the volume of books and material. One of those places you could wander through, spending hours in quiet repose. The man who originally ran it passed away and his daughter had taken over the helm. Carol turned at the creak of the floorboards as an older man approached. She took in his thin appearance and noticeable limping gait.

"You're new to town. Just visiting?" His eyes stared deep into her, prodding.

"Yes, I'm just here for a day, checking out some books on shamanism, and background history. Was told this is the place to find it." He was almost creepy, instantly her back was up. A reflex from years of dealing with unsavory types. His eyes were intense, there was so much moving behind them. Pulling at her. Reminding her of something.

"Books, yes, lots of books. Now, shamans, you say? I vaguely know of a shaman over in Skidegate. Now what was his name, a Charlie something or other?" He tapped his fingers against his chin.

"Stinkwater, Slimewater. Something S water. On, yes, it's Stillwaters. That's it, Charlie Stillwaters?" He was baiting her, Carol was sure of it. "Yes, that's the one. Right scoundrel."

"Really? What makes you say that?" Carol found it interesting a fellow that seemed to be a resident would barely know one of the locals. She also knew one other thing looking into his eyes, which kept pulling at her. The man was lying through his teeth. Those eyes, the depths behind them, were so familiar.

"He stole from me and others. Those masks of his in his cabin. Stole the most of them. Ripped me for a lot of money. A real dirty thief, I tell you."

The man clicked in sharp, staccato-like clipped tones.

"Really. I forgot to introduce myself. Carol Ainsworth, tourist."

He stared at her and when he didn't respond. "And you are…" She'd caught him off guard.

"Marten Crow, tourist likewise, although from around here. I came to find a good book to enjoy with my lunch. Hear the food is quite good in the local café. Yummy, really. I could regale you with many tales from around here. Care to join me?"

"Thanks for the information and the offer, Marten, but I must be going. I need to catch the next ferry shortly," she lied to the man, feeling her head spin as his eyes seemed to bore inside her and her stomach began craving a meal she didn't need just yet.

He'd made a fatal error, though. How would he know Charlie had a collection of masks if he didn't know him, and how would he know Carol had seen them? Too coincidental. Unless, she shivered, he was at the cabin. The eeriness outside, the feeling of being watched. She grabbed her books and headed toward the front checkout. This conversation was over and the sooner she left the better. She felt a headache building inside. The old man pretended to flip through the books in front of him, but she knew his focus was on her.

"Great store you've got here. Now, don't look up immediately, but do you know that fellow that was just talking to me?" she quietly asked the lady as she presented her credit card at the checkout.

"Never seen him before. Was he giving you trouble?" the clerk enquired, slowly glancing up.

"No, just a bit odd. Mentioned one of the locals and thought he'd be from around here. Thanks and have a good day." Carol grabbed her books and walked out. Carol shivered; she knew his dark, round eyes were following her every move as she quickly strolled out. She clicked her key fob and while wanting to jump quickly into her car and speed away, forced herself to be as nonchalant as possible. She put her books down on the passenger seat and clicked on the seat belt. There were some people that set your teeth on edge immediately and Marten Crow was one of those. Then it came to her. His eyes reminded her of the same penetrating stare of the statues at UBC.

She started the car and quietly accelerated. Once out of sight and sound of the building, Carol quickly stepped on the gas, keeping an eye out to see if she was being tailed. She wasn't.

"Most odd fellow, that one."

* * *

The Lure smiled through the woman's face, staring into the mirror of the restroom. She blinked and noticed the red lipstick, eyeliner, and blush. "Most interesting, these times. Obviously meant to attract males. Wish we had such attractive colours to paint our bodies with back in my time. Almost like the birds that strut their stuff, looking for a mate. It should be easy to attract one in this body." She straightened up and twisted around, studying herself in the mirror. "Yes, most attractive indeed." The Lure walked slowly from the washroom into the noisy, pounding music of the tavern.

The male she pulled into the portal with her, Larry, had been fun but now she was bored. He hadn't exactly enjoyed her being in charge, but that was of no concern to her. The Lure enjoyed the feel of the sheer stockings under the host's dress. "Oh, to be young and aroused." She smiled as she slinked up to the bar. Several males eyed her up; there were more than enough toys for her to choose from. Although the string that went up her backside wasn't comfortable, perhaps it was the standard item to wear in courting rituals. She'd discard it the first chance she got.

She should have finished Larry's life, but he had helped her, no matter how inadvertently. His continued existence was her way of saying thanks. Besides, he had a reason for being trapped here, the same reason that gave her freedom.

Revenge she understood very well. They would come looking and this time, unlike the last time she escaped, she would be ready. She'd planned her revenge for many years now and they would pay. Oh yes, even gods could feel pain. That she would make sure of.

"Hey, care for a drink pretty lady?" A man far older than the host body she inhabited approached her. His T-shirt proclaiming "Devil's Spawn, Already Committed to Hell." Flaming skulls were tattooed into the skin of his arms, like the native males did in her time.

"Sure, humour me."

They drank and talked for a while. He obviously liked what he saw and she didn't care. Not for what she had in mind. The music started up again. "Care to dance?"

She could already feel the host beginning to stir and gulped her drink down in one long chug. She could control the bodies even longer than Larry, but eventually, as the owner sobered up, she'd lose control.

"Look, I'd rather do something else, big boy. Can we go to your place instead?" she purred, sliding her hand along his thigh, feeling the wonderful energy she was stirring inside. He was strong and full of much desire and male energy. She searched the woman's memory. Testosterone. *Hmm, they've discovered much about the human body, even beyond the ken of some of our shamans.* "I've a hunger for something big, strong, and hard."

"Sure. Don't care for the music tonight anyways." He chugged back his beer and, taking her hand, led them into the parking lot.

All the way to his place in the car she kept her hand on his thigh, urging him on. She'd forgotten how delicious seduction was. His desire was like quicksilver in her veins, igniting her own needs, feeding her hunger.

His apartment was small, with not much more than a thing the host body identified as a TV and a small desk. On the desk sat another device called a computer, fish swimming placidly over the screen. She checked the host's unconscious mind, and was amazed at what the thing called the internet—the Web —held. The web, as in suck you in and trap you. Anything a person wanted to know about the world, great online games, and lots of sexy websites. A device that could enlighten her about this world. The Lure smiled. That was information she could definitely use later.

The man wandered over to another device. He pressed a couple of buttons and seductive music filled the room. "Care for a little smoke?"

"No thanks. I'll stick to drinking." Besides she didn't know what they smoked here, couldn't be sure of its effects on her and the control over the host. He returned with a drink he called a "beer,", and some good shit. The "good shit" reminded her of the weeds the shamans used during some of their ceremonies. She snapped back half of the offered fermented beverage before rising and slowly beginning to undo the buttons down the front of her dress. "I don't need any stuff. You've already got me very stirred up."

His eyes glossed over, more from the effects of the narcotic than her tantalizing him, but it didn't matter. He was hers.

"Did I mention how big strong burly men really excite me?" She let her dress slip to the floor and ran her hands over the supple body. "See something you like?"

"Yeah, baby, you." He rose and pitched his shirt over his head. The smell of sweat and testosterone washed over her. Now that was a drug worth taking. The Lure sensed his pulse racing, fueling the ache inside him, stirring her hunger. She let him control the action. Especially since she had no idea how to remove the encumbrance to her breasts. "Undo me, please." She uttered in a smoldering breath. He unclipped her. Cool air hardened her nipples. It appeared they were not used to exposure, or being suckled by the young. She wondered how the small, triangular bit of material covering her female parts did any good. But it didn't matter, energy washed over her as he stripped naked and stood before her. The muscles in his arms flexed as he flung his clothes to one side and pulled her into the bedroom. The sheer adrenalin rush of testosterone intoxicated her; she drank in the flex of his powerful pecs, the strong curve of his rear, the sheer thrusting power as he walked in front of her.

He was about to fling her onto the unmade bed when she spun him around and pushed him to the sheets, climbing on top. "Now, lay back and let me pleasure you."

She held him to the bed and climbed on top, pinning his arms over his head.

"Wow, you're a strong and horny bitch."

"Right on both counts." The Lure moaned as she slid down and enfolded his naked hardness, feeling the sensations of man thrust inside her. Ululations rose from her throat while the host body provided a wet slickness to aid her exertions. "Oh, it's been a long time since I had one of these. Let me show you how strong I am." She held him with perhaps too much force as she growled and continued stroking his hardness within her. The wetness became a flood, she was awash in desire.

"Christ, this is too much."

She could feel his mounting urges building. It wouldn't be long now.

"So tight. Oh God, it's like you're milking me. Damn, you're good."

He went to grab her, flip her under him. The Lure pulled his hands back over his head. "Oh no, honey, you're all mine."

"Have it your way then, baby. I don't mind letting the chicks do all the work."

"Oh, I will."

She stroked him a few more times. He flooded into her. His masculine energies spilling inside, igniting cells long dormant. Electricity surged through her soul as she continued to stroke him and he continued to pour into her. Washing himself into her.

"Oh God, so good, I feel like I'm going to die and go to heaven. I can't stop coming. Unbelievable! Baby, you're the best."

"Don't know about heaven but you are right about the first part." She kept sucking him into her. Working him like a cow's udder.

"No, I gotta stop."

"Too late to stop."

"No, stop, please make it stop," he begged.

She smiled, enjoying this part the most. Forcing him on and on until she could see his eyes flutter as he lost consciousness.

"Ah, honey, what's the expression they use here? The best way to go, in bed with your boots on. Most males would kill to expire like this."

"Please…" he whispered, fainting away, unable to move. Paleness blossoming across his face, draining of colour. She bent over and kissed his lips pulling the last of his energy in a mist into her mouth. "I was just making sure you lived up to your T-shirt." She laughed and stood up. "God, was that good. It's been far too long since I had one of those."

The Lure looked down at her arms and for a moment could see the edge of a reflection against the skin. She strode over to his bathroom and stared into the mirror. A faint image of her, the real her, stared back before vanishing.

"I never expected that to happen. There is a way back to this world and perhaps be rid of the guardians forever."

She slowly pulled the dress on, leaving the dead man lying naked, his body slightly shrunken, on his bed. She put the undergarments into her bag and quickly left the bedroom, enjoying the feel of skin, wonderful skin, beneath the dress. The Lure sat down in front of his computer, humming away, and allowed the host to show her how to access the data. The Lure had a couple of hours to kill and intended to make the most of them, especially with this tool that held knowledge of the world in which she was now carnate.

She hummed later all the way back to the nightclub, her internal instincts allowing her to find the way back.

"How are you doing?" the one called a bouncer said as she entered. "Last call is in a couple of minutes."

"Wonderful, just wonderful," she replied. And she swept from the host back into the pulsing lights and smoke over the gyrating bodies. "But I've already had my limit for the night, thanks."

Chapter Seven

Carol parted company with the last paved road and drove onto the hard packed beach just past a place called Tow Hill. She drove along the sand, wondering if even a GPS would work up here. Noting in the rearview mirror that her tire tracks were barely visible. If anything happened, she realized, no one would even know she'd been here. Minutes later she pulled up to the derelict remains of an old crushed boat wondering if this still seemed like such a good idea.

She should turn around, this was nuts. Despite two people mentioning the place, something inside seemed to call her to be here anyway, all con siderations of the investigation aside. "Crap, this is nuts, but I gotta trust my intuition on this one." Exiting the car she walked around the old boat, *Kelly Ruth* was faintly scrawled on its hull. As far as she spied along the sand there was not a soul in sight. She stared out across the waters trying to spot Japan several thousand kilometres away.

"Hey, how about some sushi to go," she yelled to the wind. Only the silence of barnacles drying whistled back. Glancing around the empty beach she realized again there probably wasn't another soul in miles. In the distance, the shadow of the volcanic plug called Tow Hill broke the horizon like a lonely outpost. "Well, to find a shaman, you must know his background, his experiences. No better place to get into his head than the birthplace of his people. I guess I really shouldn't read all those tacky tourist brochures."

Returning to the SUV she twisted the key in the ignition, faintly relieved to hear the engine jump to life.

"Just hope this isn't some crazy mistake," she said aloud, the sound of her voice reassuring in the whisper of the constant ocean breeze. Driving on, she took in the thousands of grey drift logs lining the beach. Most laying in haphazard jams, the odd ones piled upright indicating someone had made a shelter for the night.

Finally, the sight of two old upright stumps marked by buoys made her veer to the right onto a narrowing headland of grass and sand. A single radio tower signaled the last vestige of civilization as she continued, bouncing along the sandy trail. Skidding to a stop, dust flew in the air at the edge of the grassy bluff. Not wanting to take the chance of going down the steep embankment and getting stuck, Carol shut off the SUV and climbed down onto the rock-strewn beach. She spied the edge of Rosespit curving away into the distance well over a kilometre away. It narrowed as the spit sneaked away before vanishing into the belly of the sea. "It looks like an umbilical cord coming out of the ocean."

Never in her life had she ever been this far from civilization, this far removed from people of any kind. She'd been in many dangerous situations and was confident she could handle herself. But this; this was different. She couldn't recall a moment when she'd taken the time to be alone. Utterly alone, with no one even within a dozen kilometres.

Carol wandered along, idly picking up pieces of agate and crystal, stuffing them in her pockets. Like a little kid at the beach, bringing back memories of trips with her parents when she was young. Light mist hid part of the ocean as it closed on two sides as she walked along the narrowing finger of sand barely a foot above the briny depths. A rogue wave could easily wash over the glittering rocks. This section was virtually devoid of logs, long ago swept away. How did it make any sense? How did any of this help her find Charlie? The ocean breezes seem to sigh "keep walking" in her ear.

Maybe he spent most of his time alone, what else would a shaman do? Yes, in meditation, like a yogi on a mountain top. "Or along God-forsaken, crystal-laden beaches like this one."

A sharp cry overhead made Carol look up. An eagle. American bald eagle, she spotted the white of its head and tail as it circled. She remembered the eagles carved in cedar back at the museum in Vancouver, noting that probably more lived along this coast than in America itself. This one, though, could swoop down and attack her. She smiled at herself. He was perhaps more on lookout duty. Carol continued, wondering what it would be like to be free enough to fly.

Find a different tree, Charlie said. Seagulls, disturbed by her passing, squawked their annoyance as they lifted in front of her. They flapped for a few seconds before landing behind her, until she was surrounded by a curtain of birds, rising and falling, obliterating the sun for a few seconds, lost in a moving wave of squawking feathers.

A pod of sunbathing seals quietly slid into the water and watched her pass, not sure what to make of the police officer trespassing in their midst. She kicked at the pebbles, not feeling like an officer anymore. A whisper of someone's voice on the wind, calling her, intrigued her. Carol turned.

A lonely girl of six or seven strolled along the beach. It was her, alone, all by herself.

Get out to the edge, he said. Here she was listening to a mirage of a shaman, and the more she got to know him, the more she began to realize he was probably nuts. One thing she knew for sure from her years of police training, if you wanted to find a criminal you needed to get into his head. Think like he thinks, learn his environment, or as the natives would probably say out here, walk a mile in his moccasins.

Hadn't Mr. Denton and Brook said the old man travelled in dimensions we barely scratched? Maybe that was why she was here. This was where Charlie's people came from, the beliefs, the spells, it all started here. This was where the magic happened.

Memories of beaches and being with her parents on holidays as a child flooded in. Skipping rocks and chasing the edge of the tide trying not to get wet. Finally she stood on the edge of the finger of land, ocean gently crashing on three sides of her. Nothing and nobody for miles. Salt air sang, ringing out for thousands of kilometres, tides from Japan swept along the BC coast, sometimes bringing in strange bits of debris. What had she expected to find out here? What was so special about this place?

Rosespit answered as the wind sighed again and warmth wrapped itself around her. Just like her mother would when she was cold.

She touched the cool of the water lapping at her feet and knew there'd be no rogue waves out here, no danger. Safe, tears trembled on her lashes as emotions uplifted, welling up from inside. Serenity—she was lost on the edge of the world. Her soul cradled in the ocean's embrace, like a child snuggled in its mother's arms. This was the essence, the magic, of Rosespit. A tear streaked her face, and then another, as Carol began to sob. Her mother's arms No, not Mother Mom.

Not here, not now. She was supposed to be finding Charlie.

Mom. God, how she missed her. She'd never really cried, couldn't before. Carol had been afraid to let her emotions go. It was also something she'd trained to do as a police officer; stay aloof, remain observant, and detach from yourself. Emotions were so dangerous in the world of crime and her dad's military order. She watched her dad, rigid, stone-faced, and unmoving at her mom's funeral. A true soldier. Her Rock of Gibraltar. Only there was something new planted inside his eyes. The hurt, the missing. Regrets of never holding her again.

Later, over the years, she'd hear him behind the bedroom door, sobbing at night. Alone with only lingering memories and the pillow where her head once lay. He never dated.

But here it didn't matter, there was no one to interfere and Carol cried, releasing it all. The pain stored inside, the want of a child, missing something she'd always blamed herself for losing. If only she'd been better behaved maybe her mother wouldn't have left. Only she knew long ago that wasn't true. But it still remained, the hidden guilt, until now. The woman she called Mom, Catherine, was gone, all gone and here it was finally okay. Here, on the edge of reality, safe in the cradling arms of Rosespit.

Carol fell to one knee, the rocks rounded by the sea's salty caress crunching under her. She sobbed as the ocean mixed with her tears and gently washed it all away. Lost in the surf's sigh a mother sang to her daughter one last time. Carol lost track of time, crying. Then, as quickly as it had come, the wind subsided. Carol shivered in the cool ocean air and a larger wave lapped up almost to her feet.

Time to go.

"Charlie, you bastard."

* * *

Falling into oblivion, tumbling over and over. Ben lurched up and grabbed his pad, scribbling in the dark. He wasn't sure what he was writing, didn't care, and didn't want the light to awaken him more than he was. An image burned into his consciousness, he frantically drew from the fading memories, trying to place on paper what was rattling around in his nightmares.

Done, he stopped and fell back. He needed to get some sleep; otherwise he'd be a worse wreck than he had been the last few days.

In the morning he stared at the pad. A logo; it appeared to be a hastily drawn GMC emblem, and beside it the figure of a head in mist? Underneath the image was the letters LA…

That was where it stopped.

"Larry." The name from out of his mouth, but he didn't know why. He sat, staring, burning the images into his mind, as if replaying them over and over.

Ben jotted the name down and got up for work.

Outside the window four figures in black shuffled. "See he's familiar.

He will take us to her."

"Yes," they responded as one. "We will help him remember."

* * *

Big Dan slammed the door to his office, rattling glass. "You better explain this colossal waste of taxpayers' money and it better be good. Otherwise, I'll can your ass off this investigation quicker than you can say 'I can assure you sir, this ship, the Titanic is unsinkable.' I have to watch every bleeding nickel under my control and answer questions from the next pencil-pushing jerkass who takes over from our deceased mayor." He chucked a pile of expense reports in front of her as his verbal tirade continued. "It's not the first time I had a frigging rookie go on a spending spree," he bellowed.

Carol had barely set foot in her office after getting back from the Charlottes when Dan demanded to see her. He obviously wasn't happy. She didn't think he'd find out that fast about her trip and one thing she never did was lie to superiors. She had wanted enough time to hopefully get some information together to find and question Charlie, arrest him, or prove he even existed. She'd have to go with one out of three.

"Okay, here goes. There is one thing about the night of my stakeout in Stanley Park I didn't put in the official report. Late in the night, a native man with a cane came from out of the blue and started talking. Called himself Charlie Stillwaters."

"A what?" he fumed, his face turning red. But Double Patty was willing to hear her out. "Proceed."

"You've made quite evident your feelings on any woo-woo crap. I also agree with your line of thinking. I haven't much to say about, or any experiences with, anything remotely esoteric or supernatural."

"Can the buttery crap. I'm not in the mood. Just give me the straight facts." He glared at her, his face steaming.

"He talked for a while, some weird stuff that made me realize he wasn't some kind of alcoholic or crackhead. Said I was looking in the wrong tree and we'd eventually find the others. The next morning he was proved right. When he was done talking, and for the most part I thought he was probably some sort of religious kook, he started to wander off back down the trail. I went after him to question him more, as he sounded like he knew the where-abouts of the other two, but he'd vanished."

"Vanished? What do you mean he vanished?"

"He said he was a shaman. I mean, even with my flashlight there was nothing on the trail. An old man couldn't move that fast, not with a limp and a cane. I looked everywhere and in the end was a little freaked out, thinking I'd seen a ghost. And I'll be honest, sir, after our last conversation I didn't think you'd back me up on checking this out. At first, I brushed him off as a hallucination brought on by the morbid cold, but the next morning I knew he'd been right about other deaths, well, at least the wife's. As outrageous as his story sounded, I had to pursue it."

"Fuck. And that's what all these expenses are about?" Amazingly, Dan merely sat there, the redness in his cheeks subsided. His mind was chewing up what she'd spilled before him. How he'd got the expenses of her trip, Carol still had no idea. Obviously all expenditures were immediately brought to his attention. He'd put her in control of the case, but on a tight leash, and in his eyes she'd hung herself.

Carol nodded and waited for the explosive, "you're fired, pack up your bags and get back on the beat", but Dan just sat, chewing on his pencil. He spun around slowly in his chair and tapped the pencil against his temple.

He swiveled back and looked at her, throwing his pencil across his desk.

"You're saying the girl is also in the park? Dead?"

"Yes, that's what he alluded to."

"We combed it."

"I know."

"We'll comb it again. Do you have any evidence to back up this outlandish story before I elect to put you on permanent beat duty?"

"So far this is it." She pulled the picture of Charlie at Lyall Island out of her vest pocket and showed it to Dan. "This is Charlie Stillwaters, the man I met that night. He mentioned the term ska-ga, a Haida term for their shaman. I checked it out at the UBC museum. It will be in my report as soon as I can put it together. This Charlie lives in the Queen Charlottes, at Skidegate, and was involved in the Lyall Island land claims in ninety-three regarding Gwaii Haanas National Park. I found his address and went up there to ask him some questions. Oddly enough, he'd wasn't home, had just left for Vancouver the day before."

Dan blinked twice. "So, when you saw him, he wasn't actually here?"

"No."

"So you were talking to some kind of Casper the fucking native ghost?"

"Yes. Apparently he was in Skidegate at the time. I met with a reporter, Brook Grant, also, as it happens, married to Charlie's niece, who can attest to seeing him there the day before I arrived."

"Well that throws a big FUBAR into the scheme of things." Big Dan calmly looked at the picture, and then at Carol. "Grab a chair and sit down. What I'm about to say stays between you and me." His voice lowered about twenty decibels as he reached over and shut off the tape recorder she knew he kept running to record all conversations in his office.

"Yes, sir." Carol's hand shook as she pulled up the chair, afraid of where this was going to go. Big Dan angry was normal, Big Dan quiet was definitely frightening.

"Yeah, I don't believe in mystical, mumbo jumbo shit and I've come across some pretty weird crap in my days. I'll say this much about you, Carol, you've got balls hidden in those pants someplace and true detective intuition. You were right to check this lead, as bizarre as it seems. That's why I had you promoted. One of these frigging days I'll be six feet under and kicking up daisies and you'll be in this chair. I'll have to bury these costs someplace until this is over. Now I want to you to continue to try to find this man, and bring him in for questioning, but keep it as quiet as possible. If it's a real lead, it's the only one we've got at the moment. Don't like this, but I'll clutch at straws and vanishing shamans if I have to. We'll enlarge the photo and release an APB on him. Hopefully we'll get some results. I'll also talk to the Crimewatch Section and get a person-of-interest bulletin on TV right away based on this picture. Although it is a bit old."

"From what I hear, he seems to wear the same stuff all the time. Not quite what I'd have pictured for a native shaman!"

She rose from her chair, thinking a lot of good it was going to do to try to catch a shaman that didn't want to be caught. But she wasn't about to yank Dan's chain at this point. She pushed in the hard wooden chair and walked to his office door, blood draining back into her legs. At least she wasn't fired.

"And Ainsworth. Any more screwball ideas, let me know. You keep me personally informed on everything you do. Got it?" He raised his voice about five decibels closer to his usual freight-train level as his finger hovered over his tape recorder.

"Yes, sir."

"Ainsworth, this is between us for now. Totally off the record. Understand?" She nodded as he clicked the tape recorder back on.

"Now back to work. I've another suspicious death over on Hastings, involving a Spawn member. CSIs are there but cleanup will have to wait until we've had a look-see. Go ahead, I'll be right behind you."

"Yes, sir."

"And Ainsworth."

"Yes, sir."

"I don't say this often," He lowered his voice again to a level sincerity. "Good job."

* * *

Carol scrambled out of her car. The Harley lay crushed on its side awaiting the journey to the holding yard. She could tell by the polished chrome, hand-painted fuel tank and extended forks its deceased owner had taken great pride in his bike. Probably more than his own family, if he had one. The yellow, rotating lights of the tow truck waited patiently until all those who scurried about were done, and it could take the American-built legend to its final resting place.

Forensics was already having a field day studying the scene. She walked up, grabbed a smoke, and stared at the body under the blanket. "Who's the stiff?"

"Tom Braden, alias Stumpy, a leg breaker for Ryley."

Great. One of his right hand men, she thought, suddenly taking more interest in the scene.

"It first appeared that he'd slammed headlong into the dumpster. But on closer examination we discovered these skid marks and what could be paint scrapes on his bike that are not from the dumpster. Forensics is analyzing the chips. He was maybe sideswiped and ran into it." One of the guys pointed to the blue garbage bin about twenty feet away with a large scrape along it and the twin black lines scored into concrete.

"Great!" Big Dan came striding up. "Just what I need, more trouble brewing, especially with the Spawn."

"You sure he hadn't just had too much to drink?"

"He had a couple of drinks, but I don't think so. We'll test his blood-alcohol content, but usually Ryley's bodyguards are only allowed a couple. The man ain't stupid enough to get caught driving impaired."

"What if he had a night off duty?"

"Possibly."

A camera clicking away caught Carol's attention.

"I don't see how a simple road accident can draw so many officers, especially the chief and one of our newly elected detectives, do you?"

Carol knew the voice right away, she'd forgotten about Ben.

"Ainsworth, tell this reporter to piss off before I have him thrown in jail," Big Dan growled, obviously in a worse-than-usual foul mood. After his good appraisal of her work, which still shocked her, she wasn't about to argue.

"Is he usually this belligerent or has he found a bug in his Wheaties, or should I say Double Patty." Ben smiled at the two of them.

"Don't push your luck, asshole, or I'll have you arrested and strip searched quicker than I can spit and it'll be my size-twelve hands that'll be doing the cavity searching." Big Dan moved until he was face to face with Ben, who suddenly turned a little paler.

One thing Carol learned long ago; either be prepared to go all the way with Dan in a pissing contest or don't start one. Because he didn't back down from anyone.

"You. Come with me." Carol grabbed Ben and spun him around, pulling him toward her squad car. "You know you could learn something about social etiquette and charm. I figured out long ago that you can attract more wasps with flowers than with rotting cabbage, but in the end you'll still get stung if you're not careful, and Dan is like an overgrown wolverine. So a word of advice from one that knows. He don't back down from anyone."

"I've never been good at suck-holing." Ben looked her square in the eye.

This close he looked even better. "Now, if you want to get within even a mile of any further crime scenes, learn and learn quick to apologize, or you'll have a tube of jelly and those mitts of his up your backside before you know it. He can and will make it ugly for you." She tried to be serious, yet her insides were churning. Man, it had been way too long since her last date and he looked good enough to eat.

"Only if you come out with me tonight."

"Out?" Carol stepped back, caught off guard. "Out as in what?"

"As in an actual date, somewhere romantic. Out. I buy dinner, we eat too much, and drink too much. Get to know each other a bit and I take you home. If I play my cards right you invite me in for a rousing game of chess or checkers."

"Hate chess," she laughed.

"Not the way I play it."

"Which is?" She was beginning to like this fellow already. He managed to put a smile on her face.

"Strip chess. Lose a man other than a pawn and lose a piece of clothing. Whoever checkmates who gets to go on top first." He lifted his eyebrows.

"Figures. Do you not have any morals?" She smiled; her visit to Haida Gwaii had made her realize just how alone she really was without her mother or any significant other in her life. Carol was put out by the offer, it set off her internal alarm bells and her suspicious detective instincts were going off like wildfire. "You know what I think? I think you only want to go out 'cause you're hoping to get some more insight into this case."

"Actually no, I'm a bit hurt by that statement." His eyes dropped.

Judging by the reaction, he really was.

Ben looked hard at her. "There'll be no talking about this or any case. You have my word. I'll be honest. The truth is I find you quite attractive. So what is it? Another night at home watching reruns or an exciting night with me, a bottle of wine, and a loaded chess board?"

She giggled. He made her laugh. No one had done that in a long time. "Okay. Only no chess mating on a first date."

"Deal. Strip Monopoly it is. We'll meet at Earl's downtown, tomorrow night at eight."

"You're on." She felt her insides shiver. That had been too easy. She hadn't been on a date for over a year and couldn't remember when she'd last got any. Carol blinked. She couldn't even remember the last time she'd had an orgasm, self-induced or otherwise.

"Now to swallow my pride." Ben walked over to Big Dan. "Look, I'm sorry. I haven't had too many good run-ins with the police lately, the bad side of being a reporter. You have my sincere apology. I didn't mean to insult you, sir." Ben stuck out his hand.

Carol was quite impressed. Maybe he had a good side to him after all. She could feel her insides tingling. A date would be very nice, especially after her trip to the Charlottes, and if he played his cards right, who knew. Chess wasn't out of the picture, heaven knows she could stand to have her Queen royally taken.

Dan growled, "Whatever." He shook Ben's hand quickly, and as she could tell by the pained look on Ben's face, gave him one of his patented Big Dan bear crushing handshakes.

"Hey! By the way, nice tie."

"Don't push your luck, I hate suck holes."

"Okay. Actually it clashes with those tacky shoes."

Dan cracked a quick smile, "Piss off, will you already." He turned back to studying the bike lying on the pavement.

Ben looked Carol's way and cracked her a wink. Carol smiled. He had a certain charismatic charm, and balls. Something she admired in men. She wondered if that taut butt would feel as good in her hands as it looked walking away from her. "Oh, I'm bad," she muttered. Already thinking about sex and she hadn't even gone out on a date. Still, he carried himself with a lot of confidence and had a great ass.

* * *

Ben walked back to his car. He hadn't really expected to end up on a date with Carol. That was a bonus. What did he find so attractive about her? The take-charge, authority-figure role? "Here's hoping she's like that in the bedroom as well."

He looked up as he opened the door to his car. The street seemed oddly familiar, yet he couldn't ever recall being down here before. "Strange." He drove off, admiring Carol's curves in the rear-view mirror as he drove by. One thing for sure, under that uniform she was definitely no stick creature.

* * *

"So." Carol kept glancing at Charlie's picture as she typed up her notes on Stumpy's death. "The question begs to be asked, what would happen to attract the attention of a shaman? Because it sure wasn't me sitting on a park bench late at night. Nor would the death of a man, albeit the mayor of Vancouver. And you apparently were in the Charlottes at the time. If I can believe that story."

Carol stared at the wall map of Vancouver, and more properly, Stanley

Park. "He's in touch with the earth and all that mumbo jumbo, hoodoo, ho-cus-pocus stuff. Or is there something more spiritual, like another shaman or some force of nature that would call him? John Denton mentioned that to touch the bones of a shaman caused madness or some such thing. Is it possible that a village is located in the area or maybe a shaman's resting place?" She opened her browser and punched in Stanley Park history.

As far as she knew the park had been donated by an overstuffed English Pooba on the understanding it would only be used for parkland. So what was it before then?

She grabbed her phone and dialed the number on the card John gave her as she scrolled through the several pages of information the computer retrieved. "John, yes, good to speak to you again. I remember you saying something regarding the box full of shaman bones. Can you tell me, were there any native villages in the Stanley Park area before the whites came along? Or more to the point, any mention of a shaman being buried in the same area?"

"Not sure, but I think I might be able to answer both questions. Let me do some digging and email you. I do recall some natives living in the Coal Harbour area after the creation of Stanley Park," he replied.

"Yeah, thanks." She hung up and stared at the screen as a story regarding Pauline Johnson came up. Wasn't that the person with the memorial at the park? She hadn't paid much attention to the pile of stones erected to a woman back in the twenties. Now nearly forgotten under a canopy of trees. In fact her memorial wasn't even on the latest list of tourist sites that included Stanley Park.

The puzzling thing was, the mayor's car had been found in the parking lot adjacent to the memorial, and his body had been found next to the monument. But his wife; she had been found quite a distance back along the trail.

So, assuming the family arrived together, then maybe they had been attacked near where he was found, and she was chased to where they found her. Or they strolled along the trails and were attacked somewhere near where they found her body, and he staggered back to the memorial or the car. Either way didn't make any sense yet.

As sad as it was to say, Carol knew nothing about Pauline Johnson or the reason she'd been memorialized. Other than she had something to do with native stories and legends on the West Coast told by a white girl posing as a native. Okay then, not so PC now. The monument seemed almost abandoned, forgotten over time, hidden under the trees growing around it.

So many of the names used back then were inaccurate pronunciations. Siwash rock in Stanley Park for example; she'd read in the paper recently, should be properly called *Slhxi'7alsh* although virtually no one could pronounce it without spitting. Sure wouldn't help attract tourists, and now there was new talk of renaming Stanley Park to its politically correct, native name of *Xwayxway*. Man, that would just rake them tourist dollars in.

Johnson's book 'Legends of Vancouver' was written around the early 1900's. Several of her stories, supposedly based on true telling's by her native friend, Joe

Capilano, chief of the Pacific Tribes in the area, involved one of her beloved areas, Stanley Park. She called herself Tekahionwake. From her Eastern Mohawk roots.

"Mildly interesting," Carol muttered reading further on a brief summary of the stories. One story was regarding Siwash Rock, it being a man turned into a transformer rock because of his love and devotion to his wife and child.

Another of the stories was about The Lure of Stanley Park. An evil sorceress was transformed by some native godlike mythical beings called the Sagalie Tyee into a white rock etched with black, like acid. They took a group of honest men, good souls, and appointed them guardians to watch over her. Pauline stated they were transformed into the old cedar trees along the trail and the way they were placed reminded her of a cathedral, if such a thing was ever built by nature. The trail was named after the trees today.

"Hang on, what was the name of the trail where his wife was found?" Carol sorted through the police reports. Mayor's wife's body found beside Cathedral Trail in former grove area under a downed cedar tree. Now that is more than interesting. Time to visit the library and see if they've a copy of that book." She couldn't believe she was going to go to the library to research a police case. "Well, he did say to look up a different tree."

Chapter Eight

Joggers flashed by Carol as she strolled through sunny Stanley Park the next morning. Recalling how she first met Ben, she found herself absent-mindedly searching their faces for his. She smiled at an old couple strolling hand-in-hand through the trail, hoping that might be her someday. Geese honked in the background as young kids played ball on the grass. She knew the sites had been cleaned of grisly evidence and police involvement, the policy being to get back to normal as soon as possible.

Carol inhaled deeply, savoring the musky fall scent of damp earth, pine, and cedar. She exhaled slowly, releasing some of the tensions of the last few days with her misty breath. Everything was slower, more relaxed, here in the coolness of the forest. The very air lent itself to that, with the trees blocking out most of the sunlight. Humidity trapped beneath the Boston ferns growing everywhere, spread out, fanning their space. Smaller licorice ferns fought for space, budded with dainty purple flowers, and in the swampier areas, the vibrant yellow of skunk cabbage flowers. Rarely had she taken the time to simply relax and enjoy the forest.

One thing she'd established was that if the incident originally happened along Cathedral Trail, the mayor could have staggered the length of an adjoining trail before crossing the road and heading for Pauline's monument, but why? Carol pondered the question as she walked the length of Cathedral Trail. One of the shorter hikes; it had sustained the most damage with many trees shattered from the wind storms. She smiled at one downed tree near the terminus of the trail, the log split horizontally at one end, some joker had inserted "eyes" and jagged rocks for teeth so it resembled an alligator's snout. Gnarled limbs for legs completed the reptile. "Very creative." She laughed, wishing she could take some time out for simple silliness, but today was about investigation.

She walked into what she envisaged was once the clearing which Pauline Johnson claimed was the location of The Lure's rock and stopped short. It was only a few feet from where the mayor's wife had been found. Several trees lay on their sides, root balls exposed to the drying sun. Carol walked around, plotting where they once stood forming a near semicircle, almost like guardians. "God, I can almost believe this shit." She smirked at herself as she walked around the devastated glade.

A couple of the articles seemed to imply that much of what Pauline had written was in disrepute, probably because the woman was only half native and not a full-blooded aboriginal like she tried to portray. But times were different back then, and she was a pioneering spirit for not only native rights, but women's as well. "Let the critics rot." She grimaced as a spot near the centre of the trees caught her attention. "It seems those of lesser talent are always the ones to tear apart people who try to do something with their lives. Especially those of good intentions." One of her pet peeves. Being honourable and willing to uphold justice for all was something central to Carol's being. A trait her dad had instilled in her.

She stooped over and studied an area of bare earth, about two feet square. "Odd, why is this spot bare? I know we never removed any evidence other than the body." So much of the area had been disturbed in the last couple of years by the staff workers clearing the busted-up trees.

She reached down and touched the damp bald spot. Coolness of earth greeted her touch. "Why wouldn't grass have grown here after all of this time?" She could tell the soil hadn't been dug up recently, in fact if anything it was compressed, in a slight depression, like something heavy had been on top of the soil. "So perhaps something was taken away? Like a rock, in fact." She looked about. "I think I want to check the forensic photos, because I swear there was a rock here when we found her body. Didn't one of them mention the wife was hit by a rock and there was granite imbedded in her skull? Only it couldn't have been the rock that was here, not even Arnold Schwarzenegger could lift something that big."

She made a mental note to ask Ben; he jogged there often. Carol walked back along the trail, past the grimacing-alligator tree and sat in a covered shelter alone with her thoughts. She lit up a cigarette and enjoyed the peace while sorting through what she'd discovered here today. She hated the furtiveness smokers had to have these days, even in public parks, but realized that as a cop she of all people should uphold the law. In the background ducks quacked and somewhere in the limbs of the trees a crow cawed. She only had an elusive shaman and the bones of a native legend to go on. "And here I thought playing detective, like Starsky and Hutch, Kojak, and Magnum PI would be a bit more glamorous." She butted out her smoke, scooped the remains into a trash can, and scuffed along the trail to her car. "Man, was I wrong. Can't even butt a cig without having to hide it."

* * *

Back at the office, an email from John Denton was awaiting her. "Yes, there were several native villages at the south end of the Peninsula near the totems and Coal Harbour. The settlement was known as *Ch'elxwa'7elch*. There was another village near *Slhxi'7elsh*, or Siwash Rock as you would know it. Several aboriginals lived in the newly formed Stanley Park for quite a few years until they passed away, and their houses were later burned to the ground and bulldozed. In fact, the totems were erected over an area of heavily built-up clam shells, which suggests native presence for hundreds of years."

"Man, he can go on, can't he," Carol muttered as she read, but then this was his life, cataloguing artifacts and digging through the past.

"I've reports of finding a mortuary box. Legends say it was of the shaman called Kloo, possibly buried off the southern end of the peninsula or on Deadmans Island, once an island used for burials. Most likely spot. Don't know its native name, didn't think you really cared. Hope that helps. Email me back or drop by if you've more questions. By the way did you find your man?"

She responded with a quick thanks for the information and no she hadn't.

Carol read another email from Brook Grant. "Haven't heard from Charlie, I assume you have. Well, I should have bet you. The pee stick showed positive this morning. Off to see the doctor later in the week."

Carol shook her head. Okay, maybe he had some sort of ability; on the other hand it was only fifty-fifty odds. Still, how'd he know, unless Brook let it slip they were trying

She pulled up the photos of the crime scene involving Mrs. Bridge, and there it was. A white, black-etched rock in the background. "I thought as much. But where the hell is that rock now, and how'd it vanish?"

* * *

Larry puked once into the toilet. Spittles of blood coughed free, and his head throbbed insanely. This wasn't getting easier. Every time felt harder but, although he rarely admitted it, not as hard on him as on the bodies he occupied. Easing himself upright in the stall, Larry slumped on the toilet waiting for the pounding to subside before he staggered to the washbasin and rinsed his face. His hands shook as he stared at the almost-effeminate face of the young male he inhabited. As much as he hated it, this was the best chance to get close to Greasy, and perhaps to Ryley himself. Whether or not it was a wise move wasn't the only matter. What he was about to do went against everything he believed in.

He swayed over to the table of bikers, letting the host take over as much as possible, working on virtual reflex with remembered moves from the man's questionable lifestyle.

"There you are. Got you a drink." Greasy winked as Larry joined the table and sat next to the burly biker. Ryley was more interested in chatting up two blondes covered in less material than he sneezed on, as his hands caressed the stockinged thigh of one.

Typical tarts that attracted Ryley, all boobs and no brains. He'd probably get them smacked out on coke and do one or the other, or both, and give them the heave-ho in the morning. A job usually left to one of his flunkies; Larry's job when he was alive.

He growled to himself, usual fare for the area leader. The night was nearly over, close to last call. Music pounded away with its numbing techno beat. The same basic bass notes thumped over and over, which wasn't helping to ease away the distress in his head. Thank goodness that in whatever dimensional state he dwelled in over the dance floor, he couldn't hear the music banging away every night.

Larry jumped as Greasy's hand touched his thigh. "Nervous are we?"

"No, sorry, just excited I guess. Want to leave soon." He knew the host had been seen with Greasy more than once before, and Ryley felt somewhat comfortable with having him around. If he'd been a complete stranger, like the girls, Ryley would be watching him like a hawk. Larry had searched the man's memory banks and confirmed that Greasy had been with this man before.

Larry spoke in clipped tones, trying not to let his voice overpower the host's. It wasn't going to be easy; he wanted more than anything to grab Greasy's hand as it inched towards his crouch and break every finger, one at a time. Maybe he should have tried another approach. He closed his eyes, not knowing if he could go through with the charade.

Ryley was hiding something, had been even when Larry was alive, he was certain of that. But what?

A cell phone rang. Ryley scrambled to answer it. "Yes," he tried to appear calm, but something about that call worried him. Larry caught it in his voice and nothing made Ryley nervous.

The idea of being another man's boy toy rankled in every nerve of Larry's body. He'd hated being with The Lure, he despised this even more. He refused to enter a female's body, or at least the kind Ryley liked. He was only willing to go so far in order to get close, and this was too far. He wanted to puke thinking what Greasy would be doing with his boy toy later. Maybe this wasn't such a good idea after all.

"Okay, thanks. I'll be there tomorrow." Ryley set the cell phone on the table, and choked back a drink. "Come on girls, let's dance a bit before I take you home for a good time," he bellowed, relief echoing in his eyes and voice.

Ryley had plied them well with drinks, and probably coke outside the club. They were his for the night, any way he wanted them. That much was obvious. Larry glared at the cell phone. Whatever the call was about, the relief on Ryley's face was evident.

"Let's join them," Greasy whispered in Larry's ear.

He needed to act fast. "I've a better idea. Let's disappear into the washroom, grab one of the stalls. I think judging by the bulge you seem to be suffering from one of those SR headaches," Larry whispered. "Perhaps I can relieve a little of that heavy load." He had to get his hands on the cell phone.

"Now you're talking, bitch. Hey, what the…"

As they rose Larry leaned into the table and knocked his drink over. "Crap, sorry about that." Larry attempted to clean up as the waitress rushed over.

"Right. Let them clean up, I've better things to do with you," Greasy grumbled.

"Head for the washroom and I'll be right behind you. You know how management hates guys doing each other in there." Larry winked, wanting to punch the man in his grinning face.

"True. Ryley would be pissed if we got kicked out." Greasy staggered off, Larry turned to catch a glimpse of Ryley on the dance floor with his back to the table. He quickly scooped Ryley's cell phone into his pocket as he wiped up the table with a napkin. He made a quick dash for the exit door, instead of the restroom Greasy had just entered. Larry strode into the parking lot, swiped at the phone's screen and clicked on last number received. If he planned this right, he might be able to get it back before anyone noticed. "St. Paul's Hospital?" He dialed the number.

"Right, just got a call from there a minute ago, couldn't make out the room number. Too noisy, could you repeat it?" It was a long shot, but he had to try.

Someone important to Ryley was in the hospital.

"Intensive care, Room Twelve A."

"Thanks." He took another wild stab, "And you said they're going to be okay?"

"Yes, Mr. Matthews, your son is stable."

"Son!" He nearly dropped the phone. The secret Ryley had kept from everyone. A son? He never knew.

A burly hand reached out and grabbed him before Larry could move. Ryley glared at him, a rather sheepish Greasy behind him. "Now I wonder, what would a pussyboy want with my phone?"

Ryley glared back at Greasy. "You I'll deal with later. Him I watched bolting for the exit and no one at the table other than a waitress."

Larry knew one of Ryley's cardinal rules was never leave the table unguarded. But he had to get back inside. Pulling himself out of a body at this distance was brutal, as he found out once and didn't want to do again. Larry flung the phone into the bushes and kneed Ryley between the legs. The biker dropped, holding his privates. Larry ducked under Greasy's lunge.

"Get him while I retrieve my phone." Ryley moaned, doubling over. At least he gave the two girls something to kiss better tonight.

He ran back into the building, into the noise and mayhem of the dance floor, knocking a waitress aside, her drink order crashing to the ground. They hadn't expected him to bolt for the nightclub.

He released himself into the mists as the bouncers grabbed the twinky. Reality's strings snapped away in a dizzy spin as he flowed back to his home in purgatory. He felt sorry for the man. Ryley wouldn't go easy on him, if he even let him live.

He kept running the numbers over in his head. Ryley, he knew, used the alias Matthews on occasion, usually for legal matters. His real name was McLaren, or so Larry thought.

Ryley's wrath was undeniable, Larry was a testament to that, and Ryley never liked the idea Greasy was into young males, although it kept him away from any involvement with his ladies.

But a son! After all these years, he knew there was something Ryley hadn't wanted anyone to ever know. Larry had no idea. He smiled, pulling himself up into the void, away from the thump of the dance floor. The night had gone better than he could have imagined. Far better.

Chapter Nine

"Are you Sadie Wong?" Carol asked the short Chinese-looking woman at the Legends of the Moon gift shop till. Behind her the Stanley Park totems were visible.

"Yes." The woman nodded, smiling with that hint of why and what's going on here.

"I'm Detective Carol Ainsworth. You called the police and reported you've seen this man." She pulled the picture of Charlie from her jacket, along with her notebook, ready to take down any pertinent details.

"Yes, that was me. Do I get a reward?"

"If his arrest leads to solving who killed the mayor." She liked Big Dan's idea of utilizing CrimeStoppers. Putting someone's image on TV seemed to be one of the most effective ways of getting people to contact the police with potential evidence. Although it brought out the more mercenary aspects in some people, it produced results. Even though on cases of this magnitude they could spend a lot of time chasing down half-a-dozen false leads. This woman was beginning to sound like one of those more money-grabbing or glory-seeking individuals.

"I have to feed six children on this lousy park's wages. Could use the money," she pleaded. Another person who never heard of birth control; Carol hoped she wouldn't go into the sob-story rant so many people had these days.

"Don't worry, I've got your file number and you'll be contacted if this lead gets us any closer to solving the crime. Now, tell me, have you often seen him here?" She shivered, pulling her vest coat tighter. The sky threatened to unload like a typical Vancouver, pee-down-until-you're-absolutely-soaked day. But it held off for now.

"Three or four times recently. He just appears, and I thought he was a park bum at first with the dirty jeans and jacket. But the pins on his cap and that fancy cane told me he's been around here, dressed just like in the TV ads. You guys did a good job on matching his clothes."

"Probably doesn't change very often." Carol laughed. "Continue."

"Or ever. He often buys a chocolate bar and chats a little with whoever is at the till, me usually. The bums don't chat. They just buy and go, always looking over their shoulders, nervous like the cops are after them." She glanced around showing Carol what she meant. "I'm getting to the point I don't even let most of them into the store anymore."

The lady was not only very observant, but well versed in English. Not what she'd expected. Probably born here, or spent most of her life here.

"Very friendly, more so than most natives, but he's a little, how do I say...?"

"Nuts."

"No, more like some eccentric native whacko. Mutters things like astral travelling is such hard work and talks on and on about the Montreal Expos. Even I know they moved to DC."

"Well, that kinda sounds like our man. Now, you mentioned something odd." She flipped through her notebook. It was obvious the woman wasn't lying; she'd seen and talked to Charlie. "You said he just appears. What do you mean by that?"

Sadie stopped for a moment, thinking, as if it never occurred to her what she'd said. "Well, sometimes there's a crowd of tourists around, sometimes not. He's just standing there in the middle of them."

"And once." She stopped again, obviously trying to retrieve events from deep in her memory. She looked as if the truth just smacked her in the face with a twenty-two dollar bill. "And once, I remember looking up and thinking how slow the day was going to be due to the constant showers, and there he was." Sadie leaned in closer. "The odd thing now, that I never really questioned, was thinking he was barely wet when he came in. Should have been soaked, really. If he walked in from a tour bus or a car in the parking area. That's weird."

"Any patterns, set times?" Carol watched Sadie's eyes to see if she was telling the truth, but she already knew the answer. The woman was digging below the surface of her life. One of the jobs of a good detective, make them think deeply about what they'd seen and experienced. New revelations always brought up fresh insights and information.

"Oh well, yes, actually around midday, lunch. I'm usually thinking I've got to warm up my food when he comes in." Her eyes went down, the inside knowing beginning to take hold of her. Like a python slowing beginning to swallow its prey whole and alive.

"Around noon."

"No, usually one or two, that's when I go."

"Now, you said you looked up and he wasn't there, and then he was. Where is he usually, when you see him?" Carol had to keep probing, now she'd opened Sadie up to revealing things she hadn't consciously thought about until now.

The clerk thought a moment, looking around like she was mentally seeing him in the store and following him outside. "Well, now that you mention, standing right in front of the totems." She paused again. "Usually in one area."

"And you don't see him come and go? Ever see him arrive in a bus, cab?" The woman wasn't wasting the department's time, she was telling the truth. So far she was the only real clue as to the existence and whereabouts of Charlie Stillwaters. The elusive trail of smoke had begun to solidify and Carol wasn't about to let it slip through her fingers.

"No, never, like I said it's odd, he just appears. And he'll walk away, and stand again in that one spot, I look away and poof, he's gone again. Really odd." She scratched her head as if allowing the realization to sink in. The old lady's face dropped about two shades of colour. She looked agitated, a little freaked at the thought she might be seeing some sort of ghostly apparition. If she was true Chinese, then Carol knew they didn't like anything to do with the supernatural or ghosts. Superstitions ran deep in their culture.

"Show me where, Sadie." Sadie kept glancing over her shoulder as they walked to the spot. "Sorry, I don't like these totems. I feel like they watch me sometimes. Especially that one." She pointed to the carved image of Raven.

"Yeah." Carol thought of sharing her feelings in order to calm Sadie and create a common bond. "I was at the UBC museum recently and got the same feelings from the big Raven and First Men statue. Creepy really." But Carol knew that as much the lady was here for the money aspect, she was telling the truth to herself for the first time, and that could be very unnerving.

Without fail she walked up to one spot in front of a rock, about middle of the totems, and pointed. "Right here, in front of this rock."

Carol walked up, "Are you sure? It couldn't be over here or here." She pointed to the ground, trying to determine just how strongly convicted Sadie really was.

"No, from my window I can see him right here." She drew a line with her hand toward the gift area. "It's here." Sadie stamped her foot defiantly. It was out of character, Carol thought, for a Chinese person to be so verbal and adamant.

Sadie looked back at the concessions. "Gotta go, customers. And I can't afford to lose my job. But..." She was silent for a moment. "It's like he's doing more than watching the totems, nearly quietly talking with them and when he's waiting around to leave, I get the impression—this is a bit eerie—he's waiting for me to look away."

"And when you do, he's gone." She spoke softly, trying not to break the trail of unconscious thought streaking through Sadie.

"Yes, very creepy." She shivered, and with that she trundled off, glancing at the Raven perched quietly in wood. It was obvious she was not comfortable being near the totems.

"Thanks. I think I've asked everything I need to. You've been most helpful, Sadie." Carol watched her walk away. The rain had stopped threatening and the sun had begun cracking through the clouds.

Carol looked up, squinting as she tried to see through the glare with the sun breaking the parting clouds ever further open. She stared at the replica of a shaman's grave box totem, very much like the one she saw at the museum. Behind it, the sun illuminated the crowd of trees.

"Well, I'll be." Carol blinked and bent down, staring at the trees, just under the shaman's totem. One with two trunks grew directly behind it.

"Am I to supposed to think this is just another coincidence," she whispered. It was like smoke vanishing into the mist of the day, leaving her with a chill.

Carol breathed deeply, glad Sadie had left. She didn't want to see her turn even more white as logic dictated that everything she thought she knew hedged on the truth set in the space between those trunks. The shaman was right, she needed to look up a different tree and, more than anything else, begin to accept whatever he knew might indeed have some ring of truth. "Okay, if it's true he can walk through these portals, I can't, and one thing is certain, I've had enough of feeling foolish. This one I'm not about to try out." She moved around to get behind the totems and noticed, mounted in back of the Shaman's totem, was a box. She thought there should be a reproduction, only this one didn't look like just a replica. She looked around, there were only a couple of tourists, and they were leaving back to their car. Carol stepped over the small fence, ignoring the DO NOT ENTER sign, and approached.

Wood, brittle and well-aged, smelling of old bones. Carol took several pictures of the portal tree from the spot Sadie indicated. "Odd. I wouldn't think anyone would put what appears to be an original box out here and attach it to a replica totem pole. Even Mr. Denton had that box at the museum removed due to strange disturbances. I think it's time to visit our museum director again and ask a few more questions."

As Carol walked away she looked up and caught Sadie watching her. *Yes, lady, that's two of us freaked out.* She was beginning to think becoming a detective was more to do with learning about justice within yourself than within others. That, and understanding "there's a lot of weird shit out there" as Big Dan told her the other day.

* * *

Carol smiled, trying not to laugh out loud. Ben was a nut case, but exactly what she needed right now. To loosen up and have some fun. She only wished she'd found something better to wear than the one dress hanging in her closet. It was usually reserved for functions like the police Christmas party. "I won't talk about work, especially not to a reporter."

"Got it," Ben said, as he ordered a bottle of Shiraz. "No work talk. The Australians make the best Shiraz, full of flavor. Anybody, kinda like you. Only your ancestry isn't Aussie, more likely English."

She nodded. "My parents were from Cranbrook in Kent, about forty miles south of London. They came out here in their early twenties. My dad loved the country, especially Vancouver, and it didn't take Mom long to get coast fever."

He put the menu down, twiddled his thumbs, looked around, whistled, twiddled his thumbs some more. "Okay, the suspense is killing me, what's the deal with the biker stiff?"

"No! No work talk." She frowned.

"Just kidding." He laughed. "So, besides busting people's asses and nailing grannies for jaywalking, what do you do with your life?"

She pursed her lips. "This is my life. I go to work, go home. For a thrill I grab a Venti Starbucks, dark roast, no sugar."

"Harsh. No hobbies? Any crazy things, thrill or no thrill, that you always wanted to do? At least I go jogging. Works the stress off and it can get quite meditative. You almost reach this Zen-like state after awhile. It's great for thinking about writing articles."

The waitress came by and they ordered.

"U2. I've never been to a concert but always wanted to see U2." "Never been to a concert? Period?" He blinked in disbelief.

"Yeah, hate crowds." She sipped at the wine. "Hey, I was going to ask you something, since you seem to jog around Stanley Park so much. At the Cathedral Trail clearing, where we found the mayor's wife, do you recall seeing a granite rock, white with black splotches?"

"Ah, what about the no work talk clause?" He looked annoyed.

"Hey, woman's prerogative."

"Oh yeah? I call it double standards. Yes, I seem to recall a fair-sized white rock in what used to be the clearing on the Cathedral Trail. Why do you ask?"

Having got the information she wanted Carol deliberately avoided his question, with a smile she said. "Didn't I say no talk about work?"

"You started it lady. You've done nothing even remotely crazy? Or ever wanted to?" He squinted one eye and opened the other wide, giving her the third degree she usually reserved for others.

The wine was flushing her cheeks and sending heat through her, not to mention the effect his musky cologne was having. He obviously hoped the wine would loosen her up and it was doing more than that. She held the glass in her hand, watching the contents swirl around. "The PNE. I've always wanted to ride the old wooden rollercoaster. My parents took me there as a kid and I freaked out. Couldn't do it."

"Really now." They talked on during their meal. Carol found it easy to talk to Ben and he had a way of making her laugh. As they paid the bill she put her arm around him. He smiled at her and asked the hostess to order them a cab. She hoped the evening was far from over. This was the most fun she'd had in a long time, in fact far longer than she could remember.

"So where to now? Hope you're not taking me home? It's much too early."

"No." He smiled." "The PNE, chauffeur. Post haste," he instructed the cab driver as they got in.

"What? I can't." She gripped the door handle ready to leap out.

He grabbed her hand. "If, for some reason I can't fathom, we never date again, then you need to remember this night forever. When you're an old lady with twelve kids and seven grandkids you'll say to yourself, damn, what if I went up on that rollercoaster with Ben Carlton, would I have married him instead and had his kids?"

"You are nuts. Absolutely nuts." She relaxed her grip on the door. Fear stopped its initial lancing through her flight reflexes. Childish fears, he was right. She had to tackle something that put her on the edge of the unknown, like Rosespit. That was what Charlie was on about wasn't it; doing, looking at things with new eyes. The trip to Rosespit proved that, she'd never have had the guts to walk out there by herself before. More importantly, and most of all, she didn't want to spend her life alone. Looking at things with another viewpoint was catchy and frightening. But she'd learned a few things about herself up there and finally found some closure around her mother leaving her.

Carol wasn't sure if he was THE ONE. A person should know immediately, she'd read somewhere. But if he wasn't, at least she'd have some fun, a break from the stress of work. What was that book she'd been meaning to read? *Feel The Fear*? "Okay, no chess, no kid letting, but I'll do the PNE."

"Deal."

Half an hour later saw them at the front of the line. "Are you scared?"

"Yes, terrified. This is completely mad. If I had my badge on it would be shaking."

"You don't carry your gun off duty, do you? Wouldn't want you shaking so hard you shoot yourself in the foot."

She laughed. "Ben, you're impossible. Maybe after we get off this ride you can take me back to your place and check to make sure they're okay. You know they could get windburn or some sort of thing like that."

"What? Madam 'I never play chess or monopoly on a first date.'" He made an obvious attempt to look appalled.

"True, I did say that. But I'm not averse to a little tiddlywinks."

"Tiddlywinks?"

"Yeah, you tiddly, I wink."

He coughed. "Well if you insist, but I'll have you know I'm a poor learner. You may need to show me several times before I get it. I work best with the hands on approach."

She put her arm through his as they walked through the gate and sat in the car. "And you'll need to hold onto me, I may scream a little."

"As long as you don't wet yourself, you'll do just fine."

"So, Mr. Braveheart. How many times did you ride this, then?"

"None! I've been deathly afraid of them ever since I covered the story back in Edmonton about the three people that died when the car came off the tracks at West Edmonton Mall."

"Died? Hang on, I've changed my mind about this."

She tried to get up, Ben pulled her back down as the attendant walked up and clicked the bar, locking them in place. It was now too late to run. "So, we'll see who screams the loudest and wets their pants the least." He gripped her hand tight as the old cars began their clacking run up the rickety structure.

"I can't do this." Her hand crushed his until he winced.

"Well, you're about to."

"Oh shit!" Their voices rose in unison, before being lost in a scream of wind.

They rode it once more before Carol turned to Ben and kissed him on the lips. "This was fantastic! Now, take me to your place for a drink."

"I thought you didn't play chess on a first date."

"Woman's prerogative. Besides I only have to tell the truth on the job." She smiled, still clutching his hand tight. He was right—Ben. Life was too short, especially when she was in her mid-thirties, alone, and experiencing a severe shortage of orgasmic experiences.

* * *

Charlie sat down cross-legged and sank into the cool grass and moss. He'd just got into Vancouver and came straight to the grove. The rest of his trip had been uneventful, but at least Mr. Baseball Bat had changed his outlook on life.

It was early evening, Stanley Park was almost deserted. Hopefully he wouldn't be disturbed. A simple spell of displacement would see to that.

The normal guarded stillness of this place was upset. The Lure's rock was gone, her enchantment broken. Most of the cedars in the grove lay shattered. The remaining guardian cedars swayed overhead in consternation, several branches had shed their needles, as if fretting. As he relaxed he caught a twig of thought, just skirting the edge of awareness. The wind sighed, in mourning for what had happened here. Charlie could smell the earth, the cedars, pine, But more. Blood, recent blood.

Amongst all the downed trees it lingered. He sniffed again, innocence and its betrayal hung in the clearing, muddying everything, tainting the serenity with death's kiss. This was far worse than he thought.

"Relax boys, no sense letting your bark get in a knot. I'll find her or my name isn't Rumpelstiltskin." It wasn't his name, but he also knew the trees wouldn't know that. They could sense him, and the aura behind his thoughts, but English, or most languages, were beyond their capability.

Timid, furtive thoughts skimmed by. Something else remained here. He took a deep breath and allowed himself to relax, shutting down his thoughts and opening himself to everything around him. He breathed deeply and got it.

Residue, an event from the past still lingered. He sniffed again as he set his medicine bag aside. The spirits and fetishes inside his bag would not be needed, nor would they be of any use. Not with death's cloying stink all over the place.

He took out some sage and fungus. Lighting them, Charlie allowed the pungent smoke to curl lazily around him. He opened the lid to the medicine bag, just in case he might need help. Charlie allowed his consciousness to mingle with those aromas, letting them envelop him and pull him into a trance. Well practiced, the shaman slowed his breathing and quickly faded into the reality of dreamtime, becoming one of the vapors permeating the air. Drifting.

Time unfolding in thin sheets like onionskin paper in an ancient book. Tissue paper rustled as pages lifted, stirred by his breath. He shifted his essence from his body and vanished into the vellum, slowing turning page after page, looking for the needed chapter.

Shifting, drifting, ebbing. Back, into past dreamtime.

Things he could only observe, not change. Here the past was immutable; he was just a helpless observer. The shaman opened his eyes and watched as a man entered the glade. Mid to late thirties white male, scruffy looking, his best years already gone, he looked, haggard, defeated by life. On his belt hung a large, sheathed knife.

Charlie wondered what he hunted with that. Or was it a reflection of some insecurity, fear of others. Protection.

He knew the man too heard voices, but these were in his head, talking, always talking. "Money, you're going to win the big one." The one he let get away.

"Come, James, I've your lucky pendant." A soft, beguiling woman's voice spoke.

"No lose, never lose," cried the sleepy voice within, calling to his greatest desires of fame and money. Things he didn't have and so far had failed to accomplish in life.

Charlie had heard the voice before, the seductive tones, but from where?

"Come, James. You can't lose on this throw." The voice pulled him into the clearing. "No lose, never lose."

A small red and black stone on a leather string glittered amongst the grass. "Pick it up, wear it around your neck. No lose, never lose." She chanted over and over, calling to his unborn greed and desire. "Try these dice."

He stared at two dice sitting on the white and black rock. James picked them up and rolled seven after seven over the moist earth. "Yeah, that's okay. But they'll catch on the dice are loaded."

"Not loaded, your lucky dice. Try again and tell me what number you want."

"What? Okay, nine." He threw them and a nine popped up. "Fluke. How about five." A three and a two stared at him.

"Wow!" He was awestruck. What he could do with these dice. Time after time, the number he wanted appeared. He'd be rich, and better yet, his wife, Yolanda, would love him even more. He'd get her back and they'd live happy together.

"They roll what you ask them to. They're your lucky dice. Only for you."

Voices echoed in the background. "Hide, James, they're coming for you. They seek your good luck. The rich, those that already have it, want your Mr. Lucky."

"No, they can't, only me, it's mine," James growled, his hand darting to the sheath containing his hunting knife.

"Yes, just you. But they want it. Will you protect yourself, or will you let them take it?" she urged.

"No, they always take, take." His eyes clouded and he shook his head.

"Yes, they take, always. But you can stop them. Will you stop them?"

"Mr. Lucky is mine. Only mine." His hand flicked open the cover and pulled the knife free with a hiss. Razor-edged silver glinted in the dark heart of the forest.

"You have to stop them. They're greedy, want more from you."

"No, no more." His wife had just left him. He had no idea where Yolanda was. Rent was due. James' head swam.

"Concentrate. You'll fix that bitch later. Later, James. But the greedy guts need a lesson."

"Yes, greedy. Greedy guts, they can't have it."

Cole Bridge and his blonde wife came into view strolling along the trail. The couple, so obviously still in love, were laughing and holding hands. James jumped from behind the tree.

"You can't have my lucky charm. Greedy people, take, take," he screamed, grabbing Cole before he could react and stabbed at him, catching him in the throat. As Cole fell forward, James rammed his knee up into Cole's chin, knocking him out for the count. Seeing her husband unconscious, his wife began to scream. James backhanded her viciously, the knife spinning out of his hand from the force. She stumbled backwards, eyes wide in horrified shock. James wavered for a moment, unsure what to do.

"Kill them now, they will go to the authorities and throw you in jail forever. You know what they do to you in jail, don't you." The voice echoed between his ears.

James knew. He'd been in jail and never wanted to repeat the experience. Being another man's woman was a humiliation he'd die first before performing again.

"Police!" the blonde woman screamed.

"No police. No jail," he yelled as he lunged at her. The woman staggered backwards, tripping in her haste to escape. She tried to run into the forest, into the glade of Cathedral Trail, but the high heels were useless in the mucky undergrowth. James tackled her from behind as she tried to get back onto the wood-chipped trail. They landed in a pile near her prone husband. James hit her again and again until she stopped screaming.

He dragged her unprotesting body into the glade and dumped her behind a large toppled tree. Grabbing the nearest large rock he made sure she'd never put him in jail, ever.

A movement on the trail behind him brought him up short. A young girl, eyes wide in horror, stared at him covered in a bloody mess.

She'd come running down the trail from the park's interior. Recognition faltered in her vision as she blinked in catatonia's clutches. Nerveless fingers dropped the IPod she'd been so absorbed in. James walked toward her, retrieving and sheathing his knife. Children. He didn't want to harm children, but he didn't want to go to jail. He knew what bad men would do to him in jail.

"Mommy? Daddy!" she sobbed, barely able to find her voice. The girl, who'd been focused on her IPod and not the world around her, spun around and ran back up the trail into the heart of the woods. James looked at the seemingly lifeless body of the Mayor and decided to run after the panicked child instead. "Later. No jail." He knew what he had to do, the dice rattled in his pocket as he ran, "No lose. Never lose."

Charlie closed his eyes as a stab of pain speared him. He couldn't watch the horrors from the past anymore.

"Charlie."

The shaman cocked his head slightly, trying to tune in to the whisper as the girl's screams ended. But that was impossible, he was in the past. He was, in essence, an unseen observer only. The past was immutable and he couldn't be seen.

He strained to listen, perhaps more tired than he thought. Maybe he heard wrong, a bird calling or other some other sounds.

"Charlie. Help me." Louder this time, and there was no mistaking the voice.

Chapter Ten

"October 13, 1917. Unresolved case number 3124. Woman found wondering in south end of Stanley Park, west side. Incoherent, treated for exposure. Her boyfriend's body found near trail." Thank goodness someone has put the old records onto the database.

Carol smiled as she filed through all the old police records. In fact, she couldn't get the smile off her face for most of the morning. Last night with Ben had been wonderful, living in the real world with real people. Enjoying herself, laughing so much her sides ached. Not to mention the other, more pleasant, ache between her thighs. Playing chess was more fun than she thought. "Whoever called that a boring tactical game must have got the rules wrong."

She'd cross-referenced incidents of foul play with Stanley Park. "June 4, 1938. Couple found south end of Stanley Park, near Cathedral Trail. Throats slashed. No details released to public. 1953, Skeletal remains of two bodies found by Park Gardener, Albert Tong, called the Babes in The Woods Case, unsolved. August 10, 1957. Man found dead Cathedral Trail area of Stanley Park. No identification, believed to be homeless. No signs of struggle. Suspect natural causes. A Skull was found in 1990 in the park and another later in 1998 by a woodcutter. Forensics revealed they were of two friends that disappeared in 1989."

Carol copied all the files onto her laptop. "Perhaps Pauline Johnson was right. There's something odd about the area around Cathedral Trail and Stanley Park. Whether it's a witch, well that's another matter entirely."

* * *

Charlie looked around for the source of the voice and spotted movement by the trees. It couldn't be!

"It is. It is me." The woman who spoke was once so familiar to him; like his own skin.

"But you're dead!" He was stunned; it had to be a trick.

"Not here, this is the past. It was so hard to find you. I've missed you. This is where I still exist, here we can be together."

His beloved Lucy. It looked like her. The shaman threw caution aside and approached her. He inhaled deeply. It smelled like her. The aura that surrounded her was the same. Could she indeed still be alive, here in the past? He'd never thought of that possibility.

She held out her arms. "You can love me here."

He moved closer. How many years had passed since Lucy Klintu died? Over thirty. The smell, the aura; it was indeed her. This was no trap, it was Lucy Klintu. His soulmate, his twin flame, the part of his heart that had been ripped away all those decades ago. He wrapped her in his arms.

"How? How did you find me?"

"A way. It wasn't easy. I found a way in the past. Talk later, foolish man whose waters are not running still right now. Kiss me now. I've missed you terribly."

"As have I." It was her. She used to remark how his namesake was the opposite when he held her, his waters were not still. He felt like that giddy teenager again, strung out on testosterone poisoning. His heart pounded as if he were a young man again.

Her lips pressed his. The passion, dormant all this time since her death, erupted in spontaneous combustion, firing every nerve, every seething blood cell. He'd never dreamed this could happen after her...*Dream?*

"I want you, now."

His hands remembered every curve, every inch of the softness as they continued kissing. Her hunger was insatiable. He remembered how quiet and demure she was until they kissed the first time. It was like unleashing a mountain lion. The woman became this being of karmic energy and she'd ignite his every fuse. Her hands flowed over him. His manhood surged, the throb returning to his loins.

He held her close. The press of her breasts—how he wanted to touch them, kiss them. Memories of their softness.

"Oh! God!" Twin exclamations escaped in nearly the same breath.

Hunger, passion, rifling through him. So unexpected.

The self-control, the years of sacrifice, of denying his needs, evaporated under the contact of her lips.

"Take me, Charlie, take me now. I need you inside me."

"Me too." This was insanity he wasn't about to question.

Dreams?

He started to remove her clothes but she ripped them away herself, his also. The sight of her naked body set him on fire with desire. So long, too long.

Naked she pushed him to the ground where they tumbled in the grass.

Dreams? The past?

So hungry for her, they were like great hunting cats, biting at each other as she thrust forward. He entered her body, his old flesh made young by the passion.

The leather strap of the necklace he always wore rubbed against her chest. "Charlie, the strap. It irritates me. Take it off, I don't like it."

The strap held the dried tongue of his Kushtaka guardian spirit. He went to remove it, and then stopped. Lucy would never ask that of him.

Dreams; the past; the necklace.

Something didn't jive and he couldn't dance, let alone jig. The shaman tried to pull out of her body.

"No don't, you're too close. I'm so close."

She clung to him, her muscles grabbing at him, keeping him inside her wetness and heat. Almost like she was sucking at him, pulling his essence into her. This wasn't Lucy, this was a leech. A soul-sucking leech.

"No, something isn't right. I need to return to the present. Think about this with a clear head." He could feel the burning ache within his centre. He was beginning to build toward that almighty explosion he was afraid he wouldn't be able to stop.

"No. You cannot leave me again."

"Again? I never left to begin with. You're not Lucy."

"Yes, I am."

"No. Lucy was bold, but never this bold, and she would always let me undress her. It drove her wild to have me take her clothes off. It was our thing."

The talk was helping to diminish his arousal. He fought to regain control of his body. To shut down the second chakra's very powerful sexual libido awoken after its long slumber. He tried again to pull out.

"No! You can't."

Charlie felt her holding him, her wetness crying to awaken his hunger. He closed his eyes and struggled to stay rational.

"No, you won't."

The shaman pushed her to the ground, shaking with the effort to regain control. Yet that was part of his rituals, some of what he practiced, self-control. He succeeded where others would have succumbed. The shaman flung her naked body away from him.

"I can and I will." He knew now, if he'd taken the necklace off and released his energy, she would have had him, devoured his life force. "I'm leaving."

Lucy sobbed. He wanted to comfort her, but nothing seemed right. He didn't know what, but it was wrong. Everything was all wrong. He closed his eyes and released himself from the past. He began the flow into the present, pulling at the pages of time.

A door crashed closed and the lock snicked shut. Charlie slammed against it.

He tried the handle but it wouldn't budge. He was trapped.

"I said you're staying." Lucy melted away, the charade was over. Her body shifted, melding into another. An older woman, grey hair, harsh eyes with no vestige of kindness, stared at him. Her breasts sagged grossly, and wrinkles adorned her body like perverse armour. She looked a hundred, but was possibly very much older.

Charlie tried again, but the door was locked, at least from this side. He could not get out.

"I almost had you, native man. That was quite a woman you had. It is rare two people share that much passion. That much raw energy. So arousing, so deliciously filling." She swooned, swimming in the waves of carnal arousal. "I think you'll stay, we've unfinished business and I like to play with my food."

"You want to play, do you?" Charlie flung off his necklace, throwing it at the door. As he thought, it went through; the door was only locked to him. "That's okay. I like it rough, too. Let's party." He dove at her, pinning her to the ground.

"What?"

Lucy, he thought of Lucy, and pinned the old woman to the ground. The witch was off guard, she'd probably never had anyone attack her. He thrust himself into her. Tearing aside her veils of resistance.

"You bastard." She screamed in fury.

"You know what they say in the CFL, the best defence is a good offence. But then I would imagine you'd think the Americans have a better game." He laughed. He hoped the necklace would alert those whose help he needed right now. Otherwise, he was doomed to meet his demise screwing this old hag. But if he had to go, he'd make sure it was with all he had to fight with and a smile on his face.

"You're mine, bitch."

He wrapped one arm around her neck, choking her, and thrust savagely into her, going against everything he believed in. Only she wasn't a lady, nor even a woman really and hence deserved no respect. Here in the past, he was mostly helpless, she'd altered a spell to allow this much interaction. There was little his powers could do, taking her by force was his only hope.

"No." She clawed savagely back.

Charlie guessed she'd never in her life been treated like this, raped like she'd raped so many others. Taken their lives, their souls. "You bastard."

There was only one way to beat her at her own game. "Hey, I like mature women." He thrust again and again. "You know what they say about women over forty, in your case well over forty, probably a hundred and forty. They never tell. They can't swell. They won't yell. And they appreciate it like hell." He laughed madly.

"You're crazy," she screamed. "Foolish man."

"Yeah, but it takes two to whatoosie." He could feel her regaining control; he had little time before she would take over and begin sucking at him again. In desperation he backhanded her.

She screamed in rage and blinked. "Nasty man. You are indeed smart and virile for your age. Such pent up emotions. Still." Her eyes bore into him. "You cover your heart well."

Energy welled up within the shaman, but she was breaking through, his self-control ebbing. She was beginning to see through his bravado and starting to do the thrusting now, wallowing in the sheer display of power.

"Such passion. I'll enjoy taking your soul and raping it over and over again. Before I devour it." She closed her eyes, her body swelling with all of the energy he was pouring into her. "Foolish, foolish man."

"Go ahead, I'm rather enjoying watching this myself." He smiled looking down at her.

"What?" She opened her eyes, staring at the shaman standing beside her.

"*Au contraire*, it's not just you who can play the bait and switch scene. I had people tell me once, never watch yourself making love, it's quite gross. After all, we're not all porn stars." He laughed. "I'm glad I don't own a video camera, this is one scene I wouldn't want to record for prosperity's sake. Although the look on your face right now is priceless."

"Then who…" The witch looked up at the creature on top of her. A Kushtaka; half man, half land otter. It possessed no eyelids, coarse hair covered its entire body. No lips hid the unwashed teeth, brown and stained. Tiny arms sprouted straight out from its chest, its claws tearing at her breasts. The creature smiled back as much as it could, in an eerie grimace.

"Horrible, horrible man."

"Oh, I don't know, I think he likes you. He wants a kiss."

The Lure screamed in horror, flinging the disgusting beast from her. Charlie and his guardian creature bolted for the door the beast had left open when he entered this realm. "I was right. The door would be only locked on one side."

She screamed in utter rage and vile disgust. "Never! I never!" Tearing at the course hair sticking to her, pulling at her centre, wiping away the wetness left behind. The witch was so obviously disgusted at being taken by an animal she shuddered at the vileness of it all. The shaman found it amusing in a bizarre sort of way.

Charlie grabbed the handle. "Oh baby, I don't know, I guess there's no use in asking for sloppy seconds. Actually, unlike humans, they're usually good for three or four orgasms before being satisfied. Are you sure you don't want to change your mind? He's here not only for a good time but a long and hard time."

"Bastard." She flung herself toward him. Fingers like daggers raking the air.

He had broken every ounce of self-control she had and fires of fury spat from her eyes. Charlie slammed shut the door and sealed it with a spell. She thundered into it; the heavens shuddered with her rage. The door buckled, her fingers scratching and tearing. Her outrage and screams continued unabated.

"I better tell him to bring some seaweed and a couple of dead fish as a peace offering on your next date. Probably be a good idea, to soften you up."

Her fury exploded, thundering through the entire glade. Charlie returned to his body and the present, leaving her behind in the past. The Kushtaka was about to flow back into his necklace. "No, not this time. As I promised for aiding me in this unusual and disgusting task, you can return to your people below the sea. My many thanks. You have served me well and are released from my bidding." The creature smiled and vanished. "Ah, nothing like a roll in the hay with a witch to get your day off to a smashing start." Grabbing his cane, Charlie slowly sauntered from the glade, whistling.

Inside, he was not so joyful. But he knew one thing, the witch would know better the next time they met. It was she who had whispered to the deluded man and made him kill the mayor and his family. Now she was loose somewhere in the city. Worse yet, it was she who broke down all of his resolve. All of his training as a shaman; did it so fast, so easily. The witch was truly cunning. She'd fooled him because of his pent up desires, his wanting to be with the one person that mattered. Lucy, whom he thought he buried a long time ago. A weakness he didn't know still existed.

A tear scrubbed its way down his face. She was right about something, the ache in his heart where an empty place once sat lay bleeding now. How he wished it had been Lucy, the love he could never hold in his arms again. God, he missed her. In all these years the ache never lessened, nor would the memory of her kiss ever leave him.

Not in this lifetime.

* * *

The vans accelerated harshly, metal groaned under protest, sparks rained upward. Ben jumped awake. That street! He'd seen that street once before. Ben rose from his bed; the musky smell of sex from their lovemaking still clung to the bedsheets, as he flung on his clothes. Carol couldn't stay the night; she'd needed to get up early to get back on her case.

He'd love to have her in his arms come morning and, who knows, maybe make love again. Right now, he had bigger issues to deal with. He jumped in his car and drove back to Heatley Street, where the biker was found murdered. The police hadn't released a statement yet, but he knew by what he'd seen it was no accident. What was it that was so familiar about this street?

He sat for long moments, eyes closed, trying to remember when, how, and why. He shouldn't, there was never a time when he'd come down here. The growl of a Harley cut through the night air as it started up. "Where is that from?"

He drove up the street to the corner and spied the Victorian-style house, probably nearly a hundred years old, painted in a garish burgundy and teal blue. The Harley and its rider pulled out from the yard and began to accelerate down the street. Echoes of the mufflerless bike thrummed down the block. He caught the face of the rider. He knew who that was; none other than Ryley McLaren, the leader of Devil's Spawn. Ben stared back at the Spawn's clubhouse.

So familiar. He sat still as it flooded back. This was where Stumpy was heading. It was here he woke up.

The night out with Brandi. He awoke alone in the car, whisky bottle in his lap. Somewhere on this street, staring at this house. Snitches of memories flitted by. Revenge. He clenched his teeth hard. Angry. He was bitterly angry. Vengeance cried out from the recesses of his memories.

But why? Whose anger was this seething underneath? What possessed him to come here? Ben slowly drove back to his condo as the wee-morning hours became infused with dawning sunlight. Whatever happened had something to do with the biker group. Memories of staring at that address through the night, waiting for something, refused to go away. What though? Ben didn't know as he began to sweat. Reporting about the Devil's Spawn was one thing, having to deal with them, totally another. He wiped at the cold sweat forming on his brow.

Stalking them was another level closer to Harakari.

Damn it. Why? Crap, not a good crowd to be messing with.

Not now, when one of them close to Ryley himself had just been murdered.

Stalking. Did he just think that? He, or whoever was inside his head, was stalking the Devil's Spawn. He had to find out why.

* * *

The Lure pulled herself together, holding onto the walls of the bathroom stall until the world stopped spinning. She blinked, trying to focus through this new pair of eyes, head throbbing miserably. Music pounded in the background. She had to get away from this bathroom and its stink of urine, puke, and alcohol.

She stumbled to the mirrors and looked at herself. Hair shorn short, almost manly. This woman was small, slender, and had nearly no breasts and no device to hold them in place. No beautifying paint on her face. She felt something scratch her mouth and stuck out her tongue. A pearl stud jutted out. Odd. Not at all feminine.

Did this host not believe in looking after herself? How did she expect to pick up a male looking like this?

"There you are. I thought I better come in and see if you're okay?"

The Lure stared, unsure what to make of the effeminate male that walked in. Or was it a woman? Dressed in black, hair shorn, and face painted nearly white. Black lipstick made her think female, but the bulge in the tight leather trousers assured her it was probably a male. Whatever it was, it looked like death warmed over.

"I, ah, the alcohol didn't stay down, didn't agree with me," she lied, trying to grasp what was happening. Some things about this world made no sense.

"Those tequila shooters get to me as well." The person put his/her arm around her and pulled her close. "I've something that could go down more smoothly on you." He licked slowly at her ear.

The Lure shivered, feeling hands caress the thin T-shirt proclaiming Vancouver Pride Day. Her nipples reacted immediately, small breasted, but tender. Something cold and metallic hung from one of her nipples.

"My tongue," the person said as he nibbled at her ear. The softness of the others lips on hers made her think it was possibly not a male. She ran her hands up the front to discover a similar small pair of breasts, erect nipples, metal rings piercing both. Odd culture. They dressed like the walking dead or night denizens and went to bed with persons of the same sex. She was ready to storm out, but changed her mind. In her current body she'd have a very hard time picking up a male, looking so much like one. It meant not having to go looking and time was of the essence. After all, a soul to devour was a soul to devour. It did seem easy to take people to bed in this time period, or was it only this location that seemed to be on permanent potlatching?

"I'm tired of this crowd. Why don't I take you home?"

She responded by timidly kissing the other on the lips. "I'm all yours, honey." She wasn't sure if she could stomach the thought of kissing another woman all night, or was this a hermaphrodite? There was a hard bulge pressing up against her.

"Now you're talking. My kind of girl. Up front with knowing what she wants and I've plenty of that kind of loving, too. Hope you like being my bottom tonight."

Bottom? "Sure, just get me out of here and ply me with drinks. I'll be anything you want." Strange talk. "Do you own a computer?"

"Of course."

"Hey, I'm game then."

They drove to a small apartment with little for furniture and no pictures on the walls. "I like the minimalist look," the woman said, "I'll get us a drink."

The Lure called it being poor, and thought lots of alcohol would definitely help. She'd do more research later on the computer. She'd learned much the last time and needed to know more about this era. Odd things like what kind of pride they meant on Pride Day, and more importantly, all she could about those that had trapped her.

They settled onto a mattress on the floor in one corner of the room called living. Perhaps the rest were dying rooms, she thought. Not least, this one's appearance seemed to indicate so. The girl took off most of her dangling jewelry, crosses, and skulls. She had four pieces of metal in each ear and one in her navel. A fixation with death and pain obviously. The Lure eyed the woman coming toward her. She gleaned from the mind of the host she inhabited she was called Leanne. Her gaze lingered on the large bulge jutting in her pants. Now that was what The Lure really wanted to know about and hungered to get at.

Leanne handed one of the glasses over, looking much better without most of the gaudy bits of metal. The drinks had a white substance edging the rim. She called them vodka-coke shooters.

"This will relax you and loosen you up," she promised.

They both gulped them down.

The white substance was some sort of drug, obviously meant to induce pleasure. It burned at the witch's lips. Leanne's lips, while painted dark, were soft, not hard. Most vexing these times, The Lure thought, as their hands explored each other. She tugged on the metal strung through the other woman's breasts. Leanne moaned. She obviously liked some pain. That was a good thing; she liked inflicting it.

"I see the coke is beginning to have its desired effect. I give massages during the day. Care for one now? I'll definitely make it worthwhile." She stood and rubbed at her manhood.

"Yes," the witch could barely mutter. The drug was making her languid and lethargic. Let the other female do the work. The Lure was more interested in catnapping at this point. She didn't know what a massage was, but the implications seemed pleasurable and foreplay to some lovemaking. The room began to fall away in a smoky haze. She struggled to stay in control of the host's body.

Leanne brought over a padded table and set it up, lighting candles. "Take off your clothes and lay on your belly," she purred. The Lure did as asked, the cool of the leather material sending shivers through her. Leanne rubbed oils on her hands, essence of lavender, sandalwood, patchouli, and other exotic fragrances filled the air.

Expert hands began to work at her neck and shoulders, working their way down. Easing the tension away, making it flow into one part of her anatomy. The girl was very good. As she began to rub the bottoms of her feet, Leanne's touch became softer, more sensuous. Or was it the drug taking effect? She didn't care, it was too good. The Lure had heard of the women of her tribe satisfying each other when the males were out hunting, or often males would join in, have two or three women with them at a time. But she had never tried it. She might decide to change her mind on that score.

She gasped as Leanne curled her tongue around one of her toes, licking and sucking. "Oh, that's good, you were right about your tongue."

"Just wait. I've had a few years of practice pleasuring women. Always satisfy your customers, I've learned." Her hands moved slowly up The Lure's legs. She instinctively spread them wider, not sure if it was only her enjoying this or the host joining in as well. Unable to help herself, moans escaped her lips as wetness seeped from her. This one was definitely good. She moved her legs apart and let Leanne caress the centre of her being.

"Nice set of buns." Hands caressed her behind before the cool feel of her lips on her rear. She moaned again as Leanne's fingers dipped between her legs. "You're so wet, obviously enjoying this." Her talented tongue licked all around her rear. "Oh, that's so good."

"Sit up, my dear." The Lure sat up and went back on her knees, too aroused to even speak as Leanne's mouth went to her private parts, licking and sucking away. She could feel herself already building. The woman knew how to pleasure a woman, she wished most males were this good. Leanne's hot, wet tongue explored her from one orifice to another. The Lure shivered in delight as she began to suck on her womanhood.

She exploded all too quickly, coming hard as the delicious woman continued nibbling, not releasing her just yet. Another began to build.

"Oh, honey, you're so yummy and wet." Leanne continued licking at her.

The Lure began to come again. This was too incredibly good.

"Don't move." She couldn't if she wanted to, her body shuddering as Leanne unzipped her pants and climbed on the table behind her, turning her around. "Now to officially make you my bottom and put you on the moon." Her hardness thrust inside of The Lure. Rock-hard and extremely large, filling her. She could feel herself building once again.

"Oh God, no more, no more." She'd never cried that out before. She definitely would rethink her position on just being with males. This woman was much too good. The Lure collapsed in a heap, tremors rippling across her skin. "My turn."

She slowly turned over and saw the penis-shaped device strapped around the woman's body. *Very interesting invention, such ingenious technology.* They'd made some great strides in pleasuring each other in this culture.

"Take my place," she ordered, allowing her sense of control to return. She had Leanne take off the male-enhanced device and sit on her knees. Time was beginning to run short and she had to get back to the club. The Lure wasn't sure if she'd like the taste of another woman, so she just closed her mind and let the host's instincts take over. Still it wasn't bad, musky. She began to lick and suck at Leanne's womanhood.

"Oh, you've had a little practice yourself."

The witch kept licking, beginning to revel in the energy flow. Pulling at all of the built up energy, and there was lots stored in this one. She let Leanne have her release as the woman cried out in ecstasy. Hunger sang to The Lure; more, she needed more.

"No stop, I've had enough, I just need one," the woman pleaded.

But Leanne couldn't pull away, she was held in a grip of steel as the witch kept at her. Licking and sucking away. The Lure had her cumming again, and another after that. She'd forgotten the difference between male and female. Men were done usually after the first one; with Leanne the energy released kept increasing each time. The woman screamed in ecstasy as she shuddered all over.

"No more! God, I never thought I'd ever say that." She fluttered on the edge of consciousness. "Please stop, I can't take this anymore, you'll suck me until I have a heart attack or stroke and keel over."

"That's the idea."

"What, NO!"

The witch wouldn't let her pull away as the mouth kept devouring her energies, pulling it out of her, sucking it into the witch's essence. The Lure could feel her going weak, losing consciousness.

Finally the woman went limp and collapsed in a heap. Robbed of life, the body slumped onto the table, arms dangled over the edge. Her eyes glazed over in one final release of her soul into the mouth sucking on her.

"Now that was different. Don't know about living room, darling. I'd call it a dying room myself." She kissed the cooling lips. "Hate to eat and run, but I do have to get back soon, and I need time for a little research."

She sucked back another drink, making sure she wiped away as much of the drug as she could. The host was stirring, obviously upset by what had just transpired. The Lure turned on the computer and sat before it for the next hour, searching. Her mind glancing at entire pages, learning at a speed unthought-of of by society.

Done, The Lure set down the glass and began dressing herself. She watched one hand begin to separate itself from the host's body for a moment before fading back into the woman's essence. She looked in the mirror and watched her face materialize momentarily. "Interesting. One or two more absorptions might be all I need. Very powerful energy in this era." She bent over and licked at the now cold ear. "You've made me change my opinion of females though. I quite enjoyed having my cake and eating it, too." She laughed and headed for the door. "Although, I still think I prefer sausage and beefcake, as they say around here. But nothing wrong with a little something different once in a while."

* * *

Larry strode into St. Paul's hospital. He was taking quite a chance this far from the nightclub, but he had to come here. If the patient was who he thought it was, then the blow to Ryley would be enormous. An eye for an eye, he smiled. Worth the risk, and he didn't get many chances during the day. Fortunately today this fellow had come in and got smashing drunk after losing his job. Larry didn't feel remotely sorry for him; he simply wanted to take advantage of what he'd learned his last trip out.

"Lose your family, kids, wife, and your own life, see how upset that makes you," he muttered as he walked into the room. Two Spawn members he didn't recognize, or expect, sat guarding the room. He spotted the small body under the oxygen tent, all covered in bandages.

"What the fuck do you want? No visitors! Can't you read the fucking sign," one growled, rising to challenge him.

"Ah sorry, wrong room." He turned and quickly marched out. Damn, this made matters harder. The male he inhabited wouldn't be able to take out both of them, at least not unarmed.

He gritted his teeth and sauntered up to the nurse's desk. He had to wait while she talked to the nurse on duty. Although impatient to get his information he couldn't help admiring the body under the girl's shapeless scrubs. Would have taken a sack to hide those curves. Eventually, the nurse left but not before giving him a real come-on smile. He turned from her to the charge nurse. "Matthews. How's he doing?"

"You are?"

"Relative, not much liked by the family, but I care a lot about the kid." He smiled, speaking firmly. She took one look at him dressed in his suit and tie. Larry had learned long ago attitude and appearance will get you farther than swearing and belligerence. Look like a million bucks and you'd get treated the same. This body he inhabited was some sort of lawyer type, according to letters he found in the briefcase.

The nurse looked down at her sheet. "I'm not supposed to discuss his details with anyone, but the kid's a gem. We all like him here. Don't like the thugs hanging around though."

"Yeah, call me the black sheep of the family. I make a respectable living, and they deal with drugs and pimps. Say, are they here often?"

She looked blankly at him.

"Look, I just heard he was here and need to know if he's going to be okay. I might be able to get an injunction against them, stop them coming here, if you'd like."

The nurse shivered. "Everyone coming in has to sign in. Sign here." She handed him a sheet. "The fat one gives me the creeps, eyes me up all the time, like I'm some piece of meat. They're here all the time. I think his dad is some kind of biker or something. The kid's in serious shape. Car accident. Broke both legs, cracked four ribs, one of which punctured his lung. Should pull through, but he'll be here at least a couple of months yet."

Larry caught the one biker leaving the kid's room, clicking off his cell phone. He was walking straight toward Larry. Must have been talking to Ryley.

"Thanks." He smiled at her. "I'll see what I can do." And he walked briskly around the corner, trying not to look too hurried.

"Hey pal, hang on a second," the biker yelled.

Unarmed, he wouldn't stand a chance against the two goons. Larry rushed to the exit and ran down the stairs. Two floors down he spotted a cart left behind by a nurse. He grabbed a couple of new syringes and stuffed them into his pocket, just in case.

"Damn armed guard makes this difficult, didn't expect this and now they know someone is looking." But of course they wouldn't know who. He exited the hospital hoping to grab a smoke, and after ditching the goon, figure out how to get back into the room. But, it proved one thing right. Ryley had a son he kept from everyone, even Larry, his main man. At the far end of the lot, not far from where he'd parked, was Greasy. He'd just pulled up on his bike.

"Damn."

He must have been either relieving one of the two or visiting. Greasy reached into his blue jean club jacket and clicked on his cell. Larry unwrapped both syringes and kept them in his hand in his pocket as he strode straight up to the biker. Greasy was eyeing him up as he clicked off the phone. Larry pretended to pat his pockets looking for keys, and found a pack of cigarettes instead.

"Hey, bud, got a minute?"

Greasy growled as he put away the phone.

He stuffed the unlit smoke into his mouth and muttered, "Sure, got a light?"

Larry glanced around quickly to ensure there was no one in the immediate area. As Greasy clicked on the lighter, Larry pulled the two syringes free of his pocket, rammed them into the biker's neck, and kneed Greasy in the balls as hard as he could.

The biker screamed and buckled over, one hand trying to yank out the needles while the other cupped his privates. He reached down and whipped the knife free he knew Greasy kept tucked in his left sock. Before the biker could react Larry slashed his throat and stepped back as blood erupted, spraying down the biker's front. Greasy slumped to the ground in a pool of expanding crimson. "That, you fucker, was for my son."

Greasy blinked unbelievingly. He tried to speak but couldn't, gurgles simply spewed a red tide from his mouth and throat. Both hands trying to stem the red tide.

Larry glanced around, checking to see if they were still unnoticed. The body he inhabited jerked a couple of times, the host obviously reacting to the severe violence. Larry breathed deep and chugged from the small twelve-ounce bottle of whisky in his vest. He wiped his mouth and stood calmly watching the biker die. Larry grabbed the two syringes and knife; he didn't want any evidence linking the host to the crime. He stuffed the items into a large silk handkerchief he found in the jacket pocket. He scrawled LS into the pool of blood and quickly left. "Looks like the day wasn't a total waste after all." He headed back to the club, dumping the weapons into a dumpster a few blocks down.

* * *

"How many nights ago? It seems like a lifetime," Carol mused as she butted out her smoke standing by the table in Stanley Park. She'd spent virtually the entire night camped out there.

Cedar softened the air made harsh by the concrete jungle abutting it. Geese squawked over the sound of traffic bussing by heading for the Lion's Gate Bridge and West Van. She walked to the monument nearly hidden under the canopy of trees. Just behind it three trails converged. Obviously, the memorial was placed where it was just for that reason. Which made it difficult to determine exactly where Charlie came from and left. "He could have easily vanished up one of these and I missed him," Carol muttered, walking around the area. "It was dark and foggy, after all," she reassured herself.

Only why did the mayor stagger here? A parking area was just beside them. The concession area wasn't open, but it appeared from the position of his body that he sat down and died there. A bloody handprint, since faded, had been placed over Pauline's name. It appeared almost as if he had no intention of going any farther.

Carol had already followed the route taken by the mayor that night, as evidenced by the blood splatters along the trail marked Rawlings, which travelled just beside the parkway road. But why? Why end up here and not go to the road and flag down a passing car? That would make more sense.

"You don't think…" She drew a mental trajectory between the trail and his body and followed her vision to the memorial. "That he was heading here?" She got up and walked toward the spot she recalled seeing Charlie when she first met him. She flipped through her notes from the visit to the mayor's house earlier. He had an extensive library and, out on his desk with a couple of other books, was a first printing of Ms. Johnson's *Legends of Vancouver*. He'd obviously been reading it recently. "Perhaps it was part of the reason they came out here that day." She knew the mayor was an avid outdoorist and reveled in not only going to the park, but espousing its glories to visiting dignitaries. "I think the mayor came to the totems to die, perhaps unseen or not wanting anyone to stop him from getting here, knowing he was dying, but again, why? There is no evidence he might have done the killing and perhaps committed suicide after."

"Well, if I were to believe this folklore stuff about native legends, would explain why a shaman would be involved in some remote context." At the time she didn't really pay close attention, especially in the dark, at nearly two in the flipping morning, thinking Charlie was some derelict crackhead. "Still not sure about the cracked part, nor what he might smoke, snort, or ingest in his moments of spiritual meditation. But I know this, he knows something I don't, otherwise, why contact me, and would that involve her?" She stared at the stone figure of Pauline. Rubbed her hand over the canoe cast on the right side of the monument.

"We need to talk lady."

The trouble with a shaman is he travels only where smoke follows. Carol had read that in one of the books she'd picked up from the Vancouver library. To date, Brook had been right, the man had been very elusive, impossible to find. "So how does one think like smoke?"

She started down the first of the three trails where Charlie had disappeared and stopped. There in front of her stood a tree identical to the one framed in the picture window of his backyard. "Well that might explain a little." She walked up to the benign looking portal tree. Another of the books she'd read confirmed what Brook told her. Some tribes believed that portal trees were magical and a shaman could travel between dimensions through them.

Carol took a picture on her cell phone and walked carefully around the tree.

"Looks like your regular western red cedar." Reaching out she touched it. "Okay, no jolt of electricity or heebie-jeebies tingles. A regular tree. I must be nuts to think that just because this tree has a hole in its centre you can travel between dimensions, kinda like an earthly Dr. Who's Tardis. Or, of course, what's even nuttier is that I'm standing here in the middle of a forest talking to myself about a bloody tree."

Shaking her head she walked around again. "No trace of any kind of disturbances or…"

Something glinted in the hollow of the tree. Pulling out her pen she brushed aside the leaves, exposing what looked like a small plastic container. "Odd." Carol reached in her pocket and pulled out a pair of latex gloves. She pulled free the container.

"What the hell is this? Some kind of a joke?" Inside, a smiley-face badge stared at her, along with a plastic dinosaur, a little metal car, several business cards, a travel BC pin, a Peruvian worry-type doll, and a small ball of multicoloured wool.

At the bottom was a card with a website written on it. She pulled her phone free again and took a couple of pictures before calling headquarters. "Can you get me Gary in investigations? Thanks." The line clicked over.

"Gary, any ideas?" She told him about the container and read him the website.

"Yeah, gimme a second to call this up… Just what I thought, heard about this lot. A geocaching group. You basically take a set of coordinates like the ones on this site, punch them in and try to find the hidden location using a GPS device. The cache will include a log sheet or book and you write about your find and enjoy the trinkets left by others. If you take any of the trinkets you must leave behind something of equal or greater value," Gary replied.

"Thanks. Damn crazy computer geeks." She clicked off the phone and carefully replaced the container where she found it, thinking there was no sense wrecking some geeky people's fun.

"Clever boy, that Gary. So, no funny woo-woo stuff here my shamanistic friend. It only proves one thing, I'm still sane and you're still cracked. Crap! This is getting me nowhere except a trip to the loony-tunes hospital." Folding her gloves she put them back in her pocket. "Hate these things, feel like some vet about to dive into a cow's behind or feel up its udder." She'd seen her grandfather do that many times during calving season. Grabbing a handful of leaves to cover the box, Carol pulled back wincing in pain. A pin-prick of blood adorned the end of her finger. "Damn, just my luck. Probably some crackhead's needle."

She dabbed at her cut with a tissue before carefully pushing aside the vegetation with a pen, exposing a small round pin with its metal end unhinged. "Okay, so I can relax, no chance of HIV." She picked up the pin and examined it. The Montreal Expos logo stared at her. Carol's legs buckled slightly and she slowly sank down on to her haunches, feeling the world fade away from around her into stunned silence. "You gotta be fucking kidding me."

Brook's words haunted back from memory, "He watches TV in the back of his cabin. Used to watch the Expos, now catches the Blue Jays." She twirled the pin between her fingers. "Interesting coincidence?"

She clipped the badge closed and put it in a plastic baggie. "So, is he a little less cracked than I can give him credit for, or am I less sane than I thought?" She stared up into the empty space between the two trunks of the tree. "Do I actually have to believe him now? I guess there's only one way to figure this out. I might as well try it. This is absolutely nuts, and I'm the dope head for trying it, but I've got to check out all the evidence, even if that means I end up in la-la land on the other side of the world."

Laughing, Carol looked around, making sure there was no one on the trail. "Don't want the world to think I'm a complete nut case, too." She put one hand on either side of the tree trunks. "Close your eyes. Relax, think of a calm place to go to and hope I don't wake up in Kansas with Toto licking my face, a tinman looking for his brain, and a lion man crying about bravery or lack of lioness to mate with or some such madness." Visions of her visit up to Rosespit came to mind. "Let go and allow yourself to fall through, concentrate on a safe place the book said, and faith, have faith. Pretty stupid I think, but what the heck. I don't see any Stargate symbols or any DHDs, should be safe. Okay shaman prove me wrong again 'cause I'm getting tired of this vanishing smoke stuff."

Carol glanced at her wristwatch and closed her eyes. The detective took two deep grounding breaths and let go, falling into darkness.

Chapter Eleven

The drape less eyes of the purple clubhouse stared blankly back at Ben. He hadn't paid much attention to where he'd awoken after the disastrous date with Brandi. He'd been much too disorientated and badly hungover to care at the time, but this was the place, he was sure of it now.

Whatever happened to him had to do with that place. The nightmares were fading away and he could sleep through most nights. Hopefully, they'd be completely gone soon.

He yawned, staring at his watch. It was late and this second night of observing hadn't gleaned anything useful. He closed the laptop. Searching "Larry had raised about ten zillion results. He yawned again and started his car. It was time to get some much-needed shut eye. Driving away he heard the distant grumble of a big bike with little or no muffler.

Ben crawled from his car after the short drive to his home, hoping tonight he might get some decent sleep. He'd bought pills just in case. The last several nights had been full of repeating visions and very little restful sleep, other than the night with Carol.

"I gotta hit the sack tonight." He looked back up the dark street as he slunk up the staircase of his building.

* * *

Four pairs of eyes watched the man stumble up the steps of a large building. Why here, and why the Spawn?

"She is here, in this city." One of the men in black said, pulling free from the darkness. "Yes," the others whispered to each other. "The city is large, we know not how to navigate these trails of bitumen and limestone. But..." They all spoke in unison. "She is here. We can smell her."

"So, we wait." One of the four shadows spoke.

"Agreed."

"She will come."

* * *

"Absolutely stupid. That has to be about the dumbest thing I've ever done." Carol spat out grass and brushed decomposed leaves from the side of her face and hair as she sat up. A glance at her watch told her about two seconds had passed. She stood up, trying to dust herself and her pride clean. "For a bloody moment, I actually wanted to believe him."

She put her hand in her pocket and winced in pain again. Another pin-prick of blood on her finger. "Damn thing. I thought I'd clipped it shut!" She pulled the baggie free of her pocket; the Expos pin had managed to come free of its latch in the fall. "Why do I know somewhere there's a Haida nut job laughing his ass off at me?"

* * *

Carol stumbled from her car the next morning at St. Paul's hospital. All night surveillance was getting to be too much of a bad habit. Detectives routinely didn't get enough sleep, not regular sleep anyway, but it was especially rude to be shoved back into reality after that great night with Ben. The idea of a regular punch-clock job seemed like a remote dream right about now. She grabbed her paper-cup of coffee she got on the way down.

"Will need about three of these this morning," she mumbled, as the heat seared at her fingers. Before her embarrassing incident with the tree, she'd spent most of the day on research. She'd even investigated the mayor's library. One thing had been confirmed; he had several books on Pauline Johnson, her life and writings. "Obviously an avid fan. So is it possible he and that crazy native know something I don't? Besides, of course, the fact that grass and slug poo taste worse than two-week-old burgers. I think I need a holiday. Either this case or the shadowy shaman is beginning to get my goat."

She walked into the cordoned-off area of the parking lot at downtown St. Paul's hospital, entering the milieu of police forensics at its front-line worst. The white coats were snapping pictures, spilling measuring tapes across the tarmac, gesturing wildly, and articulating amongst themselves. It looked like an animated clown show, except everyone was dressed in white and the situation was far from funny.

"Who's the newbie?" She sipped on her coffee, pointing with her free hand to the prone biker. The man was saturated by the pool of his own blood, one hand still ineffectively clutching at his throat.

"He was Brady Jones, aka Greasy. Ryley's second-hand man," one of them replied.

"Well, it doesn't look like he stopped by to get a hangnail looked at." She pointed to the pool of blood around the body, trying to choke down her coffee, which was still too bloody hot, without gagging.

Dan growled as he walked up, "Someone sliced him from ear to ear." He pointed to the strap attached to the dead man's leg. "Forensics thinks he carried a knife, initial speculation is that he was done with his own weapon. Only no knife to be found."

"Most interesting. Who would be able to do that to a rough tough biker? It wasn't Aunt Milly out for a Sunday spin having her hemorrhoids checked out." Carol switched the coffee to her other hand.

"Let's move people," Double Patty yelled at the forensics. "I want this crime scene scrubbed and the body hauled down to the morgue as soon as possible before it turns into a sideshow for any damn reporters." He turned to Carol. "I'll handle the press announcement. I've enough crap on my plate at the minute without stirring up more trouble. This has to remain low key. I don't want them fanning any flames regarding a possible gang war. I'm surprised pretty boy isn't already here on another pretend jog." He glared at Carol, his surly lip curling. She hoped he wasn't going to ask any further questions involving Ben and her.

He glared and instead he focused on the job before them. "Now tell me what you see about this scene that's unusual?"

She scrutinized the parking lot, taking time to respond after a long sip of the Brazilian intoxicant. "I've only one question. Why are there three bikes parked over here? If I'm to assume he owns one, to whom do the other two belong? Who was here with him?"

"Good one, I noticed that right away. I wanted to see if you did. For a half-asleep broad you're okay in my books. No one else thought to ask. Now go ahead and ask some questions inside. Find out if the other two are still here and grill the shit out of them. Dave, run the plate numbers. I want to see if any of those belong to this asphalt-hugging gentleman and if that is the case, get the tow truck to haul it away. Check it for prints, etc. Now, I want his ass cooling on the ice in the morgue and someone start washing away the blood. Pronto!"

* * *

Police scurried like ants around a disturbed hill. Ryley watched quietly from across the street. They were obviously cleaning things up before joe-frigging-public or the flash-bulb bastards got a sniff.

"Damn." The biker boss was on the way to see his son and had just parked his Benz. He only used it on the occasions when he wanted to be low profile; otherwise it was the attention-grabbing, mufflerless Harley all the way. He dug into the pockets of his suit jacket and put a few bucks in the metre. Having shaved, donned some preppy dress clothes to hide his tattoos, and smoothed his hair in a different style, he doubted anyone would recognize him. He didn't want all and sundry knowing his business, especially not the rival gangs. His personal life was too complicated and dangerous to involve the only person he really cared about.

He squinted across at the body, trying to identify it. It appeared to be Greasy prone on the pavement, which, after the incident last weekend he wasn't too shook up about. Ryley had been nearly ready to slice him himself, and if it wasn't for the fact that he'd already lost his number one, he'd probably have done it. Surveying the scene more closely, he noticed the three bikes parked nearby. One was Greasy's. Was him, then. That saved him a job.

He'd already talked to Cinders, who had let him know everything was okay with the kid for the moment. When he reported the stranger in suit and tie that had mistakenly entered the room, skitters of unease ran down Ryley's back. When Cinders went after the intruder the man had been chatting at the nurse's desk and made a quick beeline for the exit. Had the stranger been asking about his son? Was he the one that did Greasy in? If so, he'd be long gone with the fuzz around.

Ryley was smart enough to know nothing was coincidence. And that raised the next question, which was probably what Big Dan was thinking. Who the fuck started this gang war? He'd make some calls to the other gangs and put feelers out to all the bigger drug dealers. Someone had offed his two best men which meant there was hell to pay. Ryley grinned, he was in the mood to kick some butt after the bar incident the other night.

Especially after they interrogated the gay guy that Greasy was with. Only it was a waste of effort pounding on the fruitcake Greasy was hustling earlier. He was so terrified Ryley would kill him he'd have ratted on his parents. Only he swore didn't remember anything between entering the washroom and being on the dance floor. He claimed to have no memory of taking Ryley's cell phone, yet Ryley knew he'd redialed the last number called. So if he wasn't lying, what the hell happened that night?

The big biker watched the female detective sipping her coffee as she and Big Dan glanced toward the three bikes. She was observant. They'd obviously noticed the two other bikes parked beside Greasy's, which, he was certain, would be towed away any minute. He dusted off his nice dress suit and calmly strolled towards the corner coffee shop.

He noticed Carol march into the hospital and quickly phoned Cinders, giving him the heads-up to clear the room. He didn't want the guards having to answer questions.

"Yeah, go for a coffee, have Little Tom come meet me at the corner coffee place by the hospital." He'd have him leave first to get his bike and see what questions, if any, the cops would ask him. They'd be asking plenty of questions, he knew that, and the fewer bodies around to raise eyebrows the better. Someone would be bound to know where the other two bikers had been in the hospital and Ryley has coached both men on what to say to the cops.

Walking into Starbucks, he ordered two coffees and decided to wait until the mess cleared. It would be either later in the day or tomorrow before he saw his boy now. It would be weeks before his injuries healed and the kid would be out of there, but then he could be put somewhere far away, where he'd be safe.

But the bigger question remained. Who was doing this? And why?

He hadn't a clue.

* * *

Sweat rolled in rivulets, seeping down his face. Metal screeching on the highway and death by betrayal born on the wheels of black vans.

Ben lay in bed for long minutes, unable to go back to sleep. Finally, he got up. The dream was definitely dissipating in strength but it still unnerved him. He was so tired, and the sleeping pills hadn't helped. He glanced out his bedroom window but didn't see anything out of the ordinary.

Flicking a switch flooded the room in light and helped fade the remnants of the dream. He glared at the address of the two newest deaths and plotted them on the map of Vancouver he'd put up on the wall. "Mayor's body found here," he pointed to a tack. "His wife's here and the two new deaths here." He looked at the locations and the trail, before he jabbed his finger at the location of Ryley's house off Heatley. "What is there in common, if anything?" Ben grabbed his pencil and drew lines between all of the incidents. "No way!"

Shocked, he stared at the crisscross of lines. Virtually all of the scribbles travelled over a place he'd been recently, on that bizarre date with Brandi.

O'Shanahan's Bar and Grill.

The place where, according to a very indignant Brandi, he had disappeared. The nightmares began shortly after. It fit, and she'd called the place a bit freaky.

"This is where all of this began. Not sure how or why. Time to do a little research."

* * *

Stumpy's prone body lay on the cold steel of the morgue slab; the roughly sewn *Y* incision was a wound that would never heal. The finality of it all made Carol just a little sorry for the man, even though she knew that as a thug of Ryley's he'd carried out many ruthless deeds on his behalf. "He don't look very tough or scary now, does he?" Carol muttered.

"They all don't look like much in theese place," Sanchez replied in his broken English. She liked Sanchez, his "yes" sounded like "chess." She smiled. Reminded her of Ben. The other night had been great, she should call him for another dinner date.

Sanchez was a very jovial Spaniard. She could never figure out what drove him to become a forensic pathologist, where most of the people were as animated as their customers.

"You have a COD for me, Sanchez?"

"Broke 'is neck. Don't theenk it was caused by the accident, no serious 'ead trauma to account for eet."

"So you're saying he somehow broke his neck after crashing into the dumpster."

"Chess. His injuries on the bike, ver' serious, but maybe 'e survive. Broken leg ver' bad, bleeding inside too, but don' 'ave a clue how neck get broke. Maybe theenk only if eet done for him." He grabbed the head and gestured, pretending to twist hard.

Carol grimaced, not liking this anymore than before she walked in. "So can the theatrics. You're saying someone, who knew what they were doing, broke his neck while he lay in pain unable to escape."

"Chess."

"On purpose!"

"Chess."

"Crap." Carol puzzled for a moment. This presented a big problem. Did it mean a gang war was developing? Or had Stumpy done something to fall out with his leader? Whatever happened, it wasn't the act of an innocent bystander. "Okay, let me know if you find any trace of DNA on his body.

Now for the second."

"Well, we know 'e didn't trip on the sidewalk and cut heemself."

"Yeah, and this isn't just over unpaid parking tickets either."

"Chess. Look at theese, what I find just above the cut." He angled a powerful, lit magnifying glass over the area and pointed to two marks, pin-pricks.

"He was stabbed with needles? Hypodermics, maybe?"

"Chess, possible. They were in an 'ospital parking lot. 'E get stabbed in the neck, is in shock, then…"

With a magician's flourish he whipped down the sheet covering the naked stiff.

"Great, just what I need, to look at a dead man's privates."

"Look closely." Sanchez pointed to the stiff's testicles and hefted them in his gloved hand. Carol squirmed, glad she was a cop and not an under-taker. Imagine having to touch a dead guy's set. "Quite well equipped, this fella." He bounced them in his hand. "But see, all swollen and bruised. They not see theese at crime scene. 'E'd been kneed in groin, stabbed in neck with needles, and then slashed across throat. Theese person that dot heese, think 'e planned eet, theenk it not spur of a moment."

Carol surveyed the damage. "Ryley, I think, has an enemy. I'd bet the same person did both of these fine gentlemen in." She surveyed the plethora of tattoos adorning Greasy's body. "This can get ugly. Has Dan been down here yet? Does he already know?"

The door opened. "He already knows and he doesn't like this one bloody bit." Dan strode in, his heavy steps echoing in the silence of the cold room. "Ainsworth! Just who I was looking for. Look, I want your focus on the mayor's case. Since this is developing into possibly something bigger I'm putting Boswell on this one as well."

"You're pulling me off?" She hated Boswell. He was very much a male chauvinist and would undoubtedly ride her for being replaced. She gritted her teeth.

"I need you dealing with the mayor and this shaman character. Boswell will partner you in the investigation dealing with our two bikers. Get anywhere on the mayor's case yet?"

"Yes, sir. I talked to a park employee who claims she's seen Charlie several times."

"Well, I need answers. The media and the city council are frying my ass and I don't take grilling very well. If I've a gang war developing, as well as the mayor and his family getting done in, I need more bodies on it. All this grief and I've my daughter's graduation coming up. Some days your cup is half full of crap and the other half is overflowing with shit. I'll go upstairs and let Boswell know. Remember, answers! I need frigging answers, fast." He walked out, slamming the door. Carol stood with Sanchez, who had a stupid grin on his face, as the noise of Dan's departure echoed in the grim room.

"The boss, he no ver' 'appy."

"He never 'appy. Happy," she corrected, realizing she'd started to mimic Sanchez's accent. Carol closed her eyes, pinched the bridge of her nose, and wished herself another date with Ben. She could use a little ha-ha, or at least another good orgasm.

* * *

The throb and power of driving a big old Harley was the only thing he missed from his life in the Spawn, Larry realized, as he drove up to the clubhouse on Stains' bike. The wind tearing at you, the smell of raw exhaust and the looks of contempt from all of those who either wished it were them on the bike, or the rest who just wanted to put a gun to the prick with the loud machine that rattled the front doors of law and justice. Rebels without a cause, a movie he'd seen a dozen times.

Finally, one of Ryley's own men had gotten drunk enough to let him get in to his body. Stains himself, who knew most of the codes and information Larry needed, one of Ryley's last remaining inner circle of underlings. He'd love to get into Ryley himself, but knew the man only drank enough to loosen up. Never got wasted, except on coke, and the drug put a haze over anything, which made trying to control the host body nearly impossible.

Larry parked out front and quietly entered the grounds of the clubhouse. He knew someone was on duty at the security cameras, watching, but they wouldn't raise any alarms at one of their own. He knew he only had perhaps twenty minutes or so until Ryley would wise up and come searching for the man that walked out on him.

Larry entered the camera room and Jonesy looked up as the phone rang. "Hey, you're back a little early, didn't get lucky tonight?"

Larry knew it would be Ryley calling, no one else had that number. As Jonesy reached for the cell Larry slammed Stains' meaty fist into the back of his head. The man slumped over the panel and Larry crushed the phone under his boot.

He had to move fast now. He headed for the bike sheds out back where Ryley kept containers full of gas. He spotted Ryley's rare fifty-seven Harley Sportster; first year of production and with a serial number under a hundred. The bike he treasured more than any woman and perhaps even his own son. Larry pushed it out onto the driveway, the turquoise fuel tank glinting under who knew how many coats of varnish and wax. He removed the gas cap from the container and poured fuel over the bike and trailed a thick bead into the house. In the cool damp it wouldn't evaporate for quite awhile. He moved into the house with two other containers of fuel, kicked one over in the living room and ran another bead of fuel along behind him as he moved up the stairs.

At the top, a nearly naked girl staggered out of a bedroom, obviously visiting one of the gang members. He didn't have time for small talk so he smacked her across the face, hard. She slumped to the floor, unconscious. He reached down and snapped her neck. No time for nicety.

Larry stepped over the limp body and punched the code numbers gleaned from Stains' memory into Ryley's pad. They didn't work. As he thought, the man was smart enough to change them regularly and Stains wasn't privy to them. Larry hammered on the heavy wooden door with Stains' biker boot and on the third kick it shattered inward. Ryley's own inner sanctum, where he also kept the guns. If the dropped phone call didn't send Ryley on his way to investigate, the remote alarm showing someone entering his office would.

Noises in the hallway; someone was up, awakened by his actions. Larry smashed in the glass of the gun cabinet with his elbow. He grabbed a shotgun, checked both barrels were loaded, and filled his jacket pockets with shells. Two Colt forty-fives were tucked into his jeans. A burly, half-asleep man staggered through the doorway dressed only in his underwear.

"Stains, what the fuc…" was all he cracked off before Larry leveled the shotgun and thunder blasted down the corridors, putting the biker to sleep permanently. Blood and meat splattered the room. Larry kicked over the last container of fuel. The raw stench of gas filled the room as the liquid gurgled onto the carpet.

He stepped over the messy remains of Big Doug the Wad, and moved methodically down the hallway. How many were here tonight? There was no way to be certain.

The wide-eyed face of another girl peeked from behind a door. Larry pumped the shotgun blast through it, knowing it had hit its mark.

Agony tore into his hand—blood erupting. A knife pulled free, as a body slammed him into the wall.

Another biker wrestled with him, his knife arced into Stains' shoulder. Larry screamed, dropped his shotgun, and shoved backward. The two tumbled across carpet. Both of his handguns clattered free. He smashed his good fist into the man's face, crushing his nose. Larry pulled Stains' knife from his sock, stabbed backward and twisted. The biker screamed, clutching at his spilling intestines.

Larry picked up one of the Colts, its lead voice silencing his attacker.

In the background the meaty growl of Harleys under full acceleration rumbled. This was going to be close. He yelled as he pulled the knife from his shoulder, blood poured down his chest. His right hand was useless, searing pain threatening to overcome him. He staggered down the stairs. Inside, Stains was fighting for consciousness, his body's defences kicking in and trying to fight Larry off. Larry tried to stagger toward the backdoor, another girl showed her face, young, innocent. His vision blurred, the body's owner awakening while Larry fought for control.

"Get the fuck out." He slumped against the doorway, waving his gun at her. In his state it would take too much to fight her off, and Stains too.

Thankfully, she ran out the front door as the growl of Harleys exploded into the street.

He fell through the door, dropping his gun and reaching for the lighter. The body's owner was awake and fighting him, a battle Larry couldn't win. He had to take Ryley here and now, not knowing if he'd be able to recoup his energies from this distance.

"Where am I?" Stains' voice. He was taking over and Larry couldn't stop it any longer.

Bikes pulled into the driveway. The girl screamed. Ryley leapt from his bike and backhanded her to shut her up.

"It's Stains. He's gone nuts. He's got guns and shot up everyone," she yelled, hysterically.

"Oh, this is going to hurt." Larry winced, feeling himself evaporating under the gnawing tear of a thousand rats. The first time he pulled himself out of a host at a great distance from the portal it took days to reassemble his soul. It was like dispersing it into the wind, bit torn away by agonizing bit. He learned that at all costs it was best to try to get back to the nightclub and re-enter via the funnel. It wouldn't be happening today, and he didn't know if he could return a second time. He fired a shot off which whistled by Ryley. He'd missed.

Larry and Stains screamed, madness tearing at both. Only one could remain in the body. Unable to control his arm, the gun dropped free.

Ryley pulled out his gun and pumped several rounds into Stains' body. Larry fell to his knees. Blood spurting everywhere, the shock pushing Stains aside. He flicked on the lighter and fell face first into the fuel before him.

The gas fumes erupted. A fireball travelled along the ground in two directions.

One into the clubhouse, the other to Ryley's precious bike.

"No!" Ryley screamed, not realizing there was fuel all around.

The bike ignited in a ball of fire as he ran toward it. Seconds later the other path of destruction entered the building and explosions racked the clubhouse.

Larry smiled as Stains' heart gave out and the man's soul slithered away. The body was his, but only for a moment, as fire consumed it.

He scrawled "I'm coming Ryley LS," into the blood on the concrete as the Spawns" leader ran by, yelling blue murder and trying valiantly to put out the fire consuming the priceless bike. The host's hand fell, covering the two initials.

Larry screamed in agony as pain like wild dogs, or piranha in a vicious feeding frenzy, tore at him. *So much worse this time. Torn into a million pieces. Each and every chunk torn away an agony.*

Larry vowed to all that was unholy as blackness slammed its fist down, Ryley had to die for his actions. "I'll be back."

Chapter Twelve

Smoke still ebbed from the charred remains of the Devils Spawn club-house. The white shirts were all over the place. The fire trucks had left, except the mop-up crew.

"This is far from looking good." Carol winced.

Big Dan was engaged in conversation with Boswell at the rear of the property, he signaled her over. She'd already been hassled by Boswell about his having to babysit her on the case and wished she could shove her fist down his smarmy throat. She disliked that man a lot, but orders were orders and Carol kept her tongue swallowed.

"Hey, babe, don't I know you from someplace?" Ben hailed her. She stopped as he walked up.

"Dan's here, so don't get too close. I don't want him to know I went on a date with a reporter, at least not yet. He wouldn't understand."

Ben took in Dan's glare from the burned remains of what appeared to be a bike. The big man started toward them. "Okay, but only if you go out with me again. I rather enjoyed your company. Otherwise I'm going to plant a big smoochy kiss on your lips, right here, right in front of Big Dan."

Carol smiled at him. "I think you rather enjoyed the strip chess more."

"Now that was pretty darn good, too." He smiled back, the warmth of it tingling her insides.

She put her hands on her hips. "If you insist." And turned away, blush-ing.

Dan strolled up, "Hey, is he bugging you?"

"No, he's okay. I, ah, didn't catch your name. What was it again?"

"Ben. Ben Carlton." He took her hand and shook it. "Reporter, gentle-man and chess player extraordinaire. And I must say, sir, that is a gorgeous tie. Louis Vuitton?"

"No. Sears. Eight ninety-five. Now piss off."

Shivers ran through Carol at the memory Ben's touch, his hot, hot hands all over her. She could definitely use another chess match.

* * *

Ryley watched from behind lace curtains at the cops, firemen, and white jackets swarming the grounds of his clubhouse. He'd bought the property across the street many years ago, in part as a refuge for any Spawn members that needed a place to lie low, but also to keep watch over the clubhouse. He never thought it would be him hiding behind the lace, nor why.

"Get me another coffee," he ordered one of the men in the room with him, and snorted another line of coke from the coffee table, trying to remain calm. Rage still seethed inside as he returned to the window. He knew the cops would want a word at some point, but for now he'd avoid them, let them steam. Maybe they'd think he was one of the bodies. Right now he couldn't let anger taint his thinking; he needed a day to cool down and think of what to do next.

Who was coming? He'd rubbed out the message scrawled in the blood right away, not wanting anyone else to see it.

And inside, there was another emotion he'd rarely felt clawing at him; fear.

He'd lost several of his top men. One of his inner circle had inexplicably torched his clubhouse and bike. God, he loved that bike and all the members knew it. It was an expensive work of art. The days and nights he'd spent restoring it. He shook his head at the waste.

That wasn't like Stains. Ryley knew the man well enough to know he'd never attempt anything like that, at least not on his own. The man was a true bully, which meant he was a coward more than anything, and after recent events one of the few Ryley had been able to trust.

He watched the interplay between Big Dan, Boswell, and the lady copper. From his informant, he knew the woman was newly promoted detective, Carol Ainsworth. New and already heading the mayor's death investigation. She was obviously sharp; very sharp. He'd have thought Big Dan would have Boswell in charge of the big case, the man had about the most experience on the force. Which was a shame, as Ryley knew Boswell well, and had paid him handsomely to do many favours for him over the years. Always helped to have a copper on your payroll.

Big Dan was no idiot, though. If he put her in charge, she was good. The biker watched her smirk at the questioning reporter. The way she looked at him, there was chemistry. She was attracted to him. Interesting, she had desires. Was that something he could use to his advantage at some point?

What he really needed was her eyes as he watched the interplay between the three.

"Fuck." Ryley rifled his coffee cup across the room, joining two others smashed into smithereens, spilled coffee streaking the wall.

Running scared, not knowing what was going on or what would happen next, it was a place he didn't like. The place he usually put others. Resorting to skulking behind curtains, fear biting at his ankles like rattlesnakes snapping away. Fangs full of venom, waiting to unload. "Calm down." He took a couple of deep breaths.

"Whoever this is wants me scared. Gotta think."

If Stains had an accomplice, Ryley needed to know who it was. His informants within the police ranks, including Boswell, knew nothing. And the back-up video cameras, the cameras only he knew about, didn't show anything. He had a line running to this house and the entire video surveillance, plus the footage from the secret cameras, was fed into a room shut off from the other members. He knew the reporter talking to Carol, he had been spotted outside the clubhouse on several occasions, looking for the story behind the recent Spawn deaths, probably. He'd have him tailed, also.

He knew this much, Stains had broken into his office looking for something. But what? Although mostly loyal and trustworthy, the man was a grunt and too stupid and cowardly to pull off something like this on his own. Ryley turned to the monitor screen and studied the video again. "Nothing odd."

Except. He watched the body language between the reporter and the female officer. The handshake he'd given her.

Stains. His body language was out of sync. The video? He rewound the tape again. The man moved slightly differently than usual, different posture. And?

Ryley blinked. He watched twice to make sure.

"You okay, boss?" One of his men brave enough to ask, piped up.

Left hand. He was using his left hand. Stains was right-handed. Ambidextrous? Hardly likely. Didn't you have to be smart to be ambidextrous? The person on the video was Stains alright, but his gait was all wrong. Too upright, too self-assured. Grunt that he was, the man even moved like a gorilla. Now, he had something to go on. Ryley turned off the video and glared out the window again, his mind working overtime.

Across the street, Carol bent over Stains' body pointing to the area around his left hand as she lifted it. The freaks in white converged taking several pictures. Damn. He'd obliterated the message but obviously missed something.

He clicked on his cell. "Buckley, come see me at the coffee shop over on Fifth at three."

Yeah, she was sharp. She'd spotted the one thing no one else had, not even the CSI types spotted whatever it was she found so interesting. "I think it's time I had a little private chat with Ms. Ainsworth."

* * *

Deep inside Stanley Park, Charlie sat alone beneath the open trunk of a huge portal tree. The Lure's energy was too strong to deal with directly; he had to find another way to deal with her. The shaman also needed to discover what trick she'd pulled to sneak out of the grove without the guardians catching her. Going back in time again was not an option, at least not from this realm. But there were others.

Rummaging in the pack beside him, he pulled out an old hand-held drum. Sinews gathered in the back to a centre; the faded image of an eagle adorned the taut skin. It had been made by his father and he'd watched him play many times before it was finally passed down to him upon his father's death. Charlie could still see the image of his dad, cavorting under a cedar outfit, his headgear an eagle transformer mask, lost in the energies of the dance he performed. Charlie also pulled out some sage and cedar and spread it around him to cleanse the area. The native settled down and began to drum, his voice muted, lest some passing tourist would hear. Echoing through wood and soil, his well-practiced beat thumping away, drawing him down into the earth, into one of the three realities that exist beyond our own. The upper, middle, and lower worlds. The drumbeat pulled him away like it had done many times.

The shaman found himself in a tunnel at the back of a bear's den. He slid along the ground, crawling on his hands and knees in the darkness, squeezing through tight openings, looking for the light just ahead. Claustrophobic worries always ate at him as he dug down, but he kept on, the warm earth pulsing around him as he tried not to choke. Worms and centipedes wriggled by in the darkness until he spotted the light of the lower world.

Brushing off dirt and bugs he straightened and strode into the brightness of the underworld. Several paths radiated out before him. He'd helped many new souls on their journey to the other side where his Lucy waited for him. A journey he'd take one day, one from which there was no return, but the love of his life would have to wait.

He began along one of the well-travelled paths, leading toward the middle world. Birds sang in the trees, cedar and fir filled the air.

"So you seek my help today, wise shaman." The fox spoke, appearing from the dense brush lining the path. Always a spirit creature of some sort would greet him along this path. "Well, I know of a much shorter path to the place you are trying to reach." Fox sat back on his haunches, a wry smile on his face.

"No, you seek to confuse me and get me lost, wily one." He stared back at the sly smile trying not to unwind from the hunter's grin.

"Oh, come now. You surely know me by now. I will not lead you astray. Tell me where it is you want to go or, better yet, let us have a battle of wits. See if you can make me your spirit animal." The fox lifted one front paw and calmly blew across it, confident he would win.

"Begone, oh deceiver. There are many reasons why I've not made you my spirit animal. Cockiness and deception are but only a couple." He stepped around the fox barring his path and continued walking.

"Oh, come now. Surely we can let go of old mistakes made in jest and the want of a few good laughs," the fox sneered.

The spirit would not leave him alone today, and Charlie did not have the time for his shenanigans. "At my expense. Now begone, I hear the others coming."

The fox's ears perked up, his one great fear, and pleasure, sounded. Bugles cracked the stillness, the thud of horses and dogs baying. "Spoil sport. But there are others to tease away this fair day." He slinked off into the dense brush.

Charlie smiled and let the sounds wash through the trees for a few moments as he continued up the trail. He'd been deceived once already on this quest and wasn't in the mood for much more. The Lure was stronger than he'd realized and approaching her again back in time would not be a wise move. No, on the balance between middle earth and the lower realm would be much safer.

Middle world was much like ours except all the spirits were visible. Which was a good thing, as energies of beings rushed by. "Hmm, busy today in the quiet forest. Must be something going on." He approached the area of Cathedral Trail, from below. Like a spectator looking up through a glass covered tunnel. He was in effect still in the lower world, on the edge watching events above.

"There are many ways to view the past, my dear witch. Some, I know you are not aware of. This one I learned from an old shaman. A bit voyeuristic, perhaps, but it should help me get the information I need."

The solid trunks of the guardian cedars anchored themselves into the earth. All around him blue luminescent tendrils of energy, cast by the roots, moved in slow agitation. Charlie coated himself in the blue energy and allowed himself to be drawn up into the trees. He shifted from tree to tree until he got the view he needed.

The Lure whispered into a man's ear. As she did a tiny blue elfin being swam in.

"I'll help you find Mr. Lucky," it said to the man.

"Clever lady. Letting mischievous forest sprites do your dirty work. But he is not the reason she escaped." Charlie sat in the trees and waited, having the same calmness as the wood he inhabited.

In the night another came along. A man with a soul tainted, impaired. He should have been unconscious, passed out drunk or stoned beyond the matters of this realm. Charlie spied the stunted tendrils of energy, minute and … another.

There, tucked amongst the corporeal essence, he spied another soul besides this man's. For his was indeed asleep and this other being controlled the body. Charlie squinted. "This one was meant to go to the other side of the underworld lake. He has stayed, the pain must be intense. Death does not take kindly to cheaters." He watched The Lure dance her elves and leprechauns before the man, seducing him.

As the scene played out he watched from the branches and caught the little creatures holding hands, setting up a fairy ring in the glade and around the stone that was supposed to hold her captive. "Smart lady. Like triplines."

As the man bent over to touch the rock she flew into the comatose body possessed by another. She knew it would be easy to take over the body. "Very tricky. Use the unconscious body like the other one has."

He watched the body contorting in a bizarre pantomime under the pressure of the two entities battling to control the body. "Very good. That explains her escape. Only to where? For once the owner awakes I doubt either has the strength to maintain control."

The body staggered along the trail. The guardians had set up their own triplines and somehow she'd triggered them. "Oh, oh. Time to go."

He felt the energy surging through the roots, as the beings within the trees awoke, their captive on the loose. They began to give chase. He could not be seen, by her or them. The pack headed towards the parking lot. Bright artificial lights stunned the earthly beings.

Charlie smiled. "Time later for a drink, I think." He slipped from trees, flowing down the root tendrils, he pulled himself back to his body, still chanting away. As the shaman regained his own body, he spotted four figures in black watching the tableau before them. They'd been there awhile. Called by the tree spirits, for they'd been the ones to imprison her as well as her guardians.

"Most interesting. Didn't expect to see you boys here. Hey! Nelson, Eddie, Willy, Sam. How's it going, fellas?" He walked over.

"What the…"

"He isn't supposed to see us." They waved their hands attempting to make themselves invisible.

Charlie smiled and clicked his fingers. "The ol' gang is back. Good to see you guys."

"Who is this deluded person?"

"Remember the mad shaman from Haida Gwaii?'

"Oh, that one," another replied.

"Shall we turn him into a rock?" The voices echoed in unison.

"Perhaps the hairs on the butt of a walrus would be better," another replied.

"Oh, you guys kill me, such comedians. Let's say we go down to the local pub and I'll buy you all a brew. Very interesting atmosphere there." He winked at them, waving his orca-headed cane. "Whatdya say, a round of Indian Pale Ale?"

"If this is a ruse for whatever a brew is, this is a waste of our time."

"No ruse. Just an invite for a beer amongst old friends, and there's something there that will definitely interest you. Let's say they use pubs to Lure people away from their real lives in this reality." He winked.

They all looked at him perplexed.

"Don't say you've never had a beer with your buddies. You know, beer? Fermented beverage made from wheat, barley, and hops?"

Their expressions didn't change much, except to look even more perplexed.

One finally spoke. "No, but the thought entertains the taste buds."

"Nice, good. Make a good slogan, gotta remember that one. Entertains the taste buds. Like that one. Follow me."

Will looked over at Edward, "Told you he was completely mad. Butt hairs of a walrus is too kind."

"I'd make him the rear end of a skunk," Sam added.

The others smiled, "Now that entertains the taste buds," Nelson replied.

They all howled like wolves in heat.

"Hang out in the twenty-first century and you begin to develop a sense of humour. I think I liked you guys better as dour overseeing, all-knowing guru types."

* * *

Carol stood in the glare of the shaman's totem at the museum, feeling it was studying her as much as she was studying it. The box was most definitely a replica, as John had told her, but the one in Stanley Park looked very much older.

"Hello again, Detective Ainsworth." Carol turned away from the staring eyes.

"Hello again, John. Thanks for seeing me on such short notice." He looked even more nervous than last time; some people just weren't comfortable around the law. "It's okay I've looked into those parking tickets and had them waived, you're a free man again." She laughed lightly, trying to put him at his ease.

He looked at her in terror. "I beg your pardon. I don't have any outstanding tickets."

Okay, so some people had no sense of ha-ha. "Just kidding. Sorry."

His face fell in relief. "Apology accepted. I take matters of law enforcement very seriously and would never do anything to invite a ticket, parking or otherwise. How may I help you again, Detective Ainsworth?"

God, she'd hate to see his house, sure it was one of those in which there was a place for everything and everything in its place. Woe betide anyone who didn't comply. "I've a couple of questions regarding native issues." She pulled out some of the photos. "These, as I'm sure you know, are the totems in Stanley Park. I thought it odd that behind this one, which I assume is meant to only be a replica of a shaman's totem, is what appears to be a very old, and possibly original, grave box."

"What?" He glared at the picture. "It is actually meant to be a chief's totem, similar in that they both contain the same thing; remains."

"So, it was meant to contain the bones of a chief?"

"Correct. This was one of my first jobs, technical advisor for the original design of this area. Could I please see the rest of those pictures? Something doesn't look right here." He studied the photos Carol handed him. "We chose a chief's totem as opposed to a shaman's. It was off to one side, overlooking the rest, like in real life, but there was no box, replica or otherwise. The totem was only installed for the tourists."

"So someone else has installed this grave box? And would this totem be, by any chance, Haida in representation?"

"Matter of fact it is. It was based on an original at the Ninstints site. Back in the fifties Bill Reid went with UBC staff to retrieve as many totems as they could before nature reclaimed them."

"Do you still have the originals?"

"Yes, in our vault downstairs. Why do you ask?"

"I'd like to have a look at this one, if you don't mind. Because from what I see in this picture I think the original box is now in Stanley Park, and I would like to know how it got there. Perhaps seeing what the real thing looks like would help."

"If there is an original box containing bones of a chief or of a shaman, then I have no idea how it was put there. It was certainly not authorized in any of the discussions we had with the park board. Not only that, but," he studied the photo harder, "it appears that this totem is not where it should be. I'll have to find the original design maps, but as I said, we placed it on the edge, not front and centre. The Haida were not integral to this area and the local tribes would have objected most strongly. Even with aboriginals we get politics."

"I suppose you would. The Haida were not liked in this area?" She never thought of the political angle.

"More feared. They would raid the coast for booty and slaves as far down as Oregon. The Charlottes grew the biggest cedars and their canoes held the most natives. We've had reports of some canoes even sporting sails. They were not far behind us in building ocean-going craft."

She needed to cut him off before he wandered off the subject. "And the casket on back?"

"Well, it looks original enough from this photo. But something is very wrong, like I said. I'm sure the plans called for the Haida chief's pole to be put over here somewhere, but there was no box on back." He poked at the photo. "This is an outrage. Come, let's find the original plans."

"What do you know about portal trees?" Carol asked as they walked toward an elevator.

"Some tribes, the Haida are one, believe that trees with a double trunk emerging from one are gateways, portals, if you like, that allow you to travel between dimensions. Many people around the world tend to believe in trees as sacred, and the Haida would bring gifts to a tree and pray before it before they cut it down. Celtic tradition deals with the Tree of Life, as do Scandinavian traditions. The…"

"So tell me. Do you think one could use a portal tree to, say, move from one portal tree to another?" She had to cut him off, as he was going on another divergent line of thought.

"I don't tend to believe in that sort of thing but it's an interesting theory. It sounds like a native belief. What made you think of that?"

"Just a crazy thought. You know, the green way to travel. Could do away with cars." She lightened up, but as expected he didn't really break a smile at her remark.

"Well, only if there are any trees left standing." John surprised her with a little humour of his own as they got on the elevator and headed down a floor. "Now, this area is obviously restricted to museum staff only so if you don't mind, stay close.

And don't touch anything without my permission."

Carol raised her eyebrows. She felt like some scolded schoolgirl.

"Ah, sorry, I just say that out of habit. I sometimes bring students down here. I guess being a police officer you'd not be that way inclined."

"No problem, if I see any out of line activity, I've back up." She patted her gun.

His eyes opened in shock. "Well, let's hope it doesn't go anywhere near there. By the way do you have any insurance coverage for damages incurred during investigations?"

He was a quick thinker, she'd give him that. "Oh yeah, we're insured up to the eyeballs," she lied. "Lead the way."

"Oh, good." John approached another door, stopping to enter a code into a keypad before it would open. "In this area we keep things like old wooden artifacts, skeletons and other finds, either inappropriate for public viewing or in need of special preserving due to their fragile or decaying nature." John turned on a computer. "Give me a second to track down the plans."

"Yeah, no problem." She glanced around. Dimly lit shelves held all kinds of strange artifacts and, she cringed, bones and mummified remains. "A great place to bring a colleague for some privacy, if you don't mind the stiffs. Don't you think?"

She could see the back of his neck turn red. "I can assure you that none of that kind of lewd activity occurs here. We have several security cameras." He snorted loudly without turning around.

Oops, she hit a raw nerve there. He'd probably either caught a few in the act or had some fun here with a newbie undergraduate himself. She'd put her money on the latter.

"Yeah, my turn to apologize. I can see the security is impressive," she lied again. *Just like the security cameras you turned off when we entered.*

"This way officer," he said very coldly. Yup, she'd been right, it would definitely be the latter. They walked down several rows until he stopped and stood before a tagged area that sat empty. "My God, it's gone." His eyes opened in horror.

She knew he told the truth. The man began to shake.

"This is preposterous. An outrage."

She wondered if all well-educated persons used that phrase instead of saying, "What the fuck?" like everyone else.

"The bones, the entire box, someone has absconded with it."

"Well, I guess it's a good thing I'm here. Save you from having to fill out a report." She flipped open her notepad while he stood there his mount opening and closing like some fish out of water.

Carol knew one thing; her money was on the possibility the shaman's box at Stanley Park was an original and probably at one time sat right here. The question was how'd it get from here to there, and did it have anything to do with her wayward shaman.

She was still pondering the situation as she exited the museum some half an hour later and stopped to light a smoke in front of the native statue erected with wide-spread arms. The signage spouted something about welcoming all. She was too deep in thought to focus on the statement.

With no warning from her normally acute police officer's senses a wet cloth full of coolness clasped over her mouth and nose. The smoke fell from her fingers. Carol struggled, realizing too late what was happening as the sickening-sweet smell of chloroform filled her lungs. She fought to remove the strong arm pinning the cloth to her mouth, strength ebbing away to the beckoning darkness.

198

* * *

The foyer of O'Shanahan's bar seemed eerily quiet as Ben walked in. So different here in the daytime. He'd only experienced it at night, with the music blaring, stage lights going. People jostling.

Nearly empty, the place had just opened for a lunch crowd that was soon to arrive. "Hi. Ben Carlton, reporter for the *Province*. I called earlier."

A very preppy young man sauntered over, sharply dressed in suit pants, pale pink dress shirt, and overstated Gucci glasses. He was obviously excited by the prospect of interview exposure although trying hard not to show it. "James Tucker, manager."

His handshake betrayed he was nervous, yet the grip was strong. "Hi. As I said on the phone we're thinking of doing a piece on local bars and I'm trying to get a feel for the atmosphere, food, clientele. I'd like a chat, but do you mind if I wander around and take some pictures first?" He'd lied of course, but could think of no other way that would allow him to photograph the place.

"Go right ahead. Care for a coffee or drink while you're here? On the house of course."

"Sure, black, one sugar. Thanks." Ben wandered around and snapped a few pictures. He took the coffee and set it up on the railing by the dance floor. He clicked off a few more pictures, trying to recall some of that night with Brandi. It was so different when the building was quiet and not full of pulsating lights and gyrating bodies.

Memories, vague new memories flashed into his head; her body pressed up against his, staggering to the bathroom. He watched someone standing by the bar. Whisky. He'd bought whisky. Then, in the bathroom, falling onto the toilet seat, coldness washing into him. All of it flooding in a jumble into his brain.

James came back with his own coffee. "I've time for a breather and a few questions."

Ben stared up into the dark recesses above the dance floor. "This turret affair over the dance floor. Seems odd. Any reason why it was designed this way?"

"Well, my understanding is that it was crated in from down east, I believe the Pennsylvania area. I've found some of the original papers in my office. Care to see them?"

"Sure would, although I would wonder why anyone would want to do move something like that this far?"

"Not sure. I was told the original application for the property as a private club was turned down after the building was already erected sometime back in the twenties. In order to save the investment they decided to open a restaurant at the last minute. I like it. But it does get eerie in here sometimes, especially when it's quiet and I'm alone. In the office I can hear the old floor move and creak. Bit disturbing, feels like something's pacing back and forth, only there's nothing outside. The maintenance crew say that's just the nature of an old building, it moves and shifts. Great atmosphere, but I get the feeling I'm being watched." "How so?" He looked up from his notebook.

"When enough smoke is pumped in, it begins to rotate, swirl kinda, inside the spire area. Probably has something to do with the way the venting is situated within the turret. Old church spire I was told. Like a funnel effect. The patrons love it; I find it spooky. But we pack 'em in nearly every night. The Goth and biker crowd seem to enjoy the dark aspects, but the staff gets a little freaked out."

"In what way?

"We find so many patrons passed out in the bathrooms, and the odd one drops right on the dance floor. Don't tell anyone, but I think it helps to loosen people up and lets them drink even more than usual. I've noticed many people seem to cut loose more than normal. Not that I mind, it's good for cash flow."

"I read about a death the other week? Man collapsed on the dance floor?"

"Oh, him. He was a druggie, known cokehead. OD'd. I thought it would kill us off for a few weeks, but if anything it actually stirred up even more business. I guess some people just want to walk over others' graves. Morbid lot in society these days." James glanced at the patrons slowly filtering in for the lunch rush. "I may have to go soon. Care to look at the old ownership papers? I've a few in my office."

"Yeah, I suppose." As they walked away, Ben shivered. There was something about the place that didn't fit. A creepiness, like an overbearing presence, part of the atmosphere he'd felt that night with Brandi.

James was right. Sit here long enough and you'd swear there were eyes in the roof, staring. Almost as if in those depths something waited for the music to start. The sensation was stronger when the building was quiet and empty, like now. Not so when too much was going on, obviously distracting everyone from the clinging feeling of being watched. He had no other way to describe it.

Perhaps it was the energy that many bars had when they were quiet, the essence of all those carousers and laughter stilled; good times ready to start up again. He couldn't quite place his finger on it. The other thing was age. Sometimes you could walk into a building and really feel its age. Even though the bar area had probably been revamped many times, the place had that feeling of venerability, seeming far older than it was.

* * *

A mallet hammered at tin cans in her head. Carol's eyes fluttered open. She gagged trying to speak, before realizing a cloth was stuffed in her mouth. Panic seized her as she tried to raise her hands to yank the constricting gag from her dry lips, but couldn't.

She tried to stand, but couldn't do that either. Instead, falling; her hands and feet tied to a very basic metal-framed chair, only letting her bend forward. A burly biker reached over and righted her as blood pounded into her head. The aftereffects of chloroform inhalation.

Carol had no idea who'd kidnapped her, or for what reason. She'd been caught off guard. A dozen of those slasher movies she loved to watch raged through her head. Were the scenes from those movies soon to be a reality? Sweat bit its way down her neck. She looked around trying to survey what was in the room as the throbbing subsided slightly. Bare wooden staircase, concrete floor, no windows. Basement obviously, probably more or less soundproof from outside, too. Not an encouraging thought.

"Boss, she's awake." Someone yelled up dimly-lit stairs.

She strained to open her eyes wide. How did she allow herself to get into this situation? All she remembered was standing in front of the totem at the museum lighting a cigarette before being grabbed and the drug stole her consciousness. She felt stupid for being taken so easily, her mind preoccupied by that shaman. So far he'd caused more aches than he was worth and except for one lousy night, she'd not even met the man/myth. *Fucking pecky annoyance, was he worth the bother?* Why did she persist in trying to find him? Whack job.

Another man thumped down the stairs. *Shit! Ryley McLaren.* This was not good. Not a slasher movie, more like a bad remake of some mafia, held-captive movie. *Dear God, don't let him torture me.* Thoughts of tongues cut out, toe-nails being pulled and other private parts hacked away raced through her. "You can leave now."

"But, boss?"

"Leave." The authority in his voice brooked no disobedience. Ryley was a man used to giving orders and others taking them, without back talk. Carol strained at her bonds, not liking where this was going.

"Now." He turned to her once the man left the room. "I'm not going to hurt you, not unless you want me to. Let's get this straight, right off the bat. We're here to talk. Understand?"

Carol ceased struggling, shocked at his words. Did that mean he wasn't going to harm her unless she didn't do what he asked her to? Or was the man some kind of sexual pervert? Either way, it didn't sound good, but better than which finger should we start to hack off first.

"I brought you here because I need to talk, and I need your help. Now I'm going to take out the gag, no screaming or I'll put it back in. Deal?"

She nodded, wanting more than anything to get rid of the dry, cloying taste of cotton from her tongue and throat. She needed time to gather her wits.

Ryley pulled up a second chair, sat down before her and pulled off the tape. Carol winced as he yanked the balled-up sock from her throat. She stretched her mouth and wriggled it side to side. Glad to be free of the harsh, dry taste of cotton, hoping the sock had been washed first.

"Ryley McLaren, head of the Vancouver chapter of the Devil's Spawn, main enforcer, tough guy, chief drug runner and pimp in his area."

Ryley laughed. "I haven't checked your panties to see if you've got a vagina, but you've got balls, Carol Ainsworth, Vancouver's newest detective, but I could have it arranged. Most people would be shitting themselves right about now. I can see why Double Patty's put you in charge of the mayor's investigation. Okay. Now that we know each other, let's get down to business."

He smiled, obviously more impressed than put off by her rude up-front attitude. "As I said earlier, I've brought you here to talk."

"Talk? You kidnapped me. This is a crime punishable by…"

"Can the shit. I didn't bring you here for arguments. You haven't been hurt, molested, had your tits cut off, or been threatened in any way. Although Fingers here," he pointed to a thin man in the corner who sat quietly, "sure wanted to frisk you for weapons. He's very friendly to bound women, kinda a fetish of his." Fingers grinned a smarmy smile from a place of evil intent. "He doesn't talk much, lets his hands and knives do his talking." Obviously someone Ryley trusted, otherwise he'd have been made to leave the room as well.

Carol shivered. She had to be careful, knowing what he was capable of, and cringed at the thought of his slimy hands all over her body while she was unconscious. She pulled at her bonds, remembering Ryley had the upper hand here, not her.

"However, I wouldn't allow it. Now, leave, Fingers. This is a private chat."

The thin man looked put out at being ejected but calmly walked up the stairs. Ryley waited. "Now that we're alone, I'll reiterate that unless you scream blue murder, you will be blindfolded and dropped off somewhere, unharmed. You have my word. Understand?"

Carol nodded, trying to gauge the man. "So why the heavy-handed approach? We could have chatted somewhere neutral, like a coffee shop, shared a hot espresso, or even met at the precinct. Far as I know, the last I heard they were still looking for your body in the smoky ruins of your clubhouse."

His eyes lit up. "Look, detective, don't think me a stupid man surrounded by thugs. I didn't get to my position, nor stay out of the grasp of the law, by being naïve and careless," he growled. Ryley employed several good lawyers. "When I'm paying the bill, we talk my way."

Carol already summed it up, if he did release her she'd have no evidence or grounds to arrest him. No idea where she was, no witnesses to her kidnapping, and no guarantee she'd leave here alive. Only her word against his. It was obvious he hadn't shown his face publicly since the gutting of the clubhouse. Which meant he was acting out of character. The man was running scared. "Okay, talk, it's your dime, and I hope you don't mind if I don't take any notes, my hands are a little indisposed."

He smirked. "I usually hate bitches like you. Anyway, I'm not about to give myself up and just walk into the nearest cop shop. Yet. Nor talk about what went on at the clubhouse."

Her eyes opened at the sound of "yet." What was troubling him so much that he needed to collar a cop and talk, besides the fact his guys were being offed one at a time. Unless that was it.

He got up and paced around the room. "You must understand, I'm a proud man. I've the respect and fear of all those under me and of most of my associates. They also know my word is good and when I say something, it happens." His voice lowered. "But I need help."

She was going to say slimy drug runners, but quashed the urge, wanting to hear him out. Carol knew one thing; Ryley's reputation for being a man of his word was good. If he wanted something, it was done. Good or bad. He only liked three things; women, coke, and his sacred 1957 turquoise Sportster Harley, in no particular order. And the bike torched appeared to be his Sportster, which meant someone had a real hard-on for Ryley. She needed to find out why.

"Someone is after me. They've taken out some of my top men, burned my house down to the ground, and torched my precious baby." He lowered his voice and again sat in the other chair, legs apart. "And I'm not sure how, but they've discovered my deepest secret, the one thing in life I care about more than anything else, even myself. You can't ever breathe a word of this to anyone." He held his dirty finger to her lips.

"Agreed."

"My son."

Carol was taken aback. "What? I never knew you had…" It suddenly made sense, the kid at the hospital.

"No, no one did."

"The hospital. Matthews, the boy." She'd already begun digging into the identity of the boy's parents and why the Spawnwere guarding him.

"Yes, he's mine, and I'm afraid this person may want him dead as well." His face showed the sincere kind of concern most parents had for their children, a look that surprised her. "I don't seem to be able to find out who, or how to stop them. I'd give my very life to let him live. I'm asking you to save his life and get me my man. I want him."

"I can't do that. If I find him he'll be arrested and tried for murder, if the evidence allows. But I will find him." She knew something else now; he hadn't taken her to a known place to question her. This was a hideout. The fear shone in his eyes, he was afraid not only for himself, but for his child.

"Fair enough."

"Now if I agree, and help you, what do I get out of it?"

"Your life for one. Plus all of my resources at your disposal to find the killer of the mayor, my undying gratitude, and a promise of my fealty to help you in any future dealings."

He's putting a lot on the line, she thought. Ryley obviously didn't have the foggiest idea who the killer was, and he wasn't just running scared, the man was terrified. "If I don't help you?"

"Then I'll tear this town apart myself to find him. And when I do, I'll unleash the full force of Devil's Spawn retribution on him and any that side with him. If I go down, or my son, we won't be alone."

Stirring up a gang war at any time wouldn't be a good move, worse even now. Yet this meant siding with an avowed enemy and she knew the old expression "he who rides the back of the tiger, often winds up inside" quite well.

Ryley stood up and walked behind her, untying her right hand.

"Deal?" He stuck out his hand.

"You've no idea who this person is, or why he's doing this to you?"

"None. I'm not saying I don't have any enemies, I've far too many, but none with the knowledge this person has. I trust few people, and even fewer now. That's why this conversation has to stay strictly between you and me. So you need to keep your mouth shut."

Carol stared at him. She wasn't about to back down before his penetrating gaze and she had to play this dead straight, otherwise he probably would kill her. Ryley's back was up against the wall. "I will have to tell my superior, Dan, he'll need to know why I disappeared. He can be totally trusted to keep his word. Agree, and we have a deal."

"Deal." Ryley shook her free hand. Then he pulled Carol toward him, dragging the chair, until his face was an inch from hers. He swallowed twice, letting his guard down. She caught the fear in his eyes, letting the true man inside come out again. "I love my son, and now that I've lost my bike, he's all I've got left on this world. All I've ever treasured. Understand. DON'T FUCK ME." Carol nodded.

Ryley bellowed for the others to come down the stairs. And said loudly enough for them to hear. "Fuck me over and I'll make sure Fingers has your tits in his freezer before you die a slow agonizing death. *Comprende?*"

"Yes." She went white, even though he said it as bravado, she knew he meant every word. Carol also knew what was possible from all those slasher films she watched and that kind of cruelty resided in Ryley's eyes.

"My personal cell phone. Very few have this number. Call me anytime." He reached into his top shirt pocket and pulled out a card. He slid it into the vest pocket over her left breast. "Nice tits. You probably want to keep those." He patted the card in her pocket, allowing his hand to cup her breast. Fingers snickered behind her.

Carol shuddered at the intent; he was serious. "I'll arrange to have a guard posted in the boy's room at the hospital after I talk to Dan. Can I go now?" she said firmly, hiding the shaking that was threatening to make her knees bang together like wind chimes in a hurricane.

"Blindfold her and take her back to her car. And Fingers, don't touch a hair on her head or any place else, or you'll be answering to me."

"Yes, boss." Fingers looked disappointed as the blindfold was placed over her eyes.

"Oh, and a little insurance so you don't try to remember our location." The strong odour of chloroform entered her nostrils at Ryley's last words as the headache returned and reality spun away.

Chapter Thirteen

"He WHAT," Big Dan bellowed as Carol explained. "Kidnapped me." Big Dan thudded down into his desk chair. Carol had never seen the ever confident commander caught off guard. "You're not shitting me, just because I was pissed when you didn't report in?"

"No, the truth." Her hands still shook from the ordeal as she raised them to her face.

"You better sit down and explain this." Dan pointed to one of the chairs in his office.

"I was just leaving the UBC museum when everything went black. He, or his henchmen, chloroformed me and took me to a secret location. It appeared to be a basement, maybe where he's been hiding out since the gang house was torched. He had me gagged and bound to a chair. We talked and when we were done he hit me with the chloroform again. I woke up in my car in the UBC parking lot. How long I'd been out, don't know. Wasn't long though." Carol let out a deep breath, trying to ground herself. She had to stop herself from thinking about what could have happened for the ten thousandth time. "After I came to, I called the precinct and drove straight over."

"Ryley?" Dan scratched his head. "This doesn't get any fucking simpler does it. So what the fucking hell would drive Ryley McLaren, head of the Devil's Spawn, to take the time to take you hostage to simply powwow?"

Carol looked around the room. "At first I thought he'd kill me, or worse. But the man is running scared. Someone is chasing him, wants him and/or his empire taken down. Don't know yet, but I do know he hasn't a clue as to who, and seems powerless to stop the person or persons."

"I've dealt with Ryley before, can't say I've ever seen him scared of anything.

He's one of those alpha-male types in total control of his world and everyone in it. You don't honestly think he's panicking over this?"

"I do, you weren't tied up. I know he's ruthless, but I saw the look of fear in his eyes. And I know what he's capable of." She remembered the touch of his hand on her breast as he put the card in her vest. "In fact, he handed me this, his personal cell phone number." She handed it to Dan.

The big guy twirled it around in his hand. "Ryley doesn't scare easy. He usually does the scaring. So someone is out for more than just taking over territory. Revenge, possibly? None of our ears out there have said anything about any new muscle moving into our territory."

"Or someone he is powerless to stop," she blurted out.

"True. Or he wants us to do it for him instead?" Dan queried back.

"Wants us to find his man?" She didn't think of that angle.

"Sure, why not. The man is cunning and if he can't find out who's after him, why not get someone with bigger resources to search."

"Do you think he has anything to help us with the mayor's case?"

"Doubt it, but I'll take anything for help on that one right about now. We'll bleed out to the press there's a possible gang war brewing. An Asian gang like the UN moving in and claiming territory, or something like that. Help deflect media attention off Ryley. While you do some more digging." He studied her face. "Look, I'll only ask this once. I know you're shaken. If you want off the case, tell me now, I'll put Boswell in charge. I'll understand."

She looked at him, knew Dan was speaking the truth and at the same time testing her mettle. "Tell Boswell to kiss my ass. I ain't giving him the satisfaction. This shaman character has stirred up a lot of trouble and even the Spawn aren't going to stop me from getting to the bottom of this one.

"That's what I wanted to hear. Although I will caution you to be careful and I want Boswell or someone with you if at all possible. I've seen what happens to people who cross the Devil's Spawn and it isn't pretty." "Yes, sir." She knew Dan was worried.

"There is something he mentioned that we may have found out if I'd dug deep enough. The Spawn were visiting a kid in the hospital."

"Yeah, your report mentioned someone on the sixth floor. The Spawn were guarding the Matthews kid. Still haven't got the records back on his parents' identity, other than a bogus address I had checked out."

"Don't bother, Ryley told me himself. It's his only son. He wants us to put a guard on the kid."

"Protect him?"

"I'm guessing his attacker may now know this as well since he'd gone to the hospital. Ryley also threatened to have all hell break loose if his kid is harmed."

"Double fuck." Dan crunched his eyes into the big meathook of his left hand. "Okay. Guards on the wing and on the door. I don't need the Spawn going to war while we find our man."

"Agreed." Carol rose, knowing the conversation had come to a close as Dan sat there fuming. His last words echoed what was racing through her head.

"Something tells me this is all tied together some bloody how." He was thinking out loud, probably more to himself than her.

"Agreed. Can I go now, sir?"

"Yes. Oh, Carol, be damn careful. This just got into very ugly, very dangerous territory. Understand?" He raised his voice.

"Yes, sir." She left the room wondering if perhaps entering another field of work would have been a better choice. "Didn't have this kind of shit to deal in with in the Air Force," she knew her dad would have said. He was probably right.

* * *

Carol answered her cell phone as she pulled up to the parking area next to the totems in Stanley Park. "John Denton here, of the University of British Columbia Museum." He obviously liked the sound of his title, or he was afraid of her forgetting him. It was funny how some people were. "Carol, I was right. The Chief's totem should have been on the far right. No idea who authorized the move. You could ask someone in city hall or Parks and Recreation, they might know. And I'd like to know too, if you find out."

So many questions that needed answering. It was like some line off a TV show she watched recently, "can open, worms everywhere." She knew where she needed to go for answers and who had them.

It was nearly noon. The last two days on stakeout at the park looking for an errant shaman were without reward, but today she sensed would be different.

As she got out of her car Carol caught the sight of a figure leaning on a cane. He stood with his back to her as she approached almost as if he were waiting. Just as she was going to say, "Mr. Stillwaters I presume…"

"Been waiting. Lovely day, officer. Don't reckon you take much time out of your busy schedule to stand here and study these remarkable works of art do you?" He spoke without turning round.

"How'd you know I was coming here today?"

"Lucky guess, I suppose." Charlie turned to face her, chewing on a chocolate bar. "Being a shaman, I usually don't let anyone sneak up on me unless I want them to. How'd you know I was here?" He threw her question back at her.

"I've been looking for you ever since our meeting. You are a difficult man to track down. Besides that's my job."

"I am? Didn't know anyone was looking." He smiled at her after that.

She was beginning to hate that smug smile of his. Like he knew so much more about what went on around the world, and even inside her head.

"Well, if you kept a phone like everyone else, this meeting could have been so much easier." She looked up and saw Sadie in the concession booth talking on the phone. She'd have to thank her later, she couldn't reveal her source, but then he probably already knew.

"Modern trappings. Don't need them, not when you travel by other means. I'll have to thank Sadie for the chocolate bar, grumpy for an elder, but then I've been known to be a little miserable on occasion."

He knew. He probably could read what she was thinking half the time. He'd pulled so many words out of her head. "Speaking of other means. Thanks for reminding me." She dug her hand into her pocket. "Lose this?"

"Now look at that. I hadn't realized I'd lost it. Thanks." He removed his hat and looked at it. There was a blank area near the back where another Expos pin resided. "Isn't the first time. I had to trade a lot to get the pair off some snotty French kid from Montreal on the islands for his holiday's couple years ago. Best of the collection, well next to the ball cap itself that is. Ow! Darn dodgy clip, seems to keep popping free, hope it didn't jab you as well. I've jabbed myself and lost it a couple of times." He smiled at her, as if hinting he knew.

Charlie placed the well-worn and rarely washed cap on his tied-back, grey hair blending away the railroad tracks of compressed hair. Carol kept her mouth shut, she wasn't going to give him the satisfaction of knowing she'd jabbed herself twice.

"By the way, the Expos are gone, moved to Washington."

"Yeah, but not in my heart. You know the odd thing about ball caps, when you find one that fits well it's like wearing a second skin. Now this cap and I have been on far too many adventures to discard, like so many wannabe fans did." He smiled back at her.

"Wouldn't know, don't wear any. Could wash it once every decade or so. But something curious, I did find that pin by a tree in Stanley Park. Supposedly a portal tree. I've read that shamans believe that they can travel through them. Only I discover this one tree also happens to be used by a bunch of geeks for their GPS treasure hunt. Funny coincidence or convenient fluke?" She stared at the nonplussed Charlie. He held her gaze without giving a hint of whether he thought she was speaking the truth or not.

"Now I look up and see, guess what? There's a portal tree here behind these totems, and oddly enough, just outside your cabin." She pointed to the innocuous looking tree just behind the arranged totems.

"Funny that, and the fact you found out where I live, good job detective. Fluke or coincidence, kinda like saying do you like Coke or Pepsi. I rather prefer Pepsi, although a stiff herbal concoction I make packs the same punch without the sugar. Did you meet Brook at my cabin? He was much like you, a non-believer at first." He smirked, obviously not letting on as much as he knew. They were playing a game of verbal hide and seek.

"Yes, nice fellow, for a reporter. He mentioned you bought the property just for the location of the supposed unique tree. The same kind of tree that also sits, coincidentally, right behind the area where we first met and I found this pin. Now call me naïve but I figured, let's see if there's any truth to supposed astral traveling inside trees. I tried and ended up only getting a mouthful of pine needles."

He smirked again. "Did you say abracadabra first? Or is it hocus-pocus." He shifted positions, picking at his teeth, obviously somewhat bored with the conversation as he shoved the remains of the chocolate-bar wrapper into his pocket. Where it would probably reside for the next several months, judging by the state of his clothing.

Now she knew he was laughing at her. "But I've found something even more interesting. Follow me, please." Carol walked around to the side of the totems. "Interestingly enough, when I look behind the Haida chief's totem I find a wooden box, like there's meant to be one there. Only this box looks like an original. One, I suspect, that probably holds the bones of someone. I'd guess a shaman or a Haida chief. Not only that, but this totem is not supposed to be sitting here."

She walked over to stand in front of it. "But over there, to the far right, kinda like overlooking the whole scene. Watching, protecting. Now how do you suppose that happened, because I'm guessing this isn't hocus-pocus or any kind of wizardry at all, but someone with either a big shovel or inside track to whoever put these totems together."

Charlie looked up and walked around to take a look at the box, trying very hard to look surprised, but failing. "Well I'll be. It's Great-Uncle Waasghu ll taadlat Ghadala. You found Great-Uncle Waasghu ll taadlat Ghadala. Well he's actually a great, great, great-uncle once removed on the Eagle side of the family." He stood with the most quizzical look on his face. "I guess he's made his way home after all these years."

The man was infuriating, but she wasn't going to buy into any emotional outbursts, she had to keep focused on her case. "Yes, that's lovely. I don't expect any thank yous from the archaeological society. How did Great-Uncle What's Mandala get into a box behind the totem and why?"

She stood there, arms crossed, feeling like some scolding school teacher catching one of her students out. "Not to mention who the hell put him there. 'Cause I've checked with John Denton, Head Curator at UBC Museum, and there were never plans to have someone interred here. In fact, there wasn't even supposed to be a box of any kind here, real or replica."

Charlie looked down and picked at the dirt with his cane. "It's Waasghu ll taadlat Ghudala, Sea wolf who outruns Trout. You English were good at brutalizing everything, including our language."

Carol frowned at him. "Trying to pronounce words in your language makes me want to spit. Now, quit avoiding the subject."

"Well, it is a guttural language and we Stillwaters have large families, comes from the Catholic missionaries I think, no birth control, nothing to do on cold winter nights except…"

"Charlie!"

"I was going to say play scrabble, not what you were thinking. Man, you whites, sex is all you ever think about." He cleared his throat. "I had a couple of nephews living in Vancouver. They simply did what I asked them to do, which was keep the Haida culture front and centre amongst the Aboriginals, like we were in the old days."

Carol groaned. It couldn't have been that easy. "This is not simply a case of one-upmanship? Why bones in the box, and why right in direct line with a portal tree behind it?"

"Oh, you've been doing your research then. Although, detective, it hasn't been established that there are bones in that box."

Carol gritted her teeth. He was impossible, but right. How could this have happened in the first place, and without anyone noticing, years ago? "I concede it hasn't been established that there is anything in that box. But I'm betting your dead uncle's remains are in there."

"Oh, he always was such a layabout, as the English would say. Let's say he makes a good batter's box, like they use in baseball."

"What?" She knew enough about his love of the game and his Expos, but she wasn't going to go off track with this diversion. "And no crap about the Expos and any other ball team."

"A pit stop after a long journey. One of my nephews worked at UBC."

"You've had someone steal UBC property and plant something illegal on city property. Haven't you? Nephews, it isn't that simple." And she wondered, if he was capable of pulling that off, would he be capable of murder and, why oh why, hadn't anyone seen this totem out of place before now. The man was too much and totally off course on this investigation.

He shrugged his shoulders as if to say "why not," or "don't believe me then."

"Tell me why I shouldn't arrest you for removal of public property or theft?"

"Well you can't arrest me for taking something that rightfully belongs to my people to begin with and on land that is still contested as rightfully ours. After all, you built this park and put these totems on a centuries-old village site."

He was right on that point. John Denton had mentioned the totems sat over a site where they'd found layers of clam shells metres thick. Carol pursed her lips, already knowing where this conversation was going and not liking it one bit.

"As you know, the Haida have been after having all of their ancestor's bones returned to our homeland. Great-Uncle Waasghu ll taadlat Ghadala here said that he'd rather stay in Vancouver. Loved it here. Had a thing for Squamish women. So I simply granted his wishes."

"You're telling me you talk to dead people."

"All the time. I go on visits to my ancestors, something you probably would call visiting the happy-hunting grounds. No big trick really if you know what you're doing, I could show you how if you like." He leaned on his cane. "No visitor's visa required, but they do get a little testy around white-man strangers, probably not so good an idea. I caused a near riot when I asked that arrogant American General Custer to join us in a poker game with those feather-heads from the US that call themselves Indians, like Geronimo and Sitting Bull. Even dead they haven't much ha-ha. Those plains Indians, great on taking pictures and looking all poohbah and all, but crap card players."

"Ah, no thanks." She had enough problems with the living ones, like this whacked-out shaman. Although his innate sense of humour nearly brought a smile to her lips. If this wasn't such a serious issue she'd be howling with him over a drink in the local pub and if this ended well maybe she would.

"We believe no one dies. The soul never dies. It merely transforms or goes into limbo, kinda like a holiday mode until reborn in the next generation. Standard aboriginal beliefs, you can check it out in the library or in the shaman's dictionary law thirty-two, page forty-six, clause sixteen."

"I've been to the library. You are the most infuriating man I've ever met." She should arrest him, but the thought of the whole legal process regarding aboriginal claims to their ancestors was a huge legal issue. One she or, she knew, Big Dan, didn't want to get thrown into under the current conditions. "Okay, at least for now, I'm not arresting you. I need to talk to my superiors on this matter. What I do want to know is why you came to see me that night. Do you know where the daughter's body is and did you have anything to do with their deaths?"

"No, I've merely been contacted by the guardians of the trail. You've stared right at the body in question. It's in a tree near the vicinity of the Cathedral Trail." Charlie leaned on his cane.

"Impossible. We've searched there a dozen times." He was lying she knew it. They went over every inch of ground there, close to the murder scene, even with the dogs. Other areas of the park might have been overlooked, but not there.

"I know you did. I contacted you because you're a good detective and you know evidence doesn't lie. The body is there."

Carol gritted her teeth, he was lying. "The body isn't there. We searched. But the evidence doesn't point to any of this crazy woo-woo stuff you keep spouting. So why pick me? I don't believe in magic trees and spells."

He reached up, lifted his cap, and rubbed his hair as a squad of policemen led by a detective came striding up. "Oww, dodgy pin. Like I said evidence doesn't lie, whether you believe in something or not. I think we have company." Charlie nodded to the men approaching behind Carol.

Boswell came striding up, with that male, superior grin on his face. "How the hell did he know we were here?" She glanced up and caught Sadie turning away quickly. "Bitch."

Charlie grabbed her shoulder. "Look, I haven't much time. The spirit that seduced our killer has put a displacement spell over the tree and unless you look right at it and unfocus your eyes you'll never see it."

"Unfocus your eyes? A spell? Give me a break."

"Trust me. It's like looking at those three D pictures, where the image comes right out at you." He stared at her his eyes going wide.

She'd already trusted him and done nothing but eat pine needles. "You're nuts. I tried to crawl through a portal tree and only got my suit full of grass stains. I'm not believing you again."

"I like being called an arachide, they grow in the earth, earth supports life. Go back to the trail and check it out. Meet me back here tomorrow."

Carol looked over at Boswell heading the pack. "Good job delaying him, Ainsworth. I'll take over from here. I read the report of your meeting with Sadie and had her call me if she was to see Charlie here again. I told her an informant's tip would come her way." He grinned from ear to ear.

"You scummy bastard."

Boswell read him his rights as they clicked handcuffs on Charlie. "Meet me back here tomorrow. Oh, are these those cheap Houdini specials?" He smiled as he slipped one hand around to the front, the cuff dangling from it.

"Cuff the smart-ass again, use three pairs if you need to. You, old man, ain't going anywhere soon, except a cozy jail cell for a long time," Boswell fumed, obviously unsure how the shaman had managed to get free.

Charlie winked at her as they roughly hauled him away. "Check out the trees. Like I said, you'll be surprised. Then we'll talk."

The arresting officers held the shaman tight, eyeing his hands to make sure he didn't pull the same stunt again.

"Don't suppose you've any cozy slippers and a hot cup of herbal tea at your fine establishment. Did I mention the last time I was in a precinct? Had to do with a dozen irate squirrels and one hungry skunk. Man, what a stinker of a story that was." Charlie laughed. Boswell's face just continued to grow redder.

* * *

An hour later found her back on Cathedral Trail. She felt bad about Charlie, although he didn't look too concerned. As for Boswell, he hadn't done anything to ingratiate himself into her good books. Bribing her contact and scooping the shaman from under her nose. He was already, no doubt, gloating about it to Big Dan.

Carol stood alone in the former glade on the trail. Overhead a crow cawed, the sound of geese honking washed into the background drone of traffic. A tugboat bellowed its whistle. Carol hoped Charlie was okay in detention. There wasn't a hope anyone would be released and back here tomorrow. Anyone perhaps, except him and that beguiling smile.

She'd tried trusting Charlie regarding the trees. She smiled, remembering wiping off the grass and leaves from her outfit. "Would have looked silly to any passers-by if they'd seen me falling face first into the dirt. So why should I trust him now?" Carol gritted her teeth, the closeness of the perimeter of trees did two things; kept the noise subdued and kept the sunlight's heat from penetrating the glade for the most part, except where the downed trees had swiped the green canopy clear of branches. For the most part it was cool and moist here.

She shivered. She really wanted to trust the crazy native man, others seemed to. He'd done the Expos pin thing on purpose, but that didn't prove anything, he could have planted it at any time. But if he did, why?

She sauntered into the centre of the glade. Overhead, the sun tried poking through the cloud cover. Damp earth sang to her nostrils and coolness danced over her lips. Toppled trees splayed their broken roots into the air, like some bizarre stripper's fans. "This had better work, I feel pretty silly again, Charlie. Don't know why I listen to you, I usually only let people screw me over once." She closed her eyes and reopened them, trying to unfocus. The shelter of the trees help to drown out the background noise, making the rest of the world strangely quiet.

This must be what it was like here for centuries, before we even came here, the silence of the woods. Although Carol could still feel the disturbing taint of the mayor's wife's dead body lingering here. "Probably a gold digger." Although reports were they were a very happy couple, she had been more than ten years younger than the mayor. "Still, poor lady. Whatever she was she didn't deserve this. So, woods, don't be silent anymore. Tell me what I need to know, actually more like show me what I need to see." She turned around as the wind picked up, trying to keep her eyes unfocused like he'd mentioned, but it wasn't easy. Muscles burned, trying to yank her eyeballs back to where they should be.

Rubbing at her aching eyes, after about an hour of looking like some drunk, cross-eyed, crazy person, Carol gave up. She was one of those people that couldn't unlock her eyes to see the image in buried in a three D print. "Stupid idea. Stupid man. Stupider copper."

The wind picked up again as she squinted several times trying to get moisture into the dryness of her eyes. "Oh, really bad idea. Should have brought some Visine." As the wind rustled leaves, Carol stared at one tree in the background.

"A different tree," he'd said.

The tall cedar seemed to not be moving in the sway of the wind as she walked closer. Like a lot of old cedars, the centre appeared hollow. The insides long rotted away or open-trunked, due to the nursery tree it began life on long ago decomposing. As she observed it the wind stirred again. The branches of the cedar tree didn't appear to be affected. "Odd," she muttered as she approached.

"Okay, stupid magic man, I'm trying this one last time and so help me if I end up cross-eyed you'll be spending the rest of your life rotting in jail for all I care." She unfocused her sore eyes one last time, standing before the enormous conifer.

A hazy film fluttered free from the very air extending around the tree. "What the...?" She reached forward and pulled at it, like flimsy cobwebs brushed aside the film disintegrated, falling away, collapsing on top of her. "Like walking into a spider's web. Hate that," Carol sputtered.

She gulped once, not sure what to expect and walked around the tree to another section that was open in the centre. Bending closer, half expecting another stupid box full of silly plastic articles, the smell of rot overpowered her. "Oh God." *Where had that come from?*

Getting virtually under the tree she looked up. Black and white specks of rock poked their way from the hollow centre. "The Lure's rock from the trail?" Without thinking she reached up and tugged on the rock.

"Shouldn't disturb it really, but he's screwed me around a few times." She didn't want to call in the investigation team only to have them only discover a wedged-in rock, someone's day old sandwich, or a dead squirrel. Not to mention Boswell's smug grin at her expense. The rock slid down about halfway.

"Help me, please..." echoed faintly from inside the tree.

"What the..." Carol put one sleeve over her nose. Trying not to puke from the foul smells wafting down on her, she pulled on the rock again.

It tumbled free, nearly braining her. A knife clattered on top of it. Pus, blood, bits of flesh, and millions of maggots tumbled down. A partly decomposed arm hung free. A young girl's arm.

Carol shrieked, brushing wriggling maggots from her arm and hair. Last night's dinner fought its way up her throat. In her head the voice of a young girl crying out persisted.

After retching up her dinner, she called Vancouver's Criminal Investigation

Department. "Get the white coats out here to Stanley Park, just north of the Cathedral Trail. I've found Cole Bridge's daughter." It was all she could manage before disconnecting and throwing up again as the stench crept behind her and several worms dangled, falling freely from her hair.

Carol waited as sirens sounded in the background, getting closer. She stood alone in the forest with the wind whistling through the trees. Overhead a crow cawed. She knew she couldn't leave, but her imagination replayed the muffled cries of a young girl being stuffed into a tree, screaming over and over.

"Christ, get here quick."

Sirens sounded all around, but all she could see was a little girl's life ending in darkness and the smell of cedar. The trample of feet on the trail warned her of the team's approach. She directed them to her via her cell phone. The wind fell silent and the screams ended.

Carol pointed to the tree and staggered back to her car. "No questions." She waved off the officers and ran toward her vehicle, vileness threatening to claw its way back up her throat.

What was wrong with her? She'd seen enough bodies in her day. She wiped at her nose over and over, unable to get rid of the sickly sweet smell of decay.

A young girl's arm falling free, again.

Maggots dropping and her own screams tearing at her ears. Images and sounds burned into her memory banks.

Starting the car, Carol drove the one-way system to exit the Park. The furious honking of a horn dragged her back into reality. Without noticing, she'd arrived at the two-way traffic and nearly driven into an approaching car. Waving apologetically at the irate driver, she realized she was in no state to be behind the wheel. The last thing she needed was a death-by-reckless-driving charge. "I need a drink," she exclaimed, as she drove toward the local bar. One thing she knew for sure, the shaman wasn't laughing at her now, and if he was, she'd rip the bastard's throat out herself.

Chapter Fourteen

"Charles Stillwaters of Skidegate, BC, correct?" Boswell cleared his throat, adding to his gruffness. His partner, Kowalsky, glared at Charlie in the interrogation room. The room was plain, nothing on the walls except the two-way mirror on one side. Charlie was handcuffed to the table that was, like the chair, bolted to the floor. He sat facing the doorway. Implying to him, as it did to all being questioned, that "do as we ask" and freedom is within sight. His cane was propped in the corner of the room, the detectives having been too wary of a lawsuit should the old man fall.

"Charlie. Only my parents got away with calling me Charles, and that was only when I was in trouble. Great décor by the way, I guess the police department doesn't believe in plants or pictures. Shame, would add to a homier atmosphere. Could make a fella relax, feel more like talking."

Riled by the native's comments, Boswell stood up. "Don't get me pissed off by being a smart-ass, Charlie. You're in enough trouble regarding the mayor's murder investigation. Now, if you're innocent, no problem. A few questions and you're free to walk out the door behind us."

Charlie sat quietly studying Boswell as Kowalsky tried to open the native man's medicine bag. As hard as the officer tried, he couldn't flip open the top. "Here let me open that for you. It, like you, has a secret catch. Officer...?" "Kowalsky," he grumbled, his expression wary.

"Kowalsky and Boswell, funny first names, sounds like a bad take-off on a seventies cop show. I thought you whites picked on us for unusual choice of names, like Running Deer, Brave Eagle," Charlie tut-tutted as Kowalsky sniffed at the pouch, wrinkled his nose and passed the bag to Boswell. "Or Greasy Mollusc." Boswell sniffed at the bag and fought to open it also. "For your sake, you better hope that's not cannabis residue I'm smelling."

"Could get you locked up for a while, definitely smells like Mary Jane to me," Kowalsky added as Boswell shoved the bag back to Charlie. "Open the damn thing. Keep your hands where we can see them and move slow."

Charlie moved his hand over the bag and snapped his fingers; it popped open.

"Easy when you know how."

Boswell turned red in the face.

"Secret latch, my ass." He gave it back to Kowalsky who looked inside.

"Nothing but some dust and old dried herbs. I think we'll have these analyzed for cannabis resin." Kowalsky closed the cover.

"Gimme that. There's no frigging secret latch on this old leather pouch." Boswell grabbed it back.

"Go ahead, even the man with the Houdini handcuffs couldn't get into that bag unless I wanted him to." Charlie raised his eyes.

Boswell fought for a few moments trying to tear the cover off, but the medicine bag wouldn't budge.

"See, it won't let you in. It locks out anyone with bad intentions or evil thoughts. And I'd hate to see what I'd have to charge you if you wreck it. But be careful, it's an irreplaceable souvenir from my great-grandfather. Made from the skin of a Buchwass."

"A what?"

"Buchwass, old man of the woods, sasquatch."

"Gimme a frigging break, no such thing. It's a rotten old hunk of junk is what it is. Bought in Mexico for three pesos and a round at the farmer's daughter." Boswell threw the bag into the corner. "And a waste of our frigging time. Now tell me where were you on the night of the fifth of October? And I've had enough of your smart-ass mouth, Mr. Stillwaters. Either you start to be a little cooperative or we are going to have a very long night here." Boswell leaned in, sticking his nose into Charlie's face. "Cause I've about had it with your flippant attitude."

"Long night? And no TV? I hope there's no baseball games on that I'll be missing." Charlie smiled. "Do we get any snacks at half-time? I'm getting rather hungry."

He muttered a few words in Haida under his breath and waved his hand at the bag. The medicine bag oozed a small cloud of mist from where it had been tossed behind the detectives.

"It's the fucking offseason. Listen I've had enough of your smart-mouth bullshit." Livid, Boswell stood up. He was trying to control his rage, grinding his teeth. More than anything in the world he wanted to backhand the old man, and would have if he wasn't under camera observation. Once done here he'd take him to the cells, there weren't any cameras to keep him from showing the native who was boss.

He walked around to Charlie and sat on the desk before him, half expecting the man to cower, like most did when he leaned on them. The edge of the desk groaned.

Charlie looked into his eyes and glanced at three faint marks, like scratches, on the side of his neck. "I think it is you who are the smart one." Charlie replied, looking into Boswell's eyes. "Playing two sides."

Off guard, Boswell blinked several times, "What are you…?"

"What is that stink?" Kowalsky turned as the sound of heavy breathing filled the room. "Holy shi…"

"What a stench." Boswell wrinkled his nose, looked up, and caught the reflections of creatures moving in the mirror.

"Ah, the aroma of male Sasquatch coming into heat. Quite distinct, musky and not only pungent, but it doesn't help that he hasn't taken a bath since…" Charlie tapped his fingers on the desk. "Well, I guess probably never."

Boswell stared at the reflections moving across the mirror, shadows haunted the edges of his vision and disappeared when he tried to look directly at them. Growls, the pad of paws, claws clicking on tile and the smell of large, unwashed animals filled the air. Boswell jumped and Kowalsky followed suit. He was startled out of his wits as coarse fur brushed by him. His fellow detective shrank away from some unseen contact moments later.

"What the hell is going on here?" Boswell yelled as a growl filled the air.

"Now, did I mention I'm a card-carrying, bona fide shaman, and as one, I happen to have a few spirit guides in my control. And if you like magic tricks, catch this. Learned it from old Houdini himself." Charlie clicked his fingers and both handcuffs fell away.

The detective glared at him, at Kowalsky, and at the shadows creeping around the room.

"No, probably not. You probably didn't want to hear that earlier. So first, I'd caution you both to make no sudden movements, and I'll explain. Might be best if you sat down. Boswell, English name I presume. What's the expression, oh yes, be a good chap and pass me my cane. Feel odd without it."

Kowalsky was about to object but another heavier growl filled the air. He seemed to decide the cane was little threat compared to what appeared to hover behind him. He passed the cane to Charlie, who slowly moved into one of the two interrogators' chairs. Boswell remained standing and backed up a step. Charlie stood and began to pace around the room. "I've pulled my spirit bear away from his happy hunting grounds. Its salmon feeding time, so he's not happy and feeling very peckish."

Boswell, feet skidding across the floor, felt himself being bumped forward toward the other chair by something large and hairy.

"I guess I wouldn't be happy either if someone took away my favourite, once-a-year feast, of Christmas turkey dinner. He's a griz, not very good sense of humour. I tried playing a joke on him once. Didn't go well. They're a little unpredictable, whole lot crazy, and more than slightly nasty. So if I was you I'd sit down and be quiet."

Boswell sank into his chair. A snort, smelling heavily of rotting salmon and salt water, washed over him.

"So, I've a couple of questions of my own to ask. For the most part, you can't see my helpers, except in the mirror, but you can smell them and hear them. However, make one wrong move and they'll tear you apart easier than you can say *hltangghu*, which in English means feather."

Boswell glanced at his partner as several grunts rent the air and the pungent smells of hairy creatures washed over him. Paws padded in echoes. There were shadows shuffling in the one-way glass.

"Now that I've got your undivided attention you're probably wondering how they got here and what exactly the spirit guides are."

Boswell's eyes opened up as he caught the huge shadow of the Sasquatch moving across the room. "Jesus."

"He's my newest animal spirit. Just coming into heat. But, of course that aroma might just be you crapping yourselves, in which case we should make this quick. Where was I? Oh yes, as a shaman I go on spiritual journeys and part of my initiation involves capturing certain animals to become spirit guides under my control. I've a wolf, a bear, and my newest, a sasquatch." Three growls from around the room answered him, one after another.

"I also had a kushtaka, you wouldn't know what it looks like, but it's a land otter, kinda man sized with arms coming straight out of its chest, no lips, sorta hideous really. However I released him after a rather sticky situation with a witchy woman, who incidentally, is probably part of the reason you and I are here today. But I guess you're not in the mood to hear that story now."

Both of the men stared wildly around the room, sweat standing out on their foreheads. The thud of heavy footsteps filled the room as the Sasquatch began to pace. They cowered a little and covered their noses at the incredibly ripe aroma that flooded the room.

"Definitely starting to go into heat. He's my newest and doesn't like to be confined, ah the impatience of youth. Quite simple and honest creatures really, they have no use for backstabbers. And speaking of two-timers, I think you and I, Boswell, need to talk. So, let's make this rather quick and I can leave through that door. In fact, if there was a game I'd still make the half-time show. Your partner Kowalsky here, he's on your side as well?"

"These are just illusions, they're not real, and I don't know what you're talking about." Boswell blurted out.

Charlie lifted his chin in the slightest of gestures and the wolf leapt onto the table, his shadowy form glaring off the wall's wide mirror. White teeth protruded from the massive muzzle while his growl rose from deep in his broad chest. The detectives pushed their chairs back, but the Sasquatch impeded their movement and shoved them back to the shaking table and the snarling, agitated wolf.

"Full moon coming, he gets a little testy and a bit hairier. Don't worry, no one will see or hear us outside of this room." Charlie waved his cane in the direction of the cameras and the mirror. A fog sheathed itself around the camera and the window went opaque. "We're sealed off from the outside. Whatever is now spoken will be heard only between us."

"Stop, don't hurt us. I've a wife and two kids." Kowalsky's voice cracked and he gasped for air, obviously the more cowardly of the two. Boswell went white, his expression uncertain; the realization of the situation sinking in. He glanced to the door.

"Wouldn't do it." Charlie responded to the man's thoughts. Boswell sank back in his chair.

"Family you say. Wolfie has ten in his litter, which is quite a feat. Our amiable Sasquatch, who as I said is in heat and by the way still a virgin, is younger than he looks. I'm not sure what sex he prefers, but I think he's starting to take a real shine to Kowalsky here."

The spirit ran a hand through Kowalsky's hair, searching. Fetid breath washed over him.

"Yes, I think he really likes you, quite a compliment, really, if he's checking your scalp for grubs. But don't worry, he may be called Bigfoot, but certain other parts of his body are anything but big." Charlie smiled, leaning on his cane as Kowalsky went pure white, sweat running down his face.

"Both of us are in Ryley's back pocket. Just let me go, please." Kowalsky pleaded. He darted a fearful glance at the mirror, apparently searching for a glimpse of the Sasquatch's member.

"Dammit! I said shut up," Boswell muttered to Kowalsky, "he'll kill us if he finds out."

"Thanks, that's all I really needed to find out. Any others on the force I should know about?"

"No, just us." Kowalsky fidgeted, trying to get away from the pestering Sasquatch.

"And this Ryley, did he have anything to do with killing a Larry Seigman?" Charlie glared at Boswell.

Boswell remained tight lipped. Charlie tapped his cane impatiently. The great bear moved forward until it breathed down Boswell's neck. The heat of the rank salmon breath making the man turn paler, as drool oozed down the back of his neck.

"Fuck. Okay, how do you know about Larry? Yes, Ryley did him, I led the investigation. Ryley McLaren is the gang-leader in this area. Larry was his head enforcer," Boswell blurted out as he wiped at the wetness on the back of his neck.

A low growl from close behind turned Boswell as pale as Kowalsky. A thick tongue licked the back of his neck, incisors scraped at the salty sweat oozing freely.

"He always licks his steaks before he begins supper. Gets him an idea just how tender the meat is." Charlie smiled. "And the rest of the story?"

Boswell stared at Kowalsky and back at the shaman. "No one else will hear this?"

"My word. We are sealed off from the rest of the building. They will only see us talking. This, as you guys say, is totally off the record, or of course, I could leave and let you guys deal with my friends, who are growing very impatient and hungry."

Boswell lowered his head and after a moment began to speak quietly. "The story goes that Larry was siphoning off money from Ryley's coke shipments, tens of thousands. He was either trying to retire and quit the Devil's Spawn or preparing to set Ryley up for a fall and take over his territory. Don't know which, but I do know that, in addition, he was doing the man's wife on the side. That's when Ryley found out, in fact I made the call to him to let him know I'd found the two in bed, taken pictures as evidence."

"So Ryley hired you to spy on his wife?"

"Yeah, he doesn't trust anyone, probably has someone spying on me." He glanced at Kowalsky, who merely sat looking petrified, as if trying to contain himself and afraid a stream of warmth would flood down his front.

"Don't think he's a worry, he's just a dirty cop like yourself. What happened to Ryley's wife in the end?"

"Don't know, suffice to say she disappeared. No trace ever found of her."

"And Larry. He had him killed?"

"Not at first. He wanted Larry to suffer, had him run over on the highway while he was out cruising on his bike. Ended up in the hospital with badly broken legs. Spent nearly a year there, during which time he burned Larry's house to the ground, raped his wife and kids, and then offed the lot of them. When Larry got out, Ryley knew he'd come looking. Ryley ordered him run over again, and this time he made sure the man was dead."

"Your part in all of this?"

"I was paid very well to make sure Ryley wasn't implicated. Treated it as a mere hit and run. But what has this got to do with the death of the mayor?"

"The reason I'm here. To undo the betrayal that you are part of. In layman's language, it's to set other paths to open up that weren't ever meant to be open."

Boswell eyed Charlie hard, even with the grizzly breathing down his neck. "I'll say this, don't fuck with the Spawn."

Charlie smiled. "Tell Ryley I'm the least of his concerns. I've other fish to fry and nature has its own code called karma. He'll get whatever he deserves and so will you. Thanks gentlemen, you've been most helpful I think I should be going, Kowalsky here is beginning to turn the colour of a chum salmon."

Charlie tapped his cane twice. The door to the room swung open. He retrieved his pouch from the floor and slung it around his neck. "Thanks again. I believe you said the front door is this way. Oh, and do mention to your superiors about the plants or pictures, too sterile a room, needs a little earthiness. Now, no funny business, you'll need to remain quite still for a couple of minutes while their energies dissipate. So, I'll see myself out then, shall I? Oh, and it's a shame, really, Kowalsky, I think he's taken quite a liking to you. You'd make such a cute couple."

Kowalsky gulped as the huge hands rummaged through his hair again. His throat worked as if he'd like to scream and his eyes frantically darted to the open door. Boswell sat still as his the breathing slowly diminished, the shaman was aware of the hate emanating from the man, biting at his heels as turned to leave the room.

"And you know sasquatchs, they just don't take to most people. Quite shy socially, actually." Charlie sauntered from the room, the mists following him.

* * *

"Ben, could you meet me at O'Shanahan's right away?" Carol disconnected her cell phone and with a still-shaking hand she lit a cigarette. She took several long drags before squashing it out and heading inside. She chugged down a Scotch on the rocks, and then ordered a second, promising herself to take it easy on this one or she'd be over the legal limit.

Her cell phone rang; the caller ID told her it was Big Dan. She left it for now. Images of the hand falling free, putrefying body fluids oozing free, blood, maggots raining down from the corpse kept playing in her head and, worse, a little girl screaming over and over. Where the hell was the voice coming from? Was she going crazy? Carol chugged the drink back and ordered a third. Hell, she could always cab it home.

Her cell phone rang again. Big Dan, he wasn't going to give up, obviously wanting to know how she found the girl's body. Especially since the entire Vancouver police department had scoured the area several times. She let it go to voice mail, and sent a quick text. Carol let her boss know she was unable and unwilling to talk right now, but would be in touch as soon as she was ready.

Carol shuddered. She couldn't handle the situation. Between the kidnapping and this incident, images played again: maggots raining down, pus, blood, and the arm dangling free. "Fuck, get out of my head."

The detective sat alone at the bar, listening to the clink of ice cubes as she swirled the drink around in her glass. The stale smell of wax and dry ice penetrated her nostrils. She stared at smoke currently flooding the dance floor.

"You okay?" The bartender approached her. "Sorry, we're testing the smoke machines. Had some trouble with them the other night."

She glanced at him. "Yeah," she lied. "Just fine. Rough day, that's all."

"No prob. If you need to talk I've an ear handy."

He smiled, the man was rather handsome. If Ben wasn't coming, she'd ask him home. She needed someone to hold her and right now anyone would do. In her head it was two in the morning and nobody was ugly.

The shaman knew. The scene played itself over and over in her mind. He must have known where the girl was this whole time and he hadn't said a word. Why? How the fuck could he not? Tears threatened to come free. "Get a grip, girl," she told herself, something her dad had told her many times. She could use his strong arms about now. Detachment. Normally she could remain unemotional about a disturbing event. For some reason, not this one. *Maggots rained down.*

She looked up into the mists on the dance floor and blinked, letting the whisky wash into her, numbing her. She needed to forget.

Carol blinked again, swearing images moved in the mists.

"Crap, this isn't helping." Was she going nuts? Faces blurred in and out of the mists, a young girl and others she couldn't quite make out. She closed her eyes as the haggard face of an old woman glared at her, watching her.

Carol chugged back the rest of the third drink. "Excuse me. Look at the dance floor closely. What do you see?"

The bartender obliged and surveyed the smoky dance floor. "Ah, smoke, miss. Just smoke. Should I be seeing anything else? You sure you don't need a cab home or anything?"

"I was afraid you'd say that. No, someone's coming to get me." As she said that sunlight seared the dimness of the pub. The front door opened and Ben came nearly running into the nightclub.

"You okay?"

She fell into his stunned arms. "Take me to your place. I need to get away from all of this." Images kept dancing before her. The smell of dead, decaying human being, was like no other. Rot all around her, filling her senses. Decomposing flesh.

"How do I? I mean what should I do?"

"Nothing, just hold me and make me feel like a woman. I'll explain later."

Ben put one arm around her, and threw twenty bucks on the counter. "Keep the change, buddy."

Carol leaned weakly against him as they exited, the fresh air intensifying the whisky flooding her nerves.

"You definitely aren't all right. Seen a ghost or something?"

Carol looked behind her, caught the face of the old hag in the mists, intently watching her as she left. They'd turned off the fog machines, but the image washed in and out of the dissipating haze. "Worse." The hag seemed to be running along the vanishing wisps, trying to get at her.

As they climbed into his Beamer she wiped at her nose, trying to get the stink out to no effect. "Thanks for coming. I'll explain later. I can still smell her, the stench." Carol closed her eyes, rubbing at her nose again. How could she explain to anyone what she'd seen and smelled? How could she get rid of the experience?

"Whose stench?"

Tears threatened to flood down her face. She hated being emotional, sometimes wished she could always be a strong as her dad. But even he'd cried at times, especially after her mother died. Carol hung her head down, unable to keep it in any longer. As they drove away she told Ben everything. Charlie, the bodies, everything. She knew she shouldn't, but Carol needed someone to talk to right now.

It helped as the alcohol softened the pain inside. Several tears dribbled down her face. "I thought I was tough enough to handle anything. To take whatever my job as a detective, could throw at me." Tears rolled down her cheeks. "I was wrong."

* * *

The Lure grimaced; images of a native man leaning on a cane washed into her from the woman's partly inebriated mind. Another drink and she could probably have possessed the woman and used her like she'd done the others. She was a female warrior, something this generation called the law. That would be the perfect one to possess, since the woman had already broken the spell The Lure had set around the young girl in the park. She wanted to know how the woman warrior had the power to remove the spell and how she discovered it in the first place. Unless of course the shaman from Haida Gwaii had something to do with it.

Charlie. If she had teeth, she'd be gritting them now, the shaman had interfered one time too many. He'd pay.

* * *

"All I need you to do is hold me. Make me forget."

Carol sobbed as they got into his place. Ben slowly drew the shades and put some soft soothing music on; a Delirium album. He lit a couple of candles he'd been saving for just such a moment.

"Well, not my idea of a second date." It was a little unexpected, but he knew she didn't need any psychobabble right now. Just to be loved, and to forget. That was enough.

"I need you, need you inside me."

He slowly undressed her, kissing her all over, and laid her on the bed. Then he undressed quickly, his arousal evident. He lay beside her. "Are you sure?"

"Yes, now, quickly." She moaned. She waited impatiently as he tore open the small packet from his bedside cabinet and hastily put the rubber on. Carol pulled him on top of her, completely defenceless, she submitted to him. Just a man and a woman, letting go of reality and existing as one entity. No words, just passion. The intense pleasure washing all else away.

Carol's breathing pattern meshed with his as he swallowed her moans and met them with groans of his own. The taste of her sweet on his lips.

Ben paid attention to her needs before his. Trying to delay his urges as much as possible, allowing her to build to that point of explosion, slowly. Knowing she needed to lose herself in her own pleasure.

When she reached the pinnacle, he could no longer control himself. She shuddered, hanging on him. Yielding to the waves of internal pleasure, driven by his demanding hardness.

Moaning, again and again.

"Enough."

He remained inside her long after he'd softened, her head on his chest, arms wrapped around each other. Cocooned under the sheets in the muskiness of their love-making nothing else mattered. Tears streaked her face. He wanted to ask more questions, but the time to talk would be later.

He stroked her hair as she sobbed herself into sleep's cradle. He didn't really understand what the hell upset her, but if he was being used simply to forget, Ben didn't care. It was the most intense and utterly intimate session of lovemaking he'd ever had. She fell asleep, vulnerable in his arms. What had happened to her? It didn't matter, he'd protected her, held her, and treasured her, when she needed it the most.

His fingers swept through Carol's hair as she slept. The rough, tough detective, now just a naked woman, snoring in his arms, breathe tickling the sparse hairs on his chest. The scent of their arousal was warm and musky in the room. Damn, that was good.

As she slept he thought about what she'd said. She was tracking a shaman and he was seeking a ghost. A ghost that, Ben was certain now, had possessed him somehow. He didn't understand how he knew, but that spirit had returned to wreak revenge against someone. Ryley McLaren seemed the likely target, and he was someone who probably deserved it. Only how many innocents, like him, would be affected before one man's revenge would be complete? And would the spirit stop there?

There was a connection between the two—the ghost and the shaman—Ben was sure of it. His reporter hackles were up. Investigator instincts sniffing at a faint scent. A piece that made no sense was missing.

She didn't realize it, but he begged to ask the question, after all, why a shaman? What would bring the shaman to reveal himself to Carol? She must have asked herself the same question.

A murder was a murder, even if it was the mayor and his family. It had something to do with the murderer. Ben stared at the pictures on his wall. He'd journeyed to all parts of the world, and met many people he called strange at first. But he realized eventually that they'd simply been raised in a different culture with a different way of thinking from his. Neither was right, just different views of life. So someone being a mystic didn't matter and he believed the man probably was what he claimed to be. So what would a man of the spirits need with a cop? Surely he could deal with things on his own?

And if the shaman couldn't, then how could Carol?

Ben didn't understand any of the esoteric disciplines, he only understood the sciences of English and reporting. Cross your i's and dot your t's. He knew what it took to make a good story. And there was more than one story here.

And he knew one further thing, someone, somehow had possessed him on the night of his date with Brandi. He had to go back to the bar and find his abductor, or at least garner some clues as to what happened that night. That part finally made sense. Someone with murderous intentions was on the loose. Ben didn't care if he got Ryley in the end, the man deserved it. It was the innocents like him that mattered.

And this was one story he had to stop before too many died.

* * *

Carol, young, perhaps eight, stands before the portal tree. Figures on both sides of her dwell in the darkness. She screams as a cold hand, coloured with the blood of her parents, clamps around her throat.

"You will not take my Mr. Lucky."

The girl struggles, but is back handed and barely conscious as she's stuffed into the dampness of old cedar. Colder, unforgiving steel slices across her throat. Carol's voice gurgles, unable to yell. Blood spews in a torrent down the old-growth wood. Aromatic cedar calls to her lungs, answering death's ring. Life ebbs from flailing limbs. Hard granite is jammed up under her. Sealing her from the world.

As stillness and cold creeps across her veins, another voice calls out, "You've come to play, my pretty." The entity yanks her to another realm, a scary place.

The strange voice cackles and only the scratching of wood lice scurrying about, busy with today's meal, answers.

Carol woke up trembling. Moisture clinging to her body, she rolled over and hugged Ben. Thank God he was here; the thought crossed her mind before she fell asleep again. She woke up several times during the night, each time aware of the same horror, only weaker, like sweating out a bad cold. The nightmares faded until it was only her, Ben, and the beating of his sleeping heart to calm her back to sleep. She struggled to keep one eye open and stay awake, watching the dark. If she didn't sleep, she couldn't dream.

* * *

Ryley watched people entering and leaving the washrooms of the bar. The biker was in a fouler mood than usual. He had shown up to police headquarters as he'd promised Carol he would, with lawyers in tow. He told the police what he knew about the torching of his clubhouse, which wasn't much.

His man snapped and shot up his home and was lighting Ryley's beloved bike on fire as he drove up. When Ryley arrived Stains pulled a gun and he shot him in self-defence.

Ryley had already contacted the insurance company, one thing he had lots of was insurance. It cost a fortune having his place and bike insured, but at least that drug money could be used for legit reasons. It was a good thing they never asked questions when his men turned up to pay the annual premium in cash.

Right now he didn't care if he even got a red cent back, his bike was gone and someone was out to get him. The problem was, who? The word on the street was there wasn't anyone with an axe to grind who was coming after him. The gay boy that Greasy tried to pick up the other night and had nearly stolen Ryley's cell phone wasn't much help either. The kid swore he didn't remember anything from the time he entered the john until the moment they dragged him off the dance floor and chucked him into the back of one of the vans where they interrogated him. He swore time and time again he didn't remember.

Odd thing to keep repeating when you're getting the crap kicked out of you.

No one and no evidence, other than an amnesic fag and three dead men. Why did Greasy's man try to run back inside the bar? Surely it would have made more sense to hide in the woods. The only common denominator was they were both here on the night their lives ended. So why would the fag run back into the bar, try to get the bouncers to protect him?

As for Carol, she talked bravely for a woman cop. That did impress him. But he knew she was crapping herself the entire time. Probably not a copper that he could put under his employ, like Kowalsky and Boswell. No, she wasn't one to try and bribe, had do-gooder morals plastered all over her brow.

One guy who staggered in earlier caught his eye. He watched the man as he walked up to the bar and grabbed a bottle before leaving. Stains, the body language, his left-handedness. Same with the man buying the drink. He stood and walked differently, and it wasn't just because he'd perhaps puked and sobered up. There was something seriously wrong here.

Stains was a piece of shit, but he also was a true coward. He wouldn't do what he did alone, even if by chance he was in league with someone.

Ryley continued watching. Two young girls sauntered up, obviously looking for a good time. "Piss off," he growled and waved them away.

"Wonder who stuck a stick up his ass," one muttered.

One of his men rose to deal with her. Ryley nodded him to sit back down. Two of his other men glanced at each other, clearly puzzled by his actions.

Ryley sat watching the bathrooms. Finally a girl entered, obviously well over her limit. A minute or so later she walked out. Only she wasn't staggering, and indeed, was carrying herself with a whole different posture. No, it wasn't just that, it was her demeanor, she moved differently, walked differently, and her face seemed to have a different cast to it.

She approached the bar and pointed to one row of the off-sale bottles and, like the man earlier, bought a drink to go. Odd thing to do, stagger into washroom, come out looking fairly sober and order a bottle before leaving.

"I want to talk to that girl and don't take no for an answer," he growled. Two burly bikers walked quickly over to her. One bent over and spoke into her ear and pointed in Ryley's direction. Her face grimaced, not out of fear, more from anger.

He could tell her answer was no.

His man's hand was on her back as he virtually pushed her towards Ryley.

"I hear you want to talk to me." She leered at him, not looking the least bit nervous.

The behaviour immediately struck Ryley as odd.

Her speech wasn't slurred, nor were her pupils dilated. Her breath reeked of booze, but the girl seemed in full control of her faculties. Curious, most curious. "Yes, matter of fact I do. Sit down for a moment. We need to talk about this place. I've noticed there's more that goes on around here, besides drinking, dancing, and picking up people, than is readily apparent."

She continued to stand. Ryley waved two of his men forward. "I said sit the fuck down." His man put his burly hand on her shoulder and was about to push her into the bench seat.

"You tell me what you think is going on here, but first tell Mr. Gorilla that if he doesn't let go of me he'll be eating his knuckle."

Ryley blinked in disbelief. By her attire, a miniskirt and low-cut top, large earrings and far too much makeup, she was more the image of a typical valley girl than a tough-as-nails broad. The voice didn't match the image. Fascinating.

He nodded and the men moved back about two feet.

"Now, make this quick. I haven't much time," she demanded.

"You're awfully cocky for someone who's dealing with me." He watched her eyes, there was no fear there.

"And so are you. Now like I said, you're wasting my time. You've got five minutes," she barked.

Rage flared for a second, he didn't take orders from anyone, particularly mouthy tarts. The two behind her looked perplexed as he swallowed his rage. "Okay, if I didn't need some information I'd give you to Snickers here. But I do, so you'll live this time. Tell me about this place and what exactly is going on here. I see people staggering drunk entering the washrooms and leaving them walking totally differently. As if," he glared at her, "as if someone else has taken over."

* * *

"Thanks for last night." Carol said as she poured the coffee Ben had made before he wandered off to have a shower.

"No problem." He smiled, giving her a peck on the cheek as he walked by. "It was incredible. I'm glad I could be there for you. There's bread for toast if you feel like it. I'm having my shower, but if you want to stick around, we can talk more when I get out. I'll be making my famous scrambled egg-and-peppers wrap."

Carol had already dressed, but she put a couple of pieces of bread into the toaster, reluctant to leave just yet. She knew by the number of calls from Big Dan she'd have to go in and see him first thing. Between the kidnapping and this last incident she'd already decided enough was enough. The weird thing was the smells and images seemed to be dissipating, like fighting off a bad flu. Maybe the orgasms last night helped, couldn't hurt that was for sure.

Munching on her toast, she wandered around his pad. It wasn't anything unique, just the usual Ikea-style furnishings, much like hers. She wandered over to the den area where he'd set up his computer desk. One wall was filled with books.

Obviously, being a reporter, he had a lot of books for research but on perusing his collection, she was surprised to discover Ben was also a fiction fan. Steven

King, Michael Crichton and an extensive assortment of crime novelists, Patricia Cornwell in particular. Must love those crime scenes and autopsies. Hanging on the wall was a framed quote, "what becomes reality, must first be dreamed of." Interesting, she thought, if she had one quote it would be the dead opposite, for she lived under the assumption that "life is stranger than fiction." Especially with this bizarre case, which seemed to only be getting crazier.

Above his desk she caught the map of downtown Vancouver and looked closely at the lines and pins he'd staked into it. All of them converging on O'Shanahan's.

"What?" She looked at each pin marking; the mayor, his wife, the biker deaths, along with several others.

"Interesting isn't it?" Ben sauntered out of the bathroom, hair still dripping, towel wrapped around his midsection. "I'm glad you're still here." He gave her a damp hug and kiss.

"Oh, you're still wet." Carol swallowed the last of her toast and moved away, she hadn't realized how touchy-feely he was. Perhaps a little too much for her, not really her type of man, but he was exactly what she needed last night. "Are you saying O'Shanahan's seems to be the central point all of this weirdness is emanating from?"

"I think so. All I know is there's some pretty weird things going on around here and since you spilled your guts I'll tell you my bizarre story regarding this place." Ben pointed to the bar on the edge of the park. He told her about his date with Brandi and the nightmares after.

For Carol that was the icing on the cake. Ghosts! No one said anything about ghosts; this was getting to be way too much. Now she had a reporter/boyfriend who thought the unholy dead were carousing around a bar every Saturday night. She was going to tell him about the old hag in the mists at the bar, but Carol had had enough.

"Look, I've changed my mind, go ahead and feel free to publish the story about the third body I just found. Consider it your scoop. I've had enough of this crap." She stormed toward the door and slipped on her shoes. "Again, thanks for last night. If it weren't for you I don't know what I would have done." Carol grabbed her jacket and left.

* * *

"Anytime." Ben stood naked under the bath towel wrapped around his waist, water evaporating from him. He put two of the eggs back in the fridge. "So much for hoping for a second round. That first one was fantastic." He leaned against the cool stainless steel door after closing it. "Great, I get a scoop and lose a girlfriend. Wonder what will happen after lunch."

* * *

"Carol! At last. What the hell is going on? I tried to contact you several times last night. You phone. Send the morbid white-coat gang to Stanley Park where the daughter's body has finally been located. Good job, by the way. Then you disappear before anyone can ask questions. Just little less than an hour earlier you're spotted in the park chatting with our number one suspect like it's a casual Sunday family outing, before Boswell arrests him. And not to mention, you look like shit."

Big Dan laid into her as she sat down in his office. Carol was aware the briefing wasn't going to be pleasant. He had a way of making even a man elected president of the United States feel like a bum on Hastings Street.

She shoved a sealed envelope toward him; the letter she struggled to type all morning. It was the toughest thing she'd ever had to do. "I know, I went through utter hell yesterday. Dan, I quit. I can't take this anymore."

Dan didn't even glance at the envelope, let alone open it. "Quit? You can't quit. You've cracked this case wide open. Forensics is going over the last body like ketchup over fries. They've found a knife covered in dried blood and gore in the tree with the body. If it's not the murder weapon I'm a monkey's uncle. The lab's working on DNA and prints. The autopsy confirms a very sharp double-edged blade likely was the murder weapon in the girl's case, and also the mayor's, and," he hesitated for a moment, "they've already confirmed, due to cedar dust in her lungs, that she was alive when someone stuffed her up the tree."

"I know." Carol slumped into the chair. "That's why I'm quitting. I already knew she was alive when our perp stuffed her up the tree. I've been having nightmares all night. Keep seeing her face, the hand, maggots." The detective put her face in her hands and after a moment looked up at Dan. Tears streaked her cheeks. "It's horrible. I keep hearing her screams in my head. I knew she was still alive, I knew. I just can't do this anymore. I need to talk to Charlie before I go, but I'm done. I quit. It's bad enough being threatened with your life, but reliving her death, over and over again? I think the shaman knew and tried to warn me. I never believed him. What cell is he in?" Carol stood up to leave, her hands shaking.

"Cell? You haven't heard the latest since you've gone into meltdown mode. Boswell and Kowalsky let him go, no evidence to hold him. Or so they claim."

"What?"

"Boswell jumped the gun and thought he'd pressure him, tried to make him talk. Still studying the video, but it only shows Boswell and Kowlsky talking with Charlie. Don't know how he did it but he managed to walk out of here smelling like frigging roses, with Boswell handing him the front door keys to the precinct." Dan thumped his beefy fist into his desk and rose, walking around to the other side.

That didn't surprise her. Charlie hadn't looked too worried about being taken in. She glanced at her watch. There was still time to meet him at the totems.

"Snap the fuck out of it." Dan pushed her chair back and stuck his face into hers. "He picked you, that looney tune native. Picked *you*. No one else. There's a reason for it. And the bastard bullied, or talked, his way out of here. I want to know how and why."

"Yeah, to drive me nuts." She could smell the boss's aftershave and swore she could smell the pickles on his breath from the burgers he last wolfed down. Not sure which was worse on an empty stomach.

"Neither of them is fessing up as to how he managed to scare the crap out of two experienced officers. I want that man back and I want to talk to him. That native knows something deeper. I think, like me, he knows you're a good cop. The best damn one on this case and in this police force."

"What about Boswell?"

"Too brash, cocky. Reacts too easy. Doesn't look, think about the evidence. You do, you look at all the angles, no matter how strange, and this case is one big bizarre FUBAR."

He stared at her. "I don't know the angles you've got with this Charlie character. I'm beginning to think he had nothing to do with the murders, other than being an innocent bystander. Once we confirm all the prints and DNA I'll know. But you need to sit down and talk to him, get his confidence. Boswell couldn't crack him. I think you can."

He took her resignation letter, tore it in pieces, and tossed it into the garbage. "This is a frigging cop out. The easy way out, and not your style. I'm not accepting it and know this." He edged closer until she could see the blood vessels throbbing angrily in each eye. "If you walk out on this case now, you know you'll never live with yourself. And that, sweetheart, will haunt you even more than what you've uncovered." Dan lowered his voice to a rare level of quiet, clicked off his tape recorder again. "I know from experience."

He walked back around to his chair and sat down. Carol was unsure what he was going to say, she didn't know he had any fears or haunted past.

"The Micky Dee's investigation everyone bugs me about." His voice went strangely soft. "I've never had the guts to tell anyone. You heard of the Almedi case?"

"Yeah, weren't you in that investigation? Ended up rushing into the house where the kids were being held hostage. The perp got shot and never recovered. Found the two bodies later, brutally drowned in a water tank." She knew more, there were allegations of Dan's conduct, but nothing proven.

He paused a long moment, as if unsure how to begin. "The step-dad had been holding the kids hostage, demanding a large ransom. Justine Almedi, mother of the two, was a top-notch attorney, high-profile lawyer. She was frantic. We'd found her new husband dead, shot. House ransacked and her two poodles with broken necks. Her ex was obviously making her pay for leaving, the prick. Only we couldn't find him. The fear wasn't that he wanted the money, but that, regardless, he'd kill both kids and her. Finally a break came when we got a report of him being spotted in West Vancouver, on two occasions, near Micky Dee's."

The force knew it better as the Micky Dee case. The reason everyone would snicker as he went for lunch. She knew Big Dan never talked about it to anyone, ever. "So you did stakeout there?"

"Yeah."

"The story goes that on the second night you saw him and chased him down a street on foot. In the ensuing takedown he ended up getting shot, nearly putting a bullet into you, and slipping into a coma from which he never recovered."

"Officially. If I'd been more patient, I'd have tracked him back to his lair. Only, being young and cocky, I didn't want to take the chance of losing him. He'd already delivered an ultimatum that the kids would be dead within two days if she didn't cough up three hundred grand. We were certain we'd nailed down his location and were setting up to break in as I arrested him. I thought once I had him, he'd tell us. We were certain we had evidence to suggest where the kids were holed up. I had him, but he wouldn't talk."

"Only you were wrong about the location. Rushed to the place you thought they were to find it empty."

"He moved them the night before, in fact had been moving them in the back of his car all along." Dan's face had a rare sad look to it. It was about as close to tears as Carol had ever seen him.

"Two days later you found the two bodies floating in a sealed water tank."

Dan rubbed his face in his hands, struggling with his emotions. "He was a sadistic bastard. Didn't want the money, just wanted his ex to pay. He pulled a gun and put a bullet into my shoulder before I pumped one into his chest. I intended to wing him. Only I punctured an artery and while he lay there bleeding he began spouting off about how he beat the shit out of the kids, enjoyed cutting up her old man, and tortured the dogs. I snapped and smashed his head into the brick wall several times, roughed him too much trying to get information about the kids' whereabouts out of him. With the blood loss, he slipped into a coma and never recovered. Died three days later."

Dan had lost his cool. Carol frowned, unsure what to say. "He probably deserved the beating," she said eventually.

"Yeah. I was certain we had the kids. I was wrong, the report stated we wrestled and I had to defend myself."

"Understandable."

"We found house keys and an address which lead us to the kids. They were tied, gagged, and floating in a large plastic sewage tank. He'd put them there, left a water tap slowly dripping, so that if he never returned, he'd still win. His insurance that if we caught him, we'd let him go."

"Some evidence suggests he knew he was being watched."

"Yeah, read those reports. He knew, the fucker knew. He wanted us to take him down and make the kids suffer anyway."

Carol thought a moment. "Christ, Dan, you fell into his plan."

"In the end I wanted to slash my wrists. I'd fucked up, rushed the take-down. Didn't stop to think he'd taken three burgers with him, was taking them to the kids. I didn't take the time to analyze the facts, nor wait to track him down, and two kids died horribly. Brutally. I still see their dead, bloated faces." He rubbed his face in his hands and Carol worried he might begin to break down even further. "I still see their dead eyes, pleading, every time I order another burger."

"But you know what?" He lifted his head. "There will be no more kids tortured on my shift. Not while I'm in charge. Not if I can help it." The growl returned to his voice, his usual orneriness probably instilled since that case. It was said by some of the older members that he was once known as the gentle giant. No longer.

"And no one is quitting on me. Now get the fuck out there and finish this off if you ever want to stare into another mirror squarely again and not hear that little girl's screams every fucking night."

Carol rose and left his office feeling like a monkey with a banana shoved up its behind.

She hated him, but the bastard was right.

Chapter Fifteen

A twenty-six of whisky, Crown Royal." The strong voice with a subtle American twang cut through the boisterous crowd. Ben knew the voice instantly, the voice that had once been inside him. He stared at the man ordering the whiskey. Ben had watched him moments earlier. On the way to the washroom, he'd had a slurred Newfie accent. "Lord tundering jezus. They pack the shitters in the wrong end of the bar." Now, this same man, with a different voice stood straighter, like he was much taller and meaner. Someone who didn't take shit from anyone. The man paid his money and calmly walked out.

Ben got up to start after him. The waitress cut him off. "Give me a minute and I'll get your bill." She looked like she was afraid he was about to do a runner on her.

Ben had to wait; he only had a debit card, not enough cash to throw on the table for a quick getaway.

By the time he'd paid and left, the man was nowhere to be seen in the parking lot. Ben returned to the bar and took another table closer to the washrooms. "Give me another, only make this a virgin Caesar. I've decided to stay longer," he told the waitress.

He noticed two other patrons stagger to the bathroom, both women, and leave looking noticeably different. The women walked like they'd not touched a drop all night. In fact, one of them carried herself differently; shoulders slouched, not at all like the lady that entered. The same as the man earlier.

"What the fuck is going on here?"

Another young fellow staggered by, very obviously inebriated. Ben tossed his money down, he'd risked using the bar's own bank machine just for this reason, and followed him into the washroom. "Hey, great game with the Canucks tonight," he barked at the man who ducked into one of the stalls reeking to high heaven of stale urine.

"Yeah, that Luongo could stand on his head some nights," he slurred back.

Ben entered the adjacent stall and sat down, waiting. A soft whoosh filled the air for a moment, a thump, and then he heard the fellow retching into the toilet. "Oh man, this doesn't get easier," someone spoke in a clear voice. It was definitely from the next stall, but it wasn't the same voice. Slur apart, there was a subtle difference; different accent. The man finished retching, spit twice, and exited his stall.

Ben exited just a few moments later and made a fuss of washing his hands so he could observe the man. "Great hockey game last night."

"Don't watch hockey." The guy studied his reflection in the mirror, as if it were the first time he'd clapped eyes on himself. The man seemed fairly satisfied and exited into the dry-ice fog and loud techno music thumping away.

"Don't get it. What the hell is going on here? Almost as if something or someone is…" He gulped and walked into the noisy atmosphere. The two women were still here, on the dance floor. The young man walked over and joined them like they were old friends and the three quickly left together. He didn't recall them hanging out together earlier, why now?

"So that's it. That explains what happened to me. But how?" He stared up into the rainbow-coloured mist swirling above the dance floor. His skin crawled as little faces, like the ones Carol mentioned, moved in the haze and voices echoed in his head. "Next. I'm next."

"Whatever's going on here is coming from this turret. Is that some kind of portal, gateway?" he asked himself. "A transit station for departures to and from hell?"

* * *

Carol lit her third cigarette, hand shaking, not caring if she was the legal three metres from the door or not, and inhaled deeply. She sat at an outside table at the nearest Starbucks sipping at her straight black, heavy-on-the-caff coffee. The rush of numbness helped settle her nerves, again. She cradled the hot coffee, unable to hold it with one hand and not spill any on herself. She couldn't stop the shakes, either too much coffee or the memories.

Big Dan was right, and she knew it. She wouldn't be able to live with herself if she quit and she'd probably end up like him, chomping down endless burgers trying to swallow the guilt, or some other bizarre habit. Crap, she'd probably end up being five hundred pounds.

A native man sat outside carving small wood figures, pedaling his artistic abilities, trying to make a buck. Maybe for his next drink, maybe just to earn his next meal, judging by the disheveled look to his clothes.

Inhaling the nicotine breakfast and lunch, she watched him carve. The steady hand and sheer determination in his scarred, street-hardened face; the man was intent on coaxing out of the wood the figure hidden in the depths of its grains. Carol studied what he was doing. Even though he should have been out working, he obviously enjoyed what he was doing, but it wasn't the best way to make a living.

That and focus. Single-minded focus, something she'd lost between the events of the last few days.

Carol thought of her earlier conversation with Dan. For her own sanity and peace of mind, this had to be played out. Even if it got uglier than kidnapping and dead, rotten bodies falling out of trees. She shuddered. How could it get any uglier than that?

Although, why Dan would torture himself, swallowing burgers, she didn't know. She'd probably quit eating them altogether. Carol butted the smoke and lit another allowing the aphrodisiac essence of the smoke to numb her again. She shouldn't have left Ben dangling like she had, that was unfair. She texted him an apology.

The carver worked fast, and he was good. He'd probably done carvings like this a thousand times, maybe the same figure. If he drank, it didn't show in his sure practiced hand. Maybe if he'd made different choices or got a lucky break, it would be his work displayed in museums with greats like Bill Reid. Not here making spinoffs for tourists so he could earn his next meal or drink.

Fascinated she allowed him to distract her, watched the figurine emerge from the wood. Like a mother giving birth, he seemed to know what lines were already there waiting to be coaxed to the surface. A hooked beak emerged. An eagle, he was pulling an eagle from the wood. The glaring eye, ever watchful, scrutinizing; he'd captured that too, as the rest of the head scraped its way free of the cedar canvas. She steeled herself, sucked back her fast-cooling coffee, and butted the last half of the smoke out. Enough.

Carol pulled her cell phone out of her pocket. It was a text from Sanchez. He'd left a message that Dan wanted her to take a look at two bodies in the morgue. She called him right away. "Sanchez? What? Okay, I'll be right along."

"More unusual deaths, just what I need right now." Carol shuddered; the memories of the girl still haunted her, and probably would for a long time yet.

In the background a jacked up diesel chugged past, belching a black cloud through the air while someone honked at a jaywalker. Business men in suits, cell phones hanging off their ears, women in dress jackets and, kitty corner to her, four men in black sunglasses and suits and ties stood looking like Svengali-hardline Jehovah's Witnesses. The Vancouver morning throng.

Carol walked up to the man as he proudly held the carving up to the light, checking angles, looking for the little flaws. "How much?"

"Forty-five bucks when I'm done. But it still needs a little sanding and some paint." He replied, rubbing his fingers over the rough edges of wood, as if seeing the rest of the lines already emerging.

"Can I take a look at it?"

She looked at the roughness, the hungry look in its eye, the beak waiting to tear into harmless prey, an unborn hunting cry that would never escape that wooden throat. She took out three twenties. "He's perfect the way he is. I'll take it." Like her, the roughness on the edges didn't detract from the mercenary glare staring determinedly back at her from the depths of that eye. Her respite was over, the hunt was back on, she'd find the mayor's killer.

He handed her the change. She took a ten only. "Keep the rest."

"Thanks." He beamed as he took the piece back and signed it, stuffing the money quickly into a pocket, no doubt already spent.

She was going to comment how talented he was, but somehow Carol knew that would start a lengthy conversation and she'd already wasted enough time feeling sorry for herself. "Thanks again."

Carol tucked the carving into one of the large pockets of her overcoat and walked back to the precinct. She set the carving on the small ledge above her desk. "Now, my friend, time to see Sanchez and do some hunting of our own." She thought a moment, about the eagle in the museum and the research she'd done on shamanism and the power of animals. "Well, Charles, it is. You're my power animal. Now let's go hunt something."

* * *

"Eet is peculiar, these two, both died of an 'eart attack. By orgasm." Sanchez beamed, proud of his discovery. "What?" No one could pay Carol enough to work with dead bodies. Sanchez seemed nice enough, but there had to be a cold part to his soul in order to do this job.

"Definite sexual activity. You can tell from the dried up fluids around the groin. 'Ave sent samples to be tested, should get DNA from semen and from the female fluid. Don't theenk the dead woman was with a man though, eet no appear to have semen. Maybe with another female. See also signs of a lube, maybe she 'ave been 'aving sex with dildo. Maybe she do 'erself or maybe another woman do it to her. 'Ave sent swabs for test from 'er, too. See 'ere," Sanchez indicated the woman's pubic area "Look dark and swollen, overworked maybe by dildo. She 'ave lots of orgasms, bring on 'eart attack. I'm too."

"What a way to go!" She shook her head, the other night with Ben was pretty darn good, but that was more for closeness than passion.

"Chess." He replied. "Seem in both case 'eart could not take the strain, gave out."

"'Ere, you think maybe eet same woman do both as so similar MO?"

"As if I didn't have enough on my plate you think I could have some homicidal bi-sexual killer on the loose?"

"Maybe she just 'ave bad PMS, eh?" Sanchez said with a straight face, and then laughed.

"You're really twisted, you know that? Keep me posted, Sanchez, thanks." Carol smiled and walked back to her office. Although lucky old Sanchez would never experience PMS, she did on occasion, and the idea of killing half the world's population, especially the ones with their brain cells dangling between their legs, didn't seem like such a remote idea.

Back at her desk she pulled up the notes on the investigation into Stumpy's death. Boswell had interviewed a suspect whose vehicle matched the paint transfer on the bike. Didn't take much these days to find a particular vehicle from paint transfer, could do the same with fibres from the carpets. Luckily it wasn't a particularly popular colour, there had been only a dozen or so in the immediate area and they'd hit lucky on the third interview. She jotted down his details; she'd speak to him herself.

* * *

"I already gave my statement, detective," David Donnetty said as he studied Carol's badge through the gap in the still-chained door. Satisfied, he briefly closed the door, unchained it, and let her into his apartment. "Sorry about that, but you can't be too careful."

"No problem. Rather that than another homicide on my hands. Now, please just tell me what happened the night your car mowed down one of the Devil's Spawn bikers." Carol guaranteed his co-operation by reminding him of the severity of the crime.

Donnetty sighed. "Okay, if you think it will help. Like I said before, I have no idea how my car got over there. I wasn't even planning to drive home, was gonna cab it and pick my car up next day. Funny though, didn't think I'd had too much. But I went to the washroom, and then it's all a blank until I was on the crowded dance floor at nearly closing."

"You have a gap in your memory?"

An obvious question, but one she hadn't read in Boswell's report.

His eyes indicated he was telling the truth. "Yes, a good few hours, I think. I don't remember anything between the washroom and the dance floor. It's like I completely blanked out."

"And someone else took over," Carol said, as if reading his thoughts. That's what Ben had said about his night at O'Shanahan's.

"I hadn't thought about it, but yeah that's exactly what it seemed like."

David stood there with a puzzled look on his face. "Weird."

"You ever blank out when you drink too much?"

"Only years ago, when I was young and foolish. Now I guess I'm older and seemingly still foolish." He smirked with that hurt look of regret on his face.

"Yeah, I guess. I may call you if I think of anything else. Thanks for your time." She walked down the hallway and waited for the elevator. "Well, I can say this for Ben's investigative mind. There's something very odd going on around here and evidence does point to O'Shanahan's Bar as a focal point. Only how?" She thought back to Boswell's report; he hadn't asked many questions. He didn't dig through the details carefully enough. The answer to one question should lead to another. He couldn't think on his feet like a good cop needed to. Probably like a lot of people that didn't care about doing a good job. She always prided herself on doing her best and couldn't understand anybody who would take something on just to be half-assed about it.

She'd see about getting O'Shanahan's security tapes, see what they threw up.

* * *

The Lure grabbed at the toilet as she steadied herself. "It doesn't get any easier." She fought off dizziness and the pounding throb in her head, trying to focus on her surroundings. "This better be the last time I have to do this."

"You okay, honey." A woman's voice came from the doorway as The Lure staggered toward the sinks. She put her hand on The Lure's shoulder.

She guessed by her short hair and manly dress the woman might be what they called a butch in these times. "I'm fine."

"Sure? I could take you home and make sure you're looked after." The touch turned to a caress across the cheek. The Lure knew this one wanted more; she wasn't just concerned, but the witch was after stronger stuff. She wasn't in the mood for another night of female companionship. What she really needed was powerful male testosterone energy, the stronger the better.

"Yeah, I'm just peachy, and you haven't got what I need. Wrong equipment, sister." She straightened up and walked out of the washroom. As she stood in front of the bar waiting to buy a bottle, just in case, one of the bikers approached her.

"Someone wants to see you." Crap, she didn't have time for this.

Nearly an hour later she staggered out of the bar with a male in tow. Ryley, the leader, had made an offer to set her up with a house and income. He needed a favour. She hated the idea of being a man's puppet, but she would need a place to establish herself once she entered this realm. The offer was tempting, although she didn't trust him. Men of his ilk were best kept close and on her side. They had a common problem and similar needs. She might even like to take him to bed one day. His energy was very strong.

In the shadows of the parking lot, she could smell the energy of the others, on the edge of the darkness. They hadn't sensed her yet and this would be the best time to deal with them, so she had to be quick.

Her male companion, Dennis, was very muscular. An avid weight lifter, testosterone oozed from his very pores. "Drive up the street and park in some place secluded." She persuaded him, her hands rubbing along his leg. She could smell his arousal, his need, and felt the hardness trapped within his pants.

"Park there, under the tree. I want this." She caressed him again and he moaned, nearly slamming on the brakes and driving into another parked car. "Easy, big boy."

They pulled over and kissed for awhile. "Get in the back and take off your pants, I need you inside me. Now!"

He blindly followed her orders, his own needs overriding any sense of indiscretion. Her eyes widened as she took in his hugeness. He was perfect. She tore off the host's underwear, pushed him into the seat and climbed on top. The Lure grabbed both his hands and pinned them over his head.

"Oh God, you're so wet." He shuddered, unable to control his urges as she rose up and down on him.

Wave after wave of energy surged through her. He was strong. Reveling in the release, she threw her head back and kept stroking him. "Oh, that's so good." They both moaned at the same time. She'd forgotten how wonderful a man's hardness felt inside her. She allowed the internal emotions of the host's body to wash over her, wallowing in the sheer ecstasy of the act.

"Oh, I'm gonna cum, we have to stop. I need to put on a rubber."

Well, he was considerate. "You, my dear man, just need to relax and release yourself to me and the rest will be history."

"No, this isn't right." He threw his head back and tried to throw her from him with a thrust of his hips. "Your face! It's changing. What the hell is going on here?"

It was happening already, she was shifting into this dimension. "Oh, honey, this is more than right and it's too late to be thinking about what isn't proper now, my delicious stud, far too late." She held his hands over his head with one arm and used the other to grab his hair and pull him to her. She sucked at his lips, feeling herself erupting from within the host.

His eyes cried for mercy as his body convulsed in exquisite desire, unable to stop himself. She commanded him on. Her body thrusting him into ecstasy, again and again. Drowning in the physical pleasures. She smiled.

"Good night forever, lover." She lost herself in the waves of deliciousness washing over the body she inhabited.

His eyes opened wide, pleading for the pleasure/pain to end. She drove him on, as the light faded inside, sucking at his lips feverishly as she drained the soul from the body.

"Oh, that's incredible, you just gotta love testosterone, best orgasm of my life, wouldn't you say," she blurted out. Throwing her head back in sheer delirium. His head rolled to one side, eyes wide open.

"I guess you're not the talkative type. Well, I hate to eat and run, but I've business to attend to." She lifted herself off the body and got out of the car, shaking from the energy coursing through her. The witch allowed the woman's thighs to stop shuddering before dressing herself.

The Lure looked in the rear-view mirror at her blurred reflection. Dizziness made her grab the side of the vehicle as her face shifted slowly back into the host's body. "Damnit, almost there, not quite. Fine. I've a little unfinished business to attend to tonight with some former colleagues, but after that, who knows." She jumped into the driver's seat, started the car, and drove off allowing the host body to control the vehicle they were using. "First, a trip to the local drugstore to purchase a couple of items and if the night is still young, maybe Ms. Brushcut and Affection at the night club will have someone to take home after all. I've a craving for a little dessert."

* * *

Carol hovered on the edge of the throng around the totems at Stanley Park, the tourists snapping photo after photo of the carved beaks and haughty images of a bygone age. She finally spotted Charlie standing slightly away from the others. He was like a living anachronism to our modern world, she thought, as she approached from behind. He probably deserved more pictures and attention than the totems.

Could society truly understand how much was lost with the demise of his people?

"I didn't say this before, but for the longest time I thought you were a ghost. The way you disappeared that night?"

"Odd, I didn't hear you approach. Glad you could make our date, though." Charlie replied, without acknowledging her comment.

Not this game again. "Didn't want you to. But I thought you woo-woo people could sense someone's presence, their carnal energies or force or something like that." The tourist atmosphere made her feel relaxed and jovial for a change. That was a first in many a day. Especially after yesterday, she needed to loosen up.

"You've learned something, then, since we last met." He laughed. "Oh, and that's karmic energy. You've seen too many Star War movies. Nice green socks by the way."

"Thanks," He still hadn't turned around. But he'd got her back. He'd obviously lied and sensed her approaching. Carol decided to drop it, wondering how he knew her sock colour. She had an urge to ask if he knew what colour panties she was wearing but resisted, in case he guessed that right, too.

She stared at the large cedars behind the totems. Trees. Images of the girl, arm dangling free, came flooding back, wriggling maggots raining down on her good mood.

"The girl?"

He turned to face her. "Sorry about that. The spell of displacement dispels the traumatic energy of the moment, so that even sensitive people like myself may not detect its use. Whoever breaks the illusion relives the final moments as time replays itself. The effect is kind of like bad food poisoning of the mind. Once you stop puking it up, it will eventually wash out of your system. It's all about energy, and even displaced energy has to go somewhere. Unfortunately, you bore the brunt of it."

"Why didn't you tell me?" The man could read her thoughts; she'd guessed that almost from the first time they met.

"You didn't ask, and would you really have believed me?"

"No. Guess not." Still didn't, really.

"There are times, when no matter what is told to someone, they just have to live the experience to learn the lesson. Again, sorry about that. I've experienced a few of those and they can be very horrific." He smiled, his face sincere. The man had a heart after all.

"We must appear like kids to you at times. I'm beginning to think there's a lot you know that I'll never have a hope of understanding."

"Or are even aware of. But that works two ways. I don't think I'll ever wrap my head around why a woman would try to follow the latest fashions even if it only makes her appear foolish."

He pointed to a younger lady, more than a few pounds overweight, wearing very low-slung, too-tight pants. Folds of flab hung out between the pants and hem of her skimpy T-shirt. The on-display thong was the icing on the cake. Next to her, a very overweight man, pants worn so low the crotch was around his knees, exposed his crack to the world.

Carol grinned. "Yes, nice twin pack of trucker's butts."

They both laughed. She should be angry with him and up until she'd got out of her cruiser, she had been. But somehow a lot of what he said began, in some bizarre way, to make sense. After all, the entire VPD, including herself, had combed the area around the Cathedral Trail several times and not found that girl's body. So he hadn't lied, he'd known all along she was there, rotting away. Carol shuddered. How could he?

The thought brought her back to one of her original reasons for being here. "For a while I wondered, how does a shaman come across a murder scene and why? What alerts him to it in the first place? Like I said earlier, I thought you were a ghost, until I came across this." Carol pulled out the photograph of the Haida demonstrators arrested at Lyell Island in the Charlottes. In the background, as they were being hauled off to jail, was Charlie leaning on his cane. "The way you vanished, at first I thought you were some sort of apparition. But this picture proves you're real."

Charlie patted himself. "Whew, I'm glad for that, thought for a moment I was a figment of my own imagination."

"After several conversations with John Denton, the head curator at the UBC Museum, it became evident you're no ghost. Otherwise, you'd be only talking about things you knew in the past, from whatever time period you lived."

"Oh, I don't know, you have to be careful with time. It, like everything else, evolves. Not like you whites believe. The past too changes, melds things into something different in these times. I knew of a Haida chief once, called S'Krone Micey, which literally meant Sister to the Old Mouse. Mispronounced by white settlers, he's now known as synchronicity." He chuckled. "And by the way it's Gwaii. Haida Gwaii. That's the name of the islands we live on. I don't use the white man's calling, most natives don't."

"Haida Gwaii it is." The man was definitely a little cracked. "Now, at the time I thought you were visiting me, you were actually in your cabin by Skidegate. Nice place by the way, very woodsy, and love the back-to-mother-earth look. Could use a few light bulbs though and some modern décor."

"Yes, I know you were there, I saw you in one of my travels. That's why I came here, thought I'd check out Ikea, some of those tiki-tiki wooden torches, or at least a few modern lamps would be a nice touch, could use them for tree shade or something." He laughed. "Smart marketing those Swedes, learned a few things since their ABBA days, which I thought was a definite throwback to the Viking era. But I guess there's hope for them yet."

As much grief as he'd caused her she couldn't stay mad at him. "Yes," she said. "It's a good thing Benny from that group wasn't Sven, then they'd have been called SAAB."

"Strict copyright infringement there, I think," he added and they both chuckled.

"And a bit of a dowdy name for a rock band," Carol added. "So how, then, did you know I was there on that bench?"

"Someone placed a call over the big cedar telephone and I was doing a little of that, how do you call it?"

"Woo-woo astral traveling? Call you? You don't have a phone out at your place."

"I don't need a phone, cell or otherwise. I use the best land line around. Well, it's really like an ancient version of the cell, only it never caught on. The whites couldn't figure out how to get the dial tone. And 'cause it's free to all they couldn't make any money out of it. World-wide coverage and no dropped calls. Get all of my urgent messages that way. That's how they contacted me."

"Who called? On what?" He was the most irritating man around. Carol wondered how sharp he really was and what kind of schooling he had. But then, was there a school for shamanism?

"It wasn't the Ghostbusters Gang. I was contacted through the earth, via the guardians within the Cathedral trees. I'm guessing you read about the Pauline legend regarding Cathedral Grove?"

She fell into that old gag, too. "Yes. But earth? Trees? You originally mentioned looking for the right tree. I spent countless hours trying to piece the murders together after we found his wife's body, and then the kid was stuffed in one of the old trees. From what I can piece together, the Bridges were on a picnic and decided to take a walk through Stanley Park. For whatever reason, the daughter ran off, spying something or playing hide and seek, who knows? But I never paid much attention to the area where they were murdered until I read a copy of Pauline's *Legends of Vancouver*." She paused as tourists jostled by, cameras clicking. "The mayor knew about the legends and about Cathedral Trail, he even had a copy of her book on his desk. Written in the twenties, one of the stories is about The Lure of Stanley Park. An evil sorceress is transformed by some native, godlike, mythical beings called the Sagalie Tyee into a white rock etched with black, like acid. They take a group of honest men, good souls, and appoint them guardians to watch over her. Pauline states they were transformed into the old Cathedral trees along the trail. The trees I found. Most of them toppled due to the fierce windstorms of a few years ago. Only no white rock etched with splotches of black was ever found, and I've walked that trail countless times."

"Right so far. Her stories were told to her by a native chief, Joe Capilano. So some weren't stories at all, but actual oral history of the area. Interesting stuff. I'll bet you'll never see this in an episode of CSI. Except maybe CSI. Haida Gwaii."

She laughed. "You really are a totally off-the-wall nut, unlike anybody I've ever met."

"Nuts, hey. Never cared for walnuts. I prefer peanuts or pistachios. Although, come to think of it, I do like a chew of pecans on occasion."

"As a matter of fact you're nuttier than anyone I've ever met. Going on the evidence, I should probably arrest you. How do I know you didn't stuff the body in that tree and send me there trying to cover yourself?"

"You could try, but old bonehead or whatever his name is, already tried that."

"It's Boswell."

"Yeah, that's what I said. Bonehead. He doesn't look at all the clues, but you are a little more observant. I'd keep a very close eye on him. He smells like a rotten egg, and remember, snakes eat their own kind. Besides, you won't arrest me, because you know I'm innocent."

"How do I truly know that?" *Boswell crooked? Could it be true?*

"Because when the coroner's office calls again, in addition to some unknown male DNA, there will also be unknown female DNA."

"What? How would you know that? You weren't here. Or were you? Did you see the murders taking place?"

266

"At least you can sleep knowing the visions of the young girl will wash out of your mind. I can travel through other dimensions and yes, I go to bed every night seeing that horror, over and over. There are some things that never leave your mind. As for the DNA, when the bodies are possessed, the more-awake soul's imprints will bleed through. Happens a lot, trust me." He smiled at her, the sadness evident in the depths of his eyes. Carol had seen enough horrifying experiences on the police force to know what he meant.

"You mentioned trees. I didn't really clue in until the story mentioned a couple vanished in Stanley Park after the incident with the witch woman. The man was found dead and the woman wandering around insane. I dug through old police records and discovered, sure enough, it was true. Back in the early nineteen hundreds a couple did vanish. And they were found in the vicinity of the Cathedral Trail. Since then, other incidents have been reported in Stanley Park, all coincidentally in the area around Cathedral Trail. If I'm to believe a witch is trapped in a rock there, then I would suspect she'd be awoken after the guardian trees were knocked down in the windstorm. So if I add one and one together you'd have me believing an old witch trapped in a rock woke up and did these people and the Bridges in? Only, as far as I know, Pauline's stories were supposed to be just that—stories written for the local paper and not true legends."

Charlie was quiet a moment, chewing her statements over as another bus unloaded a throng of vacationers. They stepped back to let the gawkers and picture takers shuffle by.

"Not much better than cattle, we are. How many of these actually stop to think about what they're seeing here and ask questions?" Charlie asked. "Is it enough sometimes, in one's consciousness, to simply marvel, or should one wonder 'why do you carve such entities in wood.' Let alone where these entities came from and how they evolved. Do Raven and Thunderbird exist or are they mere figments. Or, if they do exist, then the bigger question remains. Where are they today? A retired old-folks' home for last century's great deities?"

A young boy looked up at his grandparents. "If they carved their gods in the telephone poles why don't we carve Jesus and Santa Claus in ours?"

Charlie smirked. "Well, maybe some ain't so blind or naïve. You've got most of that story correct. Only she woke up alright, but someone else released her."

"Let me guess, that someone is also knocking off the Spawn."

"Yes, you *are* sharp. I presume you aren't talking the holier-than-thou kind, but the ones that can't afford mufflers and wear colours on their backs."

Carol stared at the boy, a grimacing Charlie, and at the multi-coloured totems. "Not many I guess, myself included when we first met, would believe this. I realize now what you were trying to do. Make me look at this case from a viewpoint I not only didn't believe in, but never even fathomed could exist."

"Ah," he replied. "I sensed there was hope within you, young grasshopper." He laughed. "Like the little boy asking a fresh question, it begs the subconscious to begin pondering along a whole new avenue of thought. Some of the greatest inventions or discoveries began with a single 'what if?' Open-minded curiosity of the innocents can often overpower the greatest imposed educations."

She shook her head. "And you've never gone to any colleges or universities."

He gave a gaze skyward. "Just naturally brilliant I suppose, although I've learned a lot from some of those daytime game shows and educational programs."

"You talked of portal trees. Legends spoke of trees with one stem and two main branches and if you stepped between them you could travel between dimensions. I tried it and all I managed to get was a mouthful of dirt. But, if I'm to believe the Pauline legend, suddenly the idea of travelling through trees doesn't seem so far-fetched. I did ask around and some of the park people say an old native fellow hobbling on a cane came to these totems set up for the tourists often. Investigating, I came across that portal tree behind those sacred totems in front of us. I reckon you travel back and forth on occasion, like on some mystical highway."

"Good work, newly made Detective. I knew you'd figure it out if you were worth the mettle of your badge, as opposed to metal, looking for little old me."

"The last few days before yesterday. Correct."

Charlie pondered, "I suppose you're wondering who the owner of the knife is?"

"You know? Why wouldn't you tell me?"

"At the time I only knew his face. Without evidence what would you tell the judge? Oh yes, Your Honour, a native shaman told me he had a vision after being called to astral travel through some portal trees? I think you'd be locked up quicker than a drunk driver in a Christmas parade."

"But, how could you not tell me earlier?" He drove her crazy, she wanted to grab his cane and whack him upside the head with it.

"You didn't ask and it never came up in conversation until now. You were too busy trying to put the pieces together and see things your way only. I was trying to get you to see it in a different light. Oh, and don't worry he's already well paid the price of his actions. The Lure of the others in Pauline's legends has seen to that. I think if you look for the sheath to the knife you'll find your man. Don't know his name, but he usually resides at the Royal Hotel pub in downtown Vancouver most nights. If you trust your senses and not your eyes you'll know him when you see him."

"Like the spell around the tree thing." She quivered.

Just then Carol's cell phone rang. Caller ID showed the morgue. "I have to take this. Won't be a mo'." She turned away and walked a few steps to answer the call.

"Sanchez?"

"Chess, it is me. We 'ave the DNA results. Unknown person, but the woman with the man, and with the woman, is the same woman. As I theenk!" Carol felt winded. Just as Charlie had told her.

"So the perp 'e is a she, we 'ave only woman DNA and one set of prints. Only one perp. Don't know who though, no hits in any databases."

"Damn. I was hoping it was a known felon."

"Oh," he said, "and the unknown male prints from the bikers murders 'ave just been confirmed. They needed two, three checks as they appear to be from a dead man. Larry Seigman, 'e a Eevil's Spawnmember."

"Hot damn!" *How the hell?* "Okay, thanks, Sanchez. That all?" she replied.

"You want some more mystery. Larry Seigman died last year. And I know, I remember doing the autopsy."

"Guess not. Thanks." Stunned she turned to talk to Charlie and take more of his gloating, stupid, smug grin, along with any I-told-you-so's.

Only he was gone. Carol spun around. There weren't many tourists milling around, but the shaman had vanished like a proverbial will o' the wisp. "Well, I guess this meeting is over."

* * *

His head still seethed with agony, it was hard to even think. It took days to pull himself back together after the host died at the clubhouse, like he'd been blown into a million particles of dust. So hard, Larry didn't know if he could stomach ever trying that again; he had to end this quick. It was said that in the name of vengeance many men had created great works of art, vileness, or scientific discovery. As sad as he was, he'd borne all of this to do only one thing. To make Ryley suffer and watch him die at his hands, and now this unexpected gift.

He hadn't been going to do this tonight, but the opportunity couldn't be resisted. His head still pounded furiously as Larry tried to walk as daintily as he could. It was murder even in the low heels. He cursed under his breath, swearing he'd never take over a woman's body again, but there didn't seem to be a better way to get into this room.

He didn't know how women did it. He rustled his shoulders back and forth, trying to adjust the bra just right, only there was no "just right." Especially when the bra was trying to hold up two melons. He tugged at the straps. "Hate this thing."

By fluke, he'd discovered his current host in the bar attending a bachelorette party. The same one that had given him that "come-on" smile at the nurse's desk. Larry couldn't believe his luck; thought God, or maybe the devil, was smiling on him. Having taken her over easily, he'd walked the eight blocks to her apartment and changed into scrubs. The girls at the nurse's station didn't bat an eye as she walked purposefully up to the cop on duty.

Timing would be of the essence. He'd gleaned enough from this lady's mind to know when visiting hours ended and the shift changed, along with the fact that after visiting hours, luckily, only one cop remained guarding the kid.

He tried to look frantic. "Just got a call. Your replacement is on the way up, but there's a disturbance in Emergency, some druggie freaking out, threatening the nurses. They need you down there right away."

The cop jumped up, typical macho male type. "Hurry! I'll watch until the cover arrives. Take the stairs, they'll put you right in back of the ER."

He glanced at the name tag ID, not failing, of course, to take in the mound it was perched on. "Great, some action. Can't stand sitting around babysitting all night." He sneered and sped off.

Larry knew he had maybe ten minutes before they noticed, or the night shift arrived. The stairs would take the officer nowhere near the ER.

Larry walked into the room. The child lay there sleeping, eyelids fluttering. He was still wrapped up in bandages, one arm in a sling, and his legs held in traction. "A kid! He's just a kid. But he's Ryley's." Larry put the knife he'd picked up from the host's kitchen to the defenceless kid's throat. The woman inside twitched. She aided the sick, not kill people. It would go against everything she believed in. Larry's hand quivered.

At the touch of cold metal, the child's eyes opened. He was groggy, probably on morphine to fight off the pain. Blue eyes, like Larry's son, Brandon's, stared back. Fear flared in the boy's eyes, perhaps the same look Brandon had before they took his life. His hand shook as another tremor went through him and his head throbbed from pain as much as fear.

He hesitated for just a split second staring into the depths of those innocent eyes. "Never hesitate." Only he couldn't do it.

Damn, he'd lost it. He couldn't do it. This was only a helpless child, an innocent pawn caught between him and Ryley. But he had to leave a message for Ryley. Larry whipped down the covers and pulled a pen from his pocket.

"Don't move or yell or I'll slit your throat." He put his hand over the kid's mouth. In small letters he carefully etched his initials into the kid's chest with the pen.

A shuffle in the hallway, someone might be coming. He had to go.

Done, he put away the pen and left the knife on the kid's chest. A sign for Ryley that his most precious gift was not safe. He was about to tape the kid's mouth shut before leaving when the kid spoke.

"You're a bad person. You won't get away with this. I'll tell my dad. He'll get even with you," the kid sputtered. "He'll make you pay, lady."

Larry stopped and stared at the child. Cruelty shone in the child's eyes, the same look he'd seen so often in the father's eyes when the man was ordering Larry to hurt someone. No empathy, no mercy, like Ryley had shown his own family, his kids. The boy was so obviously Ryley's son, and he would grow up to be another like him. You couldn't beat bad genes. He taped his mouth shut and picked up the knife.

The heart monitor flat-lined as Larry left the room.

Chapter Sixteen

It was late in the night when The Lure parked at the very edge of the deserted parking lot next to the totems in Stanley Park. She pulled Dennis' body from the back of the car and dragged him in front of the idling vehicle. Working fast, she ran a thin roll of thread back toward the car.

The Sagalie Tyee were nearby and already beginning to detect her presence. They would be coming. She arranged herself and Dennis in front of the car, making it look like he attacked her, his cold hands around her throat. She stilled her breathing to an almost imperceptible level and waited for nearly half an hour before footsteps sounded on the pavement. The mouse had taken the bait.

Four identical men in black walked up to the pair on the ground. They removed their sunglasses in unison. "Very strong energy." "It is her."

"Alive still, unconscious?" they said one after another.

They stood in front of the bodies and one bent over. "Cold. The male is deceased. The Lure herself, barely alive. We must move quickly. Yes, quickly. Remove her soul from this innocent. Yes, remove."

One reached down to touch the woman's forehead. Her eyes flashed open.

"You boys really are predictable."

She yanked on the sewing thread attached to her finger. Blinding light flooded the night as the high beams came to life. The Lure rolled across the parking lot and scrambled to her feet, jumping behind the wheel of the car. She threw it into gear and punched the gas pedal. Four bodies went sailing in all directions.

Working quickly The Lure grabbed a roll of grey tape and ran from the car. "I learned some interesting things on the internet the other night. In yoga you can slow down your heartbeat and appear to be in a coma like state, nearly dead.

"What you fellas fail to realize yet, is that in assuming human form, you attain certain weaknesses also. Oh yes, I know you're gods and will be able to heal yourselves, given the time. Only, you see, these times are different, no one here believes in you anymore. Most of the people who feared you are gone. Most of your powers are gone or greatly reduced." She quickly taped their mouths and wrapped their hands behind their backs as well. The Lure walked back to Dennis' dead body and dragged it into the bushes. She returned to the helpless beings.

"So simple spells may work, like the one I placed on this area of un-changing form, but more complex ones are powerless." Blood poured from their wounds, one moaned. "You may find it a little hard to remove human form in this dimension. Now, being natural gods, you've complete control over natural objects. Something I've learned though is that many objects in these times aren't natural. Like this slick little invention, duct tape. Made from totally unnatural substances. I suppose I should give you boys some credit, I figure in time, maybe a few hundred years, you'll be able to over-come these limitations. But then again, maybe not."

Rage flared in their eyes, they were not used to being manhandled in such a fashion. "Almost like being violated, isn't it? Now, let's see." She gazed at one in particular. "You are the power of the eastern oceans, shining heavens, blah, blah, blah. So you are even more powerless on land than the others." She dragged him over to a large plastic garbage can and stuffed him into it.

"By my recollections, the Vancouver disposal team will be here in about three hours. It's amazing what the internet will teach you. Oh, I forgot. You guys don't know how to read English. Darn shame. A spell of displacement, much like the one you guys put me under, and no one will know you're here. Now, you two boys." She taped their eyes. "Are rather useless in the water without junior over there. So

I figure a boat ride might be in order. But first we take care of junior."

She drove up the road, took the last one and stuffed him into a tree. The witch stood back and waved her hands. "The power of the shining heavens, dude, won't do much good inside a tree. You'll spend eternity much like I did, blinking in the dark. On the other hand, wood lice can be very chatty. Oh, okay. I lie. The duct tape has a lifespan of only a few thousand years. I can understand why the environmentalists are up in arms. Never get rid of the stuff. But I'm sure by then they'll have thought of something even better."

The Lure drove to the water's edge, near Stanley Park Marina. "Now I've figured out this much, your powers derive from being together. You know, the old Eco-term, everything is connected. Like I said earlier you two land-based boys are powerless in water. So I think a little swim will do you some good. Haven't quite figured out if you can drown, but let's test that theory shall we?"

She placed another spell on the car. Grabbing a large rock The Lure depressed the gas pedal and wedged it on. As the engine screamed she slammed the car into gear. "Hope the fishing is good." The Lure watched the car slam into a wooden fence and arc across the water. A minute later it vanished into the dark water. "That was way too easy. I've got to get back, but I think I've still time for one last dance. And who knows, maybe even a little appetizer after a rather industrious night's work." She returned to Dennis and reached into his pocket and pulled out the dead man's cell phone and rang for a taxi. "Rather amazing culture established in such a short time. I think I'm going to enjoy it here.

"See ya lover." She kissed his dead lips. "Hate to eat and run, but gotta go." She tossed the phone into the water as a yellow cab pulled up moments later.

* * *

Carol staggered into the hospital room. Midnight calls were never to her liking, especially when Big Dan was on the other end of the phone. "Get your ass down to St. Mary's A-fucking-SAP, and don't bother to grab a coffee this time." The bullhorn voice almost shattered her ear drums.

Whatever had happened was bad and she feared the worst as she staggered into

Ryley's son's hospital room. The bed was drenched in blood. "Oh shit."

A little boy's dead eyes stared up at her from above the tape over in his mouth. This was not going to be a good night.

"Jantzen reported being relieved by a nurse, Cindy Dipetro, with a story of a disturbance in the ER. Cindy works on this ward, occasionally on the evening shift, so he had no reason to suspect anything was wrong. We've already arrested her on suspicion. The problem is that at the time she was out at a stagette party at a local pub and…"

"Let me guess, O'Shanahan's. She blanked out, swears she doesn't remember anything."

Dan's eyes widened. "Yes. How'd you know?"

"Frigging story is getting old. Crap. Can't tell you here. In your office."

One of the CSI's bent over to examine the boy's cold body. "He died in seconds, sliced across the jugular. She knew where to cut him to insure exsanguination in a very short time. But look at this. Appears to be letters inked on his chest. *LS*. Found a knife, too. Blood, probably the boy's, and prints. We need to run them."

This was getting too much. "I need to talk to Ben again, and probably Charlie,"

Carol blurted out as Boswell entered the room. He took one look and did a U-turn.

"Forgot something, need to make a call, be right back," he blurted out.

"Ben Carlton? That slimy reporter?" Dan bristled.

Carol motioned to Dan after Boswell exited. They moved to a quiet part of the room.

"I learned something from our shaman earlier today. I've great reason to believe Boswell is in someone's pocket. No evidence yet, but possibly it's Ryley.

We need to keep an eye on him."

Big Dan's hands crunched into fists. "I hate bad cops above everything else, especially under my jurisdiction."

She couldn't tell him yet that she was dating Ben. "I've interviewed Ben Carlton, and as crazy as this sounds, he's also working on a story involving a Larry Siegman, who died last year quite violently. He thinks his ghost has returned to get his revenge on Ryley."

"Dead men don't walk," Dan blurted out. "But it may explain why our native friend contacted you." He glared hard at her. "May also explain why Boswell let him go."

"Well, this one does. Yes, might explain why a shaman is involved." She didn't want to reveal the other stuff she'd learned about Charlie yet. "I need to take off and speak to both." Carol stared at Dan. She could tell he was having a hard time wrapping his head around this information.

"I don't believe a word yet of this paranormal crap. But I trust you. Go, we need to move fast. I'll keep an eye on Boswell, and keep this latest development from the press. If this is true, how do you catch a ghost? And who's he going after next? Ryley himself?"

"Most likely."

"That wouldn't create any sweat on my ass." Dan moved to leave the room. "And Carol, be damn careful. I don't know how Ryley is going to react, but it won't be nice."

Her phone rang. It was Sanchez.

"I 'ave a third body, came in last night, ' 'e appears to have died from orgasms like the other two."

"Not good at all." The night was just getting better. "Was just about to call you, actually. Have you told Big Dan yet about the prints found at the dead bikers' scenes?" Carol paused, listening to his response. "Okay. Call Dan now, let him know about the Larry prints. And tell him Carol said 'I told you so.' Thanks"

As soon as she hung up, Carol's cell rang again. Without checking caller ID she answered the call, expecting Ben or forensics again, anyone but...

"They won't let me in to visit my son. There are cops all over the place. What the fuck is going on. Is he okay?"

Aw, crap. Carol hesitated, and lied. "Ah, yeah, he's good."

"Let me talk to him. Now!"

"I can't, not yet. Ryley, who's Larry Siegman?"

Stunned silence. She was expecting him to ask how she knew the name, but Ryley went straight to the point. "Larry Siegman. Was my right-hand man. I say was, because he fucked me over royally. He died in a motorcycle accident last year. Why?"

Carol took a deep breath, "I'm sorry, but your son is dead. Larry's initials are carved on his chest." She never got a chance to say anything else. "Bitch! You fucking betrayed me." Carol's cell went dead.

"Great. From bad to worse to absolute shithole."

* * *

Across town, in a different hideaway, Ryley threw his phone across the room and began tossing chairs and anything else he could throw. His two men stepped outside and grabbed a smoke as the trailer exploded from within for the next few minutes. Ryley screamed his rage into the emptiness of the mobile home.

"Get the fuck in here," he yelled, flinging open the door. The two burly guards glanced at each other, and reluctantly entered his hell. Spit rolled down his lip, matching the moisture seething in his eyes. Lines of disturbed coke scored the table.

"I've just lost the last thing in this world that means a fucking thing to me and someone is going to pay."

* * *

A shadow parted the darkness in the midst of the Stanley Park totems. It walked up to the prone body lying in the bushes. "Up to her old tricks again, I fear. Sorry, nothing I can do for you. May your soul be at rest." He reached down and closed the man's haunted eyes. Charlie looked around the area; the rustle of a large plastic garbage bin caught his attention.

The old shaman sauntered up. "Didn't I tell you boys too much has changed since you were here last? But no, you wouldn't listen." He lifted the lid to the can and tipped it over. "They say even gods can die. Well this is your lucky day, oh 'I am of the endless sea.'"

He pulled the tape free from the hands and mouth of the Sagalie. The being didn't wince. "That is what the cowboys used to call an ambush. She's quite clever you know. We'll go get the 'power of the shining heavens' dude next, before the squirrels take a liking to him, or bang nuts off his forehead for upsetting their winter storage. You're not much of a talkative bunch when you're alone, are you?" The godlike being merely stared at the ground as they walked.

"Hey, cheer up, I've had my ass kicked before, it happens to all of us. Obviously never to you lot, though. Don't tell me I'm going to have to send you guys to professional counseling. Let's see. I look in the yellow pages under butt-whipped gods, once powerful last century, now rudely humbled," Charlie blathered on as he walked up to the tree containing the second Tyee. "Hey, lighten up. How's about a knock-knock joke?" The omniscient being looked at him blankly.

"See, there is something you don't know about. Man, you guys need to read the daily papers and try to catch up to the times. Okay. 'Knock, knock.' You respond with 'who's there.'" The god glared.

"Shaman," Charlie supplied the response.

Silence.

"Now you're supposed to say, 'shaman who?' No wonder people have forgotten about you boys, can't keep up to the times. The punchline is 'shaman you, for letting your godhood get in the way of your brain cells and letting that witch outsmart you.' Okay, not in a humorous state of mind, are you. Come on, tweeedle dee, let's find tweeedle dumb, dumber, and dumbest and figure out what to do next."

The 'power of the shining heavens' god followed, his head hung low. "Hey, I thought the joke was funny. Gods! Gotta love 'em."

* * *

Looking for an earthbound angel? Meet me in the clouds of O'Shanahan's, Saturday night.

When she got to work the hand-scrawled note was on her desk. It could only have been from Charlie.

"Cryptic man, cryptic notes," she muttered. She picked up the phone and called Ben. Carol hadn't talked to him since the night they slept together, although she had sent him a couple of texts apologizing for the lack of contact. He'd left a couple of text messages on her phone. She felt bad about running out on him that morning, said so in her reply.

Ben picked up her text and called right away. "Interested in going to O'Shanahan's tomorrow night? We could talk some more there about both of our cases. You were right, they are connected, and not only that but my mad shaman friend left me a bizarre note, something about clouds. Not sure what he means."

Ben laughed. "It means you've never gone to O'Shanahan's on a Saturday night and been Thunderstruck, that's what it means."

"No, never. In fact I can't remember the last time I went to a nightclub, at least to have fun and dance, instead of arresting drunks or breaking up fights. I guess I live a rather deprived life."

"Well, maybe we can enrich it then. See you at six o'clock. We'll do dinner and head over there after that."

She wanted to tell him about Ryley and his son, but that would be a strict betrayal of police confidence.

"Sounds good. Should I bring rain gear?"

Ben laughed. "No umbrellas allowed indoors. Bad luck." Carol could imagine him wagging his finger at her. "Just bring yourself and a smile. But I'll bring a raincoat, just in case this leads to a repeat of the other night and some more extreme chess playing."

Carol smiled as she hung up the phone. The big question was… What to wear?

* * *

"We are olden."

"Out of date."

"Ancient beings."

"From ancient times," the four Sagalie Tyee said. They stood there, heads bowed. Charlie thanked his big-foot guardian spirit for swimming down to break the spell and tear open the doors of the car to free the two earthbound gods. While the big guys smelled bad, didn't swim much, abhorred the idea of soap, and their idea of personal deodorant was to wipe pesky muskrats under each armpit every morning, they were known to be good swimmers and could hold their breath for extraordinary lengths of time.

Charlie tried to stay upwind of the large animal before he departed. "Man, wet, sweaty dogs ain't got anything on you guys. Wow, now I know what that new perfume called 'Sour Smelt' would be like. Definitely not a big seller."

Charlie leaned on his cane, staring at the four black-clad, melancholy gods. Two dripped water and the others stood with their sunglasses askew on their noses. One brushed maggots off him and the other removed chocolate-bar wrappers and sticky Popsicle sticks from his black coat.

"Hey guys, come on now, it ain't so bad. I saved your asses. If it wasn't for me you'd either be fish food, wood lice dessert, or land-fill fodder."

"Yes, he saved us."

"We owe you a favour."

"A debt of gratitude."

"A thanks," they echoed together, nodding morosely in agreement, nowhere near as cocky as the first time they'd met Charlie.

Then the four said at once, "We must depart."

"Return to our realm."

"Reside in the past."

"Leave. These times, not for us."

"Hang on a minute, boys. I think it's time to dust off the crumpled angel wings, give the haloes a tilt, and put on your big-god pants and get back in the fight. Are you going to leave this realm as mice or as true gods? You know, with divine dignity like in the old days. Lay down some earth-shaking lightning bolts and hallowed art thou crap. Put a whole lot of fear into the humble masses of believers."

They stood there silent, as if unsure what he meant.

"Yes, get even. A score to settle." They nodded to each other.

Charlie breathed a sigh of relief, not sure how he would have proceeded if they'd refused to stay. How would he have managed to rebuild the confidence of four elemental god beings. "Great! How about we think about this over another round of Indian Pale Ale before you go. Remember that bar near here with the most unique atmosphere?"

They nodded in unison and followed him as he headed for O'Shanahan's.

"For a moment I thought I'd have to take you guys to the Big-Wannabe-Kahuna-Gods-Counseling Classes. Ever get Thunderstruck?"

Chapter Seventeen

"Look, I'm truly sorry about the other morning when I took off on you," Carol said, as Bryan Adams' *Summer of '69* pounded over the speakers in the background. The bar was packed. Waitresses, neon-aglow drink trays held high, buzzed the crowd. Lights flickered and pulsed. Carol and Ben were seated on high stools behind the railing surrounding the sunken dance floor, drinks balanced precariously on the small shelf in front of them. They were close enough for Ben to have his arm around her shoulders.

"This case has blown more than one of my brain cells, not to mention the fact I've stared death in the face on too many occasions." Carol had told Ben earlier about the tree with the body, Larry's prints all over the bikers' bodies, being kidnapped by Ryley, wanting to quit, and the crazy shaman. Perhaps she shouldn't break police confidences, but right now Carol needed help from someone who believed in her to make sense of this craziness.

Ben reciprocated by telling her of his diminishing nightmares of Larry, now virtually gone. What he knew of O'Shanahan's from his research at the city archives and at the bar, the experience of Larry possessing him.

"You're kidding me. You're telling me this, this, funnel affair just over the dance floor is some kind of strange dimensional vortex?"

He nodded as the music stopped, and the lights held steady for a few moments. People slowly exited the dance floor.

"It supposedly allows ghosts, spirits, whatever, to enter bodies? When they've had too much to drink? I really should have joined the navy." Yet, the evidence was compelling. She'd viewed numerous security videos from the establishment. They did substantiate that many times people staggered into the washrooms and walked out seeming virtually sober again. Many people even seemed to have different postures. It still didn't really answer who killed the mayor and his family.

Larry in another body? Perhaps Ben's?

Where was Charlie?

"The moment we've been waiting for folks. Midnight. When O'Shanahan's Bar and Grill's Saturday Night proudly declares 'you've been Thunderstruck.'"

Ben hugged her as the empty dance floor began to fill with smoke. He kissed her on the lips, whispering in her ear. "Looks like Charlie stood you up. So why don't we get Thunderstruck and head off to my place for another rematch."

He'd also told her about the other night here when he'd been observing the body snatching. So far they'd been here nearly three hours and hadn't noticed anything unusual. "Perhaps too early," Ben remarked. "Like in the movies, everything happens in the witching hour." They laughed together.

A dozen smoke machines continued wafting the thick, waxy smoke into the air. Overhead lights dimmed, and in the quiet a rumble echoed, then another and another, growing in intensity. Thunder grumbled and, as people began to fill the dance floor, lost in the fog, a crack of lightning shook the building and the overhead lights flickered in response. The bass was cranked right up and each rumble of thunder vibrated on the floating dance floor.

Carol hurried, with Ben pulling her, onto the smoke-filled floor before it became too crowded. If she was ever going to be caught in the middle of the brewing fury of a thunderstorm without getting wet, this was it.

Mixed in with the thunderclaps, the incessant tap of drumstick over cymbal began. Increasing in volume like hail pelting down over a tin roof as the steel guitars of AC/DC began to cut in. The nah, nah, nahs at the beginning of their song, *Thunderstruck,* took over.

"Why did he want to make sure I was here? Can't see Charlie hanging out here, not his kind of place."

As if answering the devil's own questions, a figure wavered in the mists. Carol blinked and blinked again, reminded of the image of the shaman disappearing into the mists when they first met.

Charlie limped toward her, dressed in his usual gear. He tried to pretend he was dancing, but gave up. "Not much for rock music. Although many of my people like the beat of AC/DC I think it is very much like the rhythm of pow-wow music. Got that warrior's beat, if you know what I mean." He nodded his head in time to the nah, nah, nahs, leaning on his cane.

Just then someone dancing moved over and slid right through him.

"Did I just see that? What? How is this possible?" Ben gasped. "Maybe they mix a little marijuana into the smoke."

"Oh, another non-believer. I love it." Charlie smirked.

Carol watched as several dancers began to waver. Thin lines of energy reached out from the dark recesses of the turret overhead, easily mistaken in the spotlights blinking around the turret. The lines pulled themselves into bodies. Some continued dancing in a zombie-like state; others turned and walked off the dance floor.

As they moved, the image of someone else overlapping the dancers moved with them for a moment before vanishing.

"This is why you asked me here, isn't it."

"Just watch. I figure, detective, you only work on facts and evidence. If I am to convince you of who really killed Cole Bridge and his family you need to see proof, and this is about the only way of showing it to you. By the way, you're a pretty good dancer."

"Thanks. Can't say the same for you."

Charlie smiled. "We all have our strengths. I came here to introduce you to someone."

"I can't stay this way long." A voice boomed in Carol's ears.

The wavering image of a large bearded man stared at her through the mists. He had the rough, hard look of a biker, leathered cheeks, tattoos on his arms, face full of light scars showing he'd been in many a fight. Life on that hard face, she recognized, hadn't come easy. The dead man walking from the police photos in the files, and the revelations of the prints found by Sanchez.

"Larry Seigman?"

"Yes. Hard to stay in focus, I need another body. But this thick fog lets you see me."

"But, you're dead."

"Should be, but I've one last thing to do before I can go."

Carol stared into his face. The cold, calculating darkness in his eyes, no light, no emotion. No heart. When he was alive this wasn't a man you'd want to cross.

"I've endured a lot to return. I'm only here for one thing before I can rest.

Revenge on Ryley for what he has done to me and my family."

Carol searched in those dark eyes for some spark, some sign of hope. But only found more darkness, despair, and anger. "You've no heart." She'd read the police reports about what happened to him and his family. Mown down minutes after being released from months of hospital care, the investigation, oddly enough headed by Boswell, had deemed his death accidental. She needed to talk to Boswell; Charlie was right.

"Used to. He took it away. Now all I have is the blackness to keep me going. That and The Code."

"The Code?"

"The Devil's Spawn' Code. Vengeance must be sought on all who betray a member.

No quarter given, none taken. That is the only thing that's kept me going and brought me back."

"You're using his hatred to come back and kill him."

A cold smile crept across Larry's face. "That's all I have left, it got me to this place." He tightened his eyes in pain. "Whatever it takes, I will get my due revenge."

Carol shivered; the cold dead smile said it all. He would do whatever it took. He had cheated death so far to exact his revenge and lost all of his humanity in the process. Although being a biker, and one of Ryley's main enforcers may have meant he didn't have much to start with. More than likely he'd done his fair share of dirty work.

Yet did it really matter? He'd already lost everything he'd loved on this world, there was nothing left to give. He was beyond caring and the price didn't matter, not when vengeance was all that was left to drive his soul. Nothing else.

He clenched his lips in pain again. "I must go now." His image wavered and vanished as the mists began to dissipate.

"My, what a tasty morsel on my doorstep. Do come in, said the spider to the fly." An older woman's voice made Carol turn. It was the hag watching her through the mist, watching her, just like the last time she was here. The same one from the photos. "Or maybe I should thank our shamanistic friend and say 'thanks, don't mind if I do enter.' "

* * *

Larry watched the scene play out. He should interfere in what The Lure was doing, but he had other business and he'd spied Ryley entering through the side door minutes ago.

The male he'd been in once already, a familiar. In the funnel it was easier to enter again. He closed his eyes.

* * *

Carol jolted, feeling herself filling up as mist seeped into her body. Memories, vile memories, erupted like fiery blossoms raging through her mind. Trapped in rock, like being gagged. Couldn't speak, no spells to be forged. Not breathing, just gagging on granite. The rage, anger seething. Not being able to yell, scream, or even cry in pity.

"Yes, my life that once was. But no longer, darling. It's not that I want to be free. Oh, no. I want to be you." She leered and grabbed Carol by the arm. The talon like fingers dug in, drawing blood.

"Carol, run! It's a trap," Charlie warned, swatting The Lure with his cane. Mist swirled about. He pushed Carol across the dance floor.

"Vile shaman," she seethed, "you I'll deal with later." She waved her hand and the shaman stopped, frozen.

"Catch me if you can," he taunted, shaking free of her spell and swirling into the mist, up into the funnel of the turret. Carol and Ben darted off the dance floor.

The Lure screamed. Without a body she couldn't leave the funnel.

* * *

Many patrons turned to study the commotion. AC/DC still thumped away as they made their way to the exit. "Hurry, we need to get out of here. She'll find another body and follow us." Ben yanked at Carol.

"I think I should go back and help him somehow," Carol said, looking across the sea of bodies in the bar. The Lure had been waiting here, and the shaman had led her to the witch. Was this another one of Charlie's stupid lessons about the other side?

She caught the sight of several bikers sitting at a table, including Ryley, gesturing at her. She thought he'd be hiding out. She didn't need the din of the music to know he was yelling at his cronies to bring her to him. The memory of his hands against her breasts and his man's background snickering. "Oh crap. I've got more trouble brewing. We need to move, and quick. I didn't expect to see him here."

Ben glared at the burly bikers thrusting bodies aside none too gently as they approached. "Get in my car. We'll outrun them."

* * *

"Damn! They escaped." The Lure glared at the bikers scrambling through the crowded bar as Ben and Carol ran outside. "Can't trust men to get your business done."

She stared up the swirling lights of the funnel as she licked Carol's blood off her fingertips. "Delicious! But there's someone I need to deal with first, someone who's interfered once too often." She swirled up into the lights. "You, darling shaman, are next."

* * *

Minutes later they were burning up the Stanley Park causeway, the road traffic was light in the midnight hour. "I think we gave them the slip." Ben glanced in his rear-view mirror.

Carol, not used to, or liking, that she was a passenger, stared into her side mirror. The old hag had only scratched her. She held her arm where the blood flow had nearly stopped. Her head was foggy, her thoughts cloudy, it was hard to think clearly and focus. Maybe it was just the rush of alcohol in the fresh air, or perhaps she'd drugged her.

Just as they were entering the Lions Gate Bridge, Carol looked up and spotted a black GM van behind them. Another appeared farther back, accelerating through traffic toward them. "Don't count yourself lucky just yet. We've a problem. I think we're being followed."

"Damn." Ben blurted out, "126 GRT," as one of the vans roared towards them.

Carol squinted. "Yes. How did you know?"

"It's Ryley's van, I've seen that plate in every nightmare I've had since the night I visited O'Shanahan's. Oh God, I've lived and died this scene over and over." The car began to slow down as Ben eased off the gas, a blank look stealing across his face.

Carol grabbed the steering wheel, adrenaline sobering her up in a hurry. She slapped his face. "Snap the fuck out of it. We're not going to die, not here."

The nearest van pulled alongside to their left, the other was still behind them. The one next to them began to edge in, shoving them closer and closer to the guardrail. Sparks exploded as metal buckled. The van moved away for a second, before trying to come back at them again.

"My beautiful car!" Ben wailed. Carol yelled, "When I say, hit it. Throw this thing into reverse, crank the wheel left and punch it."

The van swerved over again. Carol grabbed the emergency brake and yanked it up. Back wheels screamed as they locked up. The smell of burning rubber filled the car as Ben completed the Bond turn. "Hit it." Ben yanked on the steering wheel and hammered the transmission into reverse before he nailed the gas pedal to the floor. The tires squealed in protest, shooting out clouds of acrid, black smoke. They swung around, the front of the car sweeping into the side of the rear van, shoving it over. The van veered to the right, snapped the guardrail, and catapulted off the bridge.

Neither heard the crash of water below as Carol released the brake. Ben shifted the transmission into forward, punched the throttle. As the BMW shot forward Ben swerved over into the right lane of traffic and kept the throttle gunned as the other van made its own Bond turn. Tires screeched in a haze of black smoke as it spun around, slammed into another car, and gave chase.

"Where to?" Carol asked.

"Stanley Park. This has to end there."

A muscle in his jaw jumped. She wanted to say it was a bad idea, at the same time wondering what made Ben think it should end at the totems. The thought was lost in the roar of his engine as he floored the BMW and she grabbed at the dash.

She'd never seen him so intense. Was this how the reporter responded to stress?

* * *

Charlie waited, letting The Lure take the bait. Her spell had left a residue, and he knew that she could follow him.

"Now, shaman man, its showdown time, like they say here, and there will be no interference from anyone else, especially not your helpers." She snapped her fingers and transported them to a realm he didn't recognize. He reached for his pouch and cane and realized they were gone. His power animals couldn't interfere here in this shadow realm. That put a new, dangerous slant on things. This was her realm, her rules.

"Now, my darling, playtime." With another click he found himself floating in the clouds. Wind currents held him aloft on wide outstretched wings. The raptor's hunger filling him with the need to hunt. He'd been transformed into the guise of a golden eagle. His eyes that could spot a mouse scurrying through a field nearly a mile away, were rendered useless here in the shapeless clouds. Cool, misty air wisped by, water droplets unborn, ready to become rain.

The flutter of feathers, a screech, startled him. Her white head veered by, cunning and hunger in her yellow eyes. Talons raked him, and then she was gone. Blood sprayed from him, cold air seared at his side, it wasn't a mortal blow, but it could easily have been.

He was at her mercy, and she was toying with her food, like a cat, before she ended it. Wanting to torture him. Well, two could play that game.

Charlie tucked in his wings and hurtled earthward. A cry of rage came from above him and the witch did likewise. Talons extended, she caught up to him in a flash. Those razor-sharp claws held his soul, his flesh glinting off their already-red edges.

"You cannot outrun me here. You are mine."

She was right, here she was the larger of the two birds, and he had no chance. Charlie closed his eyes as her claws closed on his body. Sky and cloud transformed into a field of clover and forest. Ears aflutter, he listened to the rustle of branches and filled his nose with the scent of another of his kind. He quelled the urge to howl to his lover, the moon, as a wolfen shape stole through the brush. Each creature had its own strengths and weaknesses. She'd exploit those, as the snarl warned him, before The Lure lunged toward him.

Angry yowls rent the air as they tumbled into each other. Claws raked at him.

"You cannot get away," she spoke in his head.

She was powerful, more than he cared to admit, and darkness claimed him.

294

* * *

As they crossed the end of the park and the Georgia Street viaduct, the concrete city stared back. Ben cranked the steering wheel to the right. Rubber screeched as they tore down Chilco Street, passing in front of the former millionaire residence of some Hong Kong businessman she couldn't remember and zipped along the rich-yuppie neighborhood at the edge of Stanley Park.

She knew the reporter was right. This would bring her back to Charlie, and this time Carol knew he needed her help.

Ben drove on, like a man possessed.

"You okay?" Carol asked him. The man was quiet, driving with the confidence of a Formula One racer.

A black van blasted around a corner behind them. One of them was still on their tail.

"Fine." He glanced at her, his voice growing deeper. The smile was sincere, but the look in his eyes was haunting.

"Ben, you sure you're okay?"

Another black van careered around the corner in front of them and skidded sideways, blocking the street. Ryley sat smiling behind the wheel, headset in his ear.

"Shit! They must have kept in contact via cell phone."

Ben cranked the Beamer over, lifting the two wheels on Carol's side nearly off the ground. They crashed into Ryley as the first van slammed into the rear, spitting the car forward like a squashed watermelon seed.

Brush swatted past the doors, branches snapped as they passed. Ben punched the throttle and smashed his way into the forest of Stanley Park, dodging trees. Finally, the car slammed into a nursery log that nature had lain down centuries earlier. The moss that blanketed its flanks, and the several other trees that grew up in a straight procession along it, shook violent-ly. The airbags exploded while rotten wood shot skyward. The car crumpled into it, lifted up momentarily, and thudded back to earth.

* * *

Ben's head slammed against the side window, blackness haunting his vision momentarily as he unbuckled the seatbelt. He reached over a barely conscious Carol, blood covering her face from a head wound. Her eyelids fluttered.

He sent a solid right crashing into her jaw and pulled her gun free. Her body went limp.

"Like I said earlier, this ends. Here and now."

Chapter Eighteen

Wind groaned over the frozen desolation of the landscape. Ice snapped in brittle protest to the cold. Moribund icicles hung from every surface, painted in varying shades of white. The thick pad of his paws thumped on the hard-packed snow, the sound echoing through the frozen sheet covering the ocean below. He sniffed, his white fur blending into the sheer lack of any colour. Only unending ashen haze hung over everything.

Charlie shivered, his breath a mist, his side leaking redness onto the snow. Perhaps, this was not such a good idea. The witch would spot the colour and smell the blood with her sharp ursine nose. That was where it would end. She had fed off his life-force and the others she had killed, feeding to get stronger in order to return. He was only a distraction. How could he defeat her?

His massive bulk belied the silence of his passage, until the crack of ice shattered the misty air, and The Lure lumbered toward him. She was a fast learner, but so was he. He shifted again as she leapt onto him and they fell through the ice.

* * *

Carol cried out, trying to find something to grasp as she fell through the blackness. She tumbled in fear that any second she'd slam into a barrier, or worse, keep falling forever. A sharp cry echoed from somewhere.

"No," she sobbed. The searing cry of a great bird of prey echoed again, closer. The heavy beat of wings came closer. The approach was slow and methodical. Terrified, she instinctively closed her eyes. The sharp claws latched onto her jacket, and the tumbling stopped. The eagle's cry resonated, lifting her effortlessly with the heavy swish of strong wings.

Carol opened her eyes and squinted into the inky blackness but was unable to see her captor. The firm grip of the naked claws and the warmth of blood running down her back confirmed she was helpless prey. The wounds stung in the cool air.

The thump of tireless wings carried her through the ebony sky. After what seemed like hours of hanging like a limp rag doll, Carol caught sight of a spot of light in the distance. The spirit bird was heading for its nest. She hoped the huge bird didn't intend to feed her to its young. She struggled to figure out what was happening but could only vaguely remember Ben slugging her. Why the hell would he do that?

The slow thump of wings continued carrying her toward the speck of light. Nothing made any sense.

In an instant, the spot of light exploded, as if bursting through a screen into another world edging this obsidian one. The great bird of prey cried out, releasing Carol. She tumbled onto a rocky sand beach.

The massive bald eagle turned effortlessly in the air, thumping its wings back toward the edge of darkness. Every so often, its cry rang out, growing fainter as it moved farther away. But remained to watch over Carol.

Salt stung her nostrils, surf crashed onto the sand. She surveyed the vaguely familiar, narrow spit of beach vanishing into the grip of the ocean's tides.

"Where am I? What's going on here?"

A voice came from the depths of the sea. At the edge of the spit where it disappeared into the sea, a figure emerged. "This is the place you called me to, I have returned you."

Carol looked closer. Each step the figure took decreased its distance by a third until it stood before her.

"Mother?" Stupidity took her breath. What the hell was going on?

"Yes, and I am still dead, at least to your world. But this, while it looks like your world, is not." She held out her arms. "My daughter."

Carol cried and took her mother in her arms. It was really her; she remembered the smell of her mother. The softness as she held her as a youngster.

Carol sobbed uncontrollably. "I don't understand."

"You called my spirit from the place called Rosespit, and now you are travelling in other realms, I have called yours here. Your guardian pulled you from the path of the portals and brought you to me," she said, hugging her daughter. "I never really had a chance to say I love you before leaving your realm. You look different, happier, and content. It has been how long?"

"I am, and it has been too long. Only why now, I don't know how to travel through a portal? The only portal I tried going through was the shaman's portal tree last week."

"Time is not the same everywhere."

"Is that moment now, and this dream is remembering me falling through the portal tree?" But she'd awoken then with no change in time, or had she? That was it, wasn't it; this wasn't about Ben. This was about what happened when she fell through the tree. Maybe the shaman was right. Only why remember now?

"Yes. I have missed you. There is so much I have to tell you, but we don't have the time. My soul is on another journey now, and someday you'll be there as well."

"I have missed you, too, Mother." Tears tumbled down her face as they hugged.

Helen held her daughter tight. "I just wanted to say I love you, and while I am gone our guardian will be guiding you. I can't."

"I never thought I'd get one last chance to say I love you, too. You're the best and I miss you tremendously." Carol cried, "God, this seems so smultzy."

They hugged. Carol melting into the warmth from her mother's arms like when she was six. "I want to stay here with you, like this." Overhead the hunter's cry screeched.

"Time runs out. You can't stay, already the world you belong to calls. You must go before it's too late. Others there need your help. You cannot shirk your duties, even for me."

Something tugged at her, like someone trying to wake her from a deep sleep. It pulled at her, tendrils of reality attaching themselves to her with the grip of talons. Pulling. The realm disintegrated around her, dissolving into mist. Taking her away from the one she needed the most in her lifetime.

"NO!"

"You must go now."

"I want to stay here with you."

"As do I." Tears tumbled down her mother's face; Carol couldn't remember ever seeing her cry. "But that is later. We will have time in Tir 'n' nog, I promise. Not today."

"I miss you."

"I miss you every day, every moment, soul born of mine. Farewell, daughter, farewell."

Helen released her and Carol snapped away, rebounding into the darkness. She woke in a sweat clutching at the dash of Ben's car. "What the hell was that?"

A whisper from dreamtime from the one who called her darling whispered in the air. "The darkness. It chases you from the ancient arts. Watch it, it's the cause of many deaths of those you seek." The message wafted through her mind.

"Who, Charlie?"

The crack of bullets seared her eardrums as gunshots tore the silence of the night. "Holy shit, maybe going through a portal tree is not so stupid after all." Carol shook herself free of the visions plaguing her and unlatched the safety belt. Her shoulder slammed against the crumpled door until it gave way as the stink of raw fuel filled the air. She had to get free, before the vehicle caught fire and maybe exploded.

Her gun? She patted the holster under her arm. Ben had taken her gun.

* * *

Larry flung open the door to the crumpled BMW and sprinted across the mossy grass.

"Get him," someone yelled. Bullets ripped the ferns around him into shreds, before thudding into old wood. Tracers of white-hot death seared by him, wanting to kiss his life away, again.

Larry fired once as he dove behind a boulder. One man spun like a top, blood spraying heavenward, and collapsed. Another whipped his gun out and leveled three shots at Larry. Granite chipped skyward, wood thumped and Larry stood up. The biker smiled, wincing in disbelief as Larry drilled him in the forehead. Blood and brains splattered the old growth wood behind him.

"Who the fuck?" Ryley stepped out from behind the tree and raised his gun. Larry fired first. Ryley's gun spun away, blood flew from his hand. He screamed in agony, and tried to stem the flow of red.

Larry took two steps toward him and smashed him to the ground with the butt end of his weapon.

Ryley screamed as the biker fired at his kneecap.

The body Larry occupied jerked. He hadn't much time. Sirens were closing in on them. Ben was stirring.

Larry suddenly wondered how the man managed to stay unconscious this whole time, he wasn't drunk. Unless Ben stayed out of the way on purpose, in order for Larry to finish what he needed to? The thought struck a chord. The guy hadn't been that drunk, but the man would have lived the nightmares of Larry's life, known what he went through.

He only had mere moments to end it.

"Are you frigging nuts?" Ryley moaned in agony.

"That was for the wife. This one's for the kids."

Ryley screamed in agony as Larry blew away his other kneecap. Blood and tendons exploded.

"Don't you remember me, Ryley?" He spoke, the American twang evident in every syllable, as he bent over the crumpled man. "Your son didn't."

"Larry? You fuck. How could you kill him? He was innocent."

"And so was my family." Larry sneered, struggling to stay in control. Ben was fighting hard to take his body back.

"You betrayed me. You betrayed yourself and the Devil's Spawn and took far too many lives to be allowed to live. It ends now, Ryley. This is from me." He wanted to prolong the moment, torture him, make him pay.

Bits of acid exploded in his head. Ben's consciousness was tearing him away.

His finger tried to pull the trigger, he exerted a herculean effort, but the darkness kept pulling at him.

Unconsciousness overcame him, rendering him into atoms, again. It was like being run through a meat shredder and thrust back into the bowels of hell.

The gun fell from his nerveless fingers. He never heard if there was a last gunshot. Darkness and rage tore at him, yanking him away, it was too late.

* * *

His feline eyes searched the rocks from his outcrop. The shaman was worried, he could keep her off guard only for so long. She was learning far faster than he realized.

The cougar hurtled through the brush. Her tail flicked in delight, ears flattened to her head, and the eerie cry of the hunter catching its prey seared the mountain air.

Talons raked his side again. Dizziness sang to him as he tried to escape and she lunged onto his back, teeth clamped into his neck.

She blinked and their naked bodies returned to normal. "You are very good, my native friend. But the time to end this charade has come. I grow bored and there is another I seek. The one that will host my form until I find another and, as they say in the game you love, the bases are loaded. Two men out and that was your third strike. You, shaman, are out."

"No. That was classified as a foul ball. For you are indeed the most foul of beings, oh heartless witch."

Her eyes widened in rage. "I don't need a heart to deal with you."

Her weakness? Charlie opened his pocket. Here he couldn't use his power animals, but there was still one last resort. One place he could hope to run to.

"A soul catcher. Do you think me stupid? That would be useless on me. I know what spell resides in it. I used to possess one."

"That is not for you, but for me." Charlie flung it to the ground, allowing himself to be drawn down into its dark confines.

"You think me stupid and would follow you, shaman? I've a better idea." The Lure grabbed his cane and swung it down on the small wooden object. Light exploded as the shamanistic object exploded in a thousand pieces. All the souls trapped inside screamed, including Charlie, as they were released, vanishing from this world.

She sniffed the air. "A ruse perhaps? But don't worry shaman, if you are not dead, you are bleeding to death, and I will follow that blood trail no matter where you seek to hide. I have your scent memorized now." She licked his blood from her fingers. "You cannot escape. But for now, there is another I want and she comes this way." She clutched at his cane, holding herself up. "This has taken too much effort. I grow weary and I have other quarry."

Pulling herself down through the void into the urine-soaked toilets of the bar.

The Lure puked once, entered the nearest body, and wiped her mouth. She grabbed Charlie's cane and pouch and sauntered off. The smell of Carol's blood in her nostrils from earlier told her all she needed to know. "Good. One down. And I've still got a surly biker to deal with after that. Wonder which I'll enjoy the most? Ohh, I think I prefer beefsteak myself."

* * *

Gunshot echoed in his ears. A gun falling from his fingers. Ryley, his head splattered into the earth below him, convulsed once and lay still. "We're not on the dance floor. What the…? Ryley? What have I done?" Ben stood in shock. Blood and brain matter were splattered all around him.

Carol ran up behind him and surveyed the scene. Ben had not only stolen her gun, but done the unthinkable. "Ben Carlton, I'm so sorry, but I have to arrest you for the murder of Ryley McLaren." She cited his rights, finishing the arrest, and clinked on the cuffs.

The rest is a blur, what the hell happened? Ben thought.

Behind them, an explosion rocked the earth. "I think that was your Beamer," Carol said as they ducked down.

"My car! My beloved BMW! If you've damaged it…"

"Oh, I think it's gonna be worse than a scratch. A lot worse."

* * *

"And I'm afraid you, my dear, are coming with me." A woman's voice made Carol turn as she held the stunned, handcuffed reporter. Approaching sirens echoed in the forest.

A female she didn't recognize stood just behind her. In her eyes something sinister darted. "We, too, have unfinished business." Her image wavered and the old hag from the dance floor shifted into focus, pulling herself from the body of the person she occupied. The girl fell to the forest floor.

"Charlie?" If the hag was here, that meant…?

"Your shaman, like this woman, is dead." She tossed his cane and medicine pouch before her. "And you are now mine."

A cry came from above. In the parting of the trees, a large bird swooped toward them. The white of its head accenting the yellow hunter's glare in its eyes. The Lure leaped aside with a scream as it ripped towards her. She crashed into the brush.

"Run from the darkness." Her mother's words echoed in Carol's head. Was that guardian spirit her mother, in another form, coming to her rescue? She'd mentioned "beware the one from the dark arts." It wasn't Charlie her mother was talking about, it was The Lure, the old hag watching her from the mists at O'Shanahan's the day she found the little girl's body.

Charlie, Cathedral Trail, and The Lure. Mere legends? Everything was so confusing. Carol pushed Ben aside and tore off into the woods. There was one place in the park where something could intervene to help her. The place where everything started.

"You can't outrun me, Carol darling. For I'm also inside you." She was right, the voice didn't come from behind her, but from inside. Laughing.

Carol kept running until she reached the trail leading to the cairn. Laughter resounded in her ears as she entered the dark glade where the lonely, forgotten memorial sat under the cedars. Carol collapsed against the cold, stony visage of Pauline Johnson, breathless, gasping for air.

The Lure sauntered up behind her, smelling at her fingers, barely breathing hard. "Run all you want, but I have your scent and soon will have your soul for dessert, and before long I'll be you." She cackled like some witch from too many children's shows. "You can't hope to outrun me."

"Help me, O'Pauline Johnson. O'Tekahionwake." She ran her fingers over the stern, serene face carved from immobile granite. Sweat and blood dripped from her forehead. She must have fallen in the mad scramble through the woods.

"Ah, I see. Go ahead, seek hope from my old friend. But this, my darling lady, is merely a memorial. She isn't buried here. You can't get away from me. For you see, I need a body to take over before I can fully enter this realm. As for your soul, well that is quite dispensable, and there isn't room for two of us in there. What a better host than a police officer. I'm glad Ryley gave me the idea. Oh, you look a little shocked. Didn't he say he'd get even with you?"

"That bastard." He must have discovered the hag at the bar. She'd been hiding there the whole time. The one Charlie was searching for. Carol had to bide her time, think of a way to distract the witch, and hope she could make it to Charlie's portal tree nearby. If she could escape through the portal, maybe there was a chance. Even if the shaman was dead, maybe, just maybe, this time the portal would work. It did once before, somehow it had taken her to her mother, even though at the time it seemed like nothing happened.

None of it made any sense. If Charlie were here, he'd know what to do. All Carol could do now was trust her guts.

She thought fast. "What do you mean, you allowed me to get here?

Why? You sound like you knew Pauline, met her."

"Pretty perceptive lady. She was the first to sense I wasn't merely a legend told by old men around the campfires. Let's say I planted a seed within her. She visited me often after that, until she died. I needed her memory to be kept alive, the legend to live on after she died. So that I wouldn't be forgotten with the collapse of native society. Putting me into book form did that. Kept me preserved forever."

"But she died of cancer." Carol had read her biography; the cancer had spread very fast. Pauline had spent her last couple of years here in Vancouver, in the park.

The Lure smiled as she reached over and touched Carol. "Silly girl. I couldn't escape then, the guardians were too strong. But my spell of consumption ensured someone would come, hopefully at a time when I could escape. Oh, and look, I've snared a little birdie in my trap." She snickered.

"You killed her?" Coldness sucked at her. The Lure was like a living energy vampire, bleeding her life away with a touch. Carol remembered reading how fast the cancer ravaged Pauline's body. She tried to swat the hag's hand aside, but couldn't lift her own. Her body crumpled to the base of the memorial. It hadn't dawned on her that there were two people involved in the recent murders.

"Oh, I could do this the much more fun way, like the others you investigated. But you don't look like my type of woman. Although, this does take a bit more effort. Especially when you're not willing to let go, like the others." She bent over, obviously slightly drained by the resistance Carol was putting up. Her touch sucked the heat away. Carol's teeth chattered with the cold that enveloped her.

"And up on the hills against the sky,
A fir tree rocking its lullaby,"

A melodic voice cracked the stillness. The Lure looked up. From behind them, along the trail to Charlie's tree, a light moved toward them.

"Swings, swings,

Its emerald wings,

Swelling the song that my paddle sings."

"No, not possible." The Lure broke off her leaching caress and stared at the light moving past them through the woods.

The shimmering image of a woman with a bear-claw necklace around her neck, and eagle feathers braided into the back of her dark hair, moved along the trail. Clad in full Indian dress and moccasins, the strong features, and aquiline nose spoke of the native Mohawk blood that coursed through her. The ghostly figure of

Pauline moved serenely by, ignoring them, reciting words as if she were doing one of her famous stage recitals.

"She's dead. This isn't possible." The Lure released Carol, who fell to the ground.

"Cold. So cold." The detective shuddered, unable to move. Her energy ebbed, it was like floating on the cold ocean, she was unable to sustain her own body heat. She was dying.

"Her ashes. Pauline's ashes were scattered here," she whispered to The Lure. Her eyes opened wide, she obviously hadn't known that.

"I ended your life, why have you returned?" The Lure spoke to the disappearing image of Tekahionwake.

The woman floated along Cathedral Trail. In her hands a necklace and locket dangled.

"Catch me O' dear fleet of foot

O' Raven, master of the currents

Catch me if you dare."

Pauline's voice echoed up the trail. "I have within here that which you seek the most.

"The eagle plume that crests his haughty head

Will never droop until his heart be dead."

The Lure's mouth fell. "My heart. How could you know?"

The locket glowed. "My ashes have seen much and traveled far since we last met."

"No." The witch glared at Carol. "This is not right. And I know your mind holds no clues. You aren't going anywhere. This one intrigues me." The Lure vanished up the trail after Pauline's shimmering image.

Carol staggered to her feet. Where she touched the monument Pauline's graven image radiated warmth, allowing it to seep back into Carol's chilled body. She tried to take a small step and fell over, legs crumpling like rubber bands. "No good, need to rest," she muttered, fighting to remain conscious, holding onto the warmth of the stony image.

* * *

The Lure approached Pauline, who was standing before a large cedar tree.

"Slower and slower yet his footstep swings
Wilder and wilder still his death-song rings
Fiercer and fiercer thro' the forest bounds
His voice that leaps to Happier Hunting Grounds,
One savage yell-
Then loyal to his race, He bends to death- but never to disgrace."

Tekahionwake moved to bended knee and lifted her hands up. The locket dangled enticingly. Intrigued, The Lure took the locket and opened it.

The carved figure of a native Sisiutl fell out; Charlie's soul catcher.

"O' Harlot of the woods, I've beaten you at last. Your time to walk freely in this realm will be no more."

The Lure stood bewildered as Pauline rose, spun her around, and pressed her up against the wood of the tree. Before the witch could protest, Pauline kissed her hard on the lips.

"Man, this would give most men a real woody. Don't you think?" Pauline's voice changed. Her vision shimmered. Charlie's body swam into view.

"No!" Caught off guard, The Lure protested, her voice slow and heavy. "What is happening to me?"

She tried moving, but roots now grew from her legs, burrowing into the damp earth, anchoring her to the ground and the tree she leaned against. Thick sap flowed, adhering her like glue to the bark.

"Mere wood won't hold me shaman," her voice thickened and slowed.

"Perhaps by itself, it can't. But I will." Larry pulled himself from the boughs of the tree and wrapped his arms around her.

"Ah, who said anything about mere wood? This is a transformer tree housing our friend, Larry, here. He is done with revenge and I struck him a deal, one he relished performing. Especially since he has a bit of a grudge against you."

"I've defeated him once, I will break free," she screamed vilely, but couldn't break the Devil's Spawn grasp as her limbs continued solidifying. Creases of bark lined her body. Brown began to spread across her skin, swelling it, hardening it.

Her hair swirled into a whorl of tree fungus.

"Sometimes, darling," Charlie said with a sarcastic tone, "the old ways are indeed still the best ones. Oh, I did forget to mention something. I didn't mention who did the transforming, did I?"

Larry spoke, "Aid him we did."

"He aided us." "A fair return."

"The old ways still work."

Four different voices erupted from his mouth. The guardians had held themselves inside the very tree they'd used to hide the willing Larry, where The Lure wouldn't detect any of them.

"NO!"

"I seem to have run into some others that bear just a tad of a grudge against you as well. Peeing off people is one thing, but antagonizing gods? Ouch. I do think that sixties rock group got it right in their song 'with a little help from my good friends.' But you, you see, have no one to turn to and hey, two can play the old 'steal away inside your mind and learn what the other desires the most.' In the time we were together, I also learned what made you tick. I stumbled onto Pauline's spirit wandering this place a couple of times. So I decided to play the old switcheroo with Pauline here. Another, who I can say, was not opposed to your comeuppance. And that folks is what is called stealing home with bases loaded."

"NO!" Her face drained of colour, replaced by wood grain.

"Just one last, sloppy kiss for old time sakes. And do remember, I never French on a first date. Neither did Pauline, she was a proper lady that one." Charlie's face wavered back to Tekahionwake. He kissed The Lure. Her body pulled itself into the wood until only her face remained, burl-like, screaming her rage at the shaman and the native woman of legend.

Pauline's steady voice rang out from within the Shaman.

"Exultingly, the Haida now stands,

Appeased his hate, avenged his reeking hands:

He backward flings his head - one long, strange note

Leaves his thin lips - then up to heaven's height His war-whoop pierces
the fateful night.

A leap

While vengeance gloating, yells

The debt is paid."

A cedar tree on Cathedral Trail, large burl jutting out, stood silent in the cool of the forest.

* * *

Carol struggled to rise, legs wobbly beneath her, like she'd drunk a dozen vodka slammers on a dare after biking through the Tour De France.

Charlie came hiking up the trail. "Feels a bit odd without my cane. Hope I find it. Irreplaceable antique, you know."

"I saw it by Ryley's body, where Ben shot him." She explained quickly what had happened to her after they left the bar. "But she said you were…"

"Let's say reports of my death have been greatly over-exaggerated. Now chew on this." He reached into his pocket and pulled out a handful of herbs. "Call these my version of native power bars. Or as they used to say in the eighties, soul food, bro'."

Carol gagged as she chewed on the disgusting-smelling and even worse-tasting dried herbs. "Oh, God, this tastes like shit. What is it? But thank you, and thank you Pauline, O' Tekahionwake," she whispered to the monument. "I think she can sleep better now."

He was right; she felt the coldness leaving her as the herbs did their work.

"You don't want to know what end of the buffalo saw this last. Just chew. And you know, for a white broad, you don't look bad with frostbite for eyeliner."

"You, Charlie, are a complete nut job."

"I believe we've had this discussion before regarding my preference for nuts. Now, lean on me, and let's go find my cane and medicine bag, shall we? One last bit of business before I leave, the man responsible for your dear mayor's death."

* * *

James sat at the bar of the Royal Hotel pub on Hastings Street nursing a whiskey. Carol walked up behind him. "James Wells, I am arresting you for the murder of Cole Bridge, his wife, and daughter. It is my duty to inform you that you have the right to retain and instruct counsel without delay…" Carol continued with the arrest.

"I told you," the native woman's voice told James. "They've caught you at last.

Mr. Lucky can't help you now, dummy."

Charlie walked up behind Carol, reached over, and whispered something into the man's ear. James nodded to the empty scat beside him.

"There is one inside him that our witchy friend left behind, causing trouble," Charlie said. Carol frowned looking at the empty seats.

The shaman reached up and quickly grabbed James' ear. He pulled out the wriggling little blue-winged figure. Carol blinked. "What in the..."

It looked for all the world like one of the fairies from the Shrek movies or Tinkerbell from Peter Pan.

He opened his mouth and swallowed the creature. "Ah! An after dinner mint." He swallowed again.

"She's finally gone," James whispered as he looked around and hung his head low. "Yolanda is gone, she deserved better than me. I have done some evil things and must atone for my sins."

As they handcuffed him and hauled him outside, Charlie glanced at Carol. "You may want to check out the basement of a building that Ryley owns, green siding and red brick front. Something I saw in Bonehead's mind when I was at the precinct. Has to do with the old scratches on his neck."

"It's Boswell."

"Yeah, whatever. All I know it won't be pretty. Might let Larry rest a little more in peace." Charlie burped a puff of blue smoke. "Oops! Bad gas. Must be something I ate, a common sign of overindulgence." He pointed to the hunting knife sheath on James' belt. "I think you'll find the DNA on the sheath he's wearing will match the evidence on the knife found in the tree."

Carol smiled. "Charlie, you're one of a kind."

"Well, you know what they say. An elf a day keeps the witches away."

Epilogue

Carol stood watching the roller coaster at the PNE, working up the courage to get on the thing. She wished things could have worked out with her and Ben, but she knew in her heart the relationship was based on loneliness and not love. Ben had been acquitted on the grounds of no evidence. Only one set of prints was found on Carol's gun besides hers.

A dead man's. Larry Siegman's. How that worked, she didn't know, but was sure some psychic, or Charlie, could probably tell her. The only DNA found in blood splatters from the murder scene was Ryley's and Larry's. It was assumed Larry got himself cut up from roughing Ryley while he'd been in Ben's body. Ben had been checked and, although he had gunshot residue, no cuts, and not one sign of his prints on the gun. Only Larry's, same as the prints left around the other dead bikers and Ryley's son.

Ben had been out for a couple of months. He refused to talk to her after she arrested him, and as Carol told him the last time they talked, "I didn't smash up your lovely Beamer. Sorry the insurance company didn't see it that way. Unfortunately, they don't insure demonic possession."

Ben swore up and down he had no knowledge of events between the dance floor and being arrested. He even took a lie detector test and passed with flying colours. Maybe he'd eventually get over it; although she wasn't sure she really wanted to date a guy that treasured his car more than her.

Maybe that was why she was here. Old memories of their date and the fun they'd had. Terrifying, but good, times. She really needed some closure, to let him go. She screwed up her face and looked at the ride again.

As for Charlie, he'd been right. Dan had her re-open the investigation into Ryley's wife's disappearance, and Larry's and his family's deaths. She'd gotten a search warrant and checked out the basement of Ryley's house that Charlie described.

In the freezer they found the cut up remains of a female; DNA proved it to be Ryley's wife, and more DNA found under her fingernails proved to be Boswell's and the man Ryley called Snickers. How Charlie knew this she hadn't bothered to ask before he returned to Haida Gwaii. Both men were in custody and that was all that mattered.

Carol shuddered, still remembering the lewd smile on Snickers' face and Ryley's hand against her vest pocket when she'd been abducted.

How the Shaman knew that kind of stuff was a mystery. But he'd agreed to help her out as a psychic investigator in the future.

"Psychological Criminal Investigator, Charlie Stillwaters," he said, staring at the name tag she'd given him. She had one made up just for laughs. "You realize I'm gonna have a helluva time handcuffing a ghost? I'll do it as long as I don't have to wear the tag and I'd prefer the term 'Shaman Number One, Local Number One.'" Carol often wondered how he kept himself sane, and whether he truly was a matter of much greater debate.

Although Charlie wasn't happy about the idea, John Denton had been hired by city council to remove the shaman's box from Stanley Park and produce a replica. They agreed to repatriate the original to Haida Gwaii. Since he'd helped her out and saved her life Carol agreed that no charges would be laid. It was written off as a mix-up in paperwork somewhere back in the fifties.

* * *

Shaking out of her reverie, she noticed a handsome guy trying not to stare at her. Rugged good looks, tall, with that rare Michael Douglas bum chin. Maybe, like her, he was screwing up the courage to get on, or just enjoying watching everyone crap themselves. He'd said hi to her earlier. Maybe he was just shy, although anyone that could be the centrefold in a naked fireman calendar surely couldn't be withdrawn.

"Have you ridden it before?" she asked finally.

"Never."

"Didn't think a big strong handsome man like you could be a virgin to this kind of thing."

He smiled and blushed slightly, "John Bonetti, a fireman, and I'm only freaked out at some things. Being out of control on rides like this is one dare I promised to keep. They've scared me since I was a kid. I picked today, for some crazy reason, to challenge that fear. If you care to go out for a drink, perhaps dinner, you could find out just how experienced I am. They say firemen are good with their hoses."

"Carol Ainsworth, police officer." She giggled, feeling herself blush and appreciating the honesty on his part. She hadn't flirted or laughed in a long time. It felt good. She'd normally be put off or offended by his direct manner, but he did it so matter-of-factly, with no insidious overtones, she capitulated. He was mildly cocky and confident; that bold, forceful alpha-male type that Carol found rather appealing and a million romance novels swooned over.

"Sure," she said, "although, while we're here, care to go on the roller coaster together first and lose that cherry."

"Oh," he said. "I don't scream on a first date, but I don't mind if you do." She laughed, it felt good.

As they paid and got on, her short-sleeved blouse rode up her left arm. The three-inch tattoo of a bald eagle, wings outstretched slightly, curling around the image of the bust of Pauline Johnson, came into view. She'd just had it done two weeks earlier.

"Neat tattoo. How'd you get it?"

"One is my guardian spirit, and the other is my inspiration, and it's a long story. I can tell you about it over dinner. It revolves around an old shaman friend I didn't trust. In the end I think it was really me I didn't trust."

"Sounds fascinating, I'd like to talk to you about it. I take it that means we're on for supper if we live through the ride."

"You take it right."

They watched a heavy-set woman get off, staggering and sobbing, she'd wet herself and looked about ready to have a heart attack.

"Say, I go jogging around Stanley Park occasionally, haven't I seen you out there before? You look familiar."

"No, thanks. You probably saw me in the papers, and I've got this thing about trees, hate them." Especially walking along Cathedral Trail. In addition to the toppled cedars of the guardians and the crocodile tree someone had erected, the trail now bore an old cedar where Charlie had shown Carol the visage of The Lure re-imprisoned in the bore of a large fungal knot. The police department also had a couple of complaint calls recently, regarding sightings of a native woman in full regalia wandering the Cathedral Trail, reciting to herself.

Her face was trapped in wood for eternity, or so it was assumed. Rain would roll down the cheeks like tears. Carol couldn't bear to be there, or even in the park, especially alone. It sent shivers down her back. The memories of those bodies, the girl included, were always things the public would never know about. But she still woke in the middle of the night, visions of maggots raining down and an incredibly old hag watching her, always watching.

Larry and the four Tyee were guarding her, Carol knew she was safe. Yet wind would brush by her whenever she stood near the Johnson memorial. Caressing her; giving her the chills. She could so easily have been the one trapped in wood and The Lure looking back at her.

Since then, she'd read Pauline's biography, perhaps to understand the lonely woman with the warrior's heart better. She was a proud woman, one that didn't take crap and certainly wouldn't take if from a man. Probably why the woman never married, she would have been too much for any male to handle in Victorian times.

Pauline might have been politically incorrect, by today's sensitivities toward native issues, in some of her portrayals of aboriginals and their folklore. But she wasn't ashamed of who she was, or of her heritage, and proud to tell the tale of native societal desecration at the hands of the white race.

If she'd lived longer, she might have become a vocal voice in the women's movement. Pauline certainly lived and reminded Carol of someone like Karen Blixen, a figure that garnered respect from all that knew her back in the early part of the twentieth century, especially the men.

"Hate trees? How could you possibly hate a tree?" His strong voice broke her musings.

Visions of portals, falling into unending darkness, maggots dripping from branches and a young girl's dangling hand, images from her nightmares skimmed across her memories. "It's a long story and I'd rather not get into it here. Let's do the roller coaster, go for drinks, dinner, and after that, if you play your cards right, maybe you could get me to scream a second time."

"You're on. How's about O'Shanahan's? It's close, great pub, and the dance floor has a helluva atmosphere. Although I've heard it's gotten a lot tamer and quieter since they closed off the funnel and smoke show over the dance area."

"Yeah, can't get Thunderstruck there anymore." The police and city hall had convinced the owners to either make certain changes or face being shut down. Since then no one had reported doing strange things they didn't remember and the local crime rate had plummeted. Charlie also said he had the Sagalie Tyee seal up the rift.

"Atmosphere I can take. Along with a little thunder, lightning, and bed shaking."

He grabbed her hand. "Well, if its electricity you want, on we go. We can change our underwear after," he roared as they sat in place and the bar was clicked over them. One thing Ben had at least convinced her of, that she needed to take time off to enjoy herself and life.

The cars lurched forward, clacking away over the venerable wooden structure. Carol smiled, feeling more scared and free than she had in a long time.

The cars stood stock still momentarily at the top of the ramp. "Or we could just keep them off." Carol yelled as the wooden car tumbled earth-ward and they grabbed hands screaming.

Afterword

Other Novels In the Stillwaters Runs Deep Series

Stillwaters Runs Deep Book One: Raven's Lament

Protesting the logging of an old-growth forest, an environmentalist fells a rare tree, unwittingly releasing…something…into our world. After his subsequent disappearance, reporter Brooke Grant looks for answers. During his investigation he finds the love of his life, only to lose her to, well, he doesn't really know what. Brooke enlists the aid of his love's intriguing and extraordinary shaman uncle to help save her. Only they don't only have to save her, but save the world from being changed forever.

Book Two: The Lure

Ever go out for the evening and not remember what you did? What if there was a bar where spirits can enter your inebriated body and use it until you sober up? Well such a bar exists in Stanley Park, where the city's mayor has been murdered, his family missing, a dangerous witch has been released from her centuries-old imprisonment and an intriguing and extraordinary shaman shows up, only to vanish after leaving cryptic clues. So begins Detective Carol Ainsworth's first case.

Book Three: The Awakening

How angry would a mythical god be if he found himself awakening inside a mortal? After a strange and inexplicable death inside a jail, an intriguing and extraordinary shaman detects great unrest in the world, and breaks his way into the jail to investigate. He enlists Detective Carol Ainsworth to assist as an undercover prison officer who, rather strangely, also finds herself tasked with bringing to justice the murderer of a gentle forest being's mother.

His Ainsworth Chronicles (a urban fantasy, paranormal thriller series set in Victoria, BC.)

Ainsworth Chronicles Book One: The Joining
The Joining

Welcome to Victoria in Beautiful British Columbia, the most haunted city in North America, and to Detective Carol Ainsworth's first day undercover at the very grand old lady, The Fairmont Empress Hotel. Ready to deal with the two Italian families flying in for a wedding to unite them, she did not bargain for the ghosts, the FBI agent or the ancient curses that come along too. Add to that the very wonderful and mysterious psychic lady claiming you've invited her, the young boys disappearing, and the weird things happening to the unfortunates looking for their next fix trapped alongside spirits in the sewers, Carol found her first undercover assignment way more challenging than she could have imagined.

The one saving grace was the great Empress High Tea that Agnes introduced her to and the fabulous scones that are to die for. Literally.

Frank Talaber's Bio

Automotive Service Manager by day, writer by soul. Born on the wild Canadian prairies but immigrated to the cedar forests of coastal BC. Mated to a mad English woman, born of gypsy ancestry, him, not the wife. In the early hours of morning when the muse speaks and only cats stir and bobcats fear to tread he is writing, creating, or making coffee. Okay, he also makes some mean wine and has to chase the odd squirrel chasing his nuts in the backyard. Stranger ways exist in the backwoods of Borneo, Australia, or the American Bayou, but not here in the country of Bigfoot, Timmy's, and hockey. So with a fond "Like how's it going, eh!" Read on, at your peril.